THE LAST CLERIC

BOOK III OF
THE BLACKWOOD SAGA

Layton Green

To Number Nine

THE LAST CLERIC, Book III of the Blackwood Saga,
copyright © 2018, Layton Green
All rights reserved.
ISBN: 978-1-7338188-2-7

Published by Cloaked Traveler Press.
Cover design by Sammy Yuen.
Interior by QA Productions

Hear us, O Devla!
This dream of dreams I have seen.
A black night will come, stars asleep in their bower.
Our people scattered
Adrift in the sea of lament
Ground under the wagon wheel
When everything is ash.

Who is this savior?
When will he come?
When shall we be free?
O, Devla!
Not until the prophet shall herald
And the people shall hear
The roar of the last true cleric of the age, the Templar
Your fist, Your scorn, Your righteousness
The one who unseals the coffer
As he breaks the will of the world.

—Modern Translation of Book 14,
Stanzas 77–78 of the Romani
Canticles of Urfe, Author Unknown

Imprisoned in a cell built for wizards, kept in soul-numbing isolation with no windows, Valjean Blackwood put his head in his hands and wondered when he would die.

He felt crushed by memories of his loved ones, reeling from a future that might never come to pass. The plight of his two brothers, trapped somewhere on Urfe without him, hurt the most. Ever since their father had died and their mother was confined to a mental institution, Val had been Will and Caleb's guardian, parent, and eldest sibling all rolled into one.

Dying, Val could accept. He loathed the thought of it as much as the next person, but if execution by the wizards was his fate, then so be it.

Failing his brothers was another matter.

He stood and paced the cell, trying to come up with an escape plan for the millionth time. It felt so useless. The powerful wizards who had imprisoned him, those gods among mortals, would hardly have put him someplace he could magic himself out of.

Still, he had to try. He had to think it through.

Was he still in New Victoria, he wondered? Somewhere else on Urfe? In a different dimension? Ever since the elder mages had caught him trying to use the Pool of Souls and sentenced him to die, teleporting him straight to wizard prison, Val had not seen another human being.

A hole in the corner served as his toilet. Food and water had magically appeared in his cell forty-six times. Though he had no way of keeping time, the regularity of the meals felt half a day apart. He had tried to reverse-engineer the teleportation channel but couldn't get past the honeycombed walls. He assumed the geometry of the azantite cell, tiny pockets covering every available surface as if hollowed out by some giant race of bees, contributed to the immensely powerful wards shielding the room.

He had no idea when they were going to execute him. What he did know was that his limited magical abilities would never get him out of that prison. After assaulting the walls with every lesser spell he knew, all to no avail, he had summoned every ounce of magic he possessed and blasted them with Spirit Fire.

Not even a scratch. Drained and out of ideas, he slumped to his back and idly wondered if the honeycombed walls would prevent a powerful spirit mage, someone able to open dimensional doors and step through reality itself, from escaping. It didn't matter, because that sort of power was far beyond him.

He paced and he paced and he paced. As an attorney on Earth, he had once worked a pro bono case involving prisoners suing the state for keeping them in solitary confinement. A prison within a prison. Val knew better than most the effects of prolonged isolation: chronic headaches, heart palpitations, weight loss, muscle atrophy, and a slew of other problems.

But the real dangers were psychological. Anger, extreme stress, loss of a sense of reality, confusion, paranoia, depression, hallucinations. Many inmates became psychotic or suicidal. Sometimes both.

Val knew he had a strong mind. But the hallucinations had already begun, and his depression kept him huddled in a corner for much of each day. He could feel himself slipping into a dangerous state of despair.

When he next woke, his legs and chest felt heavy, as if a great weight bore down on him. He curled on his side, succumbing to the melancholy. *Just kill me*, he thought. *Put me out of my misery.*

The thought had slipped unbidden into his mind, and when he realized what he had said, he shuddered and forced himself to his feet. Snarling, he stalked to the nearest wall and pounded on it, over and over, until his knuckles bled and his white-hot rage beat back the despair. Anything to make him feel alive. Remembering a cuerpomancy trick Adaira had taught him, he hardened the skin on his hands and continued pounding, hammering the cell walls over and over with blows that would have shattered brick.

Exhausted, he sank to the floor again and watched the blood drip from his hands. The pale, cracked skin ignited a spark in his mind. A spark that grew to a small flame when he thought about the body-altering magic he had used to pound the walls.

So far, his escape plans had all centered around magic. He knew this was useless, but what if he took a different approach?

What if he used magic on *himself*?

He knew some wizards led extraordinarily long lives. Spirit mages lived the longest, by far, and most scholars at the Abbey believed the use of magic, especially reality-bending spirit magic, somehow altered the nature of time.

He also knew that cuerpomancers—a vision of strolling with Adaira in her father's garden seared through him—could reach inside someone and stop their heart.

Could cuerpomancers, he wondered, also slow down the vital organ?

The Congregation would never let him out of here alive. This he knew.

But what if he were dead?

The thought gained currency in his mind, and for the first time in weeks, a slow, grim smile lifted the corners of his mouth.

It took cuerpomancers years of practice to hone their craft. They had teachers, textbooks, cadavers, and live subjects on which to practice.

Val had desperation and an ironclad will.

During a dangerous trial and error period, he found that he could render his own pulse sluggish. The experiments made him dizzy, short of breath, and disoriented. He was sure he had induced a minor heart attack on at least three occasions. The question was, could he stop his pulse entirely? Or at least slow it enough to fool his captors into believing he was dead?

Just as importantly—could he do this and wake back up?

He didn't want the jailers to find an unmoving body with no visible wounds. They would probe. Doubt. Possibly tear him apart.

Instead, Val's plan hinged on faking a suicide convincingly enough to fool a mortician, and praying they stuck him in a coffin without calling for a cuerpomancer. Then praying even harder he woke on his own before he suffocated to death or was burned on a pyre. So many things could go wrong he shuddered even to think about it.

It was a desperate effort. A life and death gamble. But if he didn't try something, the wizards would execute him. Even worse, his brothers would be stuck in this nightmare world without him. Unlike Val, they had no innate magic, no way of getting home without the aid of a powerful wizard.

To carry out his plan, he decided to repurpose another cuerpomancy trick

Adaira had taught him: turning a fingernail into a small dagger. Unwilling to spend another few months growing out the keratin on his nails, he huddled on his side and pretended to sleep, hiding his hands under his stomach. In case someone was watching, he forced himself not to gasp as he used his magic to rip the nail off his left index finger. Once the pain subsided, he reshaped the nail into a stiletto-sharp file.

A shudder rolled through him. What if he went comatose and couldn't wake back up? Buried alive, trapped in a living nightmare?

With a shout of anguish, both for himself and for anyone who might be watching, he slit the underside of his own wrists with his nails.

He cut horizontally and only slit a portion. Blood poured from the wound and stained his arms. He knew he had to bleed enough to convince the guards of his death, but shallow enough to live. Yet another deadly variable.

He curled in pain as he bled, wondering if anyone would notice. He assumed *someone* was giving him food, though perhaps it was automated or teleported inside without a glance.

As blood pumped from his wounds, Val closed his eyes and reached for his magic, feeling the rhythm of his pulse beat through him. He focused his will and breathed deeply, slowly, in through his nostrils and out through his toes, entering a meditative state. This time he didn't stop when the dizziness overcame him. He kept breathing, kept pushing, kept drifting. When the mental confusion made it a struggle to stay focused, he collapsed on his back and pushed even harder, willing his heart to slow, trying to induce unconsciousness before he lost control of the magic.

Black spots filled his vision. A chill seeped into his bones and caused a wave of teeth-rattling shivers. He felt his mind drifting away from his body, untethered.

Still he pushed.

Saliva seeped out of his slackened mouth, and his muscles no longer responded to his commands. The last thing he remembered was seeing, in his mind's failing eye, one last vision of his brothers.

-2-

"Freetown is in ruins," Tamás said, quietly stating the obvious from the head of the long oaken table in the Red Wagon Tavern. He was the youngest member of the Roma High Council and the undisputed leader of the Revolution.

Lined with dusty casks of rum and ale, the tavern was one of the few buildings still intact after Congregation wizards had flown across New Albion in tilectium airships and leveled the capital of the Barrier Coast with lightning, tornadoes, and Spirit Fire. For the last few weeks, nearly everyone left in the city, Will and Caleb Blackwood included, had spent most of their waking hours searching for survivors and clearing out rubble.

As Will took in the drawn faces at the table, mostly remaining members of the council, he felt an overwhelming stab of compassion. Those unable to make the perilous trek across the continent to Freetown were forced into terrible ghettoes by the Congregation, the body of wizards that controlled the Realm. The Barrier Coast was the end of the line, the one safe place for those who refused to take the Oaths.

"Hundreds fill the death wagons," Tamás continued. "Many more crowd the infirmaries. The question is, what will we do about it?"

One of the elders, Jacoby Revansill, slammed a gnarled fist on the table. "What *is* there to do? Besides start over?"

Merin Dragici, a wealthy trader, shook his head. "It doesn't matter where we go. If the wizards wish to hunt us down and kill us, they will do so."

"Aye," Kyros Toth agreed.

"Is that what they wish?" Tinea Alafair said. She was the oldest person at the table, her face puckered with age. "If they desired to eradicate us, they could have started with this attack. Or long before. Instead, they imparted their lesson and returned to New Victoria. I say we do well to heed their warning."

"Some lesson," Kyros said grimly.

To Will's left, Caleb stifled a yawn. His eyes were bloodshot.

"Hung over again?" Will whispered to his brother.

"Not yet," Caleb whispered back with an unsteady grin.

Yasmina, seated on the other side of Will, heard the exchange. She didn't smile at Caleb's remark, but then again, the once-carefree Brazilian zoology student and budding wilder hadn't smiled at much of anything since the attack. She especially hadn't smiled at Caleb, who had slept with another woman on the return journey from the Darklands, just as he and Yasmina were starting to reconnect.

Will felt bad for Yasmina, who could have almost any guy she wanted. In his heart, he knew that while his brother cared deeply for Yasmina, he had never truly loved her.

Marek and Dalen had not been invited to the meeting. Will missed their steady presence. Far more keenly, he felt the absence of his oldest brother, Val, who had somehow made contact a week ago, just before the wizards razed Freetown. If that mysterious communication was to be believed, Val was now a prisoner of the Congregation.

How had such a terrible thing happened, and what could he and Caleb possibly do to help him?

"If our Black Sash brethren hadn't hired an assassin to kill students at the Abbey," Tinea said, "the wizards might not have come at all. An Alazashin, no less. I warned them the Congregation would find out."

Merin sneered. "Wouldn't have come? A fantasy that will endure right until the genocide is complete."

"I, for one, am glad the Black Sash gypsies acted as they did," Jacoby said. "Let the wizards feel our pain for once."

Tinea stood. "And how did the Black Sash afford an Alazashin assassin, Jacoby?"

"Enough!" Tamás said. "Killing students is wrong, but Merin is right—the Congregation made their intentions clear long before the attack on Freetown." The long-haired Roma leader swept his gaze across the table. "We have three choices: flee, stay and pray the wizards do not return, or fight. And to those who still question the motives of the Congregation, despite the death squads and Inquisitors patrolling the Ninth, there is something of which you are not aware. The flying ship that attacked our city was built with tilectium."

There were murmurs from the elders. Tamás exchanged a glance with Will. "As we were fleeing the mines," Tamás continued, "we saw more of these ships.

Many more. The end game of the Congregation, my friends, is clear: to settle the Ninth, and solve the twin problems of the Devla uprising and the Revolution by eradicating our people."

Silence deafened the room.

"We can rebuild here or we can flee," Tamás said, "but the result will be the same. Sooner or later they will confine us to the fens or put us to the sword."

"But it's the same if we fight," Tinea said, with a frustrated wave of her hand. She peered down the table at Will. "Even with the return of Zariduke."

Will's fingers tightened around the hilt of the sword his father had bequeathed him. The gypsies called it Zariduke, Spiritscourge, or Spiritwell. Devourer of magic. An artifact of immense power that could cleave through spirit and strike down wizards. Will didn't know how his father had found the weapon or what he had planned to do with it. The histories were unclear whether Dane Blackwood was an agent of the Congregation or a secret member of the Revolution, and almost two hundred years had passed since he had left Urfe.

Whatever the histories said, Will knew his father's motives had been pure. He would never have sold out his own people.

"As for myself," Tamás said, "I would rather die with honor than live as a slave. But our people need guidance. Let us put this to a vote."

"Does mine count?" said a mocking voice from the doorway.

The voice belonged to a short, lithe, copper-skinned woman with waves of dark hair and cheekbones as sharp as the vertical scar dividing her forehead. Will's pulse beat faster at the sight of her.

"Mala," Tamás said coldly. "There was a reason you were not invited. You've made your feelings on the Revolution clear."

Dressed in black leather and scarlet boots, her dangerous blue sash tied around her waist, Mala sported her typical array of pouches, weapons, and colorful jewelry. She was also holding a short bronze tube in her left hand. As she approached, she opened the tube and shook out a scroll. Will started, recognizing the red tie and brittle parchment. It was an item Mala had recovered during the expedition to Leonidus's castle. Will had forgotten all about it.

"Allow me to guess," Mala said. "You're discussing the bleak future of our people and whether the re-emergence of a legendary sword," she graced Will with one of her mysterious, sardonic smiles, "might help combat the wizards."

The council members replied with frosty stares.

"The sword is impressive, no doubt," she said. "The wizards will fear it. But it is one sword, wielded by one barely-trained warrior."

Will stiffened at her words, though he knew she spoke the truth.

Mala looked at him. "Will this warrior from another land fight for your cause? For now, the question is irrelevant. The sword is a powerful symbol, but it is not enough. Not *nearly* enough. A hundred Zaridukes wielded by paladins would not begin to turn the tide in a battle with the wizards. Do you not fully grasp the might of your enemy? If you choose to engage, if you even flit about their coattails like a gnat, the Congregation will massacre you."

"I think the might of our enemies is fresh on our minds," Tamás said stiffly. "As it should be."

"Did you come to mock us, or was there another purpose?"

Mala stepped closer to the table. "What if there was something that might, in fact, affect the outcome? Perhaps not enough to defeat the wizards—I doubt such a thing exists—but enough to force them to leave us in peace or risk a larger civil war? A war for which the common born might not have the stomach?"

"Now you do mock us," Tamás said, with an edge to his voice.

"Do I?" Mala asked. She carefully unrolled the parchment scroll, yellow from the ravages of time, and laid it on the table.

Along with everyone else, Will crowded in to observe the ancient treasure map with a series of runes along the top. The beginning point was marked by a large dot that appeared to be located, if the geography was the same as Earth, on the eastern coast of the Yucatan Peninsula of Mexico. Yet again, he marveled at the eerie similarities between Urfe and back home, and wondered what it all meant.

A dotted line wound through a representation of dense jungle, then crossed three geographical markers before ending at a pyramid in the middle of the peninsula. Instead of rising to a point, the terraced pyramid tapered to a flat summit, topped by a temple.

"I don't recognize these runes," Kyros said.

"They're Alazansa," Mala replied. "The language of the Alazashin."

From past discussions, Will knew the Alazashin was a secret society of thieves and assassins Mala had once belonged to.

She read from the scroll. " 'Herein lies the living tomb of the sorcerer king

Yiknoom Ukab K'ahk. All those who seek may enter, but none shall ever leave.'"

When Will looked up, everyone's face except Caleb's and Yasmina's had turned as white as alabaster.

"I cannot read the runes," Tinea said, swallowing and then peering closer, "but she speaks the truth about the origin. I've seen the language of the Alazashin before."

"I don't understand," Will said. "What does that mean?"

"It means," Tamás said after a long moment, giving the map a reverent look, "that if the legends are true, and the translation correct, then this map might lead to the final resting place of the Coffer of Devla."

"By the Queen," Merin Dragici breathed. The eyes of all twelve elders were riveted to the map.

"According to the Book of Devla," Mala said, "the coffer is a chest that holds not gold or silver, but the power of Devla Himself. A chest that, when opened by a true cleric, will unleash the wrath of Devla on nonbelievers."

"When it was carried into battle," Tamás said, "a victory for our people was assured. The coffer was used to level armies."

"If the *legends* are to be believed," Mala said, "the coffer was lost over twenty-five hundred years ago, when our homeland was invaded by the Babylonians. The beginning of the end for our people," she said bitterly. "The reason we wander the earth still."

Will felt a chill at the similarity of the coffer's origin story to that of the Ark of the Covenant. Apparently, Caleb was thinking the same thing. After exchanging an alarmed glance with Will, he said, "What does a pyramid in Mexico have to do with an invasion by the Babylonians?"

Mala answered, "As was common in that era, the Babylonians used mercenary armies to supplement their forces. The histories agree that the successful invasion of our homeland was due largely to the addition of Battle Mages from," Mala pointed at the map, "the Calakmul Empire."

"The true reason was the turning of our people away from Devla," Elder Alafair added. "We abandoned our god, and He abandoned us."

"Of course," Mala murmured, with a twist of her lips. "The Calakmul sorcerer king at the time, Yiknoom Uk'ab K'ahk, was notorious for sending mercenaries around the world to gather plunder. It has long been thought the Coffer of Devla was taken to his treasure room."

"Which no one has ever found," Will guessed.

Mala pointed at the map. "If this is genuine, and a past expedition successful, we would have known about it. One can only surmise the treasure remains untouched."

"Or the map isn't genuine," Will said.

Mala tipped her head. "My instincts tell me otherwise, but that is a possibility."

Tamás raised his head, a fierce light in his eyes. "The Coffer of Devla could give the Revolution a chance for victory."

"If the map is genuine," Mala said, "and *if* the coffer is real and can provide a glimmer of hope against the Congregation, then there is still an enormous obstacle to overcome."

Elder Revansill spoke in a reverent voice, as if quoting from scripture. " '*And the people shall hear the roar of the last true cleric of the age, the Templar, Your fist, Your scorn, Your righteousness, the one who unseals the coffer as he breaks the will of the world.*' "

"According to legend," Tamás said slowly, "using the Coffer of Devla requires the presence of a true cleric. The last cleric of the age. The Templar."

"Of which none have existed," Mala said, "if any have existed at all, for hundreds of years."

"Devla will provide for us," Elder Revansill said quietly. "If we have enough faith, and recover the coffer, then He will shine a light upon our path."

The other elders nodded in agreement, their excitement palpable.

"And if He does not," Tamás said, "then we are lost anyway." He stood and placed his palms on the table, his voice rising. "Our path is clear. We must form a party at once to search for the Coffer. The survival of our people depends on it."

"I assumed you might feel that way," Mala said drily, as she replaced the map in the bronze tube. "I will lead the expedition to the pyramid. If retrieved, the Coffer of Devla is yours. I retain right of first refusal on all other magical artifacts, and fifty percent of all coin. You will furnish me with a wizard of mutual agreement," she looked directly at Will, "and the addition of Spiritscourge on the journey would be beneficial."

"You offer your talents so selflessly," Tamás said, his voice dripping with sarcasm. "Would it not benefit the Revolution to retain all magical artifacts for the cause?"

Mala opened her other palm, revealing a concealed fire bead. She tapped the bronze tube suggestively against her palm with the fire bead. "Those are my terms. They are non-negotiable. If I must, I will seek a wizard elsewhere. But I prefer one I can trust." She bared her teeth in a half-smile. "Consider it my duty to my people."

The room erupted into chaos as Tamás and the elders began to vigorously debate Mala's offer. Will's head was spinning at the possibility of his own involvement. A memory of the smoking remains of Freetown filled his vision, the stench of bodies scorched by Spirit Fire. Just before the attack, Will had met Lucas and Mateo Blackwood, two cousins from his father's side of the family. Lucas had been crushed by a falling tower and died in Mateo's arms. These people—*his* people—needed help, or the wizards would slaughter them.

But was it Will's duty to risk his life? He had a duty to his brothers, too. To keep them alive. To get them home. The night before, Tamás had told Will that if Val was truly imprisoned by the wizards, then he was beyond mortal help.

Or was he? What if Will found something in this legendary lost pyramid that might help free his brother, or help them get home?

Mala watched the debate with folded arms, the corners of her lips upturned, cool as a lioness in her den. Caleb leaned over and whispered, "It's not our war, little brother."

"They're our family," Will said. "And even if they weren't, does that mean we shouldn't help them?"

"Now's not the time to indulge your hero complex. *Think*, Will."

"I am thinking. What about Val? We have to find a way to help him."

"We don't even know for sure what happened. How did he even get to Urfe again?"

"Maybe it was another key. Who knows? We *saw* him, Caleb. We heard his voice."

"Did we? That could have been a vision. A wizard trick."

"For what reason? That was Val, and you know it. He's here and he needs us."

"Yaz?" Caleb said in exasperation. "Talk some sense into him?"

Yasmina gave him a chilly glance, then resumed staring straight ahead.

The room quieted. Tamás stood to face Mala. "By unanimous consent, the High Council has agreed to your terms. You will have your wizard. We cannot, however, force this expedition upon the owner of Zariduke." Tamás turned towards Will. "What say you, Will Blackwood? Will you serve the cause of your people and help break the yoke of the Congregation? Will you search for the lost Coffer of Devla?"

"Yes, Will Blackwood," Mala said, her eyes mocking. "What say you?"

3

Val woke to a darkness that moved, and a smell so rotten it made him gag. As he fought back the bile, he realized he was lying on his stomach, on top of something rubbery. A weight pressing down on his back induced a feeling of claustrophobia.

Just as he started to panic, he had a flash of remembrance. *It worked! I faked my own death and escaped.*

Or did I? There is only darkness, and I'm moving. Did I die after all? Am I passing on to the other side?

If so, then I'm headed to hell, because this stench is unbearable.

The wave of nausea passed, and he tried to summon a light. He did it slowly and carefully, making sure to illuminate only the area right in front of his face, in case someone was watching. For his sanity, he needed a glimpse of his surroundings.

Illumination spells depended on some type of light source, however faint. There must have been a window nearby, and he guessed it was nighttime, because a halo of dull gray light appeared. Congealed moonlight.

At the same time he saw the leaden flesh of the dead body putrefying underneath him, he heard a chug of locomotion, followed by the long moan of a train whistle piercing the silence of the night.

A corpse. Val was lying facedown on a corpse. He tried to jerk back but couldn't move. He realized he was underneath another corpse, and there were more all around, piled ten deep in the compartment like a chest of gruesome dolls.

It took every ounce of willpower he possessed to suppress the horror of his situation. After considering an attempt to open one of the railcar doors and fly away, he decided to wait. Better not to chance alerting someone. If he could just endure until they dumped the bodies, he would have a better chance of escaping.

Though weakened, he had worked hard to ensure the cuts on his wrist looked worse than they actually were. His unconscious state was due more to his magical inducement than to blood loss. Still, he would need sustenance soon.

Breathing through his mouth, trying not to think about what he was touching, he wedged out from between the two bodies and clawed atop the pile of corpses. He pressed his face against a small window covered in grime. Once his eyes adjusted to the dim light, he let the light spell disperse into fading gray motes.

Outside the window, a sprawling slum seemed to suck the moonlight inside. The shantytown of wood and tarpaper shacks lasted for miles, giving way to a foggy patch of countryside. He did not think they were anywhere close to New Victoria. The landscape looked much different. Green and rolling and sodden. Minutes later, the train stopped beside a fifteen-foot iron gate. On the other side, a miniature stone city poked out of the fog. Obelisks and crypts and mausoleums, sepulchers and vaults and gargoyle-studded sarcophagi.

A cemetery. An enormous one.

The sea of age-spotted granite rippled across the landscape, dwarfing any graveyard Val had ever seen, even the legendary above-ground necropoli of New Orleans.

As revolting as it was, Val crawled back inside the pile of corpses and closed his eyes. He had to play dead as long as he could. There might be a wizard overseeing the disposal.

Soon after, he heard men's voices and the screech of rail cars opening. He risked a glimpse and saw corpses being loaded onto flatbed carts and wheeled into the cemetery. In a history class in college, he remembered reading about trains that hauled off the dead to mass graves in Victorian England.

His time came soon. The door opened, followed by the thump of bodies tossed onto carts. He went limp as gloved hands grabbed him and threw him atop a pile of corpses. He bit his tongue to keep from gagging, praying he didn't contract some ghastly disease.

As the cart started rolling, he counted off five minutes and thirty seconds. They had to be deep in the cemetery. Just before he opened his eyes, the cart tilted, and he slid into midair. After a moment of panic, he landed in a heap along with the other bodies.

Once he heard the cart rolling away, he risked opening his eyes and discovered he was in an enormous pit lined with sheer, twenty-foot sides. At the bottom, an irregular ring of earth-hewn passages tunneled into darkness. Access to older burial sites, he assumed.

Above him was a roiling fog and the faint haze of a crescent moon. Val scampered off the pile and into one of the tunnels, stopping as soon as he was out of sight. With his skin still crawling from the touch of the corpses, he waited while the workers made three more trips, unloading their grisly cargo to create a pyramid of bodies in the pit. Not until he heard the chug of the train departing did Val feel safe to fly away.

As soon as he stepped out of the tunnel and into the charnel pit, wondering why there were no signs of decomposing bodies, he saw the first ghoul emerge from one of the tunnels. Tall and thin, with stretched gray skin and limbs like steel rope, the creature scanned the top of the pit before advancing on the grisly pile. More ghouls emerged, faces drawn with hunger, and Val turned in alarm to find two of the monsters creeping down the tunnel right behind him.

In a panic, he hit the ghouls with a blast of hardened air, sending them tumbling back down the tunnel. Then he turned and sprinted into the pit, taking flight to create distance. He watched in horror as dozens of the filthy creatures spilled out of the tunnels and scuttled like cockroaches towards the bodies.

Something tugged at his ankle. Val whipped his head down, horrified to see that one of the ghouls had leaped into the air and grabbed his foot. Before he could react, another ghoul took a running start, much faster than he expected them to move, and jumped on the back of the first ghoul.

The added weight caused Val to drop five feet. He hit the two ghouls with another Wind Push, but that caused him to drop even farther. Four more ghouls took the place of the first two, grabbing Val's legs and yanking him to the ground. One bit into his thigh, and he screamed.

Forcing himself to focus, he reached for his magic and flung all four away, still pushing air, but the rest of the creatures had formed a circle around him. He knew if he took flight again they would grab him, pull him down, and devour him. Panic set in. He didn't have enough offensive spells in his arsenal.

But he did know one—and it was the deadliest force on Urfe.

Val's magic tended to work better when his life was in danger. The Spirit Fire came easily, black energy sparking and crackling along his fingertips. He flung his hands towards the pack of ghouls and the dark fire lanced into them, passing through a dozen of the monsters before arcing into the sides of the pit. The ghouls touched by Spirit Fire simply disintegrated, consumed by the essence of pure magic.

Val stared down at his hands in shock. He had never unleashed anything that powerful. It had simply come out of him.

Yet after the shock came terror. He had lost control and expended his resources too fast. Weakened by both the journey and the outpouring of magic, he knew he was too spent to call more Spirit Fire, and there were still a few dozen ghouls in the pit.

Still, he had created an opening. The remaining ghouls had fled into the tunnels or backed against the wall. The closest was twenty feet away. He reached skyward, summoned the magic to burst into flight—and found he didn't have the strength.

No no no no no.

He tried again, pushing against the ground with his mind. Nothing. A familiar emptiness loomed inside him, the mysterious well of magic gone dry.

The ghouls crept forward, backing Val against the side of the pit. He looked around in desperation. The walls were too steep to climb. A pair of ghouls had blocked the closest tunnel.

Had he escaped the prison only to die at the hands of these filthy, corpse-eating monsters? As the first ghoul reached for him, Val spun away, limping on his bitten leg. A second creature grasped him by the throat. Far stronger than it looked, the ghoul held Val tight as two more closed in for the kill, teeth bared, dirt-stained claws extended.

Just before they tore into his flesh, there was a loud pop, like a diluted sonic boom. All three monsters exploded, spraying Val with body parts and gray ichor.

As he looked around in shock, an unseen force lifted him straight into the air, out of the grasping hands of the undead. A man in a cowled, steel-gray cloak with black runes on the sleeves stood on the side of the pit with a palm outstretched. Behind him, three more men in similar garb waited beside a black stagecoach with silver trim hovering a foot off the ground.

The man standing beside the pit flicked his wrist, sending Val flying towards the coach. When the mage dropped his hand, Val collapsed in a heap. He eased to his feet as one of the gray-robed wizards opened the door to the black and silver hansom, exposing an interior of finely brocaded gold.

"Who are you?" Val asked.

"Wizard Guard to the Queen," said the wizard who had saved him, floating over to the carriage. He pointed at the open door. "Get in."

The queen? Where am I? Who are these people?

Val studied the grim faces of the wizards, sensed the enormous power they wielded. It was a battle he could not hope to win. Or even wage, in his weakened state.

Chin high, pain lancing through the thigh the ghoul had bitten, Val stepped into the hovering stagecoach and took a seat in one of the high-backed chairs facing each other in the passenger compartment. Three of the wizards took the remaining seats, and the one who had spoken stepped into an enclosed section at the front. The carriage rose a hundred feet into the air and then soared out of the cemetery.

Val watched the journey through a glass window. It took a lot of magical muscle to fly five men and a carriage.

Power, Val said to himself. That's what these strange mages exude.

Power.

Despite the direness of the situation—he assumed he was being hauled back to prison—these grey-cloaked wizards intrigued him.

After trying and failing to engage them in conversation, Val gave up and returned to the window. At first they passed the same scenery from earlier, a swath of countryside followed by a sprawling ghetto, but within minutes a massive cityscape emerged out of the darkness. Despite his efforts to appear calm and in control, Val felt his jaw slowly dropping.

Like a black mamba slithering between two mammoth circuit boards, an inky river dissected a metropolis that dwarfed even New Victoria. But it wasn't the size of the city that made Val stare in wonder. He had seen bigger back home. Instead it was the might and majesty of the wizard strongholds flanking the river, thousands of fortresses brightening the night sky with a wild array of glowing stone facades, some as squat as castles, some soaring hundreds of feet high. It was different, though: Val didn't see any of the dream-like architecture or graceful spires that marked the New Victoria Wizard District. These buildings were more traditional, keeps and barbicans topped by parapets and hulking domes, towers and obelisks accented by Gothic arches and cupolas. More brawn, less elegance.

As he absorbed the size and general shape of the city, he thought he knew this place. He had assumed the prison was near the Wizard's District of New Victoria, but he realized they had taken him to an entirely new city. A new *continent*.

"This is London," he murmured. Or Londyn, in this world. Despite the rise of New Victoria as the new power center, he knew Londyn was the official capital of the Realm and home to the monarchy.

It still looks pretty important to me, he thought, as the carriage soared right through the middle of the city, high above the river. Wizards and flying carriages filled the sky around them. As with New Victoria, there was no sign of steam power or the use of natural gas, though from his studies, he knew the wizards possessed knowledge of both technologies. It had gone unspoken in class, but he guessed they kept the population under thumb by using only magic-driven innovations. Flying carriages and sky barges, glow orbs and heat stones.

He soon realized they were aiming straight for what resembled a larger version of the Tower of London back home: a monolithic, white-gray fortress enclosed by a wall taller than most of the surrounding buildings.

The carriage descended, coming to rest in a courtyard the size of a football field. Guards were everywhere, including a quartet of giant orbs floating above the guard towers in the corners. Val shuddered when he looked closer and saw roving eyeballs and razor-tipped tentacles covering the gelatinous surface of the orbs.

One of the wizards threw a hood over Val's head before helping him out of the carriage. Judging from the increasing echo of his footsteps, they had walked him across the courtyard and into the interior of the fortress. He descended thirty-six steps before they deposited him in a stiff-backed chair. The room smelled like sage and candle wax.

Where had they taken him? Why wasn't he back in his cell?

Sensing the presence of the gray-robed wizards beside him, he didn't dare lift his hood. Long minutes later, he heard the sound of booted feet approaching, and then the swish of robes.

Someone removed his hood. Val blinked at the sudden light. He was in a high-ceilinged room with rich furnishings and tapestries draping the walls. A chandelier made of pearls and intricately wrought golden sconces provided illumination.

A squat woman with a round, shriveled face stood before him, flanked by a dozen majitsu in black robes and silver belts. All four of the gray-cloaked wizards were still present. They bowed to the woman, who was dressed in white finery and holding a diamond-topped scepter that thrummed with power.

"You may stand," she said to Val, in a haughty, upper-crust British accent.

Val stood, his head spinning from trying to figure out what was happening. The woman looked exactly like the photos of Queen Victoria he had seen back home.

"My Queen," he said respectfully, performing the same bow as the others. Resistance, he knew, would get him nowhere.

"It is not often that we are forced to imprison the mage-born. A spirit mage, no less. You may not have realized," she said, "that you were confined beneath this very fortress."

"I did not," Val said.

"A clever ruse you performed," she said. "Befitting your reputation as a man of ability. You did not, however, think to escape from the Wizard Vault so easily?"

"No," he said truthfully.

The queen's wrinkled mouth compressed. "To ensure a wizard's death, we call a cuerpomancer. In your case, however, we wished to see where you would land. With whom contact might be made."

"To see if I'm with the Revolution," he guessed.

She tipped her head. "Despite your transgressions, we do not wish to see talent such as yours go to waste. Thus our intervention in the pit, when no rebel forces came to save you. Some among us would see you executed, 'tis true. But others would see you go free–if loyalty to the Realm was proven."

Val felt a thrill of excitement, as well as surprise. Who had intervened on his behalf? Dean Groft? Adaira?

"Tell me, young one, why did you seek the Planewalk?"

Val took a deep breath, thinking as quickly as he could, electing to stay as close to the truth as possible. He didn't feel comfortable disclosing his father's identity. He wasn't sure how Dane Blackwood fit in with these people, especially given the persecution of the Roma clans, and he didn't want them targeting Will and Caleb. "My father disappeared when I was very young. We never knew what happened to him. I sought only to locate him, your Majesty. A boy searching for his father. I apologize deeply for my transgression."

"Was there no alternative?"

"I tried everything. In the end, I sought out a phrenomancer, who claimed my father was still alive." The lie about his father pained him. When Val was in high school, Dane Blackwood had perished during the archaeological expedition in which he had found the legendary sword Will now carried. His father had fallen off a cliff in Dordogne—yet how could a spirit mage have plunged to his death? Was his magic somehow expended? Or had something more sinister occurred?

"I knew of no other way to reach him," Val continued.

"Why did you not ask permission?"

"Would it have been granted?"

She took in his response, gazing at him with a neutral expression. "There exists a little known provision in the Common Law that allows a prisoner to be freed in service to the crown. Should you choose to accept it, I have a mission that, if completed, would secure your freedom."

Val was stunned. He didn't even care what the offer was. If the choice was execution, or live and have a chance to find his brothers, he would do anything she asked.

"I understand your desperation," she said, sensing his feelings, "but hear me first. You may have noticed," she turned to a raised dais that supported an empty glass case beneath the chandelier, "the absence of the Star Crown. An artifact bestowed in the Golden Age by Myrddin himself, as a symbol of the newly formed Congregation." She turned back to Val. "A year ago, the Crown was stolen."

"From here?" Val said, incredulous. "By whom?"

"A renegade gypsy spirit mage. Tobar Baltoris. He seduced one of our own to gain entrance, and fled through a spirit door. His actions alerted my guard—" she glanced at the gray-cloaked wizards "—and they pursued the thief to Exmoor. Imagine if the Star Crown, the very symbol of the might of the Congregation, were to fall into the hands of the Revolution!"

"So it hasn't?"

"Not yet. But neither do we possess it. The Crown is not just symbolic—it is an artifact of great power, to an extent we did not even realize. When our wizards located Tobar, he placed the Star Crown on his head and attempted to flee through the dimensions. One of our own mages attempted to stop him. We do not know exactly what occurred, except that our spirit mage and the Wizard Guard who went in pursuit—some of our most powerful conjurers— have not been heard from since. And the tract of heath and moorland where this battle took place—a swath of rugged countryside largely unpopulated— has also disappeared."

"I don't understand," Val said. "How can land just disappear? What's there now?"

"A strange, opaque fog. I am told it is an impenetrable magical barrier. Except, perhaps, to a spirit mage. My scholars speculate that an implosion of opposing magical forces and some unknown power of the crown was the cause. Yet no one knows what lies across the fog, and I cannot risk another spirit mage."

"Except me," Val said grimly. "You can risk a prisoner about to be executed."

She gave a curt nod. "It is, perhaps, an impossible task. Moreover, there are fates more uncertain than death in the realms of spirit. Do you still, Val Kenefick, choose to accept this mission?"

He took a deep breath, his voice more uncertain than before. "I do."

"Then go. Find a way across the barrier, and return the Star Crown to its rightful place. This is the only way to convince the Conclave that you do not favor the Revolution."

"I'll do my best."

"I wish for this mission to succeed," she continued, clasping her hands in front of her, "and fear it is beyond your limited capabilities at this stage of your education. There is another prisoner who shall accompany you, and I will allow you to select three additional companions."

To his surprise, she stood there and waited for him to choose. After a rushed but agonizing decision, he gave her three names. She inclined her head towards one of the gray-cloaked wizards, who floated out of the room.

"How long before I know if they've accepted?" he asked. He didn't relish the idea of confinement in wizard prison for another few months.

"I will give them one day to decide. Another to wrap up their affairs and gather their belongings." She gave Val a parting glance before sweeping out of the room with the imposing cadre of majitsu and Wizard Guard trailing behind her. "Lord Alistair will send those who agree through the Pool of Souls. Three days hence, regardless of who comes, you will depart."

4

"I can't believe you're going," Caleb said.

Will started donning the soft leather armor the local tanner had supplied. "You can still come with me."

"Thanks but no thanks. The trip to Leonidus's castle was one too many death-defying adventures for my lifetime."

"Maybe you wouldn't have to go inside the pyramid."

"And do what, wait in the jungle by myself?"

Will pulled a pair of calfskin breeches and a gray woolen cloak over his armor, then slid into his boots. When he finished dressing, he walked over and put his hands on Caleb's shoulders. "I can't bear the thought of splitting up."

"Then don't go. Simple as that."

"I have to, Caleb. We need something to help Val. We need to find a way home. And these people . . . our people . . . they need our help."

"Our people? This isn't even our *world!*"

"Do we refuse to help someone simply because they weren't born in our neighborhood, our city, our country?" Will said quietly. "And it *is* our world. It's Dad's world."

"This better not be about Xena the Warrior Princess," Caleb muttered.

"Don't be ridiculous," Will said, though he couldn't deny his feelings for Mala.

"Be careful, or she might sneeze and accidentally kill you. Then sell your sword on the black market."

Will strapped on his scabbard. "Mala's a good person. I just don't think she realizes it."

"My little brother, always trying to change the world."

"If everyone was a pacifist like you, I wouldn't need to." Will picked up Zariduke and held it lengthwise in his hands, studying it. When he finally looked up, he said, "I'm terrified."

"As you should be."

"I don't belong with them."

Caleb sat beside him and draped an arm around his shoulder. "That's where you're wrong. You're a warrior now, Will."

"I'm a novice."

"Not after the escape from the mines, and what I saw during the wizards' attack. Plus, you have a cool secret weapon."

"Dad's sword can't stop an arrow. Or any other non-magical weapon."

"Not that, dork." Caleb poked him in the heart. "This. More than any of them. More than anyone I've ever known. You better come back to me, little brother. If I'm going to die in this world, I at least want you by my side."

"No one's going to die in this world," Will said, trying to force himself to believe it.

Will left the room with a heavy heart, nauseated by the thought of splitting up from Caleb. Though he had to admit his brother was in no condition for a journey, and his limited skillset would make him a liability.

Before he met with Tamás, Will stopped by Dalen's room. He found his friend practicing his budding illusionist skills, using the light streaming through the window to transform a crystal in his palm into a multi-hued prism.

"Take care of yourself, buddy," Will said.

Dalen set the crystal down. "*Lucka*, I wish I was going with you."

"Next time. Keep an eye on Caleb, okay?"

The young illusionist looked doubtful. "I'll try. I've never seen anyone who can outdrink an entire clan."

"I know," Will said quietly. "Do your best."

Dalen flashed an infectious grin. "Maybe they'll let me be the wizard on the next expedition."

Will clasped forearms with him and took his leave. For all his talk about his adventures with his *Da*, Will suspected Dalen's life journey had been a rough and lonely one.

He seemed happy here, though. The Freetown gypsies had taken him in. Even better, a local illusionist had accepted Dalen as his apprentice.

After saying goodbye to Marek, who was waiting on the next caravan east to rejoin his family, Will searched in vain for Mateo. Had his cousin returned to the Blackwood Forest? Was he off mourning his brother?

Yasmina wasn't around, either. That hurt. He guessed she was off in the surrounding forest, doing whatever it was wilders did, but she had promised to meet him to say goodbye. He traipsed across the ruined town looking for her and Mateo, the smell of death and ash still lingering in the air, his stomach clenching at the extent of the devastation. The colorful tents and pavilions of Freetown lay in heaps of charred canvas, the sparkling fountains dry and lifeless, pubs and inns leveled.

The mood of the people was even grimmer. Those who remained were mostly revolutionary fighters, the injured, and healers. Others had stayed because they had nowhere to go, squatting in lean-tos on the beach as they worked to repair their wagons.

Will watched three golden-bodied, crimson-winged simorghs circle and then descend into town, their long tails fluttering behind them. The party's ride to the lost pyramid of the sorcerer king. Will hurried to the central square to join the rest of the group.

Long and sinewy like a reptile, yet feathered and beaked like a bird, the powerful simorghs were perched like regal statues in the middle of the square. Tamás was standing by the shattered beer fountain with two people: Mateo, and a slender woman wearing a forest green traveling cloak, brown boots, and a green-and-red bloodstone pendant. Their wizard, Will guessed.

"Mateo!" Will said. "I've been looking everywhere for you."

"Is that so?"

"I wanted to say goodbye."

"Why would you want to do such an unpleasant thing?" Mateo grinned, and Will noticed the rucksack and buckler at his feet, the shortbow strapped to the back of his patchwork cloak, and a thick leather belt coiled around his waist. A wooden hilt stuck out from the front of the belt.

"You're going with us?" Will said, thrilled at the prospect.

Mateo embraced him, his brown eyes tinged with sadness. "We will search for the coffer and avenge my brother together."

Tamás introduced the woman, who looked a few years older than Val, somewhere in her mid-thirties. "Selina is your sylvamancer for the journey."

Will knew sylvamancy was one of the eight core disciplines, and that was about it. Something to do with forests and the natural world, he assumed. He didn't care. He was just happy they had a wizard.

"Don't you mean *our* sylvamancer?" Will said, noticing Tamás wasn't carrying any gear.

Tamás took him by the arm and led him away from the others. "My people are in disarray. Scattered along the Barrier Coast. They need their leader here, with them."

Will didn't know what to say. He was counting on Tamás's steady presence and prowess on the battlefield.

"Mateo is my equal in a fight, I assure you. One of the best we have, an urumi blademaster. He and Selina will be valuable assets to the expedition. With you and Mala by their side . . . I have high hopes for your success."

Will felt buoyed by his confidence, though he knew Tamás was a born leader and trying to raise morale.

Tamás clapped him on the shoulder, his eyes intense. "I know you share our blood, but I also know this didn't have to be your fight. Thank you for risking your life for our people. I no longer consider you my friend, my ally, my comrade in arms—we are brothers now, Will Blackwood."

As they clasped forearms, Will felt a rush of pride, then guilt about his other motives. He truly wanted to help these people, but he also knew his first duty was to Val and Caleb.

He hoped he never had to choose.

"I have to ask," Tamás said, still holding into Will, "where you found Zariduke."

Will started; he had long been expecting the question, and knew Tamás wasn't happy Will had kept the origin of the sword a secret.

After hesitating, Will said, "Do you promise to keep this between us? At least for now?"

"As you wish. It is your knowledge to give."

He knew Val and Caleb might feel differently about revealing the secret of the sword and their father, but Will was more trusting—and more impulsive—than his brothers. "Our father was Dane Blackwood."

Tamás's eyes slowly widened. He had known only that Will and his brothers shared the common surname. "But what . . . no one knows what happened to him."

"He died," Will said. "A long time ago. I don't know where he found the sword, or why he was looking for it, but he left it for me."

After promising to relay the full story at a later time, Will left the leader of the Revolution standing stunned on the cobblestoned street. When Will turned back to the others, he saw Mala approaching the square, and felt both giddy and queasy at the prospect of a journey with the woman who haunted his dreams. Then he saw who was walking behind her with a large rucksack strapped on his back, along with a two-handed broadsword almost as long as Will.

Mala's handsome, overly muscled companion.

Boyfriend, long-term friends with benefits, partner for a seven-night stand, Will wasn't sure of the exact nature of their relationship. But his flush of excitement had melted into a puddle of dirty rainwater at the sight of the hulking warrior.

"Will the Builder," Mala said, greeting him with the familiar teasing tone. Her eyes lingered on Mateo, as if judging his prowess, and then apprised Selina.

"A sylvamancer?" Mala said. "Inside a pyramid?"

"You're welcome," Tamás said wryly. "Our remaining elder mages are needed here, and we thought a sylvamancer would be useful for the journey through the jungle. Or perhaps you wish for an apprentice geomancer instead?"

Mala ignored him, then crossed her arms in silence while Tamás gave a rousing speech to remind them of the importance of the journey. Caleb staggered up just before they climbed onto the simorghs, beer mug in hand, and Will could tell he was drunk again.

"You hang in there," Will said, crushing his brother in a bear hug. "I'll be back soon."

"Don't try to be a hero," Caleb said, his breath reeking.

Will swallowed hard. "You lay off the sauce, okay?"

Caleb looked down at his mug. "The true measure of a man, little brother, is how much fun he has in life."

"Is that why you've been working so hard to help build shelters and repair wagons for families who lost everything in the attack?"

Caleb looked down and mumbled a reply. There was something different in his voice, something profoundly sad beneath the glib comebacks, that Will didn't like one bit. Before he could reply, he saw his brother's eyes widen, and Will turned to find Yasmina striding towards them wrapped in a pewter-colored traveling cloak, her caramel hair spilling out from the hood, and with her owl staff in hand.

He thought she was coming to hug his brother goodbye, but after giving Will a warm smile, she brushed past Caleb and walked right up to one of the simorghs. The beast lowered its head to allow Yasmina access to the ladder-like harness.

"Yaz?" Caleb said.

"I'd like to join the expedition," she said, from the back of the simorgh.

Mala turned to Tamás, who looked flustered. He had harbored a not-so-secret crush on Yasmina ever since the flight from the Darklands.

Yasmina's eyes flicked towards Caleb, and Will understood. She wanted separation.

"We agreed to keep the effort small and maneuverable," Mala said. "Nor do I know this woman."

Yasmina ignored her and addressed Tamás. "I thought a wilder might be useful on the journey."

"You're a wilder?" Mala said doubtfully.

Yasmina turned to lock eyes with the adventuress, then held out her arms. Two furry moles scurried out of her sleeves and into her palms, pink noses twitching, before racing back inside. She lowered her hand, made a strange and high-pitched sound from the back of her throat, and the simorgh reared its head to allow her to stroke its plumed mane.

"By the Queen," Mala said, with grudging respect. "An actual wilder. Your talents are welcome indeed, though we both know your loyalty lies with your calling, and not with this expedition."

Yasmina didn't dispute the claim, and Will could only stare. Who had Yasmina become?

"It's settled, then," Tamás said, unable to disguise the disappointment in his voice. "The party is complete."

Guided by Yith Riders, the three simorghs climbed in a lazy spiral, crimson wings fluttering and flowing tails spread like a halo in the air as the ruins of Freetown receded from sight. The great birds hugged the coastline as they traveled south, the ocean stretched out like a vast blue painting. To Will's left loomed the dry tawny hills of central California, known as the Barrier Coast on Urfe.

The Yith Riders, Will had learned, descended from one of the first Romani clans to arrive on the Barrier Coast. They had settled in the high reaches of the Făgras and Dragon's Teeth long ago, intermingled with the native peoples, and adapted their lifestyle and customs to fit their surroundings. But they had remained close to the other clans, and always heeded their call.

Will shared a simorgh with Selina. As they swept over an undulating line of dunes, he leaned forward in his saddle, shouting over the wind. "Have you been to the Mayan Kingdom before?"

"I've never left the Barrier Coast," Selina replied, in a soft-spoken voice marked by a deep rural accent. She had olive skin, chin-length chestnut hair, and a mousy face with none of the arrogance typical of most mage-born.

"But you're a wizard—don't you have to pass some kind of test? In New Victoria?"

"Only if one desires validation from the Congregation. We train our own wizards. I would never abandon my clan simply to see my name inscribed in some registry."

So Selina was a down-to-earth, small-town girl who marched to the beat of her own drum.

Will liked her already.

"I hear the Mayan Kingdom is another world," she said in a subdued voice. "Unlike anything in New Albion."

According to Mala, the starting point on the map was a well-known Mayan coastal town named Ixmal, a lawless port on the fringes of the empire. Though dangerous, the isolation of Ixmal could work in the expedition's favor. The Mayan Kingdom had a Divine King who ruled from a giant pyramid at Tikal-Paya, but the real power lay in the two dozen or so city-states run by Arch-governors and supported by a class of Battle Mages: fearsome wizards with a reputation of seeking out and punishing intruders.

Due to Ixmal's position on the frontier, there might be less chance of running across the legendary warrior-wizards.

Will shivered. "What do you know about the pyramid tomb?"

"When the Calakmul Empire was finally conquered by Tikal, Yiknoom didn't want his enemies to possess his fabled treasure. As the story goes, he

built a pyramid deep in the jungle to entomb himself alongside his possessions."

"If it's a pyramid, why has no one ever found it?"

"He was a powerful sorcerer. No doubt he used cloaking magic."

"That lasted after his death?"

She shrugged. "No one really knows the extent of his power."

Will swallowed as he remembered the inscription. *All those who seek may
enter, but none shall ever leave.* "Are there any legends about the pyramid itself?"

"Until this map surfaced, no one had ever claimed to find it." Her face
turned grim. "But the Mayans have been building pyramids for thousands of
years, and the sorcerer kings were infamous for their cruelty."

Isn't that fascinating, Will thought.

The simorghs were incredibly strong and fast. They flew three shifts a day, of
nearly four hours each, over some of the most beautiful scenery Will had ever
seen. Swaths of wildflowers flowed like brushstrokes across the hills, golden
mountains swept down to a coastline of mist-drizzled dunes and frothy surf,
and on the second day, after turning inland and crossing a desert, the party entered a moonscape of pockmarked mesas and canyons scooped from the earth.

They stopped that night atop a sandstone pillar that emerged from the desert floor like a giant mushroom. After a cold dinner and six hours of sleep
under the stars, they took flight again, soon entering a lush mountain range
that extended to the horizon. Somewhere in northern Mexico, Will presumed.

Just after midday, as he was snacking on a piece of dried beef, the simorghs
drew together in a tight formation and slowed to a stop, hovering in midair
as if awaiting instruction. Will and Selina exchanged a worried glance as their
Yith Rider stood in his saddle and gazed at the clear sky through a leather-cov-
ered glass tube, trying to discern what had spooked the mounts.

After a few moments, the Rider said something in his own language that
sounded like a curse, then exchanged frantic, shouted instructions with the
other two Riders. Yasmina, riding behind Mateo, peered into the distance as
she clutched the owl staff bequeathed to her by a wilder named Elegon, and
which somehow enhanced her sensory perception.

In the distance, a pair of green dots appeared, gaining rapidly in size. Before anyone offered an explanation, Will saw for himself the nature of the terrifying creatures speeding towards them like colossal reptilian arrows, wings tucked in and curved talons extended. Saurian creatures straight out of every fantasy novel and role playing game, the monster no one ever wanted to face, the stuff of which dreams and nightmares were made.

Dragons.

5

A team of majitsu escorted Val to the infirmary, where a cuerpomancer bandaged his wrists and treated the bite wound by cauterizing it and making Val drink a creamy liquid that tasted like sassafras. After that, the majitsu hooded him and stuck him back in his cell.

On the third day after his appointment with the queen, a portion of the honeycombed prison wall hinged open, and the same gray-cloaked member of the Wizard Guard who had saved Val's life stepped inside.

He surprised Val by offering a forearm clasp. "We've not been properly introduced. My name is Cyrus Ravensill."

After Val accepted the gesture, Cyrus handed him a silver bracelet. "Before we leave, you must don this spirit bond. It does not interfere with the working of magic, but so long as you remain on Urfe, we'll know your location."

Knowing he didn't have a choice, Val slipped on the slender bracelet. It molded to his wrist, tight but not uncomfortable. He hid his anger at being treated like chattel.

Cyrus handed him a hooded gray cloak similar to his own, with fewer black markings on the sleeves. "You will travel under the aegis of the Wizard Guard. Honor the position."

Val gave a curt nod. "Are you a spirit mage?"

"I see the rumors are true. You're from a northern outpost, indeed." Cyrus's lips parted in a faint smile. "The Wizard Guard focuses on magic expedient to the defense of Queen and Realm. Though we draw from a variety of disciplines, and many of our spells are hybrid in nature, it is rare indeed for one with the talent of a spiritmancer to join our ranks."

Val followed him out of the cell. Cyrus waved a hand and closed the azantite doorway. As Val shrugged into the heavy cloak, they floated down a wide stone hallway lined with similar doorways spaced thirty feet apart. At the end of the corridor, they drifted up a long spiral staircase, and Cyrus hooded Val again.

Once they removed his hood, Val saw that they had led him back to the same room as before. Queen Victoria and her retinue of majitsu had already arrived. With them was a bald woman about Caleb's age, wearing a fitted black shirt and trousers. She was slight but wiry, and a majitsu grasped each arm.

"Synne will be accompanying you," the queen stated. Val wondered what crime she had committed. The majitsu released the woman, and Synne walked over to stand beside Val, eying him warily. She had an androgynous face that, combined with the bald head, Val had almost mistaken for a man.

"It is time to learn who has agreed to accompany you," Queen Victoria said.

As if on cue, he heard a dull *whoosh*, like the opening of a rubber seal. A man with skin the color of a moonless night appeared out of nowhere, between Val and the queen. Val recognized his friend Dida, a bibliomancer from the Kingdom of Great Zimbabwe. Val felt a mix of emotions: a rush of gratitude at his presence, relief that he wouldn't be alone, and a stabbing guilt from asking him to risk his life.

"Dida! I can't believe you came."

"Perhaps I will have the chance to put my esoteric skills to actual use," he said, with a warm smile. Besides Adaira, whose powerful father Val knew would never let her leave, Dida was the most accomplished mage Val counted as a friend.

Another *whoosh*, and someone he had counted as an extreme long shot teleported into the room. A one-armed, grizzled warrior gripping an oddly wide short sword in his left hand and wearing a battle-notched, black leather breastplate.

Rucker.

A legendary adventurer Val had met only once, when he and Dida had visited Rucker in a tavern in New Victoria to gain information on the assassin targeting their fellow students at the Abbey. Even in a room of hardened explorers, Rucker had commanded respect. He would be an invaluable addition.

Val was stunned. "I can't believe you came. Thank you."

"I didn't do it for ye, boy. I told ye before I don't join parties any more, unless it's something that intrigues me."

"Which almost nothing does."

Rucker barked a laugh. "Good memory."

He didn't explain further, and Val wondered at his true motive. Dida hurried out of the way as the crusty buccaneer took his place beside Val. Synne, he noted, didn't flinch as did most people in Rucker's presence.

The queen seemed to concentrate on something for a moment, then said, "It appears your party is complete. Dean Groft, I'm afraid, will not be joining you."

Though disappointed, Val was not surprised. Put on the spot by the queen, he had struggled to name his companions. He debated asking for Alrick, but feared the dissolute phrenomancer would be in no condition to travel. Who was left? Lord Alistair would never let Adaira go, and Val had worked hard to stay out of the limelight at wizard school. He had no other close friends.

He had hardly expected Dean Groft, the esteemed Dean of Spiritmancy, to leave the Abbey and join an ill-fated expedition into the unknown. He had chosen the dean for two reasons: first, because Groft was the most powerful mage Val knew, short of Salomon and Lord Alistair. Second, Val had always thought Dean Groft had a soft spot for him, and he had seen compassion in his eyes when Val was sent to prison. Perhaps the dean would send someone in his stead the queen would accept.

Apparently not.

"A bold choice," the queen said, in a neutral tone. "A pity it did not work out."

More than a pity. Val knew he had talent, and Dida was years ahead of him in his studies, but neither were a full-fledged wizard. What did the queen think two apprentice mages, an aging adventurer, and a young woman with no apparent battle skills were supposed to do about a situation the Wizard Guard had not been able to handle?

He decided to ask her. "My Queen, I mean no offense, but even if we do find Tobar, he's a spirit mage. How do we combat him?"

The queen gave a small, knowing smile, as if she'd been waiting for the question. She held a palm out, and an azantite container the size of a saltshaker materialized in her hand.

"Do you recognize this?" she asked the group.

Even Rucker looked perplexed.

"A Soul Jar," the queen said. "A most powerful device. If you manage to find Tobar Baltoris, this will allow you to trap his essence inside."

The inspiration for the genie in the bottle, Val wondered? "How does it work?"

"The jar will take the first breath it feels after it is opened," she said, pinching the intricately wrought stopper. Her parting smile was as cold as a glacier. "Take care it is not yours."

An hour later, Val found himself stepping into another flying black stagecoach with Dida, Rucker, and Synne. Dida and Rucker both carried small rucksacks they had brought through the portal.

Rucker's gray ponytail stuck out beneath a red-and-black horned battle helm. In addition to the sword strapped on his back and a spiked bronze vambrace covering his forearm, a serrated hunting knife and a set of smaller tools hung from his leather belt. A pair of wicked iron spurs protected his boots, and his gnarled index finger bore a multi-colored ring that resembled hardened lava.

Val and Synne had each been given packs with basic gear, provisions, and a valuable jar of healing salve. Synne carried no weapons, and Val wondered what use she would be. Was she a healer? Just as he started to ask her, Rucker turned to her and said, "Where's yer belt and robe?"

Synne gave him a frosty stare. "None of your concern."

Belt and robe? Val wondered. Seeing his confusion, Rucker said, "She's majitsu, boy. Can't ye tell by the way she moves?"

Val was stunned. They had sent a majitsu? With them?

Black-robed warrior-mages who enhanced their limited magic with martial art skills, most majitsu served the Congregation in some capacity, often as bodyguards. They possessed an aura of danger and competency that always left Val uneasy in their presence.

"I'm not a majitsu yet," Synne replied. "I haven't completed my training."

Val decided not to press her, at least not in front of the others. He sensed it was a sore subject.

Cyrus again helmed the carriage. With a nod to his passengers, he lifted the stagecoach off the courtyard and into the night.

"You should rest on the journey," the wizard guard said. "We arrive at first light."

"Arrive where?" Val asked.

"Porlock. The closest village to where Tobar disappeared. A legate there will inform you better."

Val had more questions, so many more, but he heard a note of finality in Cyrus's tone and decided to heed his advice. As the carriage flew high above the city, between the carnival of lights below and the dome of stars above, Val leaned his head back and closed his eyes.

It was a long time before he fell asleep, and when he finally did, he swam in memories of another night sky, in another world. His thoughts lingered on his brothers and then, surprising Val, they roamed fast and free to a young woman from Urfe, a daughter of wizards with pale skin and turquoise eyes, intelligent eyes, and a spirit as fierce and independent as his own.

Early the next morning, Val woke as the carriage set down in a cobblestone square surrounded by speckled granite buildings with thatched roofs. A soft layer of mist cloaked the village.

A crowd of people gathered as the party hoisted their packs and stepped out of the stagecoach. The faces of the villagers were wary, distrustful. Val didn't like the vibe. The gray cloaks of the wizard guard seemed to both cow and antagonize the crowd.

A rotund man in a cloak of fine wool pressed through the crowd, hurrying to greet the new arrivals. He bowed to Cyrus and then Val.

"Legate Wainwright," Cyrus said. "Well met again."

"Obliged, my lord. If you will follow me?"

The villagers muttered amongst themselves as the legate led Val and the others through a series of narrow lanes crowded with two-story wooden buildings. The destination was an inn called The Oak and Bull, which sat across the street from a red brick clock tower.

The common room of the inn smelled like wood smoke and cherry pie. Legate Wainwright commandeered a table next to the hearth. Despite the chill outside, the fire put out so much heat that Val took off his cloak.

"The villagers are unhappy," Cyrus stated, after introductions were made and a serving girl brought tea and scones. "Even worse than before."

The legate's obsequious expression soured. "A new demon has emerged. It took a boy of eighteen yesterday."

Rucker had been staring at the fire, and his attention snapped back to the group. "What do you mean, a demon?"

"Another?" Cyrus asked, ignoring the adventurer. "I was hoping it was an aberration. It's time to post guards along the border. They still blame wizards?"

"Yes, milord. Appeals to logic and patience from Londyn . . . have fallen on deaf ears."

"Is there a description?"

"Only that the beast has many arms and stands at least seven feet tall."

Rucker snorted.

"No reports of magic?" Cyrus asked.

"They say it runs faster than a galloping horse, and can swallow a grown pig whole. Exaggerations, of course."

"Maybe, maybe not." The queen's wizard glanced out the window. "Do we have any idea where it sleeps?"

"Multiple villagers have reported seeing it running towards the ruins of the old fort."

Cyrus gazed into the fire. "There has long been mistrust between wizards and common born in this part of the Realm. More deaths will only sow malcontent and embolden this loathsome Revolution."

"Shall I request a regiment, my lord?"

"I'll take care of this myself," Cyrus said, causing the legate's eyes to widen. The gray-cloaked wizard eyed the group. "Or rather, *we* will. Right now. It's early, and perhaps we can catch the demon unawares."

Rucker growled. "Stop calling it that."

"Excuse me?"

"There hasn't been a true demon in the Realm for a thousand years. Ye should know that, because yer not standing far from the town of Badŏn where they last appeared."

Dida sat up straighter. "You mean Badŏn the Damned? Is this true?"

"True as taxes." Rucker jerked his thumb at Cyrus. "It took a whole army of his kind to get rid of 'em."

"I'm fully aware of that." Cyrus stood and pulled the cowl of his robe over his head, casting his face in shadows. "And the town of Badŏn, damned as you say and destroyed by a spirit storm nearly one thousand years ago, might be exactly where the demons are coming from."

6

The dragons flew closer. As the Yith Riders shouted to each other in their own language, the simorghs hovered in midair, awaiting a command.

Will's voice felt tight when he spoke, fear clawing at his throat. "Did someone send them?"

"No one commands dragons," Selina said. "They act of their own accord."

"Can you do something?"

"It takes bigger magic than mine to fight such creatures," she said grimly. "A dragon's claws can penetrate all but the most powerful of wizard shields."

"Do they . . . breathe fire?"

"Each species of dragon possesses one or two innate magical abilities. The only fire breathers I'm aware of live inside the Mokupuni volcanoes. Far away from here."

When the pair of dragons were a hundred yards away, Will got a closer look. Both beasts had mottled green scales, four short but powerful legs, and an icy blue Mohawk of spikes running down their backs. They had enormous horned heads and long sinewy bodies, three times the size of the simorghs.

"Highland dragons," Selina breathed.

Still the simorghs hadn't moved. When the dragons drew within twenty yards, close enough for Will to see their flattened snouts and strangely intelligent faces, the great beasts opened their maws and vomited a cone of greenish-blue vapor. Will hung on for his life as the simorghs dove just in time to avoid the attack, flying underneath the dragons and hurtling towards the closest line of peaks. A sharp chemical odor emanated from the breath weapon the dragons had unleashed.

"What was that?" he shouted to Selina.

"Stone mist. They use it to paralyze their victims in the sky and drop them to the ground like stones."

The dragons wheeled sharply in midair and raced after the simorghs. At first it seemed as if the smaller birds were faster, but the dragons started to gain ground. Will guessed the Yith had planned to lose the beasts in the approaching peaks, but it was clear they wouldn't reach them in time.

After more shouted commands, the simorghs darted higher when the dragons released the next blast of teal mist. The vapor passed right beside Will, causing him to choke and feel a tingling sensation in his limbs.

"I was able to shield us on that pass," Selina said. "But we won't survive a direct hit."

Mateo fired off two arrows that bounced off the mottled hide of the nearest dragon. Will noticed Mala talking to her Yith Rider, who shook his head in disagreement at whatever she was saying. Gunnar, Mala's brutish companion, was standing in his saddle, clutching the war hammer he favored.

When Will turned towards the third simorgh, his cousin met his eyes. Though Will felt nothing but desperation, he returned Mateo's look of grim determination, drawing strength from his kin.

Yasmina stood in her saddle and scanned the horizon as if looking for something unseen. When she turned to face the western horizon, left of the peaks, she risked leaving her stirrups to edge closer to the simorgh's head. Gripping its mane, she bent down as if talking to it, and Will feared she would plunge to her death. The Yith Rider shouted and waved his hand for her to strap back in.

The peaks were a half mile away. Yasmina returned to her position right before the dragons wheeled and approached again. This time the simorghs didn't wait: they broke apart in three different directions before the dragons got close enough to release the stone mist. Will's mount banked left, and one of the dragons followed. Mala's and Gunnar's dragon veered right, drawing another.

The simorgh bearing Mateo and Yasmina executed a crafty looping maneuver, soaring over both dragons, then flew directly towards the western horizon. As it flew, the great bird emitted a piercing cry that rattled Will's eardrums.

The Yith Rider looked furious but couldn't get the simorghs to respond. *What had Yasmina told them*, Will wondered? Was she trying to draw the dragons into the peaks, where simorgh mounts had more maneuverability? They would never make it in time.

The dragon chasing Mala and Gunnar changed tactics. It broke off and flew towards Will and Selina, a hundred feet from the other dragon, cutting off the escape angles. They were going to pick them off one by one, starting with Will's mount.

In desperation, his simorgh flew higher, towards the clouds. Both dragons followed. The simorgh whirled and looped, spun and dove, but nothing it did could shake the huge reptiles. Will hugged the saddle as one of the beasts opened its mouth and breathed, causing the simorgh to veer left, directly into the path of the other dragon.

Just as the dragon reared its head to release a blast of stone mist, an even louder cry split the air, much deeper than the simorgh's shrill call, somewhere between a boom and a roar.

The dragons lowered their snouts and whipped around in midair. Will's simorgh seized the opportunity, nose-diving almost to the ground before leveling out. When he was finally able to look up, he saw an awesome sight: five gigantic birds with black feathers, each as big as a house, flying straight towards the dragons. He recognized the majestic avians from the journey home from Leonidus's castle.

"Rukhs," Selina said, in a shocked voice. "The ancient enemy of dragons, and immune to their breath."

The dragons hung vertically in the air and bellowed their rage, but instead of engaging, they took off in the direction from which they had come. The rukhs gave chase, and both groups disappeared into the horizon.

Shaking from nerves, Will felt the wind rush in his face as the simorghs raced towards the southeast horizon. They didn't stop until the moon shadowed the earth.

Two days later, Will woke to a stunning view of snowcapped volcanic peaks and rippling green forests. His breath fogged the air as he clutched his blanket tighter, yearning for a cup of good coffee.

The night before, Mala and the guides had seemed warier than usual. Over breakfast, he learned they were deep inside the Mayan Kingdom. If all went as planned, they would arrive at the Yucatan village late the next day.

He also learned Yasmina had found the rukhs that had saved their lives. She had sensed them in the mountains when they flew over. Will didn't bother asking how she knew, or how she had coerced her simorgh to summon the legendary birds. He wasn't even sure Yasmina knew. Elegon had provided her with some training, but Will sensed she had an innate talent that had opened like a lotus flower in this world, and was still unfurling.

After the party broke camp, the simorghs flew low and kept to the mountains. Will saw a number of strange avian creatures, but no more dragons. At one point they crossed a sapphire blue lake ringed by limestone outcroppings, and a group of winged humanoids rose into the air, clutching spears and flying aggressively towards them. The simorghs flew higher and faster, evading them with diffident ease.

The next day, after camping on a high meadow tucked between peaks, they crossed a long stretch of ocean and then flew over the Yucatan: a vast, flat, impossibly dense jungle broken only by scattered hills or the rare tip of a stone pyramid thrusting above the trees. Will felt both excited and uneasy at the thought of trekking through that forbidding landscape.

As the sun started to descend, the simorghs angled towards a port town sandwiched between the jungle and a coastline as pale blue as a robin's egg. The dusty outskirts sloped gently up to a plateau dotted with stone buildings in the center of town. The plateau overlooked the main harbor, where hundreds of small boats bobbed offshore.

"Ixmal?" Will asked.

"Aye," his Yith Rider called back.

The forms of the simorghs and their riders started to shimmer. A glance at Selina's face, deep in concentration, told Will she was cloaking their arrival. The Yith guided their mounts down to the tree line, which provided more camouflage, and the simorghs landed on a stretch of beach south of town.

The party thanked the Riders, who said they would camp in nearby mountains and fly over the same spot once a week for two months. After they left, Will felt a heaviness settle into his bones.

They were on their own now, deep in the Mayan Kingdom.

Mala glanced at the position of the sun as the party gathered around her. "We'll need to stay the night, and the inns are near the center of town. I have one in mind that will forge certificates of visitation from the port authority. On the way, do nothing to draw the attention of the border guard. They might ask for our papers, and we have nothing yet to give."

"Why not follow the rules?" Selina asked. "Register with the port authority?

"Has word not reached the Barrier Coast? New Victoria and the Mayan Kingdom suspended diplomatic relations months ago. It is common knowledge that Lord Alistair has his eye on southern expansion."

"Why not camp here instead?" Mateo asked.

"In the center of town, we will blend. Out here, we might catch the eye of a watchful patrol. Moreover, bandits roam the perimeter of the city at night."

"When do we enter the jungle?" Selina asked.

"In the morning, if I can locate the guide I have in mind. Two more things: the use of magic by foreign wizards is prohibited, and if we happen to pass near a Battle Mage, be particularly careful. They question outsiders more than the local patrols."

"What exactly is a Battle Mage?" Will asked.

"If you have the misfortune of seeing one, Will the Builder, you'll know."

After that ominous pronouncement, they gathered their packs and headed towards town. Dusty footpaths and scattered collections of thatched roof huts marked the settlements on the perimeter. Short, thick, chestnut-skinned women carried water jugs and pounded maize in ceramic pots as children ran among the huts and splashed in the surf. Though the party drew plenty of stares, no one accosted them.

The poor areas surrounding the town merged into a busy center of dusty stone plazas, canvas stalls, and a mix of cobblestone, dirt, and grass roads. The denizens of the town proper looked much more affluent and culturally varied than the peasants on the outskirts.

"Ixmal is not a typical Mayan town," Maya said. "It has a lax governor, and the port has imparted a cosmopolitan flavor."

The aroma of cooking lard overlaid the salty tang in the air. Will saw a few sights that caused his head to turn: a silver-haired woman selling miniature winged serpents out of cages; a group of men in loincloths practicing a type of ball game in the street; a set of deep stone pits containing emaciated prisoners withering in the sun; a painted man in a headdress spinning a giant wheel covered in runes, shouting to the heavens with his arms upraised.

Mala had to switch course a few times, and Will could tell she didn't know the town that well. At one point they found themselves crossing a courtyard that had seen better days. Weeds poked out of the stones underfoot, and crumbling limestone buildings surrounded the plaza. They had almost passed through when a scream to Will's left startled him.

He turned to find a darkened doorway leading into a decrepit old temple. Ten-foot pillars were carved into the cracked, blue-hued limestone comprising the face of the building. A swath of faded but elaborate scrollwork ran just below the roofline.

Another scream, ragged and more prolonged. Feminine. Someone in pain. Will stopped walking.

"It's none of our concern," Mala said.

The screaming continued. He realized it was a little girl's voice, and stepped towards the doorway.

"No!" Mala said, sharply but under her breath. A few other people milled about the square. Will knew she didn't want to draw attention to the party.

After another scream, he waffled and then stepped into the darkened interior. It wasn't in him to let someone suffer if he had a choice. Especially a child.

Why wasn't anyone helping her?

Behind him, Mala barked at everyone else to wait. Will focused on his surroundings and saw a temple dimly lit by torchlight. Friezes of battle scenes and fantastical monsters covered the walls, so covered in grime they were barely recognizable. A group of slender pillars demarcated a section of colored tiles where men and women in rags huddled on the ground, either sleeping or hovered over bowls with green smoke pouring out.

In the far right corner, a heavyset man was whipping a girl of no more than twelve, curled into a ball on the ground. Mala caught up to Will and gripped his arm, but he shook her off and strode towards the man. "Hey!" he said. "That's enough!"

The man with the whip didn't respond. Will walked faster and drew his sword. Just before he reached them, the man turned towards Will and grinned. Instead of taking the opportunity to escape, a dagger appeared in the hand of the girl, and she jumped to her feet beside the man.

Will whipped around. The people he had mistaken for beggars and drug addicts had raised into threatening crouches, pulling out scimitars and cutlasses from underneath their blankets. Mala was a few steps behind Will, already reaching for her sash. The rest of the party had remained outside.

As the group of thieves advanced on Will and Mala, four of the men broke off to roll a huge stone in front of the door to the old temple, sealing the exit.

Will reached for his sword as Mala swung her weighted sash in a circle of increasing tempo, until it was a blur of movement. "Well done, Will the Builder," she said. "You've a keen eye for a damsel in distress."

Will swallowed and didn't respond. Now strong enough to fight with Zariduke in one hand, he raised his sword and gripped a small diamond-shaped shield in his other. He spun back and forth, trying to keep the thieves at bay. Right before the battle erupted, the boulder guarding the door flew backwards, cracking one of the pillars.

Gunnar released a war cry as he rushed inside. Owl staff gripped tight, Yasmina surged ahead of Mateo, who had nocked an arrow to his shortbow and was swiveling to find a target. Most of the fighters pressuring Will were forced to break away and face the newcomers.

Yet it was Selina who ended the battle before it began. After stepping inside and surveying the situation, the sylvamancer raised her arms and caused a section of tiled floor to explode upward, along with a funnel of dirt. After the rubble and loose soil cascaded back to the floor, a host of subterranean creepy crawlies remained suspended in midair, centipedes and eyeless worms and stinging fire ants. Selina sent the insects hurtling into the group of bandits, causing a mad rush to flee the ruined temple. The thieves clawed at their skin as they ran, screaming "mage!"

After giving Will a withering glance, Mala shepherded everyone towards the exit. The commotion had caused a crowd to gather in the plaza, and the party did their best to blend in.

"I thought I said no magic," Mala said in a harsh whisper, as they hurried away from the temple.

"Would you rather risk lives in needless battle?" Selina said.

"I'd rather not attract the attention of a Battle Mage, when someone reports us. And let us pray no one already has."

7

Days after his brother left, mug of ale in one hand and flask of grog in another, Caleb watched with bleary eyes from the doorway of the Red Wagon tavern as Tamás addressed the crowd. The leader of the Revolution was standing on the lip of the restored beer fountain in the central plaza, calling for volunteers to warn the clans of the escalating threat. The clans liked to roam, but most had traditional settlements of some sort sprinkled up and down the Barrier Coast, from the southern deserts to the coastal forests to the Făgras Mountains in the north.

Caleb wondered morosely whether it would be more dangerous to wait in Freetown until the wizards decided to attack again, or wander the Barrier Coast and risk encountering whatever monsters and horrible surprises this world always seemed to have in store.

Better to stay here, he decided. At least there was a warm bed and plenty of beer.

"Join us!" Tamás shouted, pumping a fist as his long blond hair shimmered in the sun behind him. "Urge your kin to join the Revolution! Warn them they could be next on Lord Alistair's list!"

Though he missed his brothers desperately, and had never felt more alone, Caleb did not feel guilty about not going on that insane quest with Will, or not stepping forward to join Tamás. Caleb believed in peace and love, in having a good time and doing anything that didn't involve harm to other people. He had never cared about causes and knew he never would, but did that make him a bad person? Why be something he was not?

After the speech, the members of the council handed out assignments to a few new recruits. Most able-bodied adults had families to tend to, or were part of the Revolution's fighting regiments.

When the chaos ebbed, Tamás noticed Caleb standing by the tavern, and walked over. "You should join us, son of Blackwood. The people know you. Your exploits have spread throughout the Barrier Coast."

"That's a terrifying thought."

Tamás took in Caleb's unfocused eyes and the two drinks in his hands. "A journey would do you well," Tamás said. "As of yet, no one has volunteered to ride to the Blackwood Forest. Why not go yourself? Reach your kin and call them to arms?"

"I'm not much of a recruiter. Nor am I brave like my brothers."

"Bravery is a choice," Tamás said softly.

Caleb pointed the mug of ale at him. "Exactly."

There was a commotion in the square. Another caravan must have arrived. They were pouring in daily, gypsies and other non-citizen refugees from the protectorates, fleeing the patrols and increased persecution, confirming the dire rumors of pogroms and mass graves. Surprisingly, a growing number of Oath-takers had joined the caravans of late, citizens uncomfortable with the atmosphere of bigotry and oppression fostered by the Congregation.

Caleb was about to return inside when he saw someone who looked like a woman he had once known, a member of the Rogue's Guild who had accompanied him and his brothers to Leonidus's castle. A lover he had grown very close to, and whose grave injuries had devastated him. He didn't even know if she was still alive.

Was the ale causing him to hallucinate?

As she moved closer, he started, blinking in disbelief at the familiar waifish face, pixie-cropped auburn hair, and mischievous gray eyes that a slew of passionate nights had burned into his memory.

"Marguerite?"

The woman was facing to the side and didn't seem to hear. He said her name louder, pressing through the crowd.

She slowly turned. Her eyes popped wide when she saw him. "*Caleb?*"

She was truly there, in the flesh. Caleb tried to run and stumbled from inebriation. Marguerite dropped her rucksack and rushed to him, throwing her arms around his neck and pressing her cheek to his face. His elation was tempered by the sadness in the young rogue's eyes when she drew away and took in his condition. He knew he reeked of alcohol and hadn't washed in a week.

"You're alive," Caleb said, as a sob choked out of him. The last time he had seen her, on the verge of death after the ill-fated journey to Leonidus's abandoned keep, a pair of Congregation wizards had carried her off to a cuerpomancer in the fading hope that she could be saved from the deadly poison of a maw wyrm.

"It was dodgy for a while, but the cuerpomancer brought me back."

Caleb explained the commotion in the square. Then she told him how bad things had gotten in New Victoria, how even passive members of the public had been pressured into reporting those who refused the Oaths. Neighbors turning on neighbors. Undesirables rooted out at all costs. The Fens bloating with new arrivals.

"Lord Alistair is on a mission," she said. "One I want no part of. I 'ad to leave town."

"You came to the right place," he said, offering her a drink. "We'll drink ourselves to death while the world goes to hell."

She gave him a troubled glance but took a pull from his flask. Caleb knew Marguerite loved the Good Life as much as he did, and he was looking forward to having a drinking companion.

After accepting his offer to stay with him, she decided to wash up after her journey. He waited for her in the common room, downing another tankard and feeling tingly that she was alive and with him again. When she returned downstairs, a high-necked riding shirt outlining her lissome figure, he felt as if the room was spinning, a carousel of desire and intoxication.

Just as Marguerite joined him, Tamás walked through the door with Merin Dragici and Kyros Toth. He pulled away to stop by Caleb's table. "Have you given more thought to my proposal?"

"Save your breath," Caleb said.

"What proposal?" Marguerite asked, giving Tamás a worried glance that annoyed Caleb. He tried to shoo the revolutionary away after exchanging introductions, but Tamás told Marguerite about the need for an emissary to the Blackwood Forest.

"We've got all we need right here," Caleb said. "Bartender! A drink over here for the lady!"

Tamás laid a hand on his arm. "Maybe you should retire for the day."

When Caleb tried to twist out of Tamás's grasp, he stumbled out of his chair and smashed his head on the table. Woozy, he tried to sit but missed the chair and fell down.

*　　*　　*

The next morning, Caleb woke in his bed and couldn't remember how he had gotten there. After splashing cold water on his face, it all came back in a rush: Tamás's speech, seeing Marguerite, falling over at the inn.

Marguerite.

He realized he had never really missed a woman before. Not like that.

What was it about her that affected him so much? It was all a bit silly. He was acting like Will.

He stumbled downstairs to the common room for eggs and toast and a few cups of coffee. Once the caffeine hit, he stepped outside, squinting in the sun. As he had every morning since the attack, usually while Will was off having important meetings with the council, Caleb wandered the ruined town, looking for ways to help. He didn't have construction skills like Will, or leadership skills like Val, and he usually ended up doing menial tasks.

He hadn't had much of a chance to explore the town before the attack, which was a shame. It must have been a beautiful place. A city of bright canvas tents and cobblestone walkways, stretching for miles up and down the coast, extending to the base of the mist and wildflower-covered hills to the east. Outside of the main commercial area, the tents and wagons of the clans were arranged around large courtyards with once-beautiful fountains, where the clan members would congregate for meals and nighttime revelry. A boardwalk along the coast offered views of the ocean and play areas for children. Even now, under the grim pall of reconstruction, a spirit of brotherhood and merriment remained. People of all creeds and races worked alongside each other.

Freetown, he thought, was his kind of place.

Still, Caleb desperately missed home. America had its problems, plenty of them in fact, but at least there was semi-democratic rule and peace in most places. He could not deal with the medieval level of violence on Urfe. He had already been enslaved, forced to bend his pacifist ethos, and witnessed countless deaths and vicious battles.

His brothers were gone, Caleb had no real skills or purpose, and life's questions had only multiplied. He had long struggled to find meaning in a cruel world, and Urfe had only amplified his efforts.

Which was why he drank himself to sleep every night.

"Sir, could ye give us a hand?"

Caleb had wandered deep into town, almost to the base of the hills. Judging by the scorched earth and charred remains of the buildings, it looked as if the area had taken a direct hit from a fireball. The source of the voice was a middle-aged woman in ragged clothing, struggling with her two daughters to nail a board over a hole on the side of her wagon. The daughters were perched precariously on the roof, leaning down to try to keep the board in place.

Caleb hurried over, reaching up to hold the board while the woman stood on a stool and pounded in nails. After joining them for lunch, cucumber and cheese sandwiches made with stale bread, he spent the rest of the day helping repair the wagon. The woman's husband, who traded furs from the northern forests, had been killed in the attack.

"There ye are," Marguerite said, walking up as the sun started to set. "I thought I'd never find ye."

Caleb set his hammer down. It was getting too dark to work. "Here I am."

Attraction crackled in the air around them. Despite the time that had passed, he felt none of the awkwardness that usually accompanied a reunion.

She ran her eyes approvingly over the sweat-soaked shirt clinging to his lean torso. After the mother thanked Caleb profusely for his help, Marguerite slipped an arm through his. "Do ye 'ave plans for dinner? Or do I have to stand in line with the other lassies?"

Exhausted, he leaned on her as they walked away. "If you can get me to a tavern, I'm all yours."

They returned to the inn where he was staying, laughing and talking like old friends. Though her presence helped alleviate the ache in his soul, he couldn't stop thinking about the devastation of the attack and all the children left without mothers and fathers.

By the time the roasted quail arrived, Caleb had downed three mugs of ale, and started to slur his speech. He kept drinking despite the troubled look in Marguerite's eyes. Though he had longed all day to kiss her, he passed out at the table again.

When he next woke, he felt a cold cloth on his cheek and a hand stroking his hair. He blinked and saw Marguerite looking down at him with a warm but determined smile. After he dressed, she led him downstairs by the arm.

"Where are we going?"

"How many nights in a row 'ave ye passed out from drink?"

"I don't know," he mumbled. "Why?"

"Because it's time for a change of scenery."

"What?"

Instead of replying, she took him to the Red Wagon Tavern and walked right up to the table where Tamás was eating breakfast.

"Do ye still need able bodies?" Marguerite asked.

Surprised, the revolutionary finished chewing and took a drink of water. "Aye."

"And can ye spare two horses?"

"They won't be the best. But aye."

"Good. As soon as Caleb 'ere sobers up, we'll leave for the Blackwood Forest."

"We will?" Caleb asked.

In response, she looked up, patted him on the cheek, and ordered two coffees.

8

"I don't understand," Val said. "What do you mean the demons might be coming from a town destroyed a thousand years ago?"

Cyrus Ravensill led the way as the party navigated a rocky footpath that wound through the gentle hills surrounding Porlock. The morning dew freshened the air under a thin layer of clouds.

Val and Dida followed behind Cyrus. Rucker and Synne brought up the rear. The mysterious young majitsu was so thin she looked almost adolescent in her form-fitting black clothes.

"During the Age of Sorrow," Cyrus answered, "the town of Badŏn was an important city in the Realm."

From his studies at the Abbey, Val knew the Age of Sorrow was a time when wizards were viewed as heretics, and druid warrior-priests ruled the island of Albion, which equated to Great Britain on Earth. Most scholars of the Realm believed the "priestly" powers of the druids were magical abilities that, in the anti-wizard climate of the era, had been rebranded for political survival.

Cyrus continued, "No one knows for certain what occurred at Badŏn. It's thought that one of the more powerful druids, perhaps Cynwrig the Terrible, opened a door to a hell dimension that allowed Asmodeus and his demon horde to come through. Dark times, those."

Rucker scoffed. "Aren't ye an educated sort? Asmodeus is a name mothers use to terrify their children into behaving."

"It was *wizards* who fought back the demons," Cyrus said coldly. "And our histories mention Asmodeus by name."

"Bah," Rucker said, with a wave of his hand.

"What happened to the town?" Val asked.

"An army of druids led by Cynwrig laid siege. After suffering terrible losses trying to extricate the survivors, fearing the demons would spread, Cynwrig rounded up the most powerful wild mages roaming the island and forced them to raze the town with Mage Fire, as it was then known. Likely the primitive name for Spirit Fire."

"How does one force a spirit mage to do anything?" Dida asked.

Cyrus grimaced. "By holding his family hostage."

"Legend says Asmodeus is immune to Spirit Fire," Rucker said. "I don't suppose 'e was on a picnic during the siege?"

"The histories do not record the fate of Asmodeus," Cyrus said evenly. "We assume he returned to his own dimension."

"I still don't understand," Val said. "What does the town of Badŏn have to do with this alleged demon sighting in Porlock?"

They crested a hill and saw the skeletal remains of an old stone fort brooding atop the next hill. In the valley behind the fort, a wall of thick gray fog fell from the sky like a curtain, stretching to the horizon in either direction.

"Queen's bane," Rucker muttered. "What the bloody hell is *that*?"

"Again, we can only speculate," Cyrus said, "but we think the magical battle with Tobar Baltoris triggered an unknown power of the crown. What we do know is that the ancient city of Badŏn used to lie directly beyond the barrier of fog you now see before you." Cyrus's jaw tightened. "I was part of the original expedition. Though I wasn't chosen to cross the barrier, I did battle with one of the demons. Before I killed it, it spoke of its pleasure at subverting the town of Badŏn." He eyed Rucker. "And of laying my corpse at the feet of Asmodeus."

Dida paled, Synne's eyes flickered, and Rucker tightened his grip on his sword. No one spoke for a moment, and Val tried to process the information. *What have I gotten myself into?*

"Have you tried flying over the fog?" Dida asked.

"As the alchemancers say, 'As above, so below.'"

They started down the hill, proceeding cautiously towards the abandoned fort. Val couldn't stop eying the wall of fog. "What do we know about demons?"

"They come in many forms," Cyrus said. "Some have magical resistance of varying degrees."

"They're different," Rucker said, "but they're also the same. Wicked and cruel, every last one. They care for each other as little as they care for us. Power and pleasure—that's the only thing that drives them."

"Are you a believer now?" Cyrus mocked. "Were you not the one who said a true demon has not befouled the Realm for a thousand years?"

"That's right," Rucker replied. "*The Realm.* I've traveled the length and breadth of Urfe, and seen things across the oceans that would make yer toes curl right out of yer shoes. Including a handful of demons."

They reached the bottom of the hill, where a path of downtrodden grass led to the crumbling granite walls of the fort. A fine mist clung to the ruins. After a moment of silent contemplation, the party started up the path.

When they reached the top, Val realized the fort was a maze of broken walls and stone enclosures. Weeds had clawed through every crack. No roofs remained. There was no sign of demons, but a whiff of foul air reached his nostrils, an odor of spoiled meat and refuse, like garbage and road kill mingling in a dumpster.

They made their way cautiously through the ruins, scanning their surroundings with every step. Val's heart skipped a beat every time they rounded a corner or passed a doorway cut into the stone. It was impossible to see all the angles of the abandoned fort, and if they were indeed dealing with some kind of demon, he questioned the wisdom of heading right into its lair.

"I'm shielding us," Cyrus said in a low voice, as if hearing Val's thoughts.

It took an enormous amount of energy to maintain a Wizard Shield around one person alone. Was Cyrus using a different spell? A device of some sort?

They reached a sizeable inner courtyard, still with no sign of trouble. The stench grew stronger. Just as they were about to choose one of the passages, they saw it standing on a crenellated section of the wall buttressing the opposite side of the courtyard.

Huge and muscular, the demon had four arms, a scaly body, and an oversize head hunched like a vulture atop its squat neck. At a distance, the demon's mottled brown-and-green scales made it hard to distinguish from the mossy granite wall.

"Wait here," Cyrus said. Val heard an oddly personal edge to his voice, as if he bore the demon a grudge.

The creature was standing in the dip between the crenellations. As Cyrus advanced, it used its four arms to clamber like a spider atop the highest portion, staring down at them with saucer-size eyes and an unnaturally wide mouth. Val recalled the exchange at the inn.

No reports of magic?

Only that it moves faster than a galloping horse, and can swallow a grown pig whole.

Cyrus took flight, hugging the top of the wall and landing ten feet from the demon. It grinned wider as the mage extended his hands and formed a translucent spear that coalesced out of the mist. He threw it at the demon, landing a direct hit, but the spear shattered on the creature's broad chest and exploded in a spray of silver.

Magic resistant.

The demon opened its mouth and roared. Fear coursed like an electric shock through Val. The thing's jaws had cranked as wide as a barrel, exposing rows of teeth running down its throat in uneven lines. Cyrus flung his hands at the beast, causing the stone beneath it to explode. The creature fell on its back, stunned, as the gray-cloaked mage flew down to meet it.

"More!" Rucker roared. "Behind you!"

Val whipped around. Another demon, identical to the first, had crept up behind Rucker. The old adventurer must have canine hearing.

As Rucker raised his sword, Val saw a third one, similar to the first but with blue-green skin, launch itself off the nearest wall. It was coming straight for Val, four arms extended.

He stumbled backwards. The spell he had prepared slipped away, his mental concentration drowned in fear and adrenaline. Realizing he was about to get ripped apart, he managed to erect a Wizard Shield, though he suspected the demon would punch right through it.

He never got to find out. Before the demon smashed into him, something hit it in midair and sent it flying. Synne landed softly and faced off against the monster with her bare hands extended.

Val backed next to Dida as the battle commenced, desperate to find a way to help. He didn't have his staff, and Spirit Fire was too risky to use in close quarters. Dida was a bibliomancer, a specialist in runes and arcane knowledge, and did not possess much of an arsenal.

The demon ran at Synne, four arms beating the air. She matched it blow for blow, moving in a blur, blocking the demon's strikes and landing a few blows in between. Val watched her go on the offensive, sending the demon into the wall again with a powerful aerial spin kick.

She may not be a full majitsu, he thought, but she could *fight*.

Though Rucker wasn't as fast as Synne, he used his wide-bodied sword as both weapon and shield, turning it sideways to block the demon's strikes, then taking chunks of the creature's flesh with pinpoint swipes of the blade. The crafty one-armed warrior spun, parried, dodged, feinted, and used portions of the wall to his advantage, stymying every move the demon tried to make.

Cyrus had his opponent backed against a wall and was sending loose blocks of stone flying into its body. The demon tried to shield itself with its arms, but Val watched as chunk after chunk of stone pummeled the monster, until its chest caved and it crumpled on the ground. Cyrus extended his arm and formed it into a flesh-colored sword. As the weakened demon tried to stand, Cyrus cut off an arm with a swipe of the blade. With a snarl, the powerful mage leapt forward and jerked on one of the demon's horns to expose its neck, then severed its head.

"Behind you!" Rucker roared.

Val turned just as Dida tackled him from the side. The demon fighting Rucker had decided to break off and come for the two mages. Dripping brown ichor and missing chunks of flesh, the monster looked enraged and half-mad. Dida's tackle had saved them from the initial strike, but the demon loomed over them with death in its yellow eyes.

Val tried to use Spirit Fire but couldn't call it forth. The battle was too fluid and his mind too jumbled. Dida was frantically trying to inscribe something in midair as the demon barreled forward. Val screamed in rage and tried to produce something, *anything*, with his magic. A Wizard Push rushed out of him that barely slowed the creature.

After swiping Dida aside, the demon grasped Val with all four of its arms, and began to pull. Val screamed, feeling as if he were being drawn and quartered. Just as his tendons stretched to the breaking point, there was a blur of movement, and Synne landed on the demon's back like a gangly black spider. She gripped the demon's head and whipped its neck to the side. With a sharp *crack*, the head dropped at an unnatural angle. It collapsed in a heap at her feet.

Aching but alive, Val caught his breath and gripped Synne by the forearm. "You saved my life."

"Of course I did," she said, after she caught her breath. "They made me take an oath to protect you."

*   *   *

So many questions swirled in Val's head as the party returned in silence to Porlock. Would he ever be able to use his magic in the heat of battle? Why had Synne landed in prison, and could he trust her? Most importantly, if the ancient city of Badŏn truly lay beyond the barrier of fog, how could they possibly cope with an entire horde of demons?

The adrenaline lingering in Val's system caused the wildflowers to seem a few shades brighter, the air more fresh and clean. He took a deep breath to shake off the terror of the battle and caught up with Cyrus.

"Those demons were magic resistant, weren't they?" Val asked.

"Aye. But not all are. And spells born purely of this world will be unaffected."

"What do you mean?"

"Had I used a natural source of fire or lightning, for example, the demon would not have been immune. My spear was born of mist, but crafted of air and light. Not particularly strong—I was testing."

"I wondered," Val murmured. "And the sword arm, at the end?"

"The demon was weakened. I overpowered his resistance with a direct blow, aided by my own physical strength."

Val looked to the side, in the direction of the veil of fog. He hoped he never crossed a member of the wizard guard. "How do we survive this, Cyrus?"

"Remember that your mission is not to kill demons. Your mission is to find Tobar and the Star Crown. My advice is to avoid engagement."

"We'll be sure to ask the demons to take a lunch break."

Cyrus didn't respond to the sarcasm. "You must also keep your magic at the ready, at all times. Once you cross the barrier, you'll be at war."

"I was only a first year when I was imprisoned."

Cyrus stared at him calmly. "Then it's time to become a full mage."

Val pressed his lips together and returned the stare. Cyrus was right. This was trial by fire. If Val wanted to live, he had to figure some things out for himself.

"Do you have any idea how to cross the barrier?" Val asked.

"The ones who passed through never returned." He hesitated, and said, "Three members of the Wizard Guard were part of that expedition. My brother was one of them."

"I'm sorry. I didn't know."

"As you can see, I have a vested interest in your success."

Val gripped his arm. "If I find him, I'll do everything I can to bring him back."

Cyrus returned the gesture. "Thank you."

They returned to the village at midday. Before they entered the inn, Cyrus took his leave in the flying stagecoach after wishing them success. The departure of the powerful mage caused a lump of dread to form in Val's gut.

He thought the inn would be bustling, but the common room was empty except for a lone woman sitting by the fire. Her back was to the door, but she turned as they entered, lowering the hood of her finely made cloak. A spool of honey-blond hair spilled down her back, and Val froze when he saw her pale but beautiful face, eyes that matched her turquoise cloak, and a choker made of azantite disguised as black pearl.

Adaira.

9

No one accosted Will and the others as they made their way across the poor section of town, entered a more residential area, and checked into a guesthouse with thatched roof bungalows and an open-air courtyard cradled by tropical vegetation. They hid in their rooms until the afternoon, fearful of a visit from the authorities. When no sign of an alarm came, Mala allowed them to venture into the courtyard for a late lunch of ceviche and grilled cactus washed down with mango juice.

After they finished eating, Mala rose to approach Will. "You're coming with me."

"To find the guide? I thought you wanted to go alone?"

"I did, until your stunt in the temple. Now I must plan for the worst." She glanced at his sword. "Should the need arise, your sword is our best chance against a Battle Mage. Do you think you can leave the damsels in distress next time?"

"I'll never promise that." Mala's eyes flashed at the challenge. In an even tone, he added, "But I'll try to make sure I know who I'm helping."

"You'd better. Otherwise I'll leave you to fight your own battles."

Will snorted and looked away. When he turned back, she was halfway to the door.

"Why not Selina?" Will asked as they walked. He and Mala tried to appear casual as they strolled through an upscale part of town straddling a plateau overlooking the pale blue ocean. Two-story stone residences and commercial edifices, interspersed with manicured gardens, were woven into the remains of a sprawling temple complex.

"What?" Mala said, her eyes in constant motion. The tonier neighborhood meant fewer crowds and more chance of running afoul of the authorities.

"Why take me and not Selina?"

"Selina is inexperienced in battle, and I'm unsure of her strength. A Mayan Battle Mage is trained for war from birth."

Will's hand moved to the hilt of his sword. "I wonder whether Zariduke can cut through all magic, no matter how strong," he said quietly.

Mala eyed the blade. "Never forget that a wizard has many weapons, and the sword may not save you."

Will didn't need Mala to remind him that Zedock, the powerful necromancer who had driven Will and his brothers to Urfe in the first place, had almost killed him despite being run through with Zariduke. The mage had laid his hands on Will's chest and would have drained his life force, had Caleb and Yasmina not intervened.

They passed cafés tucked into columned patios, green spaces crawling with iguanas, rooftop terraces shaded by palms, and long colonnades with vendors selling beautiful handmade jewelry, silk wraps, and aromatic baked goods. Tall glow lamps lined the streets, the silver cages at the top carved in the likeness of jungle animals.

"What happened to all the temples?" Will asked. "Is there a ban on religion here, too?"

"Wizards will never forget the Age of Sorrows. I can't say that I blame them. My people, too, know what it means to suffer the scourge of prejudice." She scowled. "Are the Congregation wizards not self-aware enough to know they have become what they once despised? In any event, the Pagan Wars spread to other parts of the world, especially in the West. Religion was never outlawed in the Mayan Kingdom, but most of the temples have been converted to public spaces."

They followed a crumbling stone road on the far side of the plateau that led down to the harbor. Just before the bustling waterfront, Mala veered onto a footpath that angled through high grass and into a shanty town built into a jumble of stone ruins sitting at the bottom of a cliff. It looked as if some force of nature, or perhaps an elder mage, had pushed a temple complex off the precipice.

A host of street vendors had taken up residence among the ruins. The stench of fish guts mingled with the briny dry air. Mala waded through stalls hosting tradesmen of all sorts, blacksmiths and fishmongers and textile makers. The shanty town was more developed than Will had realized.

Mala kept going until she reached a cove at the bottom of the highest cliff in sight. After scanning the water, she looked up, where a quartet of dark-skinned Mayans in loincloths were clustered near the edge. Will watched in awe as one of the men jumped off and performed a looping swan dive. A group of people at the bottom clapped and tossed a few coins. The next two divers executed more daring maneuvers, but the fourth put them all to shame by completing a rapid series of back flips, flattened his body into a freefalling plank, then finished with a graceful back dive that landed between two jagged rocks with nary a splash.

When the last diver surfaced, a short and muscular Mayan with dark bangs that brushed his eyes, the crowd showered him with praise and copper coins.

"Nice dive, Coba," Mala said, as the diver collected his coins.

He turned, his eyes widening. "Mala!"

"A man of your talents, performing party tricks for the upper class? How would you like to earn some true coin?"

Coba's eyes gleamed as he grabbed a cloth towel off a rock. "What you have for me?"

He spoke in very fast broken English. To Will's untrained ear, his clipped, tonal accent sounded like a mix between Spanish and Chinese.

"I'll need to purchase your discretion before I disclose the nature of the job. What say you to twenty gold coins to guide us where I want to go?"

Coba stared at her for a moment, then did a standing back flip so fast Will almost blinked and missed it.

"I think I dive into a school of ogre sharks for twenty gold coins."

Mala smirked. "I thought so."

"So where we go?"

After glancing around to ensure no one was eavesdropping, Mala said, "To the tomb of Yiknoom Uk'ab K'ahk."

Coba slapped his knee and then brayed with laughter. "I thought you smarter than that."

"I have a map."

Coba wiped his eyes and looked at her as if she were joking. When she didn't change her expression, his smile slowly retreated, and he curled a finger for them to follow.

A series of caves pockmarked the limestone cliff behind the cove. The young Mayan led them into a ten-foot square hovel with a reed mat and a meager collection of clothes and foodstuffs. Mala took the scroll out of one of her pouches, unrolled it, and set it on the mat. Coba lit a candle and hovered over it, studied the geography, and pointed at the black dot marking the beginning of the map. "Ixmal."

Will watched Coba's eyes follow the dotted line as it wound through the jungle. The diver jabbed his finger in the air above the first geographical marker, a pool of water surrounded by life-size stone statues. "I know this, too."

Mala's eyes bored into his, and Coba said something in his own language. "The Basin of Blood," he translated. "A cenote near Chan Kawil."

"A cenote?" Will asked.

"Natural sinkholes in the limestone," Mala said. "The peninsula is riddled with them." She turned back to Coba. "What about the marker after that? The jaguar temple?"

The Mayan shook his head.

"Maybe someone else would know?" she asked, disappointed.

He gave her a sharp look. "No one knows jungle better than me. And no one in right mind goes past Basin of Blood."

"I see." She rolled the scroll back up and replaced it in her pouch. "And is my offer enough to induce insanity?"

A shrewd grin split his face. "I jump off cliffs to earn my bread. I never have right mind."

When Will and Mala returned to the guesthouse, they found everyone congregating in the courtyard. After recounting the meeting with Coba, Mala told the group to be ready to leave at dawn. Their guide said to expect a three-day hike through the jungle to the first marker.

As Selina and Yasmina conversed by a pair of potted banana trees, Mala disappeared to wash. Empty beer mugs littered the table that Will's cousin and Gunnar had claimed. The mood was upbeat, the calm before the storm, and Mateo waved Will over.

He wanted to dislike the muscled warrior who shared a bed with Mala. He really did. But while Gunnar was not the most intelligent of men, he was brave, strong, and friendly to Will. According to Tamás, Gunnar was an orphan from the Kingdom of Bavaria, found by a Romani clan and raised as one of their own.

So not only was Gunnar a six-foot-six hunk, he was an orphan. Women loved orphans.

"Join us!" Gunnar cried, slapping Will on the back and calling for another round.

A serving boy brought out three more foaming mugs of ale. Mateo raised his glass for a toast. "To a successful journey."

"Aye," Gunnar said.

Will clinked glasses with the big man. "So how did you meet Mala?"

Faded scars marked Gunnar's hands and forearms. He had short dark hair, a cleft chin, and bronzed arms that bulged out of his jerkin. "A swordsman competition in Port Nelson. I claimed second place."

"Let me guess. Mala beat you in the final."

Gunnar grinned like a schoolboy. "Half my size and it wasn't even close. I couldn't believe a woman could fight like that."

Probably not much for gender equality, are you, big guy?

"How long ago was the competition?" Will asked.

"I dunno, half a dozen years or so?"

"Six years!" Will forced calm into his voice. "You've been together that long?"

"Together? We enjoy each other's company now and again. I don't think Mala is the type for a homestead and a brood o' little ones, if you know what I mean." He winked at Will as Mala returned to the courtyard.

Freshly washed, her dark hair poured in waves over a sleeved corset that matched her scarlet boots. As usual, she wore black leather pants and an astounding array of jewelry: bracelets, rings, a silver nose stud, earrings, and a choker of intertwined bronze in place of her old medallion. She had left her sword and pouches behind, but her dangerous blue sash was tied around her waist, and Will noticed a dagger tucked into her left boot.

She put her hands on Gunnar's shoulders but looked right at Will, her eyes twinkling with roguish charm. "Your travels have treated you well, Will the Builder. Your hair has grown past farmboy length, and that fair skin of yours has a touch of sun. The women of Freetown were quite taken by you, you know."

Will took a long drink.

"Should we go upstairs, darling? It might be some time before we are presented with a soft bed again."

Mala was still looking right at Will, as if addressing the question to him. He stared right back at her, challenging her to look away.

Gunnar drained half a mug in one swallow and pounded it on the table. "What right-minded man would say no to that?"

As the big warrior rose to leave, Mala walked over behind Will, leaned down, and said, "Stay the course, Will the Builder."

"What?" The proximity of her freshly washed scent, cinnamon and rose, made him feel light-headed.

She backed away, lips curling. "With your training."

"Oh. That."

"It takes hard work and confidence to achieve your goals," she said, her smirk more devious than ever.

Gunnar, with the myopic confidence natural to physically imposing men, didn't seem to notice the exchange. Will watched them leave with a sinking feeling, so jealous it made his stomach ache.

"What, pray tell, was that about?" Mateo said.

"What do you mean?" he said dully.

"She was telling you something."

"She likes to torture me."

Mateo rubbed at his thick stubble. About the same age as Will, he had long brown hair and khaki-colored eyes. Unlike Gunnar, who favored tight breeches and leather jerkins, Mateo wore loose patchwork clothing and calfskin walking boots. "Mala's infamous along the Barrier Coast, you know. As respected for her exploits as she is disdained for not joining the Revolution."

"You don't have to remind me," Will said. "I know she's out of my league."

"Do you know what other member of our party is famous? It isn't I or Selina or Gunnar." He lifted his mug. "It's the warrior with the strange accent who helped lead Tamás out of captivity, and who carries Zariduke into battle. You've given our people hope, Will."

"I don't think Mala's very impressed."

He yawned and stood. "Cousin, there are three things I know in life: the art of the Urumi blade, the trails of the Blackwood Forest, and the wiles of

Roma women. And unless I am gravely mistaken, there is something brewing between you and Mala of Clan Kalev. Whether anything will come of it, well, prophecy is not a talent I possess."

Will didn't know what he thought, either, about Mala's cryptic words and dancing eyes.

Not much, that's what.

After his cousin retired upstairs, Will tried to join Yasmina for a spell, but she yawned and went to bed. He was disappointed she hadn't wanted to stay and chat about home. Without his brothers, Urfe sometimes felt like a waking dream, the realization of both his wildest fantasies and darkest nightmares.

He sat under the luminous silver moon for another hour, enwrapped in the tropical fragrance of the courtyard and the memories of the past. He thought about his poor mother, stranded in her mental institution like a ship lost at sea, and his old friend Lance, who Will prayed had survived the fight with Zedock. Eventually his thoughts turned to his father, whose early death Will had never quite recovered from. The thought that his father had once walked upon the soil of Urfe gave Will a small amount of comfort. Anchored him to this world.

After the hardships and terrors of the journey to Leonidus's castle, Will no longer suffered from the debilitating panic attacks that had begun after his father's death. For that he was grateful beyond words. But his recovery was a double-edged sword, since he had nothing to fall back on now. No excuses.

By all accounts, the dangers of the expedition to the pyramid would surpass any he had faced so far. Weighty things were at stake. His brothers needed him. And he, Will Blackwood of New Orleans, logic whiz and fantasy geek, struggling blue-collar worker and driver of a Honda Civic, was expected not just to survive but to perform as a full-fledged member of the party, tasked with leading the charge to bring hope to the persecuted clans of his people.

It was a hero's job—whether he was ready for it or not.

At dawn the next morning, bleary-eyed but buzzing with anticipation, Will joined the others for coffee, bread, and cheese in the courtyard. Everyone looked intense but optimistic, eager for the journey. Soon after Will arrived, Coba burst into the courtyard.

"Grab things!" the guide said. "Come now!"

"What is it?" Mala said.

"Port authority. Checking door to door for border tokens. Someone say foreign magic used in old town temple yesterday."

Mala leapt to her feet, face grim. Will grabbed his pack and felt ill. This was his fault.

Coba put a hand on Mala's shoulder, and Will saw fear in the eyes of the good-natured Mayan. "We must hurry," Coba said. "Get to jungle."

"The patrol is close?" Mala asked.

"Two streets over. And Mala—they have a Battle Mage."

The adventuress paled as she flew into action. Everyone dropped their breakfasts, grabbed their packs, and followed her in a rush out of the guesthouse.

The street was empty except for a few peasants on foot, scurrying to early jobs. Birds twittered from the trees, weak sunlight bathed the town in gold, and there was no sign of the patrol.

"Hurry," Coba urged.

Will had the brief thought that maybe their guide was leading them into a trap, but Mala seemed to trust him, and that was good enough for Will. Mala would have trouble trusting her own mother.

Coba led them halfway down the block and into a dirt alleyway. The passage spilled into a grassy cul-de-sac surrounded by a wooden fence topped with stakes. A dead end. Will's heart sank until he saw Coba making a beeline for a banyan tree near the fence. The guide shot up the aerial roots like a monkey, ran across the tree, and jumped over the barrier. Mala did the same, matching his agility. Everyone else followed suit, with much less grace.

On the other side of the fence, they dashed down a series of streets in a more disheveled section of town, a blur of ramshackle buildings with thatched roofs and clothes drying from tree limbs. At the next intersection, Will could just make out the edge of the jungle. He felt a glimmer of hope as Coba scanned the empty streets and dashed towards the smudge of green.

No one accosted them. They drew closer and closer, until one more block and a field of calf-high spiky agave stood between them and the safety of the trees.

Just before the last street ended, they passed an old woman on a balcony, wringing out a shirt. As Will glanced up at her, she pointed down at them and began to scream in Mayan.

"Go!" Coba yelled, breaking into a sprint.

They cleared the town and entered the field of agave, much bigger than it had looked from a distance. The jungle was at least a quarter mile away. Coba led the mad dash through the field as another voice joined the cry of the old woman, and then another.

Halfway across the exposed ground, a shrill male voice rang out behind them, in heavily accented English. "Halt!"

Will spotted a tiny fissure in the trees, a path into the jungle he guessed Coba was aiming for.

"Cease running at once!" the voice said again. "Cease or face your death!"

Mala turned her head as she ran. Will couldn't help risking a glance. What he saw caused his mouth to go dry and his heart to slap against his chest with fear. A twenty-foot long green snake, thick as a barrel, was slithering towards them with its torso raised high into the air. Standing atop a wooden dais strapped to the snake's neck was a man with the imperious bearing of a wizard, wearing a feathered headdress and covered in leopard body paint. He carried a hooked iron staff in one hand. A Battle Mage, Will knew.

A group of Mayan warriors followed behind their leader on foot. Shirtless and wearing embroidered kilts over their loincloths, the soldiers carried shields dyed in vibrant colors and a variety of spears, axes, and daggers.

The giant snake closed in on Will and his companions, advancing in a sinuous undulation much faster than they could run.

They would never reach the jungle in time.

10

"Could it be true that Zariduke has returned to Urfe?"

Garbind Elldorn, a sylvamancer from the Fifth Protectorate who favored worn traveling cloaks over tailored finery, had posed the question.

"Blood and Queen, Garbind," said Jalen Rainsword, a powerful electro-mancer and the lead representative of the Sixth Protectorate. "Have we sunk to the level of spreading a gypsy rumor?"

Murmurs emanated from the thirty-one archmages gathered for a meeting of the Conclave, the ruling body of the Congregation. Three wizards for each of the nine Protectorates, three representatives from Londyn, and the Chief Thaumaturge, Lord Alistair of Inverlock Keep.

Under the new constitution, Lord Alistair and Queen Victoria were equal in power. Diplomatic relations were solid between the two capitals, Londyn and New Victoria, though a number of distinguished Albion families were bitter about the shift in power.

"Perhaps it's a rumor that should be taken seriously," Braden Shankstone said, taking his cue from a private meeting that morning with Kalyn Tern and Lord Alistair. Braden was a handsome, dark-haired cuerpomancer from the Third. The youngest member of the Conclave, he owed his political success to Lord Alistair's patronage as much as to his own considerable magecraft.

"If the sword was at Freetown," Jalen said, "then why did no one notice during the attack?"

All heads turned towards Kalyn Tern and Professor Anastasia Azara, the two members of the Conclave present at the battle—Lord Alistair termed it a *lesson*—of Freetown.

"It happened as we were pulling away," Kalyn said coolly. "At that point, there was no more resistance." A sapphire dress of Himalayan silk swept the ground at her feet, and a waterfall of white-blond hair reached to her waist. She was an aeromancer from a powerful family in the First, and had helped Lord Alistair cement his power. Many thought her his political equal.

"If the rumor *is* true, the sword could be anywhere on the Barrier Coast by now," Braden said. "It could be on its way here. Imagine if it fell into the hands of the Black Sash."

There was a general rustling. With the help of the Haruspex, a Congregation necromancer who specialized in acquiring forensic knowledge from the recently deceased, Lord Alistair had learned that the Alazashin werebat who preyed on the Abbey students was hired by the Black Sash gypsies.

Wisely, the Alazashin had focused on inexperienced pupils. But an assassin wielding Zariduke could challenge a full wizard.

"Enough speculation," Lord Alistair said, from atop the silver-blue dais of hardened spirit facing the semicircle of wizards. "The return of Zariduke is of grave import. It is imperative we discover the truth."

Like everyone else, Lord Alistair wanted Zariduke safely in Congregation hands. Yet the Chief Thaumaturge had two additional reasons for believing the legendary sword had returned to Urfe.

The first was Zedock's secret mission to retrieve the sword from the world on which Dane Blackwood had found it, called Earth. *Someone* had killed Zedock and taken the sword. One of Zedock's majitsu had disappeared, as well—had he switched sides and joined the Revolution? Did he perhaps have gypsy blood?

The second reason was the Spirit Liege that Lord Alistair had sent to the Barrier Coast. The one that never reported back.

It had to be the sword.

The knowledge thrilled, terrified, and enraged him, and the words of the phrenomancer rang in Lord Alistair's ears like a thousand tower bells: *When the sword born of spirit returns to Urfe, war is imminent, and one born of gypsy blood will destroy you.*

Contrary to the impassioned speeches of his detractors, Lord Alistair did not hate the gypsies or the other Exilers, those who had settled in the Ninth to avoid taking the Oaths. He despised them, yes. Their ignorant beliefs had no place in an enlightened society.

But what he *hated* was the danger to the Congregation that religion posed. The unification of the common born.

For years, he had taken a hard line and hunted down those who foment-ed unrest or openly practiced their religion. Yet it was that damnable proph-ecy that spurred him to such extreme action. Lord Alistair had no time for superstition and false prophets, but phrenomancers had proven time and again they could foretell future events. The threat to his rule—in his eyes, to the survival of the Congregation—was real.

Yet no prophecy was assured. Phrenomancers dealt in possibilities, not fact. Man possessed free will.

Which was why Lord Alistair would create his own destiny. He would kill every single gypsy on Urfe, if that was what it took. Even better would be to find the sword and possess it for himself. Imagine the sword in the hands of an elder spirit mage, he thought, untouchable by a rival's magic.

Untouchable by anyone.

The very idea gave him a shiver of anticipation.

"And how do you propose we learn the truth?" Jalen asked.

"We consult a phrenomancer," Alistair said. "A good one."

"How can we be certain he will speak the truth?"

"Because I will gaze with him."

That silenced Jalen. Any further dissent would be a lack of trust not just in the phrenomancer, but in Lord Alistair himself.

"We should impose more restrictions until we find it," Braden said. "Increase the patrols, the checkpoints, the Oath guards. And, as needed, the executions."

Garbind snarled. "*Restrictions*? At this point, it's an ethnic cleansing."

"The law is the law," Alistair said sharply. "The gypsies are welcome to join the Protectorate."

"Yet our Oath Judges are free to reject an application on any grounds, and frequently do so," Garbind said, as he looked around the room. Not even his compatriots from the Fifth would meet his gaze. Only two wizards appeared sympathetic: Lord Jalen, and the sad auburn eyes of Dean Groft, Dean of Spiritmancy at the Abbey and the highest-ranking spiritmancer after Lord Alistair. Some would argue that Dean Groft was even more powerful than the Chief Thaumaturge, but the Dean abhorred politics and almost never intervened.

"Perhaps we should rethink the restrictions," Garbind said. "Are they really necessary in this day and age?"

Alistair pounded his dais. "I'll not harbor a discussion of returning to the old ways! The scourge of belief in false idols must never again darken the Realm."

"Freedom of choice is different from freedom of religion," Garbind argued. The Conclave was a representative democracy among wizards, not a dictatorship, and Garbind was not one to be cowed by bluster.

"Need anyone remind you," Kalyn said scathingly, "that the Age of Sorrow almost resulted in the eradication of the mage born?"

Murmurs of assent spread through the room.

Garbind laughed. "Yes, nearly two thousand years ago. The gypsies and other Exilers are hardly a threat to the might of the Congregation."

No one disputed that fact, which made Lord Alistair uneasy. He raised his palms in a conciliatory gesture. "Enough talk. Shall we bring this to a vote?"

As with the last meeting, Garbind and Jalen and Dean Groft were the lone dissenters. Alistair made a mental note to double the patrols and death squads.

A deep, tri-tone bell chimed from inside the Wizard Chute, signifying that someone sought entrance to the Gathering Room.

Lord Alistair pulled a lever beneath his dais, resulting in an answering bell below. He wasn't worried about intruders. An invisible multi-discipline ward surrounded the Sanctum, passable only by those bearing the imprimatur of the Congregation.

What about a team of assassins wielding Zariduke, he thought at the last moment? Able to slice through the wards? The thought caused his hand to clench, but instead of a sword-wielding Black Sash gypsy, a pyromancer named Rasha Tremayne rose through the chute in the corner. Rasha was assistant secretary to the Conclave and one of the stewards of the Sanctum.

Alistair chided himself. Zariduke was a powerful weapon, but hardly a threat to a roomful of elder mages. Legend had it the sword was made long ago for the captain of the Paladins: a group of warriors loyal only to the High Priest of Devla, who bestowed holy powers upon his honor guard. Sheer nonsense, of course, since Devla was a myth and his priests had disappeared ages ago. The current Prophet was heir to a long line of charlatans who stoked the flames of religious fervor for their own profit. A fervor which, if allowed to blossom, would erode the public's faith in the Congregation.

Rasha bowed as she faced Lord Alistair. He didn't like the uneasy frown creasing her face. "Milord, the Secretariat General just received word that your daughter is in Porlock."

The floor seemed to shift underneath Lord Alistair's feet.

Rasha looked as if she would rather be stretched on a torture rack than delivering her message. "Since the Conclave is in session, the Secretariat was contacted. Apparently Adaira has . . . traveled through the Pool of Souls to join Val Kenefick on his mission."

No one in the room dared move. Lord Alistair's pulse pounded in his head. The law was clear that an unauthorized use of the Pool of Souls was an act of treason, punishable by death.

"How do you know this?" Lord Alistair managed to choke out.

"The Legate in Porlock sent an emissary to Londyn as soon as he saw Adaira."

Lord Alistair fought against the rage that rose within him like a boiling kettle atop a blacksmith's fire. A terrible temper that had always plagued him. "My daughter is not a spirit mage—how did she manage the Planewalk? Avoid triggering the wards on the Pool of Souls?"

Rasha swallowed. "Milord, Adaira claims she used your seal to bypass the wards on the eldergate."

There was a long silence. Braden was the first to speak. "We agreed to commute the sentence of Val Kenefick if he is successful in his mission. I propose we extend the same clemency to Adaira."

It took all of Lord Alistair's willpower to suppress the trembling of his hands. Adaira was the one who had suggested the idea of sending Val on a redemptive mission in the first place.

Knowing she would join him.

He loved his daughter above all else, above even the Realm, above even the hegemony of the mage-born he had dedicated his life to preserving.

Yet Adaira had made a very shrewd move. If he tried to intervene to save her, he would lose face. His enemies would band together, block the move, and use the breach in protocol to usurp his authority.

What his daughter did not know was that the task Lord Alistair and Queen Victoria had chosen for Val was virtually a death mission. Useful if completed, but extraordinarily perilous, perhaps even impossible.

Yet she had left him no choice. Was she seeking to make her own mark in the Realm, he wondered? Or did she love the man that much?

He scoffed. Love had not had time to sprout. What Adaira felt was the infatuation of a sheltered child.

"I second the proposal," Kalyn said.

Lord Alistair's voice sounded faraway to his own ears. "As much as it pains the soul of this father, I fear it is my duty to make the only choice I possess a formality. All in favor of Braden's proposal, please say *aye*."

This time, no one dissented.

After the Conclave dispersed, Lord Alistair flew out of the Sanctum in a rage, his majitsu struggling to keep up. Anyone watching knew that his black-robed bodyguards were a show of power. Most wizards were vulnerable while flying, but if attacked in midair, Lord Alistair would simply create a floating dais of hardened spirit and rain death upon whoever was foolish enough to confront him.

He sailed through the pair of silent colossi guarding the midnight blue pyramid housing the Sanctum. Whisked above the tropical gardens and pathways of mosaic tile. Higher still, he soared through the forest of spires to the dizzying heights of his wizard compound, barely noticing the dun-colored stone flowing and dripping in surreal patterns, the Gothic symphony of bridges and archways.

He entered the central spire through an archway shielded by wards created by the strongest runemaster in the Realm. Past his chambers, up through a wizard chute, and into the observation room atop the tower, amber orb lights blinking on and off as he passed.

Alistair flew straight to the row of obsidian spirit helms, yanked the one marked "Inverlock Keep" off its hook, and shoved it on as he strode to his throne.

"Fesoj!" he roared, his vision blurring as it made contact through the ether.

The spirit helm nullified the sibilant lisp of the menagerist. "Yes, milord?"

Alistair's vision cleared, revealing the workshop of his cloud fortress through the eyes of Fesoj, a notorious fugitive on the run for multiple crimes. Unlicensed menagerie had been outlawed in the Realm for centuries.

A circle of five upright azantite pods dominated the center of the room. The incubators of the Spirit Lieges: Lord Alistair's secret weapon against an assault on his power. The reason he risked employing Fesoj.

Troublingly, only three Lieges remained. One had disappeared without a trace in mid-transformation. A second, he presumed, had fallen to Zariduke. Though disturbing, it would be nearly impossible to trace the creation of the Lieges back to him.

His mind snapped back to the present.

Adaira. Porlock. A doomed quest among demons.

Valjean Kenefick was the catalyst for all of this. The queen said he had spoken the truth about using the Pool of Souls to find his brothers. While Lord Alistair was furious at the outcome, he understood such a thing. The loyalty to family.

Moreover, despite Val's transgression, he liked the budding spirit mage. The young mage had intellect, instincts, and great potential. Power. He would make a fine son-in-law, despite his lack of lineage.

But, far more importantly: could he bring Adaira home safe?

Lord Alistair debated trying to send a Spirit Liege to aid the expedition, then discarded the idea. Not just because he didn't want one of his creations within a hundred miles of his daughter, but also because he didn't want her to know what he had done. Not before she understood why. She was still too principled, unaware of the harsh realities of the world. Of what it took to maintain power.

Of the fact that an empire, even one as powerful as the Congregation, must never remain static.

That it must forever conquer.

Lord Alistair's best hope was that Val and Adaira would spend weeks in a failed attempt to breach the strange portal the crown had opened. It would mean failure and a death sentence, but the attempt would buy Lord Alistair the time he needed to stifle dissenting voices, seize power, and pardon them both.

The time for his coronation drew near, but there were still obstacles. Powerful dissenting voices who might yet spark a civil war among the Congregation.

Voices that needed to be silenced.

"Milord?" Fesoj said again.

Lord Alistair shuddered away thoughts of his daughter. In times like these, he almost wished he had a god in which to believe. "I assume there is still no word from the liege we sent to find the sword?"

"Not yet."

"Then send the next two," Alistair said slowly, thinking through the ramifications as he eyed the circle of azantite pods, "on a mission to kill Garbind Elldorn."

Fesoj hesitated. "My lord?"

"Was I unclear?"

Another pause. Lord Alistair could sense the almost erotic pleasure his command had arisen in Fesoj.

"Not at all," the menagerist murmured.

11

When Val saw Adaira sitting by the fire in The Oak and Bull inn, he refrained from rushing over to sweep her off her feet. Instead he approached slowly, wary of her intent. What was she doing here? Who had sent her?

She held him by the shoulders and kissed him on the forehead, then let her hands linger as she met his gaze. "I heard Dean Groft declined your request. I thought you might need some help."

As she turned to greet Dida, Val sank into a chair, stunned. He was happy to see her, even more than he thought he would be, but he had never considered asking her. Not just because of the danger, but because her father would never consent. "How did you get here so fast?"

Her smile was warm but melancholy. "The same as you. The Pool of Souls."

"You completed the Planewalk?" he said, surprised.

"I'm afraid I haven't the power for that. I used my father's seal to access the eldergate. It's a restricted portal to the Pool of Souls beneath the Sanctum."

Val paled. "But the law, your father . . ."

He trailed off when he saw the truth in her eyes.

She had committed treason. For him.

"I haven't spoken to my father," Adaira said, "but he can't—he *won't*—make an exception for me. We come back together," she said with a thin smile, "or not at all."

Val looked away, shocked at what she had done. Sensing his mixed emotions, she took his chin in her hand. "I care for you, Val. But I did this for myself. If I want to effect change, I have to make my own mark on the Realm."

"Not like this," he whispered. "You don't know where we're going."

"I know enough."

Rucker cleared his throat. "The rooms are upstairs."

Realizing he had forgotten about the others, Val stood and introduced Adaira to Rucker and Synne. The majitsu looked stunned when she realized who Adaira was.

Rucker snorted. "If I was your father, I'd put you over my knee and wallop your backside."

"I'd advise against trying that," Adaira said icily. "I might decide to flay you alive for your troubles."

"Adaira's studying to be a cuerpomancer," Val said.

Rucker slapped the table. "Well, then. A spirited lass. Maybe ye'll be useful after all."

As they relaxed by the fire with ale and rabbit stew, the party told Adaira everything they knew, and relived the fight with the demons. She maintained a grim, determined air throughout the tale. As the discussion turned to penetrating the barrier of fog, mere speculation at this point, Val tried to process what her appearance meant.

He got that Lord Alistair couldn't risk political capital by intervening. Yet even if the party made a successful return, would he blame Val for putting his daughter at risk? What if something befell Adaira on the journey?

He tried to push away the scent of her, the look of challenge in her eyes that excited him as no woman ever had, the loyalty and bravery she had exhibited just by showing up. She was a remarkable woman, no doubt. One for whom, under different circumstances, he could see himself falling.

But Val Blackwood was a goal-oriented man, and at the moment, his goals were all-consuming.

Return from the expedition and secure his freedom.

Locate his brothers.

Get them home safe.

He would do his best to protect Adaira, but he couldn't let love cloud his judgment.

Adaira pled exhaustion and headed upstairs. Dida asked Val for a word alone, and he followed the bibliomancer to his room.

Dida shut the door. Curious, Val watched him trace a finger through the air, outlining an upright square the size of a wall safe. As the square glowed soft blue, Dida's spindly fingers danced across the surface, inscribing intricate patterns in midair. The face of the square swung downward as if hinged.

Val gaped. When Dida pushed his hand through the space behind the blue "lid," his flesh disappeared. The bibliomancer's elbow moved up and down as if groping inside the magical cavity, and he pulled out a leather bound journal and a long staff tipped with an azantite crescent moon facing upwards.

"My staff—my father's spellbook!"

Val gave his friend a look of profound gratitude as Dida returned his most treasured belongings.

"It was a strange affair," the bibliomancer said, closing the lid and then making the square disappear with a swipe of his hand. "Do you know a man named Alrick? A phrenomancer, he claims?"

Val nodded warily, remembering the strangest experience of his life. "I do."

"He visited me the day before I learned of your predicament. He claimed he was gazing and had seen your future possibilities." Dida swallowed. "He said there were many pathways, but the only one that did not end with your death included your staff and your father's spellbook. I must tell you that, even with these items, he said the pathway of success was an extremely unlikely one."

"Did he say why he was so concerned about my future?"

"He said you owed him a gazing session."

Val pursed his lips. "How did you get these?"

"Alrick gave me an address in New Victoria and said I would find them inside. I found the residence, knocked, and no one answered." Dida hung his head, sheepish. "The door was unlocked."

Salomon, Val thought to himself.

He clutched his staff and tucked the spellbook into his cloak. Pieces of his father's past he could never replace. "I know you didn't have to come on this journey, Dida. You barely know me."

"How can you say such a thing?" Dida said crossly. "In the Kingdom of Great Zimbabwe, a friendship is counted not by the days it has lasted, but by the strength of its bond."

Val was quiet for a long moment. "Then thank you, my friend," he said softly. "I feel the same."

Not yet tired, Val left the staff and spellbook in his room and returned downstairs, forcing himself to keep walking as he passed Adaira's door. He found Synne and Rucker in the common room. The grizzled fighter was hunched over a mug of ale in the corner, watching the door. The tables in a wide swath around him were empty. He saw Val and scowled. Val got the hint.

Synne was sitting near the hearth, wiry arms folded across her chest, warming herself by the fire.

"May I?" Val asked.

She looked up, then gave a curt nod.

He sat beside her. "I've never known a majitsu before."

She looked surprised but didn't respond.

"Look," he said. "I'm guessing they told you they would commute your sentence if you agreed to protect me. You had no choice in the matter."

"You know nothing," she said quietly.

Val spread his hands. "I know you're sitting alone, and I have time to listen."

Synne continued staring ahead.

"Did they tell you why I was imprisoned?" he asked.

After a time, Synne slowly nodded, then looked down at her hands. She plucked at the sleeve of her black shirt as if ashamed by the material.

He rose. "Trust takes time to build. You saved my life and have already earned mine." He refrained from a paternal squeeze of her shoulder. This proud woman, he sensed, would not take well to pity. "Good night, Synne. Perhaps one day we'll learn a bit more about each other."

Her eyes rose to meet his for the briefest of moments, her gaze unreadable, before sliding away.

Val retired to his room, unable to stop thinking about the barrier of fog. How it had appeared and whether they would be able to breach it. What they would find on the other side. Knowing he needed to prepare as much as possible, he reached for his father's spellbook, written during his time at the Abbey and containing notes and instructions on a set of spiritmancy spells that, if Val could learn them in time, might prove invaluable.

There was a knock at the door. He tensed and reached for his staff. "Yes?"

"It's me."

Adaira's voice.

He set his staff down and opened the door to find Lord Alistair's daughter dressed in a sleek blue nightgown, hair unbound. Val stood in the entrance, not inviting her in but not pushing her away.

She met his eyes, stepped forward, and kissed him in the doorway. Kissed him long and hard and deep. As her body pressed against his, he sank into the kiss, feeling light-headed with desire.

He took a step back, pulling her inside the room, forgetting his earlier promise to himself. Her eyes had a glazed look when she spoke. "You wouldn't have come to my room yourself," she said in a throaty voice, "and I don't know why."

That was not what he expected to hear. Yet he didn't deny the statement.

"There are a great many things I don't know about you, Val Kenefick. But I know you somehow managed to escape the Wizard Vault. I know my father thinks very highly of you, despite your crime. I know you completed the Planewalk, by yourself, with no instruction. I know that something happened between you and Gowan, because whenever I speak your name he recoils as if stung by a viper. But most of all, while I sense that my attraction is returned, I know that something in your life stands between you and me. Something important. I assume it to be another woman, but whatever it is, you should know that until it's resolved to my satisfaction, that will be the last kiss you receive from these lips."

She brushed a hand across his cheek, flashed a sad smile, and left him standing in the doorway.

With a shudder of attraction coursing through him, Val grabbed his father's spellbook and climbed into bed, poring over its contents until his eyes closed themselves. Yet when he slept, he dreamed not of Spirit Shields and Moon Rays and travels through the astral plane, but of a strong-willed young woman with hair like spun gold, challenging turquoise eyes, and lips so soft they brought him to his knees.

When Adaira returned to her room, she sat with her back against her headboard, her stomach churning so hard she felt as if she might throw up.

The mattress sagged. The rough woolen blanket made her itch. Still, though accustomed to the finer things in life, it wasn't the lack of creature comforts that troubled her. Adaira was nearing her twenty-fifth year and had never traveled without her father or a swarm of majitsu present. She was eager for adventure, and the hardships of the road sounded romantic to her. Wondrous new horizons to behold, sleeping under the stars, tests of will and wit.

She had known full well what she was doing when she entered the Pool of Souls. That her father would not—*could* not—allow her any concessions. Making the decision to risk one's life was one thing, however.

Following through with it was another.

Hearing about Val's imprisonment had sent her reeling. It seemed like such an unfair punishment for his crime. She had known in her heart he was not trying to commit treason.

Of course her feelings played a part in the decision. Val intrigued and challenged her like no one ever had. As if he cared not a whit about her lineage. For a young woman who found it impossible to escape her family's name, that was an incredibly seductive trait. She wanted to fall in love, not gain a political ally for her father.

Valjean was cool, confident, smart, and handsome. He gave her chill bumps when they touched and she found herself thinking of him at the oddest times.

Yet her mysterious beau wasn't the main reason she had come to Porlock.

Adaira knew her father loved her. But her mother's death had changed him. Never a carefree man, a genuine laugh had not escaped his lips in years. He had become withdrawn and sullen, and Adaira yearned to lift his spirits. Yet he wouldn't let her in. Her father saw her as a fragile thing to be protected, a reminder of his beloved wife that he must never, at any cost, lose. It was stifling. Adaira was a caged bird. Her father wouldn't let her walk down the street without a pair of guards.

She could not spend her life as the cloistered daughter of the Chief Thaumaturge. She had to make her own mark and prove her worth, to herself and to him and to the entire Protectorate. To do that, she knew, would take something extraordinary.

Something like committing treason and embarking on a perilous adventure to bring back the head of an outlaw spirit mage, thus reclaiming an important symbol of the Realm and winning back her freedom.

Yes, she thought as she curled into the blanket and closed her eyes, at peace with her choice despite her terror at what the future held, *that should do nicely*.

Val and the others set out for the wall of fog the next morning. The townspeople paused to watch them leave, leaning on hoes in their vegetable patches, slowing as they stepped out of shops, clutching children to their sides. Defiant stares were thrown, unlike when Cyrus had been present.

"Don't they know we killed the demons?" he asked Legate Wainwright. The portly bureaucrat had decided to escort them out of town.

"Another child disappeared last night," the legate said, with a nervous glance at the crowd. "A five-year-old boy."

Adaira clapped a hand over her mouth, and Val swore. "More demons?"

"The boy was taken out of a third-story window. One can only assume."

"Tell them we're doing everything we can," Val said. "And that we're sorry."

"Wizards don't apologize, boy," Rucker growled. "Don't ye know that?"

Val exchanged a look with Dida and Adaira. "These wizards do. Why haven't more guards been sent?"

"You weren't told?" Legate Wainwright asked, with a lift of his eyebrows. "Tobar was born in a wagon nearby, and the town is known to harbor revolutionaries. Why do you think I'm here?"

Adaira looked as surprised as everyone else. "I've heard no talk of an entire seditious town."

"They're sympathetic, not seditious. They pay their taxes and, for the most part, take their Oaths. Still, certain elements are present, and the queen has decided to teach a lesson."

"By letting demons take their children?" she said.

The legate lowered his eyes. "We thought you eliminated the threat yesterday."

"There should be a constant guard. I'll speak to my father . . ."

She trailed off, and Val winced at the sudden silence among the group.

Legate Wainwright dropped off at the edge of town, wishing them luck as the party set out along the road leading to the old fort. They warily circled the hill, wondering if more demons had taken up residence in the ruins.

No sign of danger. The curtain of fog was farther off than they thought, at least two miles past the fort, across a field of yellow gorse and heather. Val approached the unnatural barrier with a mixture of dread and fascination. When they drew to within a dozen yards, he realized the fog was thicker and more textured from up close, a filmy gray substance stretching from ground to sky.

"Remarkable," Dida said, leaning in to peer at the phenomenon.

Rucker waved his sword through the stuff, then drew the blade back and studied it. It came out clean.

"This looks more akin to ectoplasm than fog," Adaira said.

Val gave her a sharp look. "Ectoplasm?"

Rucker grunted. "The stuff spirits are made of, when you can see 'em in this dimension."

Val knew what ectoplasm was. He was just shocked this world used the same word, which derived from the protoplasm of cellular tissue. How much biology did cuerpomancers understand?

"Does that help us?" Val asked.

Adaira crossed her arms. "Not really."

They walked for a mile in either direction and found the barrier unchanging. Val and Adaira tried flying as high as they could, until the fog merged with the clouds and the air got too thin to fly. Still no variance. In exasperation, Synne put an arm into the fog, then held onto Val and stepped inside before anyone could stop her.

Val tensed. "What do you see?"

"Nothing," the majitsu called back, though her voice sounded farther away than it should. "Come in."

Val grimaced and took a tentative step closer, forming a chain by holding onto Adaira. As soon as he passed through the barrier, he experienced a sense of vertigo and had to force himself not to jerk back or cry out.

Once he found his balance, he realized he could barely see his hands in front of his face. Synne, who was standing right in front of him, appeared wraith-like, insubstantial.

"This is bizarre," Val said.

"Aye."

He kept a firm grip on both Synne and Adaira's hand, sensing that if they lost their connection to the outside world, they might not be able to find their way back.

Val tried peering into the distance. The longer he stared, the farther he seemed to be able to see, though maybe it was just in his mind. Everything was gray and lifeless. Odorless. He was about to turn back when he saw a shadow approaching, a winged mass darker than the gray matter surrounding it. Val got the sense that it had noticed him. It drifted nearer and began to pick up speed, growing larger as it approached, until it towered twenty feet above them.

Val hurried out of the fog, yanking Synne with him. He was breathing hard. "Did you see that?"

"Aye," she said, her eyes wide.

They told the others about the experience. Val thought about what had happened and said, "I need to go back in."

"You're certain?" Dida asked. "That does not sound like a promising tactic."

"There's something I want to try."

Synne and Adaira both insisted on coming with him. They formed another chain, with Dida and Rucker anchoring the outside.

"Probe with your mind," Val said to Adaira as they entered, remembering the earlier sense that he could see into the distance. This time, he tried to expand his eyesight using magic.

It did seem as if he could see farther, though he saw the same vista wherever he turned. Nothing but gray.

"Anything?" he asked Adaira.

"Just fog."

Val wondered nervously what that heaving dark shape had been, and whether another would appear. After a moment, he tried moving forward not with his feet, but with his mind. Pushing through spirit as he had at the Planewalk. He gathered his power and tried to sift through the gray fog, willing himself forward.

It worked! It was strange, though. He felt not as if he had moved, but as if a miniscule crack had opened in the fog. A crack to *somewhere else*. He pushed harder—as hard as he could—but it wasn't enough. Not nearly enough. Whatever this stuff was, it was the mental equivalent of trying to walk through concrete.

He just wasn't strong enough.

Disappointed, he brought Synne and Adaira back outside. "You were right," he said to Adaira, then explained his discovery.

They stopped to eat a lunch the innkeeper had packed. As Dida finished off his cheese and egg sandwich, he said, "Tellurian energy lines vary greatly in strength. What if the same variance applies to a barrier such as this?"

Rucker grunted. "Interesting theory."

No one had a better idea, so they walked another mile and Val tried again. To his surprise, he found it easier to push through the veil of spirit fog. Easier, but not easy enough. Still a crack instead of a doorway.

But the knowledge emboldened him, and they kept hiking along the wall of fog, trying to access it at various points. At times the barrier felt weaker to Val, at times stronger. Eventually he grew too tired to probe.

Rucker glanced at the darkening sky. "We should get back before dark. Conserve what you have left," he told Val, "in case we meet a demon on our return."

The frank words unsettled them, and they headed for Porlock in a single file, scanning the countryside for danger. Val breathed a huge sigh of relief when the village came into view. His relief turned to unease as he noticed the flames licking the sky above the town.

"Is that some kind of bonfire?" he asked.

" 'Tisn't the season to celebrate the harvest," Rucker said.

Val and Adaira debated flying in for a closer look, then decided not to put themselves at risk. As the party reached the outskirts of the settlement, they realized the flames and smoke pouring skyward emanated from the center of town.

Yet there were no people. It was only dusk, but the streets were strangely deserted. They drew closer and heard shouting from the town square, commingled with shrieks of agony. Rucker's sword appeared in his hand, and Synne took the lead, stalking forward like a predator.

The screams of pain increased in volume as the party hurried through the isolated streets. When they saw the source of the commotion, Val's step faltered and his stomach twisted with rage and horror.

In the center of the village square, a huge bonfire had been built, surrounded by hundreds of torch-wielding villagers. Tied to a stake atop the pyre was Legate Wainwright, screaming as the flesh melted from his bones.

Someone saw the party and started shouting. More heads turned. A woman pressed through the crowd with a dead child in her arms, mangled almost beyond recognition. She held the child out as if in offering to Val. "Do ye see what ye and yer kind have wrought? What ye've brought to our town?"

"Kill them!" someone else shouted, as hundreds of hands thrust blazing torches into the air. "Kill them all!"

12

"Turn!" Mala screamed, as the Battle Mage and his warriors approached through the field of agave. "Engage!"

Will felt as if he were moving in slow motion as he turned to face the terrifying vision behind him. The giant snake carrying the Battle Mage was a dozen yards away. Mala must have decided that fighting was better than turning themselves in, and he had no time to question her wisdom. She whipped her sash at the Mayan wizard, but it struck an invisible shield and fell to the ground. Gunnar and Mateo, who had brought up the rear, streaked forward. A flick of the snake's tail sent them tumbling through the spiky agave.

Mala managed to vault over the serpent and slice its tail with her dagger as she landed. It barely seemed to notice. As Will rushed to join her, Mala whipped her short sword off her back and began hacking at the beast while trying to avoid its flailing body.

Selina thrust her hands forward. Two vines shot out of the forest like missiles and wrapped around the Battle Mage, cocooning him atop the snake. Will got a surge of hope until the vines exploded, showering the ground with green mush. The Mayan wizard opened his fist, and a beam of sunlight shot out of it, dissipating an inch in front of Selina's chest. The sylvamancer had gone rigid, focusing every ounce of her power on blocking the lethal strike.

The group of Mayan warriors caught up with the fight, attacking with obsidian spears and cudgels. Mala and Will were forced to break away from the snake and help the others.

The Battle Mage kept shooting beams of light at Selina. As she backed away, struggling to block them, one got through and seared the side of her arm. She screamed.

"Help her!" Mala shouted to Will. "She's overmatched!"

"How?" he shouted back. His sword was ineffective against the colossal serpent, and the Battle Mage was seated too high up for him to reach.

"Be ready!" she said, leaving Will to wonder at her meaning.

The rest of the party fared better against the Mayan warriors. Gunnar fought with the kind of brutal efficiency Will imagined he would, using his power and size to overwhelm all who stood against him. Opponent after opponent fell to the swing of his war hammer.

Mateo took out two men in quick succession with his shortbow, then drew a flexible metal sword out of the belt scabbard wrapped around his waist. He slapped the sword back and forth on the ground as he advanced. Whenever the sword struck an opponent, even on the flat side of the blade, it tore through flesh. When one of the warriors parried the blade with a spear, Mateo's sword bent around his opponent's weapon and bit into his side.

Even Yasmina held her own. Will could tell she had been practicing. She led with her staff, using the longer weapon to bat away the blades and then crack her opponents on the skull with the bronze owl.

The Battle Mage must have noticed. With a wave of his staff, the snake surged forward, causing chaos by snapping its tail into the midst of Will and his companions. It caught Yasmina this time, whipping her violently to the ground.

"Yaz!" Will cried, holding off two Mayans as he fought his way to her. She retrieved her staff and struggled to her feet, shaken and bleeding.

The snake switched tactics, wrapping its tail around Gunnar and thrusting him high into the air. The big man screamed, his face purpling as the snake crushed him in its coils.

Mala shouted. "Now, Will!"

She sheathed her weapons, reached into her bottomless pouch with both hands, and withdrew two short orange rods. Without missing a beat, she sprinted to the snake and thrust the orange rods against its scales. As the rods glowed and then sparked, the beast's fanged mouth opened in a soundless cry, and it began to writhe and buck, as if Mala had administered an electric shock.

The flailing of the wounded snake knocked over Mateo and a handful of the Mayan warriors, as well as Mala. It also caused the creature's head to dip forward. The Battle Mage gripped the harness and managed to remain on the platform, but the snake's thrashing broke his concentration and stopped the barrage of laser-like sunbeams that were pinning Selina down.

Will took the opportunity to leap onto the wooden platform. The Mayan wizard saw him coming and shot twin sunbeams from his eyes, but Will had his sword up and ready, and Zariduke swallowed the magic.

The Battle Mage's eyes widened in shock. From up close, Will realized he was a boy of no more than eighteen.

"How?" the Mayan wizard said, then swung his hooked staff. Will blocked the blow and kicked the boy in the stomach, sending him flying off the snake. Will jumped down and stalked him. From his back, the young wizard sent a flurry of sunbeams at Will, at different parts of his body. Will couldn't block them all but his sword must have had a halo effect, because it absorbed each ray with a *snick* of blue-white light.

Will put his foot on the chest of the Battle Mage, the tip of Zariduke against his throat. The snake writhed towards them but stopped when the boy held out a palm. Proud defiance sparked in the Mayan's eyes.

"Who are you?"

"We came from the Barrier Coast," Will said. "From Freetown. We seek only to enter the jungle."

"And your purpose in our land? How do you deflect my magic?"

Enough talk. Will was in a position of strength and worried more forces were on the way. After a glance at Mala, who gave a tip of her head, he pressed his sword into the hollow of the mage's throat. "We're seeking something lost in the jungle. If I let you live, will you let us continue our journey?"

The battle around them had ceased. Will knew everyone was waiting to see the outcome between him and the Battle Mage. He looked into the Mayan's eyes, seeking trust instead of dominion. "We're part of a Revolution against the Congregation. The survival of our people is at stake. If we don't find something to help us, they will destroy us."

The Battle Mage's face tightened. "The Congregation is no friend of ours. It is common knowledge Lord Alistair plans conquest to the south."

"Then let's be allies instead of enemies."

A line of blood trickled down from the tip of the sword pressed against the young Mayan's throat. He locked eyes with Will and said, "Go. You have my word we will not follow."

Will hesitated, then withdrew his sword and helped him to his feet. In return, he clasped Will by the forearm. "My name is Aahpo Hun-Ahpu. I am a full Battle Mage of the Third Order of the Kukulcan Caste." He handed Will a silver token. "By my permission you are welcome in the Mayan Kingdom, so long as you obey the laws of this land." In a lower voice meant for Will alone, he said, "Thank you for sparing my life. I shall not forget it. But go with haste, my friend. My elders may feel differently than I."

Will couldn't be sure that Aahpo wouldn't turn on their group as soon as Will turned his back, or that a whole platoon of Battle Mages riding giant snakes wasn't headed their way, ready to tear down the jungle to find them.

But Will had made his choice. He wasn't going to kill someone at his mercy, not even his enemy. He gripped Aahpo's hand a final time and, with a nod to Mala, turned and followed Coba into the jungle.

The foliage was thick and dry, the trees and vines so dense they blotted out the sun. All vestiges of civilization disappeared, drowned amid the chatter of birds and insects.

They were lucky no one had been seriously injured in the fight, though Selina winced in pain as she wrapped her burned arm in a bandage. The High Council had gifted them three small bottles of healing salve, but the sylvamancer never asked for one.

The footpath allowed two people to walk abreast. All manner of animal sounds emanated from the jungle: the booming roar of a howler monkey, the far-off growl of a jungle cat, the piercing screech of a bird of prey.

No one said much for the first few hours, nervous of pursuit. Only Yasmina seemed unaffected, studying her surroundings with a single-minded purpose.

Aahpo stayed true to his word. By the time the party stopped for lunch beside a sluggish, copper-colored stream, the tension had eased and everyone's spirits had risen.

After he ate, Will walked down to the stream to wash his hands. Mala walked up behind him, surprising him by laying a hand on his forearm. "You performed well back there. With the Battle Mage."

He had always felt she was different when they were alone. Softer, more approachable. It could be his imagination, but he felt he brought out a side of her that no one else knew.

"Thanks," he said. "I had a good teacher."

"Had?" she said, her eyebrows rising as the teasing tone returned. "Are we equals now?"

He looked right at her. "Maybe not on the battlefield."

She met his gaze, and her fingers caressed the length of his arm as she pulled away, giving him goose bumps.

When he returned to the others, he asked, "How dangerous is this part of the jungle?"

Coba was peeling a mango he had found. "Jungle always dangerous. First day, big trail, calm animals. After that . . ." He shrugged but didn't elaborate, and Will wasn't sure he wanted him to.

"This cenote we're seeking," Mateo said. "Why is it called the Basin of Blood?"

"Most cenotes in the Yucatan were used for ritualistic purposes," Mala answered. "By that I mean human sacrifice."

Coba nodded. "Chan Kawil very important to ancients."

"You've been there?" Will asked.

"When I was a boy."

"What about the second marker, the jaguar temple?" Mala asked. "Do you have any insight as to that?"

The guide wiped mango juice off his chin. "Many temples in jungle. Old gods. Better not to disturb."

Mala scoffed, took a long drink from her canteen, and shouldered her pack. As the party set off again, Will couldn't help but feel a thrill of excitement at the adventure of it all. Sylvamancers and wilders, rukhs and dragons, Battle Mages riding giant snakes, lost tombs full of treasure. This world was more wondrous and strange than Will could ever have imagined, its magic real and potent, its myths still true.

Yet the one thing that surpassed Urfe's marvels were its terrors. Some nights, he couldn't sleep without convincing himself it was all a dream, that he would wake up safe in his own bed in the apartment he shared with Caleb on Magazine Street in New Orleans. Fighting boredom and high rent instead of terrifying monsters and wizards that could raze whole villages.

Had it been any different for the old explorers of Earth, braving high seas and an unmapped horizon, plunging headlong into brand new continents? Campaigning was like free will, he mused. Without true danger—imminent, soul-shrinking, teeth-rattling danger—there was no true excitement.

*   *   *

The party traveled light. On Mala's instructions, they had packed dried provisions and tiny silk hammocks in Freetown. They spent the first night in a moldy-smelling collection of huts used by trappers. To save supplies, Coba procured their dinner from the jungle: fruits, nuts, berries, and an enormous rodent he caught with a net and roasted over a fire.

The next two days passed largely the same. Hot and humid and exhausting. Coba provided for them well, no monsters threatened, and except for a few pythons that slithered away and a tarantula in Will's shoe that almost induced his first panic attack in weeks, there were no surprises. They spent the third night tucked inside a grove of Yucatan rosewoods, safe in their hammocks, sheltered high above the scorpions, spiders, and squadrons of leafcutter ants that patrolled the forest floor.

At dusk the next day, they reached the Basin of Blood.

A mile before they reached the infamous cenote, the ruins of Chan Kawil salted the jungle in every direction. Clumps of moss and lichen draped hulking slabs of granite pitted from the ravages of time. Steps led to broken altars that seemed disembodied, random archways dripped with vines and tropical foliage. At some point, Will realized they were walking along an old stone highway smothered in vegetation, and he wondered how far the might of Chan Kawil had once extended.

The road led right to the edge of a jagged circular depression that stretched at least twenty yards across. Will stood at the lip and looked down.

Fifty feet below, bored out of the limestone like a well of the gods, was a pool of metallic blue water so clear he could track the schools of brightly colored fish. He could also see the knobby ends of human bones poking out of the sandy bottom.

Upright stone slabs surrounded the cenote: steles that stood taller than Will, carved with Mayan pictograms divided into blocks of intricate figures and symbols. Gigantic ficus trees loomed behind the steles, their aerial roots descending into the water like petrified ropes. Yasmina joined Will at the edge, awed by the last vestiges of sunlight dappling the beautiful cenote. Bats circled the shaft of the hole, gobbling up insects.

Will cast a nervous glance into the jungle, remembering Coba's words that no one ventured past the cenote. "What now?"

Mala dropped her pack. "We set camp while Coba searches for a path on the other side."

Exhausted from the journey, Will fell asleep before Coba returned from his mission, and woke to the smell of sizzling rodent. The party gathered around the morning fire, eager to hear what Coba had discovered.

Their guide bit into a papaya and said, "No path."

"You're sure?" Maya said. "How far out did you go?"

"Far. Climbed trees, too. No path."

Frustrated, Maya unrolled the map again. A dotted line led from the cenote to the representation of the jaguar temple. There were no distinguishing features in between. The final marker, a small lake backed by hills, was positioned just before the pyramid at the end of the map.

"Maybe this is the wrong place," Mala said.

Coba tossed a chunk of rind into the jungle. "No other cenote with statues."

"That *you* know about," Mala said, then flung a bangled wrist at the jungle. "There's probably hundreds of lost cenotes out there."

Coba finished his papaya and stood. "This is right one. Make sense on map." He wagged a finger. "One place I still not look for path." As everyone watched, he ran straight to the edge of the cenote and jumped off, arcing into a swan dive.

"He's so melodramatic," Mala muttered, as Will ran over in time to see Coba swimming along the bottom of the cenote. When he reached the edge of the sinkhole, he disappeared from view.

Mateo frowned. "Where did he go?"

"I don't know," Mala murmured, "but underground streams have chewed through the limestone like termites."

After two hours passed, the worry became palpable. They didn't have a chance without their guide, and a return to Ixmal was just as risky. Just as Mala and Selina prepared to probe the water themselves, Coba darted out of some unseen passage and back into the cenote, swimming over to grab one of the vine-like roots that connected the ficus trees to their water source like arboreal straws.

"Map," Coba said brusquely, after he shimmied up the long root. "Show me map."

Mala unfurled the scroll while he stood and peered at it, dripping water. The guide pointed at a symbol in the upper left corner that Will had noticed but not really paid attention to: a curved dagger piercing a seven-pointed crown.

"What's that?" Coba asked.

"A symbol germane to the cartographer, I assume," Mala said warily, as if leaving something unsaid. "Why?"

Coba pointed at the cenote. "Because it down there."

13

"How dangerous is this journey going to be?" Caleb asked, as he and Marguerite spurred their horses along the scenic coastal road.

"Not as dangerous as your drinking schedule in Freetown."

He muttered to himself and took another swallow from his canteen.

"I know ye like 'elping others, don't try and pretend otherwise. This is just another way."

"Are there any monsters on the Barrier Coast?" he asked.

"Plenty. Gorgons, giants, genies, and shamblers, to name but a few." She cast a worried glance at the sky. "Not to mention the dragons."

Caleb's shoulders sagged. She rode close enough to give his arm an affectionate squeeze, then laughed. " 'Tis not without peril, but the Barrier Coast valleys are the safest in the Ninth. There are no dragons until ye reach the Făgras Mountains, and precious few even there."

"I don't know how I let you talk me into this."

"Ye didn't," she said lightly. "I made the decision for ye."

They rode over golden dunes laced with sea grass, through meadows of clover and wild strawberry, atop emerald ridges and promontories that jutted over the ocean like bread loaves. In the distance, the mountains seemed formed of mist, soft and ephemeral.

He couldn't deny that it felt good to get out of Freetown. Taste the fresh air and take a break from the misery. Most of all, though, he was glad to be with someone familiar. Especially someone who looked fantastic in leather breeches.

Around midday, the road veered off the coast and into the foothills. Caleb kept up a steady pace of drinking during the ride, and was nice and relaxed by the time the sun began to descend. It was a week's journey to the Blackwood Forest, and he had brought a fortnight's supply of the stiffest grog in Freetown.

The road passed through a primordial forest of old growth redwoods whose bare lower branches stuck out like swords. Marguerite set up camp by the road, looking nervous as she eyed the full moon and the fog that seemed to drip off the trees.

Caleb eased off his horse, aching from the ride. "I thought it was safe around here?"

"We've gone inland a ways, and there's a full moon tonight."

"Which means what? Werewolves?"

She didn't laugh at his joke. "I'm a superstitious lass. One never knows what kind of trouble a full moon brings. Just don't wander off."

"Um, I wasn't planning on it."

He set up camp while Marguerite prepared a basic dinner of cured fish, bread, and dried fruit. After dinner, when he offered to fill her canteen with liquor, she refused.

"Did you join a cult?" he asked.

She squeezed his cheek and settled into her bedroll.

After a moment, he eased down beside her. "You used to love a good time."

She clasped her hands behind her head and gazed up at the canopy of stars, her smoky gray eyes mirroring the mystique of the moon.

"I like to drink," she said softly, "but I like ye more."

He grew quiet, touched by her words. For some reason, in that instant, he realized he had never been ready for love, didn't even know what it meant.

Yet as much as he enjoyed life's carnal pleasures, he reviled his own shallowness. Why hadn't he been able to love Yasmina after all those years? Why didn't he feel guiltier about the legions of women he had discarded? He teased Will all the time about his love life, but Caleb always had the feeling that it was he, and not his younger brother, who was really missing out.

"G'night, Caleb."

He turned to face her, surprised. "You're going to sleep?"

"Isn't that what one does after a long day's ride?" She leaned over and gave him a kiss on the mouth, just long enough to give him chills.

Before he could respond, she faced away from him and curled into a ball, leaving no doubt as to her intentions.

Though Caleb was surprised, he had sensed something different about Marguerite the first time he had met her, a strength of character behind her laid-back façade. Secure in her own skin, she had never tried too hard, either in love or in life. That relaxed confidence had always attracted him.

Staring at her resting form and splayed auburn hair made him nervous. As if there was a hollow space forming in his stomach that he had barely known existed.

Annoyed by the feeling, he decided to stop thinking and start drinking. He worked himself into a stupor, fell asleep, and woke sometime during the night with a violent urge to pee. Not wanting to disturb Marguerite, he stumbled away from camp and urinated next to a tree. He must have fallen asleep in the process, because the next thing he knew he was lying on his back and the air smelled like cloves and girlish voices were singing in a language he didn't recognize. He opened his eyes, blinked twice, and realized he was in the center of a grove of redwoods with trunks as wide as small houses. The moon shone like polished pewter through a hole in the canopy.

Those were the normal things.

The rest of it had to be a dream.

A circle of huge, glowing, brightly colored mushrooms lined the edges of the grove. Inside the mushroom ring, a dozen creatures no taller than his forearm flitted about on tiny diaphanous wings. They were naked to the waist, their lush female forms in perfect proportion to their diminutive stature. Caleb caught a good look at one, expecting to see a transcendent faerie's face upon-which-he-dared-not-gaze, but instead found himself staring at an ugly mug that resembled a cross between a bull dog and an Oompa-Loompa.

Caleb pinched himself. It hurt.

He scrambled to his feet as the foul creatures darted to and fro, cackling and making lewd gestures in his direction. Still inebriated, he stumbled towards the edge of the ring, but the creatures flapped their wings and released a flurry of bolts of colored light. He blocked a number of them with his vambraces, but a few got through and pricked him in the back. At once he felt weakened and disoriented, his energy siphoned away. He tried to keep going but the nasty little sprites caught him by the arms and legs and dragged him to the ground. The last thing he remembered was the creatures dancing madly above his prone form, taking puffs from a smoking brazier and quaffing drink after drink from cups hollowed out of mushrooms.

Caleb woke in darkness. His hands were bound behind his back, feet tied at the ankles, mouth gagged. He gave muffled shouts for help anyway, to release tension. After the initial terror subsided, he tried to learn more about his environment, which smelled like a Christmas tree lot.

He grasped the ground and felt dirt. After managing to roll his body along the ground for eight awkward revolutions, he hit a wall. At least he thought it was a wall: the surface felt like a piece of polished wood with ridges, whorls, and knobs. He stood and felt his way around the edge of his prison and knew he was going in a circle, albeit a large one.

Was he inside a *tree*?

He slumped to his back and thought about how badly he wanted a drink. His head was beginning to pound. By the time a section of the wall hinged silently open and moonlight poured in, Caleb's hangover had reached epic proportions. He barely resisted as a team of lump-faced fairies dragged him out of the hollowed-out trunk of a giant redwood and into a circle of glowing mushrooms. He thought the scenery looked different, but he wasn't certain.

He looked to his left and saw the fairies dragging someone else out of a different tree. The other prisoner was a stocky man in his early fifties, almost as tall as Caleb, with bushy long hair and a dark, unkempt beard infused with gray.

The two men eyed each other as the fairies laid them on their backs in the middle of the mushroom ring and repeated their performance from the night before, singing and carousing like some kind of twisted sorority party.

Caleb's throat felt like sandpaper. His stomach churned with hunger, and his limbs ached from his bonds. His head throbbed worse than it ever had, on the level of a migraine.

But he had to get out of there. When he thought no one was looking, he started rolling towards the edge of the circle, faster and faster, hoping the other captive would take his cue and start rolling in the other direction. Maybe one of them could escape and go for help.

Before he got halfway out, the fairies cackled, flapped their wings, and shot Caleb and the other prisoner with more bolts of colored light. Once the drug from the psychedelic darts took effect, the nasty creatures untied their captives and shoved cups of water and a small loaf of bread in front of each man. Caleb was parched and drank greedily, then stuffed the bread in his mouth. Not until the loaf was gone did he turn to the other man and woozily ask him what the hell was going on.

"You've been captured by a troop of wood sprites. Don't you recognize the mushroom rings? Or did you just drop in from Earth?" The older man grinned dreamily as Caleb gaped at the familiar accent.

"Did you say Earth?" Caleb asked.

"They call me the Brewer around here, but my real name's Bruce Levine. I'm from the south shore of Long Island."

"Now I know I'm dreaming," Caleb said, resisting the urge to giggle. Whatever the fairies had shot them with, it was potent stuff, like a Novocain shot laced with magic mushrooms.

Which made perfect sense, Caleb thought, as he tried to focus his gaze on the colorful array of giant fungi ringing the clearing. A pimply, pug-faced faerie darted over to pinch his cheek, turned to thrust her buttocks in his face, then cackled as she flew off.

"I'm trying to figure out who the fairies sound like when they sing," the other prisoner said dreamily. "Pantera fronting Enya? I was in a rock band back home, you know. Lead guitar. Kinda famous."

"Oh yeah?" Caleb said. "Who?"

"Ant Patrol."

"Never heard of them."

"You're not from Long Island. You're also not fifty."

"Cool, man."

"Hey kid, how'd you get here?"

"My brother stuck a magic key in a door," Caleb said. "You?"

"I was playing a gig in Istanbul—believe it or not, they loved me over there—and the day after my show, I popped into a curio shop. I was really into music history and found an old tablet with these stick-like marks carved into it. Cuneiform. The old geezer who owned the shop claimed it was a really old piece of sheet music, the oldest song in the world. I laughed and asked him how he got it. He said his son was a treasure hunter who found it on a dig near the Syrian border. It sounded like a sucker's story to me, but I was curious and rich and bought it anyway, along with an ancient Sumerian lyre. I found a scholar to help me translate the tablet, then went home and sang it. When I finished, I started feeling really weird, like my body was dissolving. I blacked out and ended up here."

"Righteous," Caleb said.

"Yeah."

"Hey, Bruce—"

"Call me the Brewer. I've gotten used to it."

"Sure, man. So what's up with these gnarly pixies?"

"You think the hot ones want humans? That's a male fantasy. We get the Woodland Fairies, kid. Bottom of the barrel."

Two of the fairies started arguing, and one dumped the contents of her mushroom-shaped cup on the other's head. The dispute dissolved into a hair-pulling fistfight. The other fairies joined hands and flew in a circle around the combatants, cheering them on.

"This is awful," Caleb said, as colored spots filled his vision.

"Yeah."

"Do the mushrooms give the wings their power?"

"I think so. The shrooms only pop up around a full moon."

"So what happens next?" Caleb wrinkled his nose. "They have their way with us and let us go?"

"Only the queen gets those honors. She shows up on the last night of the cycle." The Brewer glanced at the moon. "Two or three nights away, I'd wager."

"Does she look any better?"

"You see these ugly mugs flying around? They're like Brazilian supermodels compared to her."

Caleb swallowed. He glanced around the circle, then back at the Brewer's filthy clothes and dirt-encrusted nails. "You look like you've been here awhile."

"About a year."

Caleb started to laugh hysterically. "A *year*?"

"I'm lucky," he said, flashing a lascivious grin. "I keep the queen entertained."

One of the fairies took a puff off the brazier and blew a cloud of smoke in Caleb's face. It smelled of sassafras and rotten eggs. Above his head, the moon started to rotate slowly in place and then enlarge, until it was a spinning top that dipped and whirled across the night sky. Caleb felt himself losing his grip on both sanity and consciousness. "What happens when the queen gets bored?"

The Brewer let his cheek sag against the ground, his face slack as he stared at the circle of mushrooms. "She turns us into one of those."

14

The raised torches of the villagers glowed brightly in the night. It seemed to Val as if the entire town surged towards them. He and Adaira and Dida bought them a few seconds by tossing the front line back with a Wind Push, but hundreds more rushed forward.

The legate and the queen had badly miscalculated the effect of the deaths of the local children. The village had gone mad with grief.

"Retreat!" Rucker bellowed. "There's too many!"

Synne pulled Val into a sprint. Adaira ran beside him, turning while she fled to swipe a hand through the air. Atop the pyre, a fountain of blood erupted from Legate Wainwright's throat, silencing his screams. The legate's body shuddered and then sagged, his spirit released. *Good girl*, Val thought grimly.

The party ran for their lives, knowing the villagers would not want to leave witnesses to their crimes. The queen would send the Wizard Guard to slaughter them.

"If we can reach a building," Dida said, huffing as he ran, "I can ward us."

"Better to get to open ground," Rucker countered. Easily the oldest member of the group, he wasn't even breathing hard from the sprint. "If they don't lose their appetite soon," he gave Adaira and Val a hard look, "make an example."

Whenever one of the faster villagers drew too close, or someone launched a brick, Val or Adaira or Dida would send them flying backwards. By the time the party reached the edge of town, the crowd had fallen back and the closest pursuer was fifty yards away. Just as Val began to relax, he realized something was missing he couldn't leave behind.

"My father's spellbook," he said. "It's in my room."

Rucker waved a hand. "Leave it, boy!"

Val was already hovering in midair. "I can't do that."

Adaira and Dida rose with him, but he put out a hand. "Stay with Rucker and Synne. They might need you. I'll meet you at the fort."

Without waiting for a response, he extended his arms and soared into the night sky, high above the angry villagers, heading back into the center of town.

He looked down and realized the enraged mob had stopped chasing after the others, instead focusing on the wizard who had foolishly decided to return. Fearing arrows were being notched, he flew higher and faster, relying on speed and darkness.

His room was on the second floor. As the villagers poured into the inn, he crashed feet-first through a window, blowing out the glass as he went through. He slowed, landed on his feet, and crunched on broken shards as he strode to the bed and lifted the mattress. The spellbook was still there. With a sigh of relief, he tucked it inside his cloak.

He turned to leave as the door flew open. Five men burst into the room holding torches and swords. A sixth lagged behind with a bow and arrow trained on Val, negating the option to fly away.

He kept them at bay by swinging his staff in a wide arc. One of the men tried to block the staff with a wooden shield, and the azantite crescent moon sliced right through it.

The men approached more carefully, backing Val towards the window. The archer released an arrow. Val put up his Wizard Shield just in time. The archer grinned and notched another, waiting for Val to fly away and negate his Wizard Shield, sensing they had the advantage.

Footsteps pounded on the stairs. Val had to think of something fast. He used his staff as a deterrent while he worked to summon bigger magic. Focus, he whispered to himself. Focus the will and release. Focus and release. Focusreleasefocusreleasefocusreleasefocusrelease

Black lightning crackled at his fingertips. He was backed against the open window, but the men stopped moving when they saw Spirit Fire emerge. Still, he wasn't sure how much energy he could expend. What if he killed three of the men and ran dry of magic, leaving him defenseless against the others?

He should have worked harder to understand his limits. And now it was too late.

As they rushed forward, Val made a snap decision. He pointed his hands downward, at the men's feet, and disintegrated the wooden floorboards. Arms flailing, all five men fell through the jagged tear in the floor.

Val extinguished the sparks. He had to conserve enough energy for flight. The archer released another arrow that fell harmlessly to the floor, turned aside by Val's Wizard Shield. He sent the archer toppling backwards with a strong push of air, then turned and flew out of the window, soaring high to escape the marksmen below.

He caught up with the others before they reached the old fort. After checking to ensure no new demons infested the ruins, the party decided to camp for the night, in case the villagers mounted a pursuit. They reasoned the twin threat of demons and angry mages would deter them.

"Ye learned an important lesson tonight, boy," Rucker said as he and Val took first watch. The sky above the village still smoldered, though not as brightly as before.

"You don't need to tell me how vulnerable I am," Val muttered. "Isn't that why wizards formed the Congregation in the first place? To protect themselves against the prejudice of angry mobs?"

The old adventurer eyed him carefully. "Aye."

"What if the town had attacked a few elder mages?" he asked, still seething at the senseless murder of the legate. "I doubt they would like the outcome."

"I doubt it, too." Rucker spat. "But are ye an elder mage? Or high in a tower in the Wizard District? Didn't think so. The lesson was for ye, not them."

Val gripped his staff and peered into the blackness. "Lesson learned."

No one approached them during the night. The villagers probably thought they had returned to Londyn. At first light, the party set out for the wall of mist, tracking it to the southeast. They moved slowly so Val could test the strength of the barrier periodically.

There was no breakthrough, and they spent the next night camped atop a high, sloping moor with nothing but wild countryside as far as the eye could see. The air smelled damp and earthy.

"We're running into peat bog territory," Rucker said. "We'll have to watch our step."

Synne took first watch by herself. Val laid his sleeping roll next to Adaira's, studying his father's spellbook while the others slept. He examined a number of spells, including Spirit Radiance, which allowed a mage to create a light source directly from spirit, and Moon Ray, a cousin to the Sun Ray spell that, his father had noted, the Battle Mages of the Mayan Kingdom employed.

Val read about a spell called Mind Whip, though he didn't understand the principle or the execution. He also started practicing an advanced form of Wizard Shield called Spirit Armor.

When he finally turned in, Adaira stirred on her sleeping roll beside him and reached for his hand.

"It's beautiful out here," Adaira said dreamily, still half-asleep. "So many stars."

Val had to agree. As he lay on his back and stared at the constellations speckling the firmament like exploded silver, he wondered how many worlds his father had seen.

She murmured, "Did you know Londyn has an underground transport system with wooden rail cars powered by wizards?"

He smiled at her half-conscious rambling. "I did not."

"Let's ride it together one day. Good night, my love," she said, so softly he wondered if he had heard her correctly. He turned his head, but she was already asleep.

Another frustrating morning probing the mist. What if they failed before they even began? Would the queen send him back to prison, and Adaira along with him? Would they execute them?

He didn't want to find out. They *had* to break through.

"What about your magic?" he asked Dida, as they delved deeper into the countryside, traipsing through tangled woods and mist-soaked valleys. "Is there anything you know that might help?"

"Bibliomancy spells often intersect with other dimensions, true, but we employ mathematics and principles of physics, combined with runeology and general principles of magic. We do not manipulate spirit itself."

Rucker grew increasingly skeptical of their chances, until Val worried he would abandon the quest. Knowing his loss would be catastrophic, Val began trying inventive methods to breach the barrier. He sent Spirit Fire arcing into the wall of fog, tried a light spell to burn away the mist, and joined forces with Dida and Adaira to produce a hurricane-force Wind Push. Nothing seemed to affect it. Caring less and less about his personal safety, Val tied together every bit of rope and loose clothing he could muster, attached it to his waist, and ventured deep inside the fog.

No black shadows approached him, but neither did he make any progress. As far as he could tell, the world inside the mist was gray and unchanging.

They ate a cold lunch beside a waterfall that tumbled off a steep embankment right at the edge of the fog. Forced by the villagers to set out prematurely, they carried but a week's worth of emergency provisions in their packs. Munching on his ration of dried beef, Dida stood and walked to the edge of the waterfall. He closed his eyes as if deep in concentration. Val wandered over and asked him what he was doing.

"The tellurian energies are strong here," Dida said. "Not the highest we have seen, but potent." He wagged a finger. "Something else comes to mind. Flowing water interacts with different energies in different manners, sometimes enhancing, sometimes retarding."

"And?" Val said, intrigued. "Can you sense a difference here?"

"Only a slight one. But part of the waterfall is flowing inside the wall of fog."

"You think that might matter?"

Dida gave a helpless shrug. "I'm unable to judge the strength of spirit. But I think it bears investigation."

Val pressed his lips together and nodded. As he stood beside Dida and began to gather his will, the bibliomancer grabbed his shoulder and pointed at the waterfall. "I would advise standing there," he said. "Right where they meet."

"Underneath the waterfall?"

"I'm afraid so."

It was cold, maybe fifty-five degrees. Val grimaced and stripped down. Adaira wandered over, chuckling. "Are you that desperate for a wash?"

"Get everything packed and ready to go," he said, forcing conviction into his tone. "Just in case."

Adaira's eyebrows rose, but Val had already started to wade into the freezing water. His legs numbed by the time he reached the waterfall, and when he stepped underneath the flow that abutted the wall of fog, the shock of cold water made him gasp. He hoped he could endure long enough to test Dida's theory.

As Val concentrated, sifting through spirit while inside the fog as he had done a hundred times already, he was shocked to notice an immediate difference. Instead of pushing through wet concrete, it felt like he was trying to catch a greased pig. The stuff of spirit slipped away from him as if buffeted by the falling water, and it took everything Val had to hold on.

But when he finally grasped it, good and true, the barrier felt much weaker.

"To me!" he roared, fighting to maintain his mental hold. "Grab on!"

His back was to the party, his eyes closed so he could focus, but soon he felt hands grabbing onto his arms and waist. Moments later, Adaira shouted that they were ready.

Val pushed. Hard.

And felt himself moving forward, through the veil of spirit.

He worked to control his excitement. It was the first time he had made real progress. As with the Planewalk, the task grew more difficult over time, each step heavier and less steady than the last, until he felt as if he were trying to control an oil-drenched boulder on a Slip 'n' Slide.

It was too hard. He couldn't do it. Muffled shouts of encouragement from the others reached his ears, as if coming from faraway. While it bolstered his spirits, his greatest motivation came from inside.

You have to get through the barrier, Val. Failure is not an option. It never has been. It never will be.

He thought of his brothers and the threat of execution and reached deep into his well of power, opening himself as he never had before, feeling the magic burn through him, not caring if it ripped a hole in him. He was getting through this invisible barrier he didn't even understand. He was getting through it right damn now.

With another roar, he made a final push, *willing* his way through, and then he felt as if he were falling. After a moment of panic, he landed on a spongy but firm surface, and got a whiff of morning dew.

When he opened his eyes, the world had changed.

15

Mala kept two waterproof lanolin bags in one of her pouches. The sacks were as thin as silk, magically enhanced by artisamancers. The party stripped down, then split the provisions and clothes between the two packs. Gunnar took one, Mateo the other.

Coba dove into the cenote again, treading water while everyone shimmied down the ficus roots. Mala and Will brought up the rear, and he worked hard not to stare at her naked, athletic body.

Or at least not to let her catch him.

The water was much chillier than Will expected, and quite deep. As he neared the bottom, he noticed a number of uneven passages that erosion had bored into the limestone. As Coba led them through one of the larger openings, he pointed above the hole, to where a small dagger-and-crown symbol had been carved.

They followed the watery passage, swimming behind a school of green-and-white striped fish. Just as Will began to worry about his oxygen, the channel poured into a half-submerged cavern. Far above their heads, shafts of sunlight streamed through holes in the limestone.

The party emerged wet and freezing from the sump. Hundreds of stalagmites and stalactites lined the floor and ceiling like the maw of some great beast, and Will had an unpleasant flashback to the journey through the Darklands. Unlike that subterranean environment, deep and dark and smothering, the Yucatan cavern had a pungent mineral smell, moist walls, and vines creeping down from the ceiling.

As if the cavern were a living, breathing thing.

"Come," Coba said, once everyone had dressed. He led them behind a huge stalagmite near one of the walls in the dry half of the cavern. The rock formation concealed a narrow opening that blended into the wall, unnoticeable from a few feet away.

Shivering, they followed a damp, uneven passage through a series of caverns with varying levels of water. Will took off his boots and waded through two of them, his feet slipping on algae. The journey was quiet except for the drip of water and the soft rustle of bat wings.

As Coba ranged ahead, Will and Mala walked side-by-side, ahead of Mateo and Yasmina. Gunnar and Selina guarded the rear. Whenever more than one choice of passage appeared, a dagger-and-crown symbol marked the way.

In a low voice, Will said to Mala, "You know something about that symbol, don't you?"

She gave him a sidelong look. "Aye."

"Does it have something to do with the fact that you can read the runes on the map?"

Her eyes sparked but she didn't respond.

"You never offered an explanation," he said.

"Perhaps there was a reason for that."

"I'm sure of it. You want to tell me what it is?"

After a moment, she said quietly, "As I said, the runes are written in a code language used only by the Alazashin."

"Marguerite told Caleb you were once a member."

"Desire produces loose lips."

"Why did Leonidus never send an expedition here? Because he couldn't read the map?"

"He could have hired a linguist. Or made inquiries. I have to assume it was a recent acquisition, a mission known only to him and interrupted by his demise."

"Do you have any idea why the Alazashin might have sent someone looking for the tomb in the first place?"

"They are always looking for items to improve their craft, or to barter with."

"What're *you* looking for, Mala?"

"Is a fabled treasure hoard not reason enough to search?"

"Maybe. That doesn't mean you don't have another reason."

"You think too much, Will the Builder."

"Is that a crime? Or do you prefer companions who think with their sword arm?"

He felt bad as soon as he said it. Her face darkened as she strode ahead of him.

*   *   *

Even when the light grew dim, enough natural illumination seeped through the cracks in the ceiling. Still, Selina cast a light spell at times to aid their passage, both to check for traps and to expose any dangers lurking in the shadows. When the lengthy passage they were following spilled into an intersection, Will was surprised to find an alcove with a flight of roughhewn steps descending into darkness. Beside the steps, another dagger-and-crown symbol had been carved.

Coba stood rigid atop the steps. Maya said something in his language, and the guide responded with a curt nod. It made Will uneasy to see the easygoing Mayan so on edge.

"His people believe the deeper caves in the Yucatan lead to Hell," Maya said. "These steps probably lead to a ritual chamber of some sort."

"That's comforting," Will muttered.

Mala lit a torch. Selina used the flame to ignite a light spell that lit the way with a dull orange glow, reinforcing the imagery of a descent into the mouth of Hades.

Will counted three hundred and fifteen steps. A short passage at the bottom led to a spacious natural cavern converted into a temple that sent chills along his arms.

A blocky limestone pyramid filled the center of the grotto, surrounded by steles with carved demonic faces. An emerald pool the size of a hot tub fronted the pyramid, ringed by a stone ledge covered in runes. The pyramid had no apparent entrance, though Will had the strange feeling it wasn't empty.

Multiple passages led out of the cavern. As the party spread out to look for the Alazashin symbol, Will approached the nearest wall and realized the surface was inset, top to bottom, with human bones.

The entire cavern was one giant ossuary.

"Over here!" Mateo said, pointing out another dagger-and-crown above one of the passages.

The entrance grotto was just the beginning. The cave system below the long staircase turned out to be a vast network of bone-strewn pools and ruined temples, mysterious stone columns, and elaborate sets of runes covering the walls and steles. Water was everywhere, trickling from heights unseen, pooling at their feet, dripping off the jagged tips of cave formations.

The floor grew so muddy that Will's boots squished with every step, and his fascination with the ancient scenery ended when the damp earth revealed something ominous: footprints.

Coba grimly pointed out the first set: two feet twice the size of a normal man's, but with a uniform, flattened surface. As if the owner had no toes or arch. Even stranger, the footsteps continued for ten yards and then abruptly disappeared.

"Any idea what they are?" Mala asked.

As the guide gave a grim shake of his head, Mateo rose from inspecting the footprints. "What lives down here?"

"Frogmen, giant salamander, bats, harvesters, troglopods." Coba shrugged. "This far out? Who knows what else?"

They had no choice but to warily continue. The footsteps appeared and disappeared in random fashion, vexing all attempts to decipher their pattern, causing everyone to grow increasingly tense. The only consolation was that the passage sloped gently upward. Maybe they would reach the surface before they met the owner of the strange tracks.

Will had lost track of time. It felt as if they had been trekking for two days straight, and Mala finally called a halt when they reached a muddy cavern dotted with man-size stalagmites. Multiple openings led out of the grotto. After locating the next dagger-and-crown symbol, they set camp on a dry patch in a corner of the cavern.

After a meal of cured beef and water that Coba had drawn from the nearest sump, Mala declared a double guard. She and Will took first watch. Selina and Mateo volunteered for the second. Will had noticed the two of them exchanging approving glances, and often walking side by side.

Mala shook out a glow stone and sat cross-legged with her back against the wall. Normally Will would have welcomed the chance to try to chip away at her armor, but both of them were focused on staying quiet and watching the entrances to the cavern.

As his adrenaline ebbed, he couldn't stop yawning, and as soon as Mala signaled their shift was over, he bent to wake Selina. When the sylvamancer opened her eyes, Will thought he saw movement behind her. He blinked. Though he might have been hallucinating from exhaustion, he could have sworn the cavern floor just rippled.

"I think I saw something," he whispered.

Selina sat up and expanded the dull gray light from Mala's glow stone, illuminating the cavern. Will gasped: the entire cavern floor seemed to be moving. As he watched in disbelief, the foot of thick mud covering the ground flowed together at various points and then heaved upward, coalescing into a dozen eight-foot tall mud creatures with melting faces and vaguely humanoid shapes. The creatures had giant spikes along their backs and horns jutting out from their heads, camouflaged as stalagmites from a distance.

In silent unison, they advanced on the party. Will scrambled to unsheathe his sword.

"Rise!" Mala shouted. "Gunnar, Mateo—to arms!"

Will rushed to her side as the sleeping members of the party gained their feet. Out of the corner of his eye, he saw Selina thrust her palms at the nearest mud monster, driving it backwards. It flowed back into the ground, dissolved, and reformed.

The monster closest to Will swung a huge fist at his face. He ducked and cleaved through the limb. Instead of falling off, the arm resealed without visible effect.

Beside him, Mala had a similar experience. Her short sword whisked through the mud creature, carving it up a dozen times before it reached her, but the creature kept coming and backhanded her across the cavern floor.

"Sharp-edged weapons don't hurt them!" Will shouted.

The party was backed into a corner of the cavern. Will tried to run to open ground, but the two monsters chasing him turned to mud and flowed along the ground faster than he could sprint. One emerged right behind him and grabbed him by the waist. The other creature lowered its head and thrust its spear-like horn at Will's chest. Just before it connected, Gunnar's war hammer smashed into the horn, shattering it. The mud monster made a low-pitched moaning sound that set Will's teeth on edge.

"Duck!" Gunnar cried.

Will lowered his head as the big man swung, then heard a thud as the mudman's arms released him. Will turned and saw the thing stumbling in a circle, its head lopped off. As Will watched in horror, it sank into the mud and rose with a new head, even taller than before.

A group of the creatures had Yasmina surrounded. She whipped her staff in a circle, knocking off chunks of mud but barely slowing them. Will ran to help her, raising his shield to protect against the fists and horn thrusts, then using the shield as a battering ram. Mateo noticed and used his buckler in the same manner. They managed to reach the wilder, but more mudmen flowed in to surround them. Another group had Gunnar and Mala pinned against a wall. It was only a matter of time before they broke through.

Mateo used his sword like a whip, slicing up the mudmen but barely slowing them. Coba was running and flipping around the cavern, trying to stay alive. His only weapon was a small, ineffective dagger. At one point he shimmied up a ten-foot stalagmite, but one of the creatures dissolved at the bottom of the cave formation, flowed up it, and reformed at the top with Coba in its grasp. Selina saved him by causing one of the broken horns on the cavern floor to fly into the air and drive into the mudman's back. The thing flinched long enough for Coba to flip off the cave formation.

"Fire!" Mala said. "Try fire!"

Selina grabbed a torch and flew high above the cavern to light it. She blew on the flame, igniting it like a blowtorch in the face of the nearest mudman. The creature moaned and hardened, slowing as its flesh dried out. It toppled to the ground, dissolved into the mud more slowly than usual, then reformed once again.

Will's arm burned from using his shield as a battering ram, and he could see that everyone else was tiring, too. He doubted they could hold on much longer.

"Mala!" Selina shouted. The sylvamancer was wreaking havoc by violently pushing the creatures together, causing them to merge and reform. "Get everyone through the passage!"

Keeping the sash in her hand, Mala spun like a whirling dervish, using the weighted ends of the weapon to distract the creatures. "I'll try!"

"Do it now!"

Mala reached into a pouch and withdrew a handful of firebeads. She threw them at the mudmen surrounding her and Will. The flames hardened their heads and torsos, allowing her and Will to break through. Mala shoved a pile of beads into his hand, and together they freed the other members of the party from the enclosing circles.

Will didn't know what Selina had planned, but the monsters were regrouping quickly, and a number of them still blocked the exit passage marked with the dagger-and-crown symbol. "You have to fight through," Selina said grimly. "What magic I have left I will need."

Will held out his hands to Mala for more firebeads. She shook her head. "We used them all."

Gunnar roared and charged the group of mudmen, clearing away the front line with a huge sweep of his hammer. The rest of the party followed, using shields to break through. One of the mudmen speared Gunnar in the side with a horn, and another two grabbed Mateo. Yasmina pried one off by using her staff as a lever around its throat. Will bellowed and grabbed an arm of the other mudman and used his powerful grip to wrench the arm off at the shoulder. It felt like tearing apart rubber with his bare hands. Spotting a gap between the monsters, the party sprinted for the passage.

Selina remained alone in the middle of the cavern, surrounded. As a cadre of the subterranean creatures flowed towards Will and the others, rippling through the mud, Selina raised her arms, and Will heard a sound like thunder. Rocks and debris tumbled to the cavern floor as dozens of thick vines and tree roots shot down like missiles from the cavern ceiling. Just before they reached the floor, the organic projectiles angled towards the dagger-and-crown marked passage, poling straight through the mudmen. One of the vines wrapped Selina around the waist and carried her along.

Will watched in shock as an entire ficus tree, jerked by its roots from the world above, broke through the ceiling and fell to the cavern floor, joining the shower of rocks and dirt. The creatures flowed into the mud to escape the destruction. As soon as Selina joined them on the other side of the passage, she caused the mass of vines and roots to twist into an impenetrable barrier blocking the passage.

Not an ounce of mud seeped through.

Another day traversing long passages and wading through half-submerged grottos. Will flinched every time the ground squished underfoot. The party hadn't slept in two days, but they stumbled forward, wary of another night underground.

Mala had applied a thin paste and a bandage to the wound in Gunnar's side. The big man had grunted in pain when he took a few practice swings, but declared himself able to fight.

Will asked Yasmina if she could call for help as Elegon had in the Darklands. She replied that she didn't have the skills of a mature wilder yet, and didn't know the ecosystem. Call out to the wrong creature, she warned, and it might doom them all.

Just as Will thought he would collapse from exhaustion, they traversed a long passage that led to an above-ground cave marked by the Alazashin explorer. Will felt like whooping for joy as they emerged squinting into a jungle clearing dominated by a huge structure made of interlocking, flinty black stones. The construction was quite skilled, like nothing Will had ever seen.

At least a hundred feet across, and as high as a two-story building, the sinuous roof and bulky support columns gave the impression of a crouching animal. Though the structure appeared extremely old, no vegetation encroached. Mala studied the facade and turned to Coba. "Have you ever seen anything like this?"

The guide shook his head, peering uneasily into the jungle.

The vegetation surrounding the clearing was oddly sparse, as if thinned by hungry elephants. Coba pointed out multiple paw prints, all of them more than a day old. Jaguar, he said. The party branched out, looking for a clear path or another dagger-and-crown marking. An hour later, as the sun sank behind the trees, they returned to the clearing without a clue as to the way forward.

"This must be the place," Mala said.

"If the map is real," Gunnar pointed out, turning away when Mala stared him down.

Will turned to face the strange edifice. "There's one place left to check."

Though no one had stated it, everyone seemed wary of stepping inside. The ancient structure had an anthropomorphic presence, as if it were a sentient thing, watching over the jungle.

"Something wrong with jungle," Coba said. "No small animals."

Mala scoffed, but Yasmina said, "I sensed it, too. The animals avoid this place."

"Unlike them, we haven't a choice," Mala said, and then strode towards the building. Everyone followed, though Coba kept glancing nervously into the jungle.

"It looks like obsidian," Will said as they approached, "but you can't build *this* out of that."

"You can if you're an artisamancer," Mala said.

Archways spaced a dozen yards apart provided access to the interior. A cavernous main entrance dominated the western-facing side, bookended by two slender black towers.

Mala entered first. Will followed, gaping when he saw the prehistoric drawings covering the walls in faded pigments. Most of the artwork depicted half-human, half-jaguar creatures engaged in a variety of tasks: carrying water from a cenote, building dwellings in the trees, hunting game in the jungle.

A row of iron hoops inset into the ceiling confused him. He had no idea of their purpose, except to thread a curtain or tapestry through. In the northwest corner, rudimentary steps had been cut into the rock wall, leading to one of the towers. As Will walked over, he noticed a mural showcasing a group of jaguar-people cringing in awe before a giant cat. Outlined in black pigment with charcoal streaks, the monstrous feline stood higher at the haunches than the shoulders of the tallest human bowing before it.

Will glanced around and noticed similar scenes interspersed among the drawings. "Guys," he said slowly, thinking about the sinuous shape of the building, "I think this is some kind of temple."

"To what?" Mateo called out.

Will pointed at the gigantic cat. "To that."

"Typical superstition," Mala scoffed.

Coba couldn't seem to take his eyes off the ancient rock drawing. "There are rumors of old races deep in jungle," he said. "Worshipping old gods. Before my people, before sorcerer kings."

"Everyone keep searching," Mala said. "We need to find the next symbol."

Will drew closer to the tower steps and, with a whoop of excitement, pointed out a small dagger-and-crown etched crudely into the black rock. With Mala on his heels, he climbed the steps and emerged on a crenellated platform at the top of the tower, just above the tree line. They scanned the jungle and saw nothing unusual.

Still no clue as to where to head next.

They showed the others, then descended as the last rays of sunlight slithered out of sight. "We have to find shelter in jungle," Coba said.

"No," Mala said, catching his shoulder as he turned to leave. "We camp in here tonight. It's the safest place. We'll set a watch on the tower."

Coba did not look happy. The party ate a cold dinner, and Mateo volunteered for first watch. After Will thanked Gunnar for saving his life in the caves, the big warrior laid out his sleeping roll and wrapped his arms around Mala. In disgust, Will took his own roll and followed Mateo up the steps, deciding to sleep under the stars. He gazed at the twinkling heavens, the jungle a vast and tenebrous thing below.

"Will," his cousin said, in a disbelieving voice. "Look down."

At first Will didn't understand. He was looking at the jungle and couldn't make out a thing. Then Mateo pointed at their feet, near the edge of the tower, where a dagger-and-crown symbol glowed a soft silver-gray, as if painted with congealed moonlight. Just beside it shone the luminescent outline of a basic compass, with an arrow pointing due west, right off the edge of the tower.

When they shouted for the others, Mala led the charge up the stairs, her eyes widening when she saw the symbol. "Moon Paint," she said, excited. "A favorite marker of the Alazashin."

"What's it made of?" Will asked. "It's been here, what? Fifty years? How does it last so long?"

"Mage-enhanced phosphorescents," Mala said in a distracted voice, peering off the ledge and into the darkened jungle. "I feared we had lost the way."

They decided to celebrate the discovery—and calm everyone's nerves— with a shot of grog. After the excitement waned and everyone except Will and Mateo returned below, Will fell into a deep, troubled sleep. He dreamt of his childhood, only instead of languorous days by the levee in New Orleans, he and Caleb had been raised as orphans in the slums of New Victoria. They were caught for not taking the Oaths and banished to the Fens. Disease ridden, emaciated, and on the verge of death, Will lost all hope until Val flew onto his and Caleb's rotting plank one day, carrying their father's staff and wearing a cloak with the insignia of the Congregation.

I've come to free you, Val said.

As Caleb held out his hand in supplication, Will pushed to his knees to greet his oldest brother. His mouth was too dry with thirst to speak.

Val smiled down at them. *All you have to do is take the Oaths.*

Will stared at his pockmarked hands, then lifted his eyes. *Take us out of here, Val. Please.*

That's my greatest wish, brother. As soon as you swear allegiance to Lord Alistair.

Two men on the plank ran at Val, screaming *filthy wizard*. Val held out a hand, not even looking at them. Black lightning lanced from his fingertips and swarmed their bodies, reducing them to dust.

What have you done? Will whispered as he stumbled away from his brother. Those men had been friends. *Who are you?*

With Spirit Fire still dancing at his fingertips, Val raised his hands towards his brothers as if to burn them. He reached forward and Will woke in a cold sweat, opening his eyes to find Mateo sitting cross-legged beside him, gazing into the darkness.

Sweating from the nightmare, Will rolled onto his side just in time to see a man with the furry face of a jaguar climb over the eastern edge of the tower and leap straight at Mateo. Unsure if he was still dreaming, he tried to cry out, but a fur-covered hand slipped over Will's mouth from behind.

He bucked to free himself as more hands grasped his arms and legs, holding him down. Someone shoved a root that smelled like cinnamon and diesel under his nose. Within moments, he felt woozy and his eyelids fluttered. The last thing he saw was Mateo slumping to the ground, surrounded by jaguar men with long slinky tails, tufted ears, and muscular bodies covered in yellow and black fur.

16

Lord Alistair brought Professor Azara, Dean Groft, and a small team of majitsu with him to Bohemian Isle. The denizens of the densely packed section of the French Quarter gaped as the bejeweled wizard carriage drifted across the dirty canal, soared above the rickety buildings, and alighted in the central square.

The Chief Thaumaturge wrinkled his nose at the smell of stagnant water commingling with garbage and spilled ale. He had long wanted to expel the hordes of artists, drifters, street urchins, and grifters who populated the isle. Half of them were gypsies, he was sure of it. Not to mention the freaks of nature trolling the streets, lepers and half-breeds and worse. A public fondness for the eccentricities and cheap pleasures of Bohemian Isle had stayed his hand, but one day he would stuff them all in the Fens.

People parted like water in a boat's wake as the elder mages exited the carriage and floated down a decrepit side lane with gargoyles leering off of every peaked roof. Lord Alistair could feel the threads of old magic lurking far beneath the worn cobblestones, a nameless tickling in his skull.

Alrick's phrenomancy sign was located halfway down the street. Lord Alistair climbed the short flight of steps to knock on the wooden doorway of the boarded-up structure, annoyed at the look of boredom on the phrenomancer's face when he answered.

"Greetings, Alrick."

Holding a battered wormwood gourd, the phrenomancer looked as disheveled as always: coarse stubble obscuring his handsome features, tangled hair spilling onto a cotton shirt, pantaloons that looked as if they had never been washed. "Alistair."

Not *Lord* Alistair. The Chief Thaumaturge's face tightened. "You refused my request to gaze."

"I refused your request to leave Bohemian Isle." Alrick waved a hand, his words thick with intoxication. "I prefer not to leave my palace."

"Even at the behest of the Chief Thaumaturge, in a matter concerning the defense of the Realm?"

Alrick gave a lazy smile.

Rage fluttered in Lord Alistair's breast. He could have forced Alrick to come to the Sanctum, but he couldn't force him to gaze, and he didn't want to antagonize the phrenomancer before the reading. A former spirit mage, Alrick had spent two years as an itinerant wanderer after graduating from the Abbey. He became hopelessly addicted to wormwood water in the Bavarian Kingdom, left the Congregation in disgrace, and became a gazer because he was unfit to do anything else.

At least that was the story. True or not, Alrick was the best gazer in New Albion, and notoriously difficult to corral. He had once refused to gaze for the queen during a state visit.

"I need to know if you can trace an inanimate object," Lord Alistair asked.

"Of course not. You know this."

"What if it were made of hardened spirit?"

Alrick's mandarin eyes sparked with interest. "Then I wouldn't know. I've never tried such a thing."

"Would you care to?" Lord Alistair said, more a command than a request.

After taking a sip from a copper straw protruding from the gourd, Alrick stepped aside and ushered them through.

All of the majitsu except Lord Alistair's two personal attendants remained outside. Professor Azara and Dean Groft followed the Chief Thaumaturge and his bodyguards down a stone hallway lit by guttered candles and into a windowless room painted black. Two chairs on either side of a stained wooden table supported a device called an oculave: a brass stand branching into circular apertures spaced a foot apart. As Lord Alistair settled into the leather chin pad and tightened the knobs on the device, he worried about placing himself at the mercy of a soul gaze.

Which was why the Chief Thaumaturge had chosen his companions carefully. Alrick unnerved Lord Alistair, and he wanted Dean Groft and Professor Azara present in case the phrenomancer harbored any treacherous ideas. Gazing was a poorly understood activity, fraught with peril, and he didn't want to be at Alrick's mercy.

Alistair could have just brought Professor Azara, but he wanted Dean Groft to bear witness to the day's event. Groft would squirm, and that was fine. The dean was soft. Perhaps he would commit treason by intervening.

Alrick lit a candle on the table and shut the door. After inserting two colored drops into Alistair's eyes and two in his own, he secured his side of the oculave and asked Professor Azara to snuff the candle.

Darkness reigned.

As the drops took effect, Alistair experienced the weird sensation of falling towards Alrick's leonine eyes and into a wall of blackness crisscrossed by silver filaments, weightless in his chair, a growing prickle in his brain. Alrick's twin golden orbs rushed past him, leaving him suspended in a three-dimensional world of silver lines and endless dark.

Lord Alistair guided Alrick with his mind through the maze of filaments, concentrating on the last time he had seen the sword. Deep into the past, images rushing by with the clarity of consciousness and the power of a dream. Lord Alistair choked up as he witnessed the tragic death of his wife and the birth of his daughter, his ascension as Chief Thaumaturge, dueling a Dragon Mage in the Place Between Worlds and almost being caught by the Astral Wind, watching in agony as his younger brother took flight with their father before the late-blooming Alistair could leave his feet, the bond his father and brother had shared that would never be his, the lost inheritance that had driven Alistair into a murderous rage.

More images, coming so fast he had to slow them.

Remember the sword.

Focus.

Branches and branches and branches, swooshing down silver pathways, Lord Alistair holding Zariduke as he strode into the throne room in Londyn to confront the queen, striking down the Mayan Overlord in battle, flying an airship above the Ninth Protectorate and then across the Eastern seas, dueling a faceless warrior atop the Sanctum as a battle raged below, tearing apart the Wizard District—

No, Alistair whispered to himself. *The pathways are both past and future, fact and possibility. Concentrate.*

An unpracticed gazer, Lord Alistair was unable to shield all of the future probabilities. Alrick had already seen too much.

An outcome which Lord Alistair had fully anticipated.

Images whipped by in a blur. Finally he saw it, the strange world called Earth that was almost devoid of magic, full of bizarre and powerful machines.

The adopted home of Dane Blackwood.

In the past, the moment Dane had found the sword, Lord Alistair's Spirit Ward had been triggered, and he had stepped through a dimension door to confront the gypsy mage. Though the Conclave had sent Dane on a mission to find the sword, Lord Alistair had uncovered Dane's secret allegiance to the Revolution, and decided to accomplish two of his greatest objectives in one fell swoop.

Find Zariduke, and rid himself of the treacherous gypsy spirit mage once and for all, somewhere far from prying eyes.

They fought. Though Dane Blackwood was even stronger than Lord Alistair had realized, the Chief Thaumaturge prevailed in an epic battle. Just before Dane died, hovering high atop the ground, he used the last of his magic to force Alistair through a portal back to Urfe and scramble the dimensional pathways. It had taken long decades for the Chief Thaumaturge to find Earth again, and send Zedock after the sword.

Thankfully, Lord Alistair managed to shield the battle with Dane Blackwood from Alrick. The phrenomancer would know he was doomed if he witnessed the true fate of the legendary gypsy mage.

After Dane disappeared from view, the sword hovered in darkness, and it took all of Lord Alistair's immense mental power to slow the images and drift near the sword. He shivered with excitement. This was why he had come to gaze with Alrick.

What had happened to Zariduke?

The other phrenomancers had failed to make it past this point, unable to track the sword on its own. After a long pause, a new set of silver pathways appeared, branching out from the sword. Exultant, Alistair felt his hands clutching the table. Alrick had done it!

As Lord Alistair whooshed forward down a new silver line, he realized it must take a spirit mage to gaze upon a thing of spirit. The pathways flew past, he forced his thoughts elsewhere, and then an older man with a trimmed beard and clothes from Earth was holding Zariduke, gazing upon it in wonder. The silver lines branched and the man took the sword to a city in a swamp that looked vaguely like New Victoria, and then the sword lay in darkness for many years until the same man took it out and carried it inside a motorized carriage to an alleyway and gave the sword to—

A scraping sound interrupted the gazing session. The acrid smell of sulfur. As the light from a match expanded into a sickly yellow illumination, jerking Lord Alistair back to the present, Alrick extracted himself from the oculave and said, in a husky voice, "The session is over."

"Take me back," Lord Alistair shrieked. "We were there!"

"No, milord. I will not."

Alistair stamped his feet and shouted. "Who are you protecting?"

Alrick refused to answer. Professor Azara and Dean Groft looked between the two in confusion.

Lord Alistair pointed a finger at Alrick, so enraged that spittle flew from his mouth. "You *will* answer me!"

A slow, knowing grin crept onto the phrenomancer's face.

"Traitor! I charge you with treason under the law and sentence you to the Wizard Vault, effectively immediately!"

"No trial?" Alrick mocked.

"You can rot in gaol until you change your mind!"

Lord Alistair waved a hand, opening a portal to a cell lined with honey-combed azantite walls. As his two majitsu rushed at Alrick, Lord Alistair stood ready to follow the phrenomancer if he fled through spirit. Just before the warrior-mages reached him, the phrenomancer whipped a needle from his pocket and jabbed himself in the arm. His mocking grin faded, and he slumped in the arms of the majitsu.

Lord Alistair took him by the collar and peeled back an eyelid. Alrick's eyes were dull and lifeless. "Fool," Alistair roared, shoving the phrenomancer away.

"What is it?" Professor Azara asked.

Dean Groft walked over and lifted Alrick's slumped head by the chin. "He appears to have injected himself with a highly powerful gazer sedative, allowing instant retreat into his mind." The dean stepped away from the phrenomancer, his eyes sad at first, and then accusing as they met Lord Alistair's. "And I suspect he won't be coming back."

17

Drained from breaking through the wall of fog, Val found himself standing in a mossy field full of age-spotted boulders. A blue-tinged mist cloaked the landscape, making it hard to see more than a few hundred feet in any direction. Short, gnarled, windswept trees dotted the moorland like babushkas in silent contemplation. Five feet behind him, a waterfall tumbled off a steep embankment, just as it had before.

"Fascinating," Dida said, as he absorbed his surroundings.

The air was moist and peaty. Val realized he was freezing. After toweling off with a spare cloth, he donned his woolen trousers and high-necked shirt, then wrapped his gray cloak tight. The air was a few degrees colder now.

"Here," Adaira said, taking his hands in hers. A warm red glow spread outward from her palms, slowly infusing him.

"Thanks," he said, after his body heat started to regulate. She smiled back.

Everyone was staring around in confusion. Val walked over and stuck his hand in the waterfall, concentrating. He felt no residual trace of the spirit barrier. "Whatever portal we just went through," he said grimly, "is gone."

Rucker growled. "You mean we're trapped."

"I mean we're not going back the same way."

Synne remained quiet, eyes narrow as she probed the landscape. Staying close to Val as always.

"Are we on the other side of the mist, in our world?" Dida asked, wrinkling his long forehead. "Or in another one?"

No one had an answer.

"We should find a town and figure out where in the Queen's Blood we are," Rucker said finally.

"I second that," Val said.

Adaira consulted a compass. "If the geography is the same, we should aim east, towards the plains."

Rucker led the way. Val's feet squished into the spongy ground, and after Adaira sank to her thighs and scrambled out of the muck, they realized the brownish-green groundcover was deceiving. The whole area was one giant peat bog.

Rucker broke off a desiccated limb and snapped it into pieces. "Use these to probe."

They plodded through the soggy moorland for hours without a sign of civilization. The eerie blue mist hung omnipresent around them, never thinning or thickening, as if part of the air itself. They had not seen the sun since they arrived. Oddly, night had not fallen, despite the fact they had traveled through the portal in the late afternoon.

The shadows of monstrous birds could be seen soaring high above, some with wingspans as long as a bus. Whether they were demons or something else, perhaps the same inchoate forms Val had glimpsed before, no one knew.

Rucker stopped beside a series of tracks, scratching his chin as he studied a cloven hoof print with three curved, spur-like markings sticking out on each side.

"Do you recognize them?" Val asked.

With a grunt, Rucker shook his head and pushed to his feet.

Dida said, "With how many species of monster are you familiar?"

"In Albion?" Rucker said. "All of them."

The peat bog grew more and more treacherous, until it was hard to take a step without sinking. The wizards could fly if needed, and Synne could skim atop the ground in that feathery jump-stride the majitsu used, but no one wanted to expend magical energy in such an unfamiliar setting.

Rucker planted his sword on a patch of moss. "We need a better plan."

"It's possible no one lives here," Dida said philosophically, "or that it's been decimated by demons."

"Wherever *here* is."

"If the mist would clear," Adaira added, "one of us could fly higher, to a better vantage point."

"I wonder if we could fly above it?" Dida asked.

Val shook his head. "Too dangerous with those things in the sky."

The bibliomancer wagged a finger. "I could try a Tellurian Disruption."

"A what?" Rucker said. "I've never heard of that spell."

"An enchantment that sends magical energy in a shockwave along the nearest tellurian lines. If something impedes the flow, such as a town or a sizeable manmade structure, I will know."

"What's the range?" Val asked.

Dida stroked his narrow chin. "Perhaps twenty-five miles."

Rucker clapped him on the back. "What are ye waiting for?"

"There is . . . complication."

"Spit it out, mage."

"When I cast the spell," Dida said slowly, "a rather large magical signal will result. Any wizards or creatures attuned to tellurian disturbances within the spell's radius will know exactly where we are."

"What kind of wizards are attuned to a tellurian disturbance?" Val asked. "I don't even know what that means."

"Not many, outside of a bibliomancer or perhaps a well-learned sylvamancer," Dida admitted. "But one class of creature in particular might notice," he said, with a pointed look at Rucker. "One more attuned to the primeval elements."

The adventurer grimaced. "Demons."

"Yes."

Rucker jerked his sword out of the muck. "Then we cast the spell and get our arses out of here. If there are demons around, they'll find us anyway, wandering around like lost pups."

Everyone agreed they should take the chance. Dida cast a spell that reminded Val of what he had once thought real magic would look like: hand waving, chanting, and marking symbols in the earth. Later, he planned to ask his friend if the gestures had any true effect.

After several minutes of intense concentration, Dida announced he felt a disruptive vibration almost due west of where they were headed. The party hurried off in the new direction, trying to distance themselves from the source of the signal.

Hours later, they still had seen no sign of civilization. They voted to take a quick break and keep walking. The mist and sky were unchanging, despite the fact that it should have been dark.

Val sat on a large rock and munched on a beef stick, lost in his thoughts.

What was wrong with the sky? What had happened to the previous wizards who had breached the barrier? How would he and the others get home? What *was* this place?

As he reached for his canteen, he saw Adaira hugging her knees, also deep in thought. Dida was examining a patch of moss, and Rucker was sharpening his blade.

Where was Synne?

Val whirled, used to seeing his protector close by. Perhaps nature had called? Before he could yell out for her, he noticed a ripple in a watery patch of peat bog a few yards away. He walked over to inspect the disturbance and saw Synne submerged in the bog, fighting to free herself from two creatures with mottled green skin.

Val bellowed for help as more of the bog demons crawled out of the watery quagmires pockmarking the landscape. Once they emerged, their long muscular arms dragged the ground, and he noticed in horror that their hands, which resembled five suckered, rigid octopus tentacles ending in dagger-sharp tips, opened and closed as they advanced. A mass of short tentacles writhed around an oval maw that puckered like a fish's mouth.

Val thrust his staff in the water and cut deep into one of the creatures holding Synne. Green ichor gushed forth, obscuring his view, but moments later she reached a hand out of the water. Val extended his staff, and she clutched it. As the second demon burst out of the water, he pulled Synne out of the bog while using Wind Push to thrust the demon back.

Synne pushed him aside and attacked another demon right behind him, hitting it so hard with a double punch that her fists sank into its chest. She yanked her hands out, gutting the creature, then kicked it back into the muck.

Val spun. Adaira had taken to the air to avoid the initial attack, Rucker was fending off three of the creatures, and two more were dragging Dida towards a bog. From the corner of his eye, Val noticed another pair crawling out of the water.

Adaira let herself plummet as she waved her hands in the air like knife strokes, cutting deep into the legs of one of the creatures holding Dida. By the time she arrested her fall, landing hard on the ground at the last moment, the demon she was attacking had collapsed, its legs sliced open in a dozen places. Val swung his azantite staff at the other creature holding Dida, cutting off the monster's legs at the knees. One of its long arms whipped forward as it fell, piercing Val's side with two dagger-like fingers.

Adaira looked stricken as Val staggered to a knee, but he waved at her to help the others. Another demon lurched out of the nearest bog and loped forward, swinging its deadly arms. She flew backwards to escape its grasp.

A demon wrapped Rucker from behind. He jerked his head back and stabbed the creature in the face with his horned helm. When it bucked in pain, Rucker turned and sliced open its torso with his blade. Two more came at him. He kicked one in the chest and caught the other with an elbow to the maw, his spiked vambrace ripping its jaw open. The demon he had kicked came at him again. Rucker roared and advanced, whipping his blade back and forth to block the long-armed strikes, then stepping inside and using his helm as a battering ram, spearing the demon through the chest.

Val sank to the ground, pressing his fingers into his side to try to staunch the blood flow. He tried to summon his remaining magic but the pain interrupted his concentration. Dida picked up Val's staff to fend off an approaching demon, but Synne got there first, leaping past them both in a blur, her hands and feet a concerto of violence. She spun behind the creature and broke its spine with a forearm strike so hard it made Val shiver. *God, majitsu are scary.*

Three creatures remained. Instead of attacking, they communicated with a series of slurping sounds and retreated to the nearest bog, sinking into the water while casting malevolent stares at the party. The intelligence in their eyes caused gooseflesh to prickle along Val's arms.

"Gather up!" Rucker commanded. "They might be going for their friends."

"Agreed," Synne said, still dripping water, flush with adrenaline from the battle. She wouldn't meet Val's eyes, as if ashamed the first two monsters had gotten the drop on her.

"We'll go when I say we go," Adaira said, easing Val onto his back. She tore away a portion of his shirt, cleansed the wound with water from the canteen, then handed Val her rucksack.

"What's this for?"

"The pain. We don't have time for a long procedure, so I'm going to cauterize the wound and burn away the poison."

He gasped and looked down. Greenish pus was oozing from the stab wound. The flesh beneath felt as if insects were crawling around inside, stinging in a thousand places.

Adaira put her hands on the wound until her palms glowed red. She directed heat into the wound with precise aim, and Val bit down on the leather as the pain seared through him and the smell of burning flesh flooded his nostrils.

When it was finished, he shuddered and started to pull away. "Not yet," she said. He gasped as Adaira slowly closed the wound, the pain duller but more prolonged than the previous bout.

"I'll work on the scarring later," she said. "Can you walk?"

Val limped to his feet. His side still ached but the pain was far better. Tolerable. "Thank you."

"I'm glad the wound was not more grave," she said softly.

"May we go now, Your Highness?" Rucker said.

"With all due haste."

Doing their best to avoid fens and standing water, the party hurried through the soggy stretch of moorland, eventually reaching firmer ground that had a smattering of hardy grass. As they crested a long ridge that seemed to last for miles, Synne pointed out a circular stone wall in the distance. Inside, a handful of towers and peaked roofs poked above the fortification.

Rucker clapped Dida on the back as they stopped to absorb the view. "Well done."

Val felt a surge of relief, but also trepidation. What if the town was abandoned, or overrun by demons? What if nothing but horror lay on the other side of those walls?

With a snarl, Rucker started clomping down the opposite side of the ridgeline. Val and the others hurried to catch up.

18

Will woke hanging upright in midair, his arms stretched above his head, wrists and feet bound with some type of vine. The vines wrapping his wrists had been tied off to a rope that looped through the hollow stone rings set into the ceiling.

At least he knew the purpose of the rings. Dying with a construction puzzle plaguing his final thoughts would be a terrible way to go.

Mateo and Yasmina and Coba were hanging to his left, Gunnar and Mala on his right. Everyone blinked and struggled as they came to. One of the jaguar people, a slender female with mahogany spots, held herself upside down on the rope above Gunnar, as if she had just finished stringing him up. She somersaulted off, landed silently on the floor twenty feet below, and hurried to the entrance, where a large group of her kin filled the main opening. Will swiveled and saw the strange hybrids pressing into all of the doorways.

Selina, where was Selina?

He swiveled on the rope to peer around the temple. There was no sign of the sylvamancer, and he paled when he realized what must have happened.

Of course there's no sign of her. You can't tie down a wizard. They surprised her and killed her.

Mala and Coba were kicking their feet, trying to swing back and forth. Gunnar struggled against his bonds, muscles bulging as he tried in vain to rip the vines free. Will yanked on his bonds as well. They felt as strong as steel cables.

"What do you want?" he called out. "We're not here to harm you!"

The jaguar people seemed startled, almost frightened, at the sound of Will's voice. Almost as if they didn't realize he possessed the power of speech. One of the females, as tall as Gunnar and wearing a garland of thorny vines, dropped to her knees and supplicated herself on the floor. The rest of the tribe followed, except for another female. At first he thought they were worshipping him, but then the lone standing jaguar woman held up an enormous gourd, raised it to her lips as she turned towards the jungle, and blew into it. A deep, booming note issued forth. She varied the pitch as she drew the note out, repeating the call three times.

When she finished, the jaguar people bounded out of the temple and into the darkened jungle as if the hounds of hell were behind them.

"That can't be good," Will muttered.

Mala bent her knees to her chest and started shimmying up the vines upside down, despite her bound hands and feet. When she reached the iron ring, she started tugging on the knot. When that didn't work, she put her mouth against the vines, trying to bite through.

A weird coughing sound echoed in the distance, followed by a prolonged growl and a throaty roar that echoed through the trees.

Coba stopped struggling, his face drawn with fear. "Jaguar," he said.

Will lifted himself up so he could gnaw on the knot around his hands. He made some progress before his muscles gave out and he had to drop back down. Still, with enough time he knew he could break free.

So why tie them up with vines?

Moments later, another roar came from the jungle, this one much closer. As if whatever had made it had traveled a few miles in less than a minute. The sound was so thunderous it reverberated through the temple.

He answered his own question.

Because we don't have time to escape.

One of the jaguar people dashed back into the temple, surprising Will. He thought they would all be far away by now. His shock grew as the female creature in front of him began to shift, her body morphing in seconds to the naked form of a human woman—one Will recognized.

Selina.

Mala gasped. "A lycamancer," she said, staring down at her in shock.

Selina whipped out a knife, flew into the air, and cut everyone down. Another roar vibrated the air, so close it sounded right on top of them. Mala darted to one of the western entrance portals and peered outside. "It's still clear," she said, in a loud whisper.

"It will smell us," Coba said, in a trembling voice. "Follow us everywhere."

"You're right," Mala said, as she pulled out a vial from one of her pouches. She uncorked it and doused everyone with an oily substance that smelled like cheap soap.

Selina retrieved her clothes as the party hurried to scoop up their belongings scattered around the temple. They recovered everything except Mateo's longbow and Will's shield, last seen atop the tower. They dared not take the time to search.

Will had never felt so vulnerable as he sprinted out of the temple and dashed across the jungle clearing in the moonlight. As they reached the edge of the trees, a huge shape bounded out of the jungle, traveling fifty feet with one leap.

"Stop!" Yasmina ordered, in a harsh whisper. "He'll sense your movement!"

Will stilled with his head turned, watching in dread fascination as a jaguar as big as a bus slunk towards the temple. The monstrous feline was black with gray spots, and resembled the sinuous form of the temple itself.

The cat entered the cavernous main entrance and unleashed a mighty roar, turning Will's nerves to jelly.

"Now," Yasmina said softly. "Run now!"

"It will hear us!" Coba replied, almost too panicked to speak in a coherent voice.

Mala yanked him forward. "This is our only chance. Take us due west. *Now.*"

Coba eyed the moon and then darted through the jungle, moving without a sound. As everyone hurried to keep up, Yasmina made a series of bird and animal calls. The jungle came alive in response, helping to mask their progress.

Will turned and saw the cat pausing in the clearing, trying to discern the source of the disturbance. Cats had night vision, he knew, and they hadn't run that far. With his heart pounding and his palms slicked with sweat, he looked over his shoulder again and noticed a strange sight: the foliage closing in behind them, obscuring his view of the clearing. Then he noticed Selina looking back as they fled, locked in concentration as branches bent double and vines snaked down to cover their passage, the forest responding to the sylvamancer's call.

More ear-shattering roars and rumbling growls pierced the night, but as the party fled through the jungle, not daring to slow as the vines and branches whipped into their faces, the cries of the mighty jaguar grew farther away.

How can such a thing exist? he wondered. *Is it the creation of a menagerist? A holdover from the dinosaurs? Are there more of them around here?*

As they ran, a thunderous cacophony of animal and insect life assaulted the party's ears, a stark difference from trekking during the daytime. Fleeing through the uncharted Mayan jungle in the dead of night was one of the most terrifying experiences of Will's life. Almost as frightening as facing a jungle cat that could take a swipe at King Kong.

They pressed grimly forward, through an endless series of shrieks, chitters, snarls, howls, and bellows. Nothing as intimidating as the roar of the giant jaguar, but the pitch of some of the nocturnal sounds was almost more disturbing, aggressive and deranged, strangely intelligent.

Yet they dared not stop. They could still be within the jaguar's range. Coba's skills and Mala's compass kept them heading west, despite the lack of a path.

"Do you recognize these sounds?" Will asked Yasmina, keeping his voice to a whisper.

"Some. Not all. This is a very different jungle from Brazil."

"But you're learning, aren't you?" he asked, noticing her eyes in constant movement, fingers brushing trees and bushes, slender nose turned to the air.

She nodded.

"What's it like, being a wilder?"

A soft smile appeared on her lips. "It's beautiful, Will. I feel so attuned to nature. It's as if this part of me I never knew existed has been unlocked."

"Do you think we all have it?" he asked. "It sounds pretty good."

She gave a quiet laugh. "Maybe to some degree. I do feel like it's . . . natural to me. And there are things to learn, of course. Many things. Elegon taught me so much in the short time we had, but I think I could spend a lifetime in study and barely scratch the surface."

A shrill, ragged cry pierced the night, almost human in its distress. Yasmina cocked her head. Moments later, the cry repeated, insistent. It wasn't far off, and sounded different from the other night calls. Vulnerable. Pleading.

"I know that call," she said, her face crumbling. "It's a harpy eagle, and she's in pain."

The cries continued. A hundred yards later they found the source: a huge but emaciated eagle, dark gray with a white head and breast, trapped inside a bamboo cage. The cage had been strung from the branch of a tree and tied off with vines, reminding Will of their own capture. He glanced uneasily into the jungle.

"There's no time," Mala said, but Yasmina, with a look of pure revulsion, ignored her and used Will's sword to slice open the cage. The sickly, two-foot tall bird cawed and fell over as it tried to hop out. Its wings and talons had been clipped.

Yasmina picked the bird up and tucked it into her arms. "It's my duty. She won't slow me down."

Mala flung a bangled wrist in annoyance. "I hope not."

Will helped fashion a sling out of Yasmina's cloak, and tucked the bird inside. The party continued slogging through the jungle, exhausted beyond reason, desperate for the dawn.

A hundred yards later, Coba stopped and put a finger to his lips, calling for silence as he pointed into the canopy. Looking up, Will could just make out an elaborate, open-walled tree house made of living vines and giant leaves. He swiveled and saw more of the arboreal dwellings. Dozens of them.

"Jaguar people," Mateo whispered. "We saw these homes on the temple walls."

Yasmina's eyes flashed as she stroked the head of the harpy eagle, which had nestled against her chest. "The bird was a sacrifice. An offering from their village."

"It appears empty," Mala said. "They must hunt at night."

Gunnar nudged his head to the left. "We can backtrack and circle around."

"Or save time by going straight through," Mateo said.

Will sided with his cousin, Yasmina with Gunnar. "I vote for a direct approach," Selina said in a hard voice. She had kept to herself during the night trek. "I won't be taken by surprise this time."

"Maybe, maybe not," Mala countered. She stood with her hands on her hips, debating her choices. "But speed is of the essence. Let's continue straight through. Quickly, now."

The party stepped as lightly as they could beneath the tree houses, trying not to make a sound in case the canopy concealed any of the residents. On the other side of the village, just as Will began to relax, a group of jaguar people emerged out of the jungle dragging nets full of freshly killed game.

The hunting party looked stunned when they saw they were still alive. Will wondered if he could somehow communicate with them. Over Mala's whispered objection, he stepped forward with a palm out, beseeching them to talk instead of fight.

At first, he thought he might be getting through, but then the first low growls issued forth. The warriors raised short rods of bamboo, and a pair of females crept forward with a net held between them. A dozen or so others slunk into the jungle, disappearing from sight.

"Stay tight," Mala said, eying the jungle as she whipped her sash off and raised her sword. "Will and Mateo, watch the flanks. Yasmina and Coba, guard our rear. If we can strike a decisive blow, maybe they will lose their appetite for battle."

"I was hoping they'd let us through," Will muttered. "Isn't our survival a sign from their god?"

Mateo slapped his sword back and forth on the ground, drawing attention. "Maybe they think they've failed in their duty."

Will heard a sound in the background, a steady hum that seemed to be increasing in volume. He didn't have time to process what it might be, because Mala had initiated the battle by letting her sash fly at the front line. The weighted projectile was a darkened blur of movement, but the lead jaguar was even faster. He whipped his bamboo rod forward and used it to catch the sash in midair.

Not a good sign.

The weird buzzing in the background increased as a wave of jaguar people attacked, leaping and clawing at Gunnar and Mala. Though more agile than the adventuress and stronger even than Gunnar, the duo's skill and superior weaponry kept the exchange even. More jaguar people leaped out of the jungle, striking at the party's flanks, throwing nets at Will and Mateo. When Will sidestepped the throw, two of the jaguar people pounced on him. It took everything he had to force them back. The length of his sword negated their physical advantages, but there were simply too many of them.

Out of the corner of his eye, Will saw Coba trapped in a net, and watched Mateo rush to help Yasmina, who was fending off a pair of attackers with her staff. The wounded harpy eagle was perched on her shoulder, shrieking her rage. Mateo's whip-like sword seemed to confuse the jaguar fighters, and he beat them back.

The background noise grew so loud it paused the battle. As friend and foe alike stopped to discern the source of the ear-splitting ruckus, Will saw Selina standing on a tree branch high above the party, her lean form silhouetted in the moonlight. In the chaos of battle, he realized he had forgotten about their most powerful ally.

The sylvamancer spread her arms wide, shouting but barely able to be heard above the din. "You left us to be consumed," she screamed, "and so consumed you shall be!"

As she swept her hands forward like a conductor, the jungle exploded around them. Millions of insects swarmed out of the foliage, from all directions, covering the ground like a moving carpet. As Will stared slack-jawed at the swarm, something long and sinewy grabbed him by the waist and jerked him into the trees. He panicked before realizing it was a vine and not a serpent. About the time he realized vines shouldn't grab him around the waist and lift him into the air, he was deposited on a branch near Selina and Mala, who had recovered her sash. More vines deposited the other members of the party in the same place.

When Will looked down, he saw the jaguar people leaping madly into the trees to evade the swarm. One of them was too slow and the horde devoured him like a vacuum cleaner sweeping up a pile of dust. Not to be deterred, the insects rushed up all of the trees except the one holding Selina and the party, forcing the jaguar people to flee through the canopy.

Clacking and chittering, the swarm of bugs followed their prey into the jungle, disappearing as quickly as they had arrived.

Remind me, Will thought as the vines lowered everyone to the ground, *not to piss off a sylvamancer in the woods.*

Mala gave Selina a nod of thanks, checked her compass, and started walking. No one wanted to find out whether more jaguar people would arrive, or how little magic Selina had left in reserve.

Hours later, the jungle broke, and the party found themselves at the edge of a lake whose far shore remained unseen in the dark of night.

"Here," Mala said, as everyone leaned against the nearest tree or rock, pushed to the point of collapse. "We camp here."

The terrain was dense but quite dry. They retreated a short way into the jungle and, drawing on vines and fallen trees, Selina used her magic to weave together a crude shelter and shield them from view. Everyone crowded inside, shoved down cold rations, and collapsed. Praying nothing disturbed their little hideout, Will fell asleep to the gurgle of a stream in the distance.

*   *   *

Both the dawn light and the loudest, most obnoxious cawing Will had ever heard disturbed his sleep. His head still fuzzy, he rolled over and saw Mala sitting cross-legged by the leafy entrance to their shelter, studying the map. Will joined her as the others roused.

He could see the lake a few dozen yards away through the trees, and he gawked at what the daylight revealed. The surface of the lake had a dreamy, vivid pink hue, a sunset trapped in water. It was a breathtaking contrast to the deep green hues of the surrounding jungle.

Mala pointed out a rune on the map. "Roughly translated, it means rose water."

Excited, he looked from the map to the lake. "This has to be it."

Mala nodded, then put a finger to her lips and pointed at the water's edge, where a cluster of thick-bodied birds with brown feathers and long, curved talons was causing the awful ruckus. As Will wondered why there was a need for silence, two of the birds started fighting and one turned its head in their direction, causing him to gape for the second time that morning.

The bird had the face of a human female.

It was not a pretty sight. Framed by coarse feathers, the face looked stretched and rubbery, unnatural, as if the face of an old crone had been ripped off and fused onto the bird.

"The Arpui are known for their vicious natures," Mala said quietly. "And they are quite territorial."

Arpui, Will thought. *Harpy*. In Greek mythology, the harpies were human-bird hybrids known as the hounds of Zeus. Jason and the Argonauts had encountered them in Virgil's *Argonautica*.

Looking back and forth between Yasmina's eagle and the Arpui, wondering if they shared a common ancestor, Will shuddered and looked down at the aged parchment. The lake was the third and final marker. On the map, the terraced pyramid lay just beyond, surrounded by a group of thimble-like symbols denoting hills. Mala handed him a bronze monocular. The miniscule telescope allowed him to see past the opposite shore, where a long slope marked the beginning of a region of low hills.

"Judging from the map, we should be able to see the pyramid from here," he said.

"Perhaps," she said, sharing the monocular with the others as they gathered around.

They decided Selina should take flight and do a reconnaissance of the terrain. She didn't return until the late afternoon, stumbling out of the jungle and looking raw with nerves. Mateo caught her as she almost fell into the shelter. She dropped gratefully into his arms, smiling up at him and brushing aside a lock of his hair.

"Why did you come through the jungle?" Mala asked.

"I circled the entire region of hills," the sylvamancer replied, after catching her breath and accepting a canteen of water. "It is not extensive. When I failed to spot a pyramid, I decided I needed a better view of the center. I flew too close to the roost of the Arpui, who spotted me and gave chase. They fly much faster than I, and I was forced to shift into their form to escape. I took evasive action and attempted to blend, but somehow they . . . knew me." She shivered. "I was forced to stop and do battle, and barely managed to re-enter the jungle. I couldn't risk another flight."

Mala leaned forward. "The pyramid. Did you see it?"

Selina took a long pull from her canteen, then slowly shook her head. "I saw the top of every hill. I'm sure of it. There was no deviation."

Mateo pointed at the map. "Perhaps it's nothing, but notice how the pyramid is drawn. Not on top of one of the hills—but standing alone."

Gunnar frowned. "And?"

Will squeezed Mateo's shoulder as he stared at the map. "What if the pyramid *is* one of the hills? Buried inside or overgrown? This thing is thousands of years old—of course it's not sitting there like the Parthenon."

"The what?" Mateo asked.

"Nothing," Will mumbled. Yasmina gave him an amused glance.

"An astute observation," Mala said, "but which hill? We hardly have time to excavate each one."

"There are a hundred hilltops, at the least," Selina added. "Most of them within view of the Arpui."

Will looked up from the map, thoughtful. "What's the story with them? Are they menagerist creations?"

"No one knows their true origins," Mala said. "In fact, they were believed to be extinct. What we know is that they breed amongst themselves, hate all living creatures, and are loathe to leave their roosts. Legend holds they were first bred as guardians for the stronghold of an ancient menagerist."

Mala's eyes widened as she realized the implication of her own description. She gave Will a brief, expressionless glance, then turned to the sylvamancer. "Selina, were the creatures roosting on one hilltop in particular?"

"It appeared so, yes. But there are far too many Arpui for us to engage in battle."

The party fell silent for a moment, until Yasmina looked back at the jungle and said, "I think I can help with that."

After breaking camp, the party watched anxiously as Yasmina left the safety of the shelter and walked alone towards the beach. None of the Arpui was within a hundred yards, but once the closest ones saw her, they lurched into the air, claws extended, and flew at her with their horrid faces twisted into snarls. Will realized the eyes of the avian hybrids bothered him the most, the mixture of human intelligence and animal cunning. They stared at Yasmina with pure hatred, as if the Arpui knew what perversions of nature they were.

In keeping with the mystique of her new profession, Yasmina had refused to divulge her plan, saying only that friends were watching and making everyone promise to stay behind her until she gave the signal.

Knowing the Arpui would tear her apart if she were wrong, Will could hardly bear to watch as the troop of foul avians, at least a hundred strong, bore down on her. Yasmina kept walking towards them, unflinching, her eagle cawing madly from her shoulder. Will couldn't take it any longer and ran out of the shelter. Just before the creatures swarmed her, he saw a pack of huge gray bodies surge out of the jungle and fly straight at the Arpui. The new arrivals had wingspans as wide as three men and bulbous feathered heads, silent assassins targeting their enemies without warning or mercy.

Owls, Will realized as he watched the two flocks engage in midair above Yasmina. Terrifyingly giant owls.

It was no match. Though inferior in numbers—perhaps two dozen strong— the owls had far superior power and speed. They also had claws three times as long as those of the Arpui, curved and strong as meat hooks, and their thick bodies looked impervious to normal blows. As the first wave routed the front line of smaller birds, more owls poured out of the jungle to join their brethren, scattering the Arpui across the sky.

Yasmina waved furiously. The party rushed over to find six owls waiting by her side, necks bent. "Hang on," she said. "They're not used to riders."

Clutching the owl's broad neck, praying Selina would catch anyone who fell, Will felt his heart leap into his throat as the great bird took off like an arrow. Somehow he managed to hold on, and in minutes the bird had deposited them at the apex of a low hill, indistinguishable from the other hilltops except for the Arpui roosts nestled like brown wicker cages amid the trees. The owls chased away the few remaining birds, mostly mothers with their young.

Warily eying the sky, Mala asked to borrow Will's sword, then drove the magical blade straight into the earth. It went a foot into the ground and struck stone. She returned the weapon and gave the owls a worrisome look, as if they might decide to leave. "Selina, have you fully recovered?"

"No, but I can manage this task." The sylvamancer moved off the summit of the hill and waved everyone behind her. As she raised her arms, the roots of the trees and other vegetation popped and slithered out of the ground in a large radius around where the sword had struck stone, toppling the smaller trees. Face straining with effort, she summoned a fierce wind to blow away the topsoil and remaining roots, exposing an iron pull ring in the center of a grid of giant limestone blocks, stained brown from the earth.

19

After two more days of imprisonment inside the tree, with nothing to do except dwell on his terrible fate at the hands of the Fairy Queen, Caleb spent hours feeling around in the darkness for the hinged door he knew was there. The door he had *seen* them open.

But he never found it.

Some thief he was.

Caleb had discovered that if he lay on his back in the mushroom ring and didn't move, the woodland fairies wouldn't drug him. It was a far worse fate, soberly enduring their taunts and crass behavior and putrid incense-breath, but he forced himself to lie still and observe.

Unfortunately, he didn't learn anything new, and the fairies always drugged him before they stuck him back in the tree. One thing: He was pretty sure they had changed redwood groves again.

The next night, the fairies dragged Caleb into the mushroom ring with more gusto than usual, swarming around him as if charged with licentious energy. The Brewer had already arrived, lying on his back in the center. Zipping around the mushroom ring above them, holding a crystal wand in one hand, was the ugliest creature Caleb had ever laid eyes on.

As naked as a baby hippo, the grotesquely fat Fairy Queen was twice the size of her fairy brethren. She had saggy skin the color of a dead mouse, redwood bark for wings, and a face like a bowl of mashed potatoes. As soon as she saw Caleb, the Fairy Queen stopped in midair, forcing two other fairies flying right behind her to crash into her ample backside. The queen licked her lips and snorted like a wild boar, almost hyperventilating as she drifted over. Caleb recoiled and then jumped to his feet, waving his arms for someone to shoot him up with colored bolts.

The queen batted him in the face with her wings, knocking him down. She straddled him and kissed him full on the mouth with lips that tasted like sour milk. He thought he might gag. He bucked wildly but couldn't budge her.

As she ripped off his shirt and snorted again, something pinged off the side of her head and fell on Caleb's chest. He looked down. It was a small rock.

Another rock whizzed into the circle, and then another. In a rage at the distraction, the queen flew off Caleb, looking for the offending fairy.

"Over here, ye ugly brute," Marguerite said. She was standing ten feet outside the mushroom ring, one hand clutching her trident dagger, the other holding a canvas bag. She withdrew another rock from the bag and threw it in the circle, felling a smaller fairy.

The queen shrieked and pointed at Marguerite, then began babbling in a strange tongue. All but six of the woodland fairies darted straight at the rogue. Once the wood sprites left the mushroom circle, their wings changed instantly to a dull brown color, but they whipped tiny daggers out of the pockets of their leggings as they flew. The daggers resembled large thorns affixed with wooden handles.

As the angry sprites closed in, Marguerite picked up a fishing net with weighted ends and whisked it through the air, catching three of them. After that, she rolled to the side, jumped up, and stabbed two more with her dagger. Plenty remained, whisking around and bloodying Marguerite with their thorns. She fought back with a vengeance, and Caleb wasn't sure who had the upper hand.

But Marguerite had created a diversion, and Caleb seized it. He scrambled to his feet, praying the queen and the remaining fairies wouldn't notice. If he could just escape the mushroom ring, he knew those colored bolts couldn't harm him.

The queen shrieked. Caleb dashed for the edge of the ring. In the corner of his eye, he saw a silent flap of wings, and felt a prick in his back.

Oh no.

As usual, the drug took effect immediately, blurring his vision and causing his knees to buckle. But he was going to make it. Only three steps to go.

More bolts stung his back. Didn't matter. He just had to pitch forward and clear the faerie ring and Marguerite would drag him away. He looked up and saw her backed against a tree, trying to fend off the enraged fairies. She stumbled to a knee, and one of the fairies stabbed her in the arm. Marguerite screamed.

She was losing. Caleb had to help her. Just as he lurched for the edge of the mushroom ring, his toes inches away, someone yanked him backwards by his hair, dragging him to the center of the ring. The queen batted him in the face with her wings and two other fairies held him down. The monstrous leader opened her hand and the crystal wand flew into it. With spittle flying from her mouth, she pointed the wand at Caleb and began babbling in her language.

Caleb's fingers felt numb, and he looked down at his hands in horror. They had turned green and lumpy. The queen kept chanting. As the fungal growth spread to his forearms, painfully scraping against the vambraces, a powerful male tenor rose above the din, belting out a ballad that projected through the forest, causing a feeling of well-being to flood Caleb's senses.

The queen slowly lowered her wand and stood in a daze with the other fairies, mesmerized by the voice. For a moment, Caleb joined them. He forgot about the fairies attacking Marguerite, the ring of glowing fungi, and the deadly power of the queen that was turning him into a mushroom. Everything was drowned by that incredible voice and the numbing effect of the fairy bolts. All he wanted to do was drift and forget, spend the rest of his life sinking into blissful nirvana.

Someone darted into the circle and grabbed Caleb underneath the arms. In a dim corner of his brain, he realized it was the Brewer. His voice didn't have the same power in the circle, and the fairies started to blink and recovered from their stupor. The older man dragged Caleb backwards as fast as he could, towards the edge of the circle. Just before they made it out, the Brewer tripped over a prone fairy.

As Caleb started to giggle, watching the Brewer try to extricate himself from the ugly little sprite, the Brewer stumbled to his feet, pulling Caleb with him and using him as a shield. Caleb felt a flurry of colored bolts sting his chest in the process. He couldn't tell if any had hit the Brewer, but once they reached the edge of the mushroom ring, the older man resumed singing, even louder than before.

Marguerite screamed Caleb's name as the eyes of the nearest fairy began to gloss over again.

The Brewer pulled faster.

Caleb passed out.

20

A civilian guard clutching a halberd shouted down at Val and the others as they approached an entrance gate set into the north side of the town wall. "State yer name and purpose here!"

Rucker gave their names and claimed they were travelers passing through from Londyn, seeking a warm bed for the night.

"We 'aven't had news from Londyn in a year. It's still standing, is it?"

Val and Adaira exchanged a glance. *Still standing?*

"We're here, aren't we?" Rucker said, with a flawless rendition of the man's archaic accent.

The guard glared at Val. "Yer staff—'tis not a wizard's?"

Rucker brayed with laughter. "A wizard? 'Im? 'Tis a fancy walking stick."

"Londyn's a long way to travel through demon territory."

Demon territory? Val thought. *What happened here? Has this town been stuck inside the mist for an entire year, or are we someplace . . . else?*

Rucker twirled his sword above his head in a figure-eight pattern, the blade whisking through the air. "I never said we didn't have some fun along the way."

The guard nodded grimly and ducked below the wall. He appeared at the gate a few minutes later with a dozen armed men. One by one, the militia let the members of the party through, searching their belongings and performing a strange ritual: they checked everyone's wrists, neck, heels, and back.

Searching for signs of a demon.

"We'll tell the Dwyn yer here," the guard called out, as the party went through. "He'll want to talk to ye."

"Dwyn?" Val whispered to Adaira.

"Another name for a Druid, though not in a dialect common to this part of Albion. At least not anymore. I'm not sure why . . ."

She trailed off, perplexed by the mounting questions.

Taking in the village, Val saw timber-framed houses squeezed together on muddy cobblestone streets, carts and wheelbarrows and buckets full of bricks, the smell of fresh bread and compost heaps, barking dogs, smoke pouring from the chimneys. Despite the signs of everyday life, the village had an ominous feel, encased in the eerie blue mist, devoid of street vendors and laughing children.

They followed the main thoroughfare to the center of town, where they discovered a crowd of people congregating in a courtyard marked by a clock tower with a peaked red roof. Candlelight gleamed from the second and third story windows of the angular townhomes overlooking the square.

The gathering appeared to be some kind of worship service, led by a bearded man in a hooded white robe on a podium, waving his hands as he called out for succor from a deity named Arawn. He prayed for good crops, warm hearths, and protection from the demons.

"The local Dwyn," Adaira said quietly.

The man on the podium shook a fist to the sky, resulting in a flash of lightning that awed the crowd.

Val moved closer to Adaira. "Electromancy?"

"A trick of the light. He's a low-level wizard passing himself off as a priest. Historians have long suspected that was the *modus operandi* of the druids."

A middle-aged man and a woman pushed through the crowd, right to the edge of the podium. The man was cradling a little boy wrapped in a blanket and writhing in pain. The Dwyn leaned down and took the child in his arms, then laid him on the podium. Val caught a glimpse of a horrible, blistering burn covering the boy's chest.

The Dwyn performed a series of hand gestures above the child, then bent his head in prayer. The crowd stilled while the boy whimpered and tried bravely not to cry out. When the Dwyn raised up, a look of infinite sadness lengthened his face. "It is not the will of Arawn for me to heal this child. He suffers for the good of all."

"Charlatan," Adaira seethed, and took a step forward. Val grabbed her arm.

The mother wailed as the Dwyn returned the boy to his father. Trying to comfort the distraught child, the parents left during the service. Before anyone could object, Adaira skirted the edge of the crowd and chased them down an alley.

"It's not our problem, girl," Rucker called out, but Adaira ignored him and caught up to the family. The little boy was wailing in pain, squirming back and forth in his father's arms.

"I can help," Adaira said. "I'm a healer."

The father wheeled to face her, mistrust darkening his brow.

The mother took Adaira's hand. "Please. 'Elp 'im if ye can. 'E's suffered so much."

"What happened?" she asked gently.

"An accident in the smithy," the mother said, glaring at the father. "Put 'im down, Warwick."

The father, a burly man with red-veined jowls, shot a worried glance towards the crowd in the square. Finally he swallowed and said, "Okay. But not 'ere."

They followed the alley to a tight cul-de-sac packed with two-story cottages with thatched roofs. In whispered voices, the party debated using one of the two healing salves, but everyone agreed using one of the precious ointments so soon was a bad idea. Unable to change Adaira's mind, Rucker finally stopped protesting and turned his attention to watching their backs. He, Synne, and Dida remained outside while Val entered the dwelling with Adaira and the family.

The father laid the boy on a coarse rug by the hearth, cradling his face as Adaira peeled off the blanket. The boy's upper chest was a morass of raw and blistered flesh.

"Water," Adaira commanded. "Lots of it."

The mother ran off, and Adaira put her hands on the boy's temples. "Sleep," she said softly. Nothing happened at first, but eventually the boy's eyelids began to flutter. After a few long minutes, his head lolled to the side, and the father's eyes widened. "You're not a Dwyn."

"No," Adaira said evenly. "I'm not."

"I won't 'ave a wizard touching me boy!"

The mother returned and put a finger in his face. "She wants to 'elp. And yer going to let her, do ye hear me? I don't care who or what she is. *Yer going to let her.*"

The father looked away from his angry wife, down at the sleeping boy, and then cast a suspicious glance at Adaira. The mother pushed him aside and set two buckets of water on the rug. Adaira traced her fingernails across the boy's thighs. Blood seeped through the pores where her fingers grazed. The mother gasped. After Adaira had outlined two sections roughly equal in size to the boy's chest burn, she slowly raised her hands off the boy's thighs, bringing a thin layer of skin with her.

The father made a choking sound. The mother shushed him with a furious glance.

The boy stirred, eyelids fluttering. Adaira paused to stare into his eyes until he resumed sleeping. Val then watched in amazement as she floated the two rectangular sheets of detached skin onto the boy's burn and fitted them into place.

She's performing a skin graft. Without any instruments.

After the skin settled, Adaira sprinkled water over the new layer of flesh, placed her hands lightly atop the boy's chest, and closed her eyes while the skin absorbed the water and attached. She repeated those steps time and again. It took two hours to finish the task, and Val could only imagine the complexities involved, but after a final application of water Adaira pushed to her feet and declared the job finished. The boy was still snoring peacefully.

"The pain will be mostly gone by week's end," Adaira said. "He'll have minor scarring."

The mother hugged Adaira and began to sob. The father looked ill but took the boy's hand and squeezed it, a tear falling onto his son's cheek.

"We should go," Val said.

Adaira gave a weary nod.

A few hours later, after they had rented rooms at an inn and washed up, the party gathered in the wood-beamed common room. Even Synne joined them by the wide stone hearth for a pint of golden ale and a platter of roasted quail and vegetables.

Rucker devoured his meal and pushed his plate aside, twisting his colored ring as he stared into the fire. Val ordered a bottle of port and five glasses, but only Adaira and Dida joined in. The aroma of wood smoke, spice-scented candles, and Adaira's damp hair was an aphrodisiac after the hard days of travel.

The atmosphere in the inn was somber. A table of four men took the table next to them, and Val recognized the bearded guard who had accosted the party at the entrance gate. The guard sent wary, curious glances in the party's direction. Halfway into a pitcher of ale, he decided to speak. "Londyn, eh? All of ye?"

Rucker turned and scowled, causing the entire table of men to flinch. "Aye."

Next to the guard, a swarthy man with an axe strapped to his side leaned forward. "When was yer last nightfall or sunrise?"

"Same as ye. Too many moons to count."

The men seemed to deflate at the answer. "We was 'oping it was different outside the moor. That if we could just get through . . ."

Rucker growled. "Sorry to disappoint ye."

" 'Tis the same in Londyn? Demons outside the city walls? Everyone afraid to leave?"

"I'm afraid so."

"We need supplies," the guard said. "Medicine. Since ye got through . . . do ye think ye can send word? When ye return?"

"Aye. *If* we return. We're traveling the countryside, taking stock of what's left."

The men nodded sagely. Val was glad Rucker had taken the lead; the crafty old warrior seemed to be saying the right things.

"Where ye 'eaded next?" the swarthy man asked.

Rucker downed his last swallow of ale. "The next town over."

Mugs stopped in midair. The faces of the four villagers drained of color, and they wouldn't look Rucker in the eye. The guard's voice lowered almost to a whisper. "But there's nothing between . . . the next town over is Badŏn. Ye can't go there. No one goes there. That's where *he* is."

Rucker wiped his mouth and set his mug down. "He who?"

The guard's face twisted in confusion. "The mad king Tobar. The vile wizard who brought the demons."

The door to the outside flung open, banging against the wall. The Dwyn strode in, fully robed, carrying a staff topped with an iron oak leaf. The tips of the leaves looked dagger-sharp.

Massed in the street behind the druid, Val saw scores of angry villagers carrying torches and a variety of weapons, some of them hoes and pitchforks. Warwick, the father of the boy Adaira had healed, stepped forward beside the Dwyn. Warwick cast his gaze around the stunned common room and pointed at Adaira. "That's her! She's a wizardess, I swear it."

The men at the table next to Val's leaped out of their seats and backed away.

The mother of the healed boy stumbled forward as if someone had pushed her. "Is this true?" the Dwyn asked. "Two witnesses are required to condemn a wizardess."

The mother looked down at her hands and shuffled her feet. Val gripped his staff and saw Rucker's hand slipping to the hilt of his weapon.

"May I remind you," the Dwyn said in a stern voice, "of our pact with Arawn. Why do you think this village still stands? Speak, woman. Is she what your husband claims?"

The mother slowly raised her head, looking in Adaira's direction but not meeting her gaze. "She is," the mother said, in a pained voice just above a whisper.

Adaira leaped to her feet. "I healed your *son!*"

"Silence!" The Dwyn thundered. He pointed his staff at her. "Take the wizardess to the execution tree. Leave the others outside the gate, and may Arawn have mercy on their souls."

A burly, red-haired man holding an axe rushed Adaira, his face twisted in hate. Before Val or Dida could react, she held a ridged hand out like the side of a knife, holding the man in place. Seeing the effects of her magic first-hand enraged the crowd, who surged forward as the Dwyn raised his arms and began to chant.

Villagers poured into the common room, bursting through the door and climbing into windows. Val pushed the first wave back with a strong wind. That whipped the villagers into a frenzy, and the room erupted with cries of "kill the wizards!" and "their kind brought the demons!"

As more people poured inside, the nearest villagers advanced on the party with swords and knives, some even raising beer mugs and chairs.

"Push them back!" Rucker roared. He overturned the table in front of the guard and the swarthy man, who had not joined the collective madness that had overtaken the crowd. "Secure the inside, if ye can!"

"Protect me, and I can ward the entrances!" Dida said, his hands already waving through the air.

Villagers rushed them from all sides. The meal had restored some of Val's strength, and he tried to think of a spell that would work on a large group of people. Synne bought them some time by tearing through the crowd like a tornado in a mobile home park, felling large men with one blow, caving in chests and punching through wooden tables raised in defense, dancing through the room in a ballet of violence. The vicious display seemed to cow the crowd, until the Dwyn advanced on Synne with his staff, whipping it back and forth with inhuman speed. She tried to hit him, but her blows stopped an inch from his body.

Wizard Shield, Val knew.

Synne lost ground against the stronger wizard, who hit her with blow after blow from his magically-enhanced staff, taking her knees out and driving her to the ground. He stood above her, poised to impale her with the tips of the iron oak leaf, when Val called out. "Dwyn!" he screamed, enraged at the sight of his protector lying in a pool of blood. "You want to duel with magic?"

The druid turned, his eyes popping in fear when he saw black lightning dancing at the ends of Val's fingertips.

"Then try a spirit mage," Val whispered to himself.

Knowing they had to make a statement or all risk being killed, he thrust his hands forward and sent twin lances of Spirit Fire arcing into the Dwyn. The magic consumed his body in moments, silencing his terrified screams, leaving a heap of ash on the floor as Val extinguished the magic.

The death of the Dwyn broke the will of the villagers. Most stumbled over themselves to flee the inn. Rucker and Synne, who had managed to struggle to her feet, chased away any that remained.

"The room is warded!" Dida called out.

Though relieved beyond words, it seemed to Val the victory had come a shade too easily. There had been hundreds of people gathered; had word of the Dwyn's death spread that quickly? Why had they all dispersed?

Val whipped his head back and forth, realizing what was wrong. "Adaira? Where's Adaira?"

The members of the party looked at each other as if someone, surely someone, knew where she was. Once it was obvious she wasn't in the room, Val raced through the door in a panic, knowing Dida had shielded the room from the outside in.

Val flew above the street and spotted her at once, a hundred feet away, being hustled towards a scaffold in the town plaza by a group of villagers. That was why they had hurried off, he realized. They wanted a sacrifice for their god. They wanted it so badly they would risk the wrath of wizards.

He took flight and headed straight at the crowd, noticing Adaira's hands were tied behind her back, a black hood pulled over her head and secured with rope. At times a blast of Wind Push or a blind Invisible Knife stroke would buy her a moment, but the villagers shoved or hit her to keep her moving and off-balance.

She's drained, and can't see to use her magic. They knew how to take her.

Blinded by rage, he landed behind the group and raised his staff. Someone grabbed him from behind and Val jabbed the azantite tip backwards like a sword, without looking. It connected with flesh and he jerked it out. After swinging the staff in a wide arc, clearing space, he brought forth Spirit Fire again, letting it arc high into the sky, scattering those who bore witness to his fury. Adaira's kidnappers dropped her on the ground, and not until every villager in sight had fled did Val quench the awful flames, his body vibrating with adrenaline, humming with the power of his magic. He wanted to burn the entire loathsome village to the ground.

"Val? Dida?" Adaira said, her voice muffled and unsteady. "What's happening?"

When Val took a step towards her, his knees buckled. He was completely drained. With a deep, shuddering breath, grateful beyond words Adaira was unharmed, he shuffled forward and sliced through her bonds. She ripped the hood off as Rucker, Synne, and Dida raced down the street, slowing as they approached.

Dida was staring at the ground behind Val, his eyes wide and uneasy. Val turned to find a red-headed girl of no more than sixteen huddled on the ground, her hands holding her stomach to keep her insides from spilling out of a long gash.

It took Val a moment to realize what had happened, but then he rushed to the girl's side, his stomach bottoming at the knowledge of what he had done. "Adaira!" he roared. "I need you!"

As Val dropped to his knees and cradled the girl's head in his hands, he saw the dark tint to the blood pooling around her body, the glassy stare and limp arms. "Help her!" he screamed, collecting the girl in his arms as he stood. "Do something!"

Adaira felt the side of the girl's neck. "She is beyond my power," she said quietly. "I'm sorry."

There was no weapon on the ground. In the heat of battle, Val thought an angry villager had grabbed him, but it had just been the girl, probably someone who had seen him burn the Dwyn, trying to plead with Val not to kill her parents. He rocked with the girl, who felt as weightless as a baby bird, as shouting arose in the distance and booted feet pounded on cobblestones.

Rucker jerked Val around. "Let it go! There are hundreds more in the square!"

"What was she doing?" he asked, in a daze. "Why did she have to grab me?"

Adaira gripped his arm. "Please, Val. We have to go. Can you fly?"

He closed his eyes and tried to force away the image of the girl. He reached deep for the magic and felt nothing. He shook his head, uncaring of his fate.

"Everyone link arms!" Adaira said. "Dida and I can get everyone over the wall and away from the village."

Torches and weapons in hand, a horde of enraged men and women rushed around the corner, shouting in frustration as Adaira and Dida lifted the five members of the party above the town. They rose quickly out of arrow range.

Encased in the eerie blue haze, they sped off into the countryside, in desperate need of a safe haven. Yet not even the presence of the huge winged creatures wheeling through the mist above them could tear Val's thoughts away from the memory of the girl lying in a pool of blood on the cobblestones, killed by his own hand.

21

As Will and the others bent to observe the iron pull ring, he noticed two things marking the surface of the limestone block. The first was a roughly carved dagger-and-crown, the symbol of the Alazashin. The second, chiseled by a much steadier hand, was a two-line runic inscription in a language unfamiliar to Will.

Coba murmured *ancient Mayan* and then translated the inscription, reciting the same ominous words that had stuck in Will's mind since Mala had first uttered them.

Herein lies the living tomb of the sorcerer king Yiknoom Uk'ab K'ahk. All those who seek may enter, but none shall ever leave.

For a moment, no one spoke, staring in awed silence at the entrance to the ancient tomb. What wonders and terrors would they find inside? Would the inscription prove prophetic?

"Someone managed to escape the tomb," Mateo said. "Or we wouldn't have the map."

"I don't think so," Mala said. "I believe the Alazashin explorer who found this place sent the map back with a messenger before he entered the pyramid, in case he failed to return. I don't know what happened, but if the assassin had plundered the tomb and lived, history would record the deed."

"The trees at the apex of the hill are much younger than those below," Selina pointed out. "Half a century old, rather than hundreds of years."

"So the Alazashin explorers dug it out fifty years ago," Will said. "Or there was a wizard with them."

With a nod from Mala, Gunnar stepped forward and heaved on the iron ring. It took a few tries before the heavy block groaned, but it opened to reveal a darkened cavity yawning below. Will dropped a large rock inside. It made no sound.

"How can that be?" Coba asked, leaning over the opening.

Mala shook out a glow stone and tried to illuminate the darkness, but her light failed to penetrate even a foot inside.

"It's a magical ward of some sort," Selina murmured. "Sound and light proof."

"Can your own magic penetrate?" Mala asked.

The sylvamancer concentrated for a moment. "I don't believe the ward will bar us from entry, but I cannot undo the spell. Whoever made this was stronger than I. *Much*."

"The sorcerer king," Mala murmured.

"I know enough about wards to know this is a one-way passage. Once we enter, we cannot go back the same way."

Coba gave the cavity a nervous glance. "Dark hole is symbol for Xibalba. No one knows what comes after death."

Xibalba, Will knew, was the name of the Mayan underworld.

"I should go first," Selina said, as she stared down at the hole.

Mateo took her by the arm. "What if it's an ambush? Take me with you."

She kissed him on the lips, causing him to blush. "I can maneuver more easily on my own."

Mala stepped to the edge of the hole. "How do the rest of us get down?"

"I'll float you down as you enter," Selina said, "two at a time."

"What if you're unable to?"

"That's a chance we'll have to take," she said grimly.

As everyone prepared to descend, Yasmina took Will by the hand and said, loud enough for everyone to hear, "I'm staying behind."

Mala turned to stare at her, waiting for her to continue.

Yasmina's grip on Will's hand was firm, her voice strong and composed. "I'll be of limited use to you inside the tomb, and I have . . . things I need to do." She glanced at the eagle perched on her shoulder, whose feathers had already taken on a brighter sheen. Yasmina shook her head. "I'm not even sure I can explain. I'm a steward of the land, not a seeker of treasure, and I sense I'm needed elsewhere now."

"Where?" Will asked. He could tell by her voice she had made up her mind. Not only that, but as much as he would miss her companionship—she was his only link to home—he preferred her out of harm's way.

"To the north," she said mysteriously. "But first I'll return to the meeting place and direct the Yith Riders here, instead of waiting at Ixmal. I'll also attempt to have the owls clear the Arpui from this roost for good, so you may exit with impunity."

Mala stepped forward and clasped her forearm. "Thank you, wilder. Your assistance on this journey has been much appreciated."

Unsure how Mala would react to her departure, Will breathed a sigh of relief. He suspected she appreciated Yasmina's fierce independence and dedication to the code of the wilder.

And, ever the pragmatist, Mala probably agreed with the decision. A wilder, especially a new one, would not be of much use inside a pyramid.

After Yasmina said her goodbyes, Will hugged her tight. "Take care of yourself," he whispered.

"I will. You, too."

"Are you going back to Freetown?"

"No," she said sadly. "Not there."

"I understand. What about getting home? How do we find you again?"

Yasmina smoothed the harpy eagle's feathers as she stared at the shaggy sweep of jungle extending to the horizon. "I think I've found my home, Will." Though her words were not unexpected, he was still stunned, and didn't know what to say. She gave him an oddly knowing look. "Maybe you have, too."

He glanced at Mala and then down at his hands, but didn't respond. He had been avoiding those thoughts. His only goals right now were to help Val, get Caleb, and find a way home. Then they could all make decisions together.

"I'll miss you, Will. Your brother always made me cry, but you always made me laugh."

He felt himself choking up. He hugged her again and didn't want to let her go. She eased away, squeezing his hand a final time. Staff in hand and head held high, her long stride carried her swiftly to the nearest owl.

"Wilder," Mala called out.

Yasmina turned.

"Take Coba home, please."

The sturdy Mayan was sitting cross-legged on the ground. He jumped up and opened his palms. "The treasure—you promised!"

"You've guided us well," Mala said, staring at the maw of the tomb. Though his fee had been paid, she had also pledged him a share of the loot. "But this place is not for you. If we find coin and return alive, I'll deliver your share my-self. You have my word."

Coba hung his head for a moment, then broke into a wide grin and did a standing back flip. "Good deal for me," he said, walking backwards towards Yasmina. He pointed at Mala. "You stay alive so I be rich."

The hint of a smile lifted her lips. "I shall try."

Will felt a heaviness descend as Yasmina and Coba climbed onto a pair of owls and took flight, soaring towards the southern coast. Mala turned to address the group. "Without the wilder, the other owls could leave at any mo-ment. I, for one, do not wish to be here when the Arpui return to their roost."

Everyone peered nervously into the entrance. "Wait a count of twenty," Se-lina said to the group as she clasped Mateo's hand, "then descend one by one."

After Selina stepped into the hole and disappeared, Mala counted off the seconds, then asked Gunnar to go next, followed by Mateo. They both dropped into the blackness.

Will took a deep breath. "Go ahead," he said to Mala. "I'll go last."

She smirked. "Ever the chivalrous one, Will the Builder."

"I saw what you did for Coba. That was kind."

"Down there, he would be a liability. A risk to the safety of the group. I did what was necessary."

Will laughed. "Whatever."

"Tsk tsk. I'm afraid you'll never learn."

"Learn what?"

They were standing at the edge of the hole. She swayed right up to him and cupped the back of his neck, her body brushing against his. A tingle shot through him as she pulled his face close, eyes dancing, full lips parted. Just before their mouths met, the warmth of her breath against his, she pushed him backwards, into the hole.

"That I act in my own interest," she said, as he tumbled headlong into the tomb.

Will was falling through blackness. Arms and legs flailing. Unable to hear his own shouts for help.

Long seconds later, he emerged into an enormous chamber illuminated by a dull crimson glow. Still in free fall, he noticed a sandstone floor thirty feet below, covered in life-size statues. Just as his voice returned so he could yell for help, Selina arrested his fall, floating him gently downward.

As he descended, Will craned his neck to get a better view of his environs. Visibility extended at least a few hundred feet, but he couldn't see the walls. The limestone statues were placed five feet apart throughout the chamber; there must have been thousands.

The air was cool and dry. Fresh. No discernible odor. The source of the red glow was a mystery. Will glanced down as he landed and noticed that large, dun-colored stone blocks comprised the floor, each carved with a prominent Mayan glyph. He looked up and saw, except for the shaft of darkness through which he had fallen, the same construction on the ceiling.

From up close, the statues looked incredibly lifelike. Most depicted a man or a woman in various upright postures, though a few displayed mythological beasts and godlike beings. Will joined the others as they craned their necks to gawk at the awe-inspiring scope of the underground structure. He had expected a claustrophobic apex chamber, the dusty tip of a pharaoh's tomb. Instead he got a buried sandstone museum of unbelievable size.

Selina flew up to the entrance shaft and confirmed the journey was a one-way ticket. Will felt a sense of oppression at being trapped within the ancient tomb. He approached the statue of a young warrior raising a spear, dressed in a loincloth and an elaborate headdress. The statue's chest felt as solid as it looked. Will ran his hands across the smooth surface, then looked up at the proud face and frozen eyes staring back at him.

The statue blinked.

Will stumbled backwards. It blinked again, and then the pupils flicked to each side.

"Did you see that?" Will asked, his voice hoarse.

"Aye," Mala said.

The stone eye started roving in its socket, frantic, as if seeking to escape. Will looked at the next statue over and noticed the same thing. He whipped around and sought the eyes of every statue within sight.

They were all in motion.

Weapons raised, the party bunched together, unsure whether they would animate and attack them.

"Wait," Selina called out, in a shaky voice. She stood inches away from a statue of a beautiful woman wearing a cloth wrap and covered in jewelry. The statue's eyes blinked in a regular pattern, and Will had the impression the statue was staring at Selina as much as the sylvamancer was staring at her, trying to communicate.

"I've seen living stone before," Selina said, "and the eternal sleep of an Encasing. This is neither. I believe," she swallowed, "I believe these people are still alive, somehow trapped within the stone. *Part* of it."

Will couldn't tear his eyes away from the statue of the Mayan woman. "How old is this tomb again?" he asked.

"Thousands of years," Mala said, unusually somber.

Will felt himself start to shake. "That's . . . that's an abomination," he whispered. He raised his sword and, after an approving nod from Selina, held it up in front of the statue of the woman. The statue squeezed her eyes shut, and Will could *feel* what she wanted him to do. He touched the tip of Zariduke to the woman's chest and began to slowly thrust forward. With a snick of blue-white light, the sword pushed through the stone with the resistance of warm butter. The eyes of the woman flickered with relief, then turned still and lifeless, just before the statue dissolved into dust.

"Magic," he said through clenched teeth. "Not stone. Magic."

Mateo's knuckles tightened against his buckler. "All these people . . . free them, Will. Free them all."

In a rage, Will howled and cut down the statue to his left, and another, and another.

"Stop!" Mala called out.

Will completed his swing, freeing another trapped soul, then turned.

"Don't make a sound," she said.

He corralled his anger and heard a low susurration, somewhere between a hiss and a rattle, faint but growing in volume. As the noise level increased, he realized it was not one prolonged sound but multiple bursts of shorter ones. It brought to mind the sound of a thousand shaking maracas.

A scorpion came into view, scuttling down one of the rows towards Mateo. The foot-long creature moved in short bursts, pincers extended, the rustling of its segmented body producing the sound they had heard.

When it drew close enough, Mateo whipped his sword at the arachnid, cleaving it down the middle with a crunch of exoskeleton.

Three more took its place. Will swiveled and saw them coming from all directions, rushing down the rows of statues, hundreds of them, stingers poised and ready.

He had once read that the bigger the scorpion, the less dangerous the sting.

But he didn't want to test that theory.

Especially not on Urfe.

"Fly, Selina!" Mala said. "Find the exit!"

The sylvamancer took to the air as Will and the others prepared for the onslaught. As they formed a loose circle and spread out to give themselves room to fight, Will wondered what had caused the scorpions to attack en masse and realized that, like the Arpui, the hand of nature had probably not designed the colossal arachnids.

Zariduke emitted no *snip* of blue-white light when Will cut the first scorpion in half, but it died just the same. The monstrous things were quick, darting at sharp angles as they approached, and Will found that a spearing motion worked best. A single scorpion was no great threat, but they came in waves, pouring into the room like grain from a silo. He wished he hadn't lost his shield. It would have proved invaluable against the stingers.

Mateo's weapon proved the most useful. Will watched in awe as his cousin wheeled back and forth, using his sword as a whip, crushing the backs of multiple creatures at a time with the flexible urumi blade.

Mala fought with her usual brilliance, spinning and weaving with both blades, using the base of the statues to guard her back, scooping the scorpions away with the tip of her sword if they got too close. Stronger but slower than his companions, Gunnar looked awkward against the scuttling creatures, having to bend almost double to strike them. One reached his boot but Gunnar kicked it away.

Selina swooped back into the fray, alighting atop one of the statues. "There's no exit I could see!" she yelled, causing Will's heart to sink.

"The walls?" Mala shouted.

"The chamber is square. Solid all around. Scorpions everywhere."

As if in response, two of the creatures scuttled up the statue on which Selina was poised, causing her to take flight again.

Mala swore. "There has to be a way out. My guess is a concealed door along the wall. Everyone—stay behind me. Watch your flanks."

The scorpions followed the party as it moved through the chamber. The numbers were not yet overwhelming, but they were steadily increasing. Will knew it was only a matter of time before someone got stung or tired.

Mala moved as straight as she could, vying for the nearest wall. Whenever Will got a second to breathe, he destroyed a statue with his sword, unable to bear the thought of damning someone to an eternity of living stone if he could prevent it. When he tried to swipe through a man with the head of a deer, his sword passed right through the statue, and he almost lost his balance. Confused, he tried waving a hand through the statue.

Empty space.

Forced to resume fighting, a few yards later he tried to slice into the next mythological creature, a statue of a multi-limbed serpent standing on its tail. Again, nothing but air.

Will stepped into the base of the statue, reasoning it might conceal a hidden exit. His boot never touched the ground, and he stumbled at the edge of a shallow pit filled with a writhing mass of scorpions. He yelled and lost his balance. Just before he fell, someone caught him by the back of the shirt.

As Gunnar jerked him away from the pit with one arm, Will felt a pincer latch onto his boot. He shook his leg to get it off, then looked down and saw a mass of scorpions darting in and out of the bottom of the pit, as if it were riddled with tunnels.

"The statues of monsters are illusions!" he called out, as Gunnar set him down. "With pits beneath them!"

Someone screamed in reply. Will whipped to his left and saw his cousin holding his hand, backed against a statue and surrounded by scorpions. Mateo's buckler was nowhere in sight. Before Will could reach him, Selina landed atop the statue and cleared the scorpions away with a Wind Push. She turned in a slow circle, thrusting the army of arachnids back, giving the party room to breathe.

Will felt little relief. The scorpions were already scuttling back down the endless lines of statues.

Selina jumped down to embrace Mateo, then gasped when she saw his hand. Will looked down in horror. The skin around his cousin's palm was slowly turning gray and hard, petrified by a creeping stone poison.

"You were stung?" Mala asked.

He gasped. "Aye."

She dug into her pouch and shoved a stoppered container the size of a perfume bottle at Mateo. "Drink," she said.

He quaffed the healing potion and poured the last few drops on the injury, but there was no effect. Millimeter by millimeter, his left hand kept solidifying into gray stone.

"What do I do?" he cried.

Even Mala looked at a loss.

The scorpions returned, and Selina blew them back again. "I can't expend all my power," she said, her voice thick with emotion as she cast a sidelong glance at Mateo. "We must find the exit."

They fought their way to the wall. The engraved stone blocks looked identical to the floor and ceiling. Mateo's sword arm was intact, but the petrification had reached the fingers of his left hand.

Will felt nauseated. He couldn't lose his cousin. Mala pushed against the wall to no effect, then ran her fingers along the seams of the blocks.

"Solid," she said. "We'll have to work our way around the perimeter. Go!"

The group formed a protective semicircle around their leader, moving along the wall as fast as they could. After they had progressed a few hundred feet, they finally hit the corner. The adjoining wall looked the same as the first. Will risked a glance at Mateo. The stone had crept to his wrist.

Think, Will. There has to be a way out. This is a test of brains, not brawn.

But he couldn't find an answer, and the scorpions kept him too busy for prolonged thought. When the party reached another corner without finding an exit, Mala banged her fist against the wall in frustration. A scorpion broke through and almost stung her from behind, but Will batted it away at the last instant. He spun and stabbed another that tried to take advantage of the distraction.

His arms were tiring. Was there even a way out, he wondered? Was this room nothing but a deathtrap, a cruel joke by a long-deceased despot?

The scorpions grew denser. Selina looked tired. Mala shouted at them to keep going, pinning all her hopes on a secret door. Halfway along the third wall, Gunnar broke from the group and strode down one of the rows. "Take my back!" he yelled.

Will followed, wondering what he had seen, hoping Gunnar didn't stray too far. Will braced as a powerful wind blew by, Selina covering their flanks. He noticed Gunnar heading straight for a statue of a putrefying corpse with the head of an owl.

The scorpions seemed thicker than ever near the grotesque figure. A group of skeletal statues surrounded the corpse, and Will watched a pair of scorpions jackknife and then scuttle through the feet of the skeletons, as if clambering out of one of the hidden pits.

What is Gunnar thinking?

Will and the big warrior tried to push forward but the scorpions attacked en masse, causing them to retreat. Selina flew to their side, clearing the way once again. The effect of her Wind Push seemed weaker, but in the interlude, Gunnar rushed forward and knelt next to the corpse statue, waved his hand through it to confirm the illusion, then stuck his head through the floor.

"There's a staircase!" he shouted, jumping to his feet.

Their hopes renewed, the rest of the party fought their way to the owl statue. Hundreds of scorpions surrounded them, pincers clacking, stingers poised. Mala herded everyone onto the staircase as Will followed Gunnar down, feeling blindly through the illusion for the first step.

22

Garbind Elldorn soared high above the Canal Bridge as he flew back into New Victoria after a long weekend exploring the wetlands south of the great city. As always, the sylvamancer from the Fifth Protectorate was not eager to return to his urban stronghold. A sylvamancer's true home was the jungle, the swamp, the forest. Though an ambitious man—one had to be in order to claw one's way into the Conclave—Garbind had never felt at ease in the intrigue-soaked halls of the Sanctum.

He dipped low enough to inhale the exotic aromas of the Goblin Market, then basked in the aura of unbridled might as he entered the Wizard District and gazed upon the domes and obelisks and poly-sided towers, the gleaming fortresses of the Realm's most powerful wizards.

Slowing as he entered the thicket of colored spires, he floated past the Hall of Wizards and the serene groves of the Abbey, then wheeled to the right and flew into his citadel. Compared to most of his peers, it was a simple affair, thirty thousand square feet of teak and forest-green marble shaped by a master artisamancer to evoke the subtropical rainforests of the southern reaches of the Fifth Protectorate. Of course, the vegetation surrounding the stronghold concealed a host of nasty defenses.

Garbind's thoughts turned pensive as he glided into the arboretum. Taking up an entire level and heated by solar walls, the indoor botanical garden showcased a stunning variety of tropical plants. Garbind's wife Elena loved the arboretum almost as much as their twin eleven-year-old daughters did. He always felt close to his family here.

Two more weeks, he thought, until he returned home for the second half of the year. Most members of the Conclave brought their families to New Victoria, but Garbind preferred to raise his daughters in the less cosmopolitan atmosphere of Port Nelson. *Let them remain children a while longer.*

These days, preserving his daughter's innocence wasn't his only concern. Lord Alistair's new policies bothered Garbind a great deal. He knew his voice of tolerance was an unwanted one, but Garbind was from a port town with a stew of people and cultures. His mother was Egyptian. His father Basque. Garbind had long opposed Lord Alistair's discriminatory policies, and lately they had taken on an even darker nature.

And for what? The modern era was eons removed from the Age of Sorrows. It was laughable to think that anyone, especially gypsies and other Exilers, could challenge the might of the Congregation.

As Garbind removed his traveling cloak and strolled through a grove of red coconut palms, he noticed a shadow pass through the glass wall, out of the corner of his eye.

A shadow? Passing through *the solar panel?*

He turned and saw something foreign to his hundred years of travels drifting towards him, creating a swath of destruction through the dense vegetation. It resembled, he thought, a coagulated shadow.

Streaks of silver light darted like heat lightning through the man-shaped form, its white eyes glowed as if heated in a forge, and the face of the thing, akin to a sculptor's mold cast in shadow, seemed strangely familiar to Garbind.

Expressionless, it drifted towards the sylvamancer with arms outstretched. Though stunned, Garbind was a powerful wizard in his own home, surrounded by layers of defenses. He had no idea how the shadow thing, whatever it was, had bypassed the wards. But an elder mage had many defenses.

Garbind extended his palms and summoned a Wind Push so fierce it made the red palms bend. He aimed to blow the shadow thing out of his residence and reseal the wards, yet the entity drifted right through the powerful gale.

Though a sylvamancer by trade, all Congregation mages were familiar with the basic forms of magic. Garbind could not summon a fire spirit or create a multi-pronged Flame Scourge like a pyromancer could, but he could use fire against an enemy vulnerable to that element. He whisked a glow orb into his hands, smashed it with his mind, and sent a Fire Sphere spinning towards the shadow creature.

No effect. After that, Garbind tried a blast of water from an overturned urn. That also failed. Next he tried to suffocate the being with a mountain of soil, overturning half the room in an explosion of power.

Still nothing.

Garbind felt a stab of fear.

Air, fire, water, earth. Nothing had slowed it. Harnessing spirit, the only basic element left, was not within Garbind's power.

The thing was ten feet away and closing. The sylvamancer's instincts screamed that a touch would mean his death. After what he had just witnessed, he did not even trust his Wizard Shield.

Something else: from this distance, Garbind finally recognized the face of the shadow creature as belonging to a spiritmancy student named Alfor Tremayne who had perished three years earlier, while attempting the Planewalk.

Or so they had been told. An elder spirit mage oversaw each attempt at the Planewalk, and Lord Alistair himself had proctored Alfor's exam.

Garbind's face drained of color. Lord Alistair. He knew the Chief Thaumaturge had long detested Garbind's voice of dissent, but he never dreamed he would take it this far.

The others had to be warned. He would call a special meeting of the Conclave and accuse Lord Alistair in person. Ideally, he would bring what remained of Alfor as evidence—except he had no idea how to capture him. Better to find someone else to bear witness. Jalen Rainsword lived nearby and would support him.

As Garbind decided to flee, he realized the shadow creature—he could not think of the thing as Alfor, a studious and well-mannered lad—had drifted over to block the exit. No matter. Garbind flew to the northwest corner of the arboretum and up through the wizard chute, all the way to the highest room in the stronghold. He would use the portal at the top.

When he exited into the high-ceilinged chamber called the Eagle's Nest, a beautiful space filled with ethereal orchids in hanging baskets garnered from cloud forests around the world, he saw the shadow creature drifting upward through the floor to block his escape.

Furious, Garbind made the room come alive, sending hundreds of vines and creepers to entrap the shadow thing. All passed right through him. Garbind cursed. He could think of no spell or magic item that would affect the wretched thing. Not only that, but it was drifting towards him again, deceptively fast, and he didn't have time to think of creative options. He was forced to return to the wizard chute and try another level. If he had to, he would blast through the walls of his own stronghold.

He wheeled and dove into the wizard chute—and saw a second shadow drifting towards him from below. In a panic, he wheeled to return to the Eagle's Nest, but the first shadow creature had entered the top of the chute.

Garbind was trapped between them.

Now with the rancid taste of fear coating his mouth, Garbind whisked down four levels and quickly disabled the wards around the secret escape passage halfway down the chute. He could sense the shadow creatures converging on him. Images of his wife and daughter filled his mind as he released the wards and extended his arms, blowing out the hidden door and revealing the horizontal chute that led to the exit.

He thought he was free when one of the shadow things appeared ahead of him in the escape chute, drifting through the wall and trapping him inside.

Desperate, Garbind tried to blast out the thick walls of the escape passage. He had almost succeeded when one of the beings flowed on and then into him. Garbind screamed as the hottest fire imaginable seared through his body, from the tips of his fingers to the soles of his feet, and then he ceased to exist.

23

Val and the others flew through the mist for as long as they dared. Not a mile from the village, the shadows of the flying things roaming the ghostly blue sky drew closer, exposing the bottoms of forty- and fifty-foot membranous wings.

That was enough for the party. They had no desire to combat whatever strange species of demon or other creature thrived inside the aerial nether-world. After flying low enough to ensure no search parties had followed, they set down atop the highest ridge in sight.

Except for the lonely speck of gray marking the village walls in the distance, nothing but bleak moorland rippled the landscape.

Dida glanced at the sky and cringed, as if expecting something to swoop down and snatch him up. Adaira simply sagged, exhausted. *How long had it been since they had slept?* Val wondered

"I s'pose we're off to Badŏn to find Tobar," Rucker said. He pawed at his stubble, consulted a stainless steel compass attached to his belt, and pointed. "Taking into account where we started, and assuming this world's anything like ours, Badŏn should be about a three-day journey that way."

"I don't understand," Adaira said. "Tobar brought the demons to Badŏn? A year ago? And he's some sort of . . . *king* here?"

"Lassie, I don't know much of anything about this world, except it's bloody dangerous. But wherever we are, we need shelter. A place to rest where we can defend ourselves."

"What about right here?" Val asked, forcing his thoughts away from the redheaded girl. As much as he wanted to curl into a ball and wallow in grief and self-pity, he had others to think about. The members of his expedition. His brothers. "It's high ground, with a good view of the moors."

Rucker shook his head. "Too close to the town, and I don't care to be ex-posed. Not with demons roaming the land."

"Traveling also poses danger," Synne murmured, eying Val with a worried expression. "Especially without your magic."

Neither Dida nor Adaira took offense at her words, and Val knew what the majitsu had meant. Dida was a bibliomancer, Adaira a healing-focused mage. Both could defend themselves and were powerful in their own right, but neither of them possessed Val's innate strength or offensive skill set.

Or a staff that can disembowel a teenage girl.

Val pressed his lips together, forcing the memory away. "She's right. I'll need to rest to regain power."

"I propose we start towards Badŏn," Adaira said, "and impose a half-day limit on the journey. If no better option arises by then, we camp on the nearest high ground."

"Reasonable enough, Your Highness," Rucker said. He started warily down the ridge, sword in hand. "I hope we last long enough for it to matter."

A wary, contemplative silence encased the group as they trudged single-file through the mossy terrain. Thankfully, the direction they chose was free of bogs. Val tried to focus on his surroundings, but the village girl's sightless eyes found his no matter where he looked, pleading for her future, asking why Val had taken her young life.

Adaira stepped beside him and squeezed his hand. "You didn't know," she said softly, gleaning the source of his distress.

"I lost control."

"You were trying to save me. They were trying to kill us."

Val lowered his head. Nothing mattered when you took a child's life, intentionally or not. The black sash gypsy he had crippled in New Victoria, Mari's murderer, flashed through his mind. While the violent act had made him ill, the man had deserved worse.

Nor did Val feel remorse about threatening Gowan, and even preparing to torture him if he didn't cooperate. Val had needed to find his brothers. He had given Gowan a choice. He would do it again if he must.

The same with the Dwyn. He had ordered his followers to kill Adaira. Val could protect himself and his loved ones with little remorse, though he now knew that the taking of another life, whether justified or not, took something from him, too.

But the redheaded girl had taken more than everyone else combined.

Much more.

Who am I? What have I become?

He blew out a breath and let Adaira's hand fall away. He didn't need sympathy or self-pity; he needed better control of his magic. He needed more spells. He needed to plumb the depths of his limits and increase his magical reserves, work to ensure he never had to blindly lash out again.

The party walked beside a steel-gray creek for the better part of an hour. After that, they skirted a boggy valley, picked their way across a boulder-strewn plateau, tramped up and down a series of hills and dales. Val analyzed his spells in his mind, trying to dissect how they worked, thinking of ways to improve his arsenal. The odds they faced seemed so daunting. A city full of demons? A terrifying entity named Asmodeus? A powerful and insane spirit mage whose head he was supposed to deliver to the queen?

They didn't even know the way back.

Five hours in, as they topped a hillock covered with stunted trees and dark green moss, another smudge of gray emerged out of the mist in the distance. A collection of granite stones too aligned and purposeful to be random. Hands gripping their weapons, the party pressed forward, eyes in constant movement. As they drew closer, Val realized they were looking at dozens—hundreds, even—of enormous standing stones formed into house-like structures of varying shapes and sizes.

Not houses, Val corrected himself.

Crypts.

They had stumbled upon an ancient cemetery.

Imposing and silent, the necropolis seemed rooted to the ground, present since the dawn of man, defying the ravages of time to protect its inhabitants from desecration. Runes and crude iconography marked many of the stones, and Val noticed a number of crosses with short arms and elongated bases carved into the granite.

"Well?" Dida asked. "Will this suffice?"

"Maybe," Rucker said, his eyes roaming the perimeter of the cemetery. "If it's not infested."

Val gripped his staff, shuddering as he remembered the ghouls in the tunnels beneath the Londyn graveyard. "Infested?"

The old adventurer waved a hand. "Demons, undead, scavengers. A cemetery's no place for the living."

The vaults and mausoleums sprawled across the moor with no apparent order or formal entrance. The party stepped warily past the perimeter, weapons
drawn, keeping a tight formation.

"We need a place we can barricade," Synne said.

Val noticed the tombs near the perimeter were either too small to be of use,
not enclosed, or had no visible door.

Rucker gripped his sword. "Aye."

"Adaira and I can seal one of the open tombs with a standing stone," Dida
said. "I can then set a ward."

Rucker grunted. "Not a bad plan."

Adaira pointed towards the center of the cemetery, where the top of a large
oval structure was visible. "I wonder what that is?"

Rucker twirled his sword and started walking. "It might be our inn."

As they delved deeper into the cemetery, Val had a strong sense of being
watched. In addition, a whiff of something foul lingered beneath the smell
of loamy earth and old stone. Perhaps a recent burial was the culprit, though
judging from the remoteness of the site and the besieged state of the villagers,
Val doubted anyone had visited the cemetery in some time.

He mentioned his suspicion to the others.

"There's something in here, all right," Rucker said. "The question is how
dangerous it is."

The structure Adaira had seen, a huge block of smooth gray granite looming over the center of the cemetery, came fully into view. Judging from the
seamless construction and the size of the mausoleum—fifteen-feet high with
at least a hundred foot diameter—Val guessed a wizard had been involved.

As they circled the giant tomb, they found a bronze door etched with three
lines of runes. On either side of the door, pillars protruded from the granite in
bas-relief, carved with intricate renditions of forest life.

Adaira and Dida stepped forward to study the runes. They started to translate at the same time, but Dida flourished and allowed Adaira to continue.

"Herein lies the tomb of Myrddin of the Demetae, Lord of the Wild and
Scourge of Albion, defeated in glorious battle in 1201."

Adaira's reading had slowed to a crawl by the time she finished, her face
pale. "But that can't be."

Val looked to the others, who also seemed disconcerted. He tried to remember his lesson about Myrddin at the Abbey. "1201. That was the Battle of Londyn, right? The one that established the Conclave?"

Adaira covered her mouth in horror. "The wizards didn't win here. But this place, it looks so old . . . I've been under the assumption that we had somehow traveled into the past—but could this be an alternate present? One where the druids and common born rule Albion, and wizards are still oppressed?"

Dida stepped forward to run his hands along the door. His head cocked to the side, contemplative. "The entire structure is warded. Quite powerfully, I might add."

Rucker snarled in annoyance. "Can you break them?"

"The rune craft is impressive. The wizard who made this was much stronger than I. But, yes, I can disrupt them. The technique is outdated. If I had to guess"—he looked at the bronze door and then at Adaira—"twelfth century is about right. The art of bibliomancy is much evolved since then."

Rucker turned in a wary circle, eying the cemetery, before letting his gaze rest on the open moor in the distance. "Assuming we get inside the tomb, how strong are your wards?"

"I scored four hundred and seventeen on the runic tensile exam," Dida said proudly, "and my strongest sigil-glyphic continuum possessed a density rating of thirteen psi."

"What the bloody hell does that mean?"

The bibliomancer stroked his chin. "For a space this size, I surmise I can effectively ward against an assault by most races of giants. Perhaps even a stone golem."

Rucker looked impressed.

"As for human wizards, it is unlikely that anyone below an elder mage could unravel a runic construct of my design. Excepting bibliomancers, of course." Dida bowed his head, embarrassed. "I am still quite young."

"Good enough for me," Rucker said. "Get us inside."

Synne grabbed Dida's forearm. "What if the tomb conceals something dangerous?"

"Unlikely," Adaira said. "Myrddin was a benign wizard—at least in our world—and did not keep worldly possessions. Nor was it customary in ancient Albion to safeguard tombs."

"Then why the wards?" Val asked.

"To prevent desecration, I would assume."

"Bah," Rucker said. "It matters not. We have to take a chance. We need rest."

It took Dida the better part of two hours to break the wards. A sense of foreboding plagued Val the entire time, and more than once he heard scuffing and gnawing sounds coming from the recesses of the cemetery. Small animals, Rucker surmised, after casing the immediate area and seeing nothing. A cane rat or a squirrel. Maybe a wild dog.

Remembering the ghouls outside Londyn, Val wasn't so sure.

Wiping sweat from his brow, Dida took a deep breath and pushed on the center of the crypt door.

It swung inward without a sound, and stale air rushed out of Myrddin's tomb. Adaira's light spell illuminated the interior with a weak sapphire glow, drawing from the veil of mist outside.

Frescoes of forest scenes covered the ancient stone walls. A ring of rune-covered pillars supported the high ceiling, and inside the circle, an azantite sarcophagus rested on a platform of green marble. The outline of a human figure was carved into the azantite.

"The walls and pillars are warded," Dida said, turning in a slow circle, "though not as strongly as the door. And the wards have degraded over time."

After ensuring nothing lurked in the recesses of the tomb, Rucker approached the coffin. "That's a king's bounty of azantite."

"I wouldn't touch that," Dida warned.

"It's warded, too?"

"Not on the outside. But the azantite will shield any wards hidden underneath."

Rucker slowly withdrew his hand.

"Are we in agreement," Dida said, "that this location will suffice? If so, I shall prepare our defenses."

No one dissented. Adaira left the door cracked, to allow sufficient airflow. A sealed entrance would not add much to Dida's wards, and he created the illusion of a closed door to discourage casual discovery.

Rucker and Synne guarded the entrance while Dida worked. The rest of the party laid down blankets and set out rations. After dinner, Val collapsed next to Adaira, too exhausted to take off his boots. A pillar shielded them from the others.

Adaira's light spell had dissolved into barely visible motes. Synne took first watch, sitting cross-legged by the entrance. As Adaira lay next to Val, the warm contours of her body fitting snugly against his side, she traced a finger along his cheek. He shifted to face her. Despite the chill of the tomb, heat rose through his body, and he had an overwhelming desire to press his lips against hers.

He moved to close the last few inches between them, aware of the warmth of her breath on his face. She put a finger between their mouths and said, "Are you ready to tell me what stands between us?"

Her hair brushed his cheek, and Val shuddered with attraction. As close as he had grown to Adaira, as much as he craved her touch, he didn't want the daughter of Lord Alistair to know that he was looking for his brothers. Better if they stayed off the Congregation's radar.

But he didn't want to lie to her, either. "It's not another woman."

He could see the relief in her eyes. She removed her finger and brushed her lips against his. "Whatever it is," she said in a throaty whisper, "you can trust me."

Val took her hand and interlaced their fingers. She had risked everything to join him, and he could see the depth of her feelings in her eyes. A starved radiance he suspected she had concealed from him for fear of rejection. Instead of shying away, he was surprised to find that he, too, was caught in the glow.

"One day," he whispered back.

She gave a sad smile in response. They lay facing each other in the darkness of the tomb, breathing the same breath, slipping silently into sleep.

"To arms!"

The voice was a shouted command in Val's dream. He shrugged it off, deep in slumber, but it came again and again, insistent and fierce.

"Raise yerselves, wizards! To arms!"

Rucker's voice. Val blinked and realized Synne was shaking him awake.

He jerked to his feet. Adaira leapt up beside him. Synne pointed to the far side of the tomb where, opposite the entrance, a shirtless male warrior formed of liquid silver stood watching them, holding a spear and shield formed of the same material. The figure looked oddly one-dimensional, as if cut from a mold.

Rucker stood between the group and the silver warrior. He held up his meat cleaver of a sword, backing away as his opponent advanced. Sheathing his longer blade, Rucker drew his hunting knife and sent it spinning through the air at high speed. The being melted and flowed to the side—Val could describe it no other way—then reformed as a wolf of the same color and with the same flat dimensions, head reared in a soundless howl.

Val felt air *whoosh* by as Adaira tried to push the thing back. The gale passed right through it.

The wolf advanced with ungainly steps, as if it had just learned to walk. Rucker stepped forward and connected with his sword, cleaving through its torso. The liquid silver closed behind the slash as if it had never been cut.

Rucker looked down at his sword and cursed. The middle portion had blackened and started to crumble where it had touched the wolf. After a moment, the entire blade turned to dust.

Synne darted forward. Rucker dropped the useless hilt and fell back. The wolf melted and reformed into a cloaked figure holding a staff with a raven's head. Synne sparred with the figure, blocking its blows with hardened skin and delivering blow after blow of her own, though the creature evaded each one by melting and reforming before her eyes.

"It changes too fast," she yelled.

"Wizards, what is this creature?" Rucker called out.

Adaira backed towards the entrance. "I've no idea."

Dida's hands waved through the air. "Neither me. But it walks through my Shield Runes as if they were air."

The cloaked figure seemed to be gaining in coordination, and Val realized the staff had disappeared and it was fighting like Synne, utilizing the magic-infused martial arts system peculiar to the majitsu.

Was it *copying* her?

The thing broke through the majitsu's defenses, landing a blow to her left arm. Synne screamed, and her elbow blackened where the being had touched it.

"Step back, Synne," Val said coldly. He had slept enough to recover most of his power, and he felt the magic thrumming through him, begging to be released. Synne dove away as he summoned Spirit Fire and sent it arcing into the cloaked figure. The thing exploded into a million drops of silver and yet, before the drops hit the ground, they reformed into a shiny oak tree, a dozen branches lashing out at the party.

The tip of a branch caught Val on the back of the hand. Pain seared through him, as bad as the time he had thrust his hand into molten lava to pass the Abbey's entrance exam. He screamed, stumbled backward, and lost his grip on his magic.

"I've no answers," Rucker shouted. "Fall back! Into the cemetery!"

Everyone raced for the entrance. The creature morphed again, this time into a beautiful woman with a mournful expression and her hair in a waist-length braid. Faster than Val could follow, the silver woman streaked forward, cutting off Adaira's access to the bronze door. Adaira had no choice but to fly backwards. The creature held out its hands as if imploring her for something, then walked towards the cuerpomancer, cutting Adaira off whenever she tried to escape, trapping her against the far wall. Adaira flew straight up but the woman rose with her. Adaira descended and, out of options, fingered her black choker and shrank against the wall. Silver hands reached for her throat.

"No!" Val roared. Spirit Fire had already proved ineffective, so he knew Adaira's choker wouldn't help her. Without thinking, he flung a hand through the air, sending the azantite sarcophagus flying across the room with a burst of power. It thudded into the silver woman and pinned her against the wall.

"Run!" Rucker cried. "While it's down!"

Val met Adaira in the middle of the room, took her by the hand, and they flew out of the entrance together. On the way out, his eye caught some of the recurring images on the frescoes covering the walls: wolves baying in the forest, cloaked figures striding through the woods, fair maidens lounging under oak trees with forlorn expressions.

When he and Adaira exited the tomb, they found the others surrounded by a horde of grave wights with maggot-eaten faces and ragged clothing. Before the party could take flight or formulate a plan, the wights attacked, pressing forward with grasping hands.

The shape-shifting creature from the tomb, still in maiden form, burst out of the door behind them. It might have been Val's imagination, but he thought she looked less substantial than before. She grabbed a wight from behind and the undead creature dissolved in her grasp, blackening and then crumbling into ash.

Val paled. That could have been Adaira. Everyone scrambled to get out of the thing's reach, even risking the unclean touch of the wights. Val pushed a group of them back with hardened air, but more poured in to replace them. There were dozens of the filthy things.

Despite cradling her injured arm, Synne attacked like a spinning top. Having lost his sword, Rucker fought with his spiked vambrace and helm and boot spurs, knocking back wight after wight as he tried to reach Dida and Adaira, who were surrounded. Forced to take flight, the two mages rose defenseless above the fray. The silver woman followed Adaira, flowing through the air faster than the cuerpomancer could fly, and forced her back down.

They were losing the battle. Val had to do something. He cleared away a group of wights with Spirit Fire, then thought about what had happened inside the tomb. What he had seen. He still didn't understand what the thing was, but he had an idea.

"Everyone back inside!" he screamed. "Adaira, you and I go last!"

One by one, the party fought their way back to the tomb. Instead of attacking the silver maiden, who seemed impervious to magic, Val used a wizard wind to send wights flying at her to distract her. When everyone but he and Adaira had scurried inside, the silver maiden came straight for her, just as Val had planned. He grabbed Adaira and they flew into the tomb together.

Seeming more at ease with her form, yet even less corporeal, the silver maiden tore through the wights like a scythe through grass, steps behind Val and Adaira. It was going to be close. As soon as they entered the tomb, he summoned his remaining power and, with a gargantuan effort, picked up the fallen lid of the azantite sarcophagus and shoved it upright across the doorway, blocking the entrance.

Darkness. Silence.

Rucker lit a torch.

As everyone tensed, waiting for the creature to burst into the tomb, Dida gasped for breath and patted Val on the back. "Quick thinking, my friend. Azantite is the only thing that has slowed it."

"Except now we're stuck in here with limited air and a very angry . . . *something* . . . on the outside," Rucker said. "In all my years, I've never seen such a creature."

Val pointed out the frescoes on the wall that corresponded to the entity's various forms. "I don't know what it means, but I think it was mimicking the artwork."

Everyone turned to view the forest scenes. Rucker stepped closer and squinted, then sucked in a breath. "By the Queen. Yer right, boy."

"Was it put here by an ancient wizard?" Adaira wondered. "Surviving all this time?"

Dida was staring thoughtfully at the wall. He ran a hand down one of the rune-inscribed pillars. "Perhaps it was not a guardian. If not dispelled, all wards disintegrate over time, though the most powerful can last for hundreds—thousands—of years. These oldest of wards have been known to slowly dissolve and can . . . leak . . . magic."

Adaira frowned. "I've heard of this phenomenon, but how does that account for the creature we fought?"

"Given the power in these runes and the time that has passed . . ." Dida shrugged. "I cannot be sure, but I suspect the entity was a residue of old magic. Ignited perhaps by oxygen or even our light spell, forming a half-life, imitating the only forms it knew."

"So magic—spirit—is *alive*?" Val said.

"No one knows the answer to that question," Dida said.

Adaira shivered. "How do we fight it when we leave?"

Dida stroked his chin. "Did anyone notice that it seemed less substantial before we re-entered the tomb? My guess is that it will dissipate with time, absorbed into spirit."

"How long?" Rucker growled.

"Hours, perhaps."

"And if yer wrong?"

No one had an answer.

As they waited inside the tomb, Adaira tended to Synne on one of the blankets. Half of the majitsu's arm had blackened from contact with the silver entity, and she couldn't seem to bend it. Adaira closed her eyes and laid her hands atop the wound.

The back of Val's hand had also blackened, and he watched in pain while

Adaira worked. Though he had lost the use of his hand, he could still cast spells. The loss of Synne's fighting prowess would be catastrophic.

While Adaira worked on the majitsu, and Dida puttered around the runes and scrollwork, Val shook off his pain and followed Rucker to the sarcophagus of Myrddin he had tossed across the room. He felt a heaviness descend as they approached the remains of the legendary wizard. Alternate reality or not, this was a man who had affected the course of history on at least two different worlds.

Hesitant and looking strangely bare—but not defenseless—without his wide-bladed sword in hand, Rucker leaned over the tomb. Val stepped beside him and peered inside.

It was a fleshless corpse like any other, gray and lifeless, a discarded puppet of bone. But the remains of Myrddin were not the only contents of the tomb.

A gleaming battle-axe lay across the torso of the corpse, clutched in spindly fingers. Strange, rune-like markings covered the weapon's azantite handle, and a parallel latticework of silver lines, like the branching of a tree, had been engraved into each half of the two-sided blade.

After finding no sign of a trap, Rucker eased the weapon out of the skeleton's grasp. The twin blades flared like the wings of a bat. He gave it a few expert twirls. "Azantite handle, and the weight's not too different from me own blade." He spat. "Like a son to me, it was. Took it off the champion of the Sultan of Mazdag."

Val wondered just how many lifetimes of adventure Rucker had experienced.

And why an aging, one-armed warrior, tough as he was, had risked his life to follow someone he barely knew into the void.

"Why'd you come here, Rucker?" Val said softly, out of earshot of the others.

"I told ye why."

"And I didn't believe you. I just didn't ask any questions."

"Then don't start now."

Rucker wheeled and stomped back to the entrance. Val had no choice but to let him go. On a hunch, he inspected the tomb more closely, tracing his fingers along the cool surface of the azantite and finding nothing. He tried probing in another way, with his magic.

He concentrated on pushing his mind through the azantite, working his way around the sarcophagus. Just beneath the skull of Myrddin, he felt a weak spot in the seemingly impenetrable stone. Val gently lifted the base of the skull and pushed against the surface of the tomb. The pressure of his hand alone did not suffice, so he supplemented again with his mind.

And felt his hand slip through the surface of the azantite, into a concealed opening the size of a grapefruit. Just wide enough for a hand to fit through.

He probed the compartment and felt a metal object inside. Smooth. Circular. A ring.

Val took it out and examined it. Formed of a bluish-white material similar to Salomon's keys, the ring was crafted in the shape of the ouroboros, a serpent eating its own tail.

The same symbol used by the Myrddinus.

Intrigued but wary, Val pocketed the ring, not yet ready to slip it on. When he returned to the others, Adaira was shaking her head, though Synne's arm looked much improved.

"What happened?"

"It was beyond my power," she said. "I had to use one of the healing jars. The entire contents."

Val laid a hand on Synne's shoulder. "How does it feel?"

"Fine," she said curtly, as if embarrassed by the display of weakness.

"You're next," Adaira said to Val. "Where's the final jar?"

"In my pack." He shook his head. "I think we should save it. It hurts, but I can still work magic."

"We don't know what effect that wound has," Adaira said. "I worry if untreated, it will seep into your blood."

"She's right," Rucker said. "Yer the only one who has a chance of getting us back home. We can't risk ye."

They compromised on using half the jar. Adaira worked on the back of his hand, using both the healing salve and her own magic, until the pain disappeared and a pink scar formed.

Val let out a long breath. "Thank you."

After that, he sat with his back against a pillar, simmering in silence and dark thoughts as everyone waited for the air to thin. The death of the girl was still fresh on his mind, a stain of a memory he feared would never go away.

"It's time," Rucker said at last.

Val had started to grow dizzy from the lack of oxygen. He rose to his feet and, worried the silver creature might be waiting for them, slipped the ring he had taken from the tomb onto his left index finger. As far as he could tell, there was no effect.

Synne stood poised at the entrance. When Rucker gave the signal, Val moved the azantite lid and, before anyone could protest, flew out of the tomb with his staff raised.

Scores of blackened, unmoving bodies were piled up outside the bronze door. Wights. Val blew them back, clearing the way. He stepped farther out, adrenaline surging, his head on a swivel as he strained for a glimpse of silver.

Nothing.

The party didn't delay. Bunched together, they picked their way through the bodies and around the maze of deserted stone tombs, Val's stomach fluttering every time they stepped out from behind a mausoleum. The silver maiden never appeared, seeming to validate Dida's hypothesis that the eldritch magic had dissipated into spirit.

They left the graveyard and returned to the windswept moor.

24

As Will descended through the illusion, he saw a wide stone staircase leading to the next level. A soft silver glow, the color of a clear stream in moonlight, illuminated the steps.

Will shuddered with relief when the scorpions didn't follow them down. Once they reached the bottom, Mateo moaned and clutched his petrified hand. The stone extended from his fingertips to an inch past his wrist, and was still progressing.

Mala approached with her sword raised.

"No!" Selina cried. She flung herself at Mateo, but Mala pulled the sylvamancer away. "If we don't arrest the poison, we will lose him."

Mateo raised his arm. "Do it," he said, through clenched teeth.

Will stepped forward, forcing the words out. "Let me. The blow will be cleaner."

"What if your sword destroys him?" Selina said. "Like the others?"

Will hesitated. He didn't think the sword would affect any part of Mateo other than his stone hand, but he had no way of being certain.

"Hurry!" Gunnar said. "Before he loses more than a hand."

Mateo waffled, then held his arm out towards Mala. Will nodded and gripped his cousin's good hand for support. Selina kissed him and stepped back, tears blurring her eyes. Mala raised her short sword, counted to three, and brought the enhanced blade down in a swift blow, slicing cleanly through Mateo's wrist just a millimeter past the stone.

The petrified hand thudded against the floor. Mateo sagged and squeezed Will's hand, but didn't cry out. As blood spurted from the wound, Mala pulled a cloth from one of her pouches and wrapped the wound tight.

"Give him a potion," Selina said.

"We only have two left," Mala said.

The sylvamancer stepped forward, eyes blazing. "Give it to him!"

Mateo grimaced. "She's right," he said to Selina, his voice laced with pain. "I've already used one."

"He can't fight like this," Selina said to Mala. "Surely you understand *that*, if not sympathy?"

Mala stared back at her, eyes unreadable. "We can spare enough to seal the wound." After unwrapping Mateo's hand, she took another stoppered bottle from her pouch, and poured a few drops onto the wound.

Mateo's eyes rolled back as the potion took effect. Will kept his grip on his cousin's hand, gaping as the bleeding stopped and the flesh around the wound congealed. When it was finished, Mateo fumbled to take his water skin out of his pack with one hand. Selina rushed to help him. Will looked away, distraught, and studied their new surroundings. The staircase had brought them to the center of a spherical room crafted entirely from black marble. Eight archways signaled exits from the chamber.

"Where's the light source?" Will asked. "Has this been lit for thousands of years?"

"More likely a delayed spell," Selina said. "Triggered by our entrance."

"How did you know?" Mala asked Gunnar. In the excitement, everyone seemed to have forgotten he had saved them all.

The big man looked embarrassed. "I read a tome on Mayan culture before we left. A corpse with an owl head is an avatar for the Mayan god of death, and I thought the statue might be symbolic. Telling us that death lies below."

A moment of silence followed the humble admission. Mala squeezed his arm and kissed him on the cheek. "We should all have been so wise. Thank you."

Will fought against the pang of jealousy that swept through him. He had been right about Mala's taste in men—she didn't suffer fools.

Gunnar was proving himself more worthy at every turn.

"Those statues . . ." Selina said, casting an uneasy glance at the staircase. "Were they the sorcerer king's friends, or his enemies?"

Will gripped his sword. "Does it matter? No one deserves that."

"At least three were Alazashin, dressed in the fashions of the last century," Mala said. "One of them bore the insignia of a Prince of the Seven Mountains. Certainly the highest ranking member on the mission." She approached one of the archways and ran her hands over it, then made her way around the room, inspecting each one. Beyond the archways, identical tunnels of black marble curved out of sight, illuminated by the same silver light.

No one had any insight as to which passage to choose. Mala pursed her lips and selected an archway at random, creeping down the corridor with sword and dagger drawn. Everyone fell into step behind her. The air smelled clean and fresh, as if purified. A hundred feet down, the curving passage intersected with another corridor that twisted deeper into the interior.

They kept to the original tunnel. Another intersection appeared, and then another. Because of the non-linear nature of the passageways, it was impossible for Will to keep track of which direction they were headed.

"We're bearing mostly northwest," Mala said, consulting her compass as if reading Will's thoughts.

Assuming they were inside a pyramid, the corridor couldn't last forever. Mala marked their way with chalk to ensure they weren't moving in a giant circle. The passage soon spilled into a small alcove. A silver lever with a star-shaped handle was set into the center of the far wall.

Before approaching, Mala made sure the floor and walls were clear of traps. "Do you detect any magic?" she asked.

Selina shook her head, still cross with her.

Unsure what to do, Mala placed her hand on the lever without pulling it. Will walked over to inspect the vertical slot where it fit into the wall. "It should move," he said. "There's a three-inch gap."

"Everyone out," Mala said, without turning. "There's no reason to put the whole party in danger."

After the others backed out of the chamber, Will stayed and put his hand over Mala's, on top of the star-shaped handle. She looked up at him, eyes hard but grateful, and they pulled the silver handle together.

It slid to the bottom of the slot with minimal resistance, making a barely perceptible grinding sound. Will felt her hands tense, but nothing happened. The lever stayed in the bottom position. Mala removed her hand. Will pushed the lever back up, then down again. Still no effect. He shrugged and returned it to the original position.

They informed the others and kept walking. After trying one of the side passages, they came to another silver lever with a star-shaped handle.

Same procedure. Same result.

More exploration led to more levers, curving intersection after curving intersection. It was too convoluted for Will to keep the pattern in his head. He suggested they make a map, and Mala withdrew a mother-of-pearl fountain pen and a moleskin notebook from one of her pouches. Will helped her chart where they had walked so far, denoting the chambers with a silver lever.

They resumed walking, everyone on high alert. Will mapped as they went, leaving Mala free to inspect for traps. Despite the gravity of the situation, Will couldn't help but think of mapping dungeons on graph paper during a D&D campaign back home, snacking on Doritos and Mountain Dew with his gaming friends while Caleb disappeared into the bedroom with some girl.

Thinking of home caused a pang of ache for his brothers so strong it made his knees go weak. Yet the memory also caused him to flex his sword arm and notice how his muscles rippled. Muscles he had never had before, not even as a contractor. Muscles that could hold their own against delver warriors, Mayan Battle Mages, and creatures out of nightmare.

Things had changed a little since back home.

Pay attention, Will.

They found another twenty-seven levers. Mateo peered over Will's shoulder, his eyes widening. "It's very detailed."

"Yeah," Will said. "I sort of see it in my head. How," he hesitated, "does it feel?"

His cousin's eyes slid to the stump of his left hand. "The pain is mostly gone. But it . . . I won't be the same warrior. Not without my buckler."

"You're better than most without it. Aren't there shields that attach to the forearm?"

Mateo glanced away.

"I've been wondering," Will said, both to distract his cousin and because he was curious, "about my father's home. The Blackwood Forest."

"You've never been?"

"No."

Mateo's eyes took on a faraway cast. "It's the most beautiful place on Urfe. Trees that kiss the clouds, meadows as bright as the sun, streams as fresh as snow."

"Is it peaceful?"

"In a wild and rugged way, yes. No place in the Ninth Protectorate is free of danger. But it's a good life, Will. *Our* life. Free to live as we please." He clenched his good hand. "If something isn't done, all of that will change. We've been living a fantasy, believing the Congregation will leave us in peace."

"How long has our family lived there?"

Mateo shrugged. "Five hundred years? Six? They say we're descendants of Fieran Blackwood, you know."

Will marked the position of another silver lever. "Who?"

Mateo chuckled. "I forget you're not from the Realm. Still, has the lore of Fieran Blackwood not reached your ears? He was a true Paladin, perhaps the last. He fought for Priestess Nirela at the battle of Lupen-Breza." His mirth faded, and Will gathered the battle was important. And had not gone well.

"The Paladins—Tamás mentioned them. Who were they?"

Pride infused Mateo's voice. "The most powerful common-born fighting force in the history of our people. Perhaps in all the Realm. They were loyal to the High Clerics of Devla, and unable to be bought. Incorruptible."

"Every man has a weakness," Will muttered, his eyes flicking towards Mala.

"True enough, my cousin. But the Paladins were special. Some say the High Clerics imbued them with unique holy powers. If only we lived in such a time..."

Interesting, Will thought. His father used to tell stories about the exploits of the twelve paladins of Charlemagne. Zariduke was Charlemagne's sword. Had true Paladins been sent to Earth to protect the sword?

At the next intersection, Selina stopped and looked up. Will followed her gaze and saw a green mist seeping out of the ceiling. He whipped around. Down each corridor, the vaporous green substance had infused the air, mixing eerily with the silver light.

Will couldn't smell whatever insidious gas was being emitted, but as soon as it reached his nose and mouth, he and everyone else began to cough.

"Acid Smoke," Mala said, covering her nose and mouth with her hand. "If we don't find the exit soon, it will kill us all."

The gas tickled the back of Will's throat, and he couldn't seem to stop coughing as everyone sprinted down the passage in a desperate attempt to out-run the toxic clouds of smoke seeping into the black-walled maze.

"How long?" he asked, trying not to inhale the lime-green gas.

"I would say we'd be dead already," Mala said, "except we're still on our feet. The concentration must be weaker."

Mateo cast a worried glance at Selina, who was coughing heavily. "A test, then," he said grimly. "Escape the maze before the gas kills us."

"Aye."

Everywhere they ran, the acid smoke was present, seeping into the corridors from the ceiling, swirling within the soft silver light. The toxic substance had infused the entire level. Seeking an escape, the party backtracked to the staircase and huddled in the middle of the room, choking and coughing. Will felt his limbs weakening.

Gunnar bounded up the stairs, reaching for the ceiling. Instead of pushing through an illusion, his hands met solid stone. He felt around in disbelief.

"A one-way illusion," Selina said, with a mixture of dread and awe. "We're trapped."

"There's a way out," Will said. "We just have to find it in time."

"The levers must be important," Mala said. "They're the only anomaly."

"I agree. But why?"

"Pull them all?" Mateo offered.

Will frowned. "It seems too simple. And I doubt we have time."

"Do you have a better idea?" Selina asked, and then doubled over coughing. "We have to try something."

Will looked down at the map. They had found over one hundred levers, the positioning of which appeared to be random. Judging from the map, he estimated they had covered three-fourths of the level. The short, twisty passages formed no discernible pattern. "I vote for finishing the map."

"Is there time?" Gunnar asked, with a worried look at Mala. Uncharacteristically, and though she tried to hide it, she seemed the most affected by the gas. Will wondered if her slight frame made her more susceptible to the poison.

He jerked his gaze away and studied the map. It was hard to be sure, but he guessed they had been down there for an hour and a half. Which made sense, if the twisted creator of the maze had given them just enough time to map it. "I think we can do it. If we hurry."

"What if it's a waste of time?" Selina asked.

"What if it's not?" he snapped.

Mala was already walking towards one of the two archways they had yet to try. The others hurried to keep up, and as they ran through the silent passageways, Will sketched as quickly as he could. More levers appeared, and Will racked his brain to find a pattern.

Should he assign a number or letter value to the levers? Did they form a word, a symbol?

A terrible thought: what if the levers were a distraction? Nothing but a cruel twist? What if the exit was another illusory wall, or a secret door they had passed without noticing?

"Remind me what we know of the sorcerer king," Will said as they ran. His fingers and toes had numbed, and breathing had become a chore. They had all slowed to a trot to conserve what strength they had left.

"The Calakmul Empire reached its height under Yiknoom Uk'ab K'ahk'," Mala said. "He was known to be absolutely ruthless in battle, a legendary commander as well as the most powerful sorcerer of his era. His enemies called him the Crocodile of Calakmul. A vain man, he preferred the titles his constituents bestowed: Emperor of the Stars, Bull of the Heavens, Supreme Ruler, Lord of All Suns. He loved gems and coin and arcane items, and he sent his mercenaries across Urfe on missions of plunder. Some say there has never been a treasure amassed such as his, not before or since."

"Did he have a special number or word?" Will asked. "A favorite child, pet, staff?"

"I've no idea," Mala said. "Gunnar?"

The big man coughed. "He had hundreds of concubines, and thousands of children. He respected the Egyptian and Babylonian wizard-kings, saw them as gods among men like himself, but . . ." He gave a helpless shrug.

"What about the number of pyramids he built?" Will asked, growing desperate. "Cities he conquered, battles he won? *Anything*."

Gunnar looked down.

Will's hand shook as they rounded a corner and found a final lever, completing the map. The toxin had started to affect his nervous system, blurring his vision and making him dizzy.

The central staircase was just around the corner, through the eighth archway. As they returned to the starting point, Will took a deep, shuddering breath and laid the map on the stone floor. The others crowded around.

"So many levers," Selina said. "We'll never reach them all in time."

She was right, Will knew. He wanted to kick himself for not pulling the levers from the beginning, just in case, but they had worried about pulling the wrong one, and had not anticipated the acid smoke.

Mala was on her hands and knees, probing the bottom of the staircase. Gunnar struck portions of the black marble wall with his gloved fist, over and over, to no effect. Selina paced back and forth, deep in concentration, searching for a trail of magic.

Will stared at the map so hard his eyes hurt. He knew in his gut the answer was in the seemingly random placement of the levers.

Think, Will. Where are you? What is this place? Who built it?

He glanced at the walls and silver light infusing the chamber, thought about the odorless air, the levers, and the various titles attached to the sorcerer king. *Supreme Ruler. Emperor of the Stars.*

He looked again at the black marble walls and ceiling, then down at the map. The dots represented levers with star-shaped handles.

Stars sprinkled among a web of black passageways, lit by a silver glow. His skin tingled with knowledge.

The entire level was a representation of the night sky, the heavens above.

And the levers were the stars.

"They're constellations!" he shouted, springing to his feet and pointing at the map. "That's the pattern—we're looking for a constellation!"

It was obvious, once he knew what he was looking at, that the levers formed star patterns. He was no astronomy expert, but he recognized Orion and a few others. And the biggest star of all—the sun—was the spherical room in which they were standing.

Faces pale, the others stumbled to his side in the green mist. Will rushed through his theory. Mateo and Gunnar clapped him weakly on the back, and Mala put her palms on the stone floor beside the map and peered at the images.

"Yiknoom fancied himself a ruler of heaven and earth," she said, after a coughing session bent her double. "Yet even if you're right, do we know anything about Mayan constellations?"

"I know a little," Gunnar said, almost shyly. Will's light-headedness had progressed, and he found it rather absurd that, with everyone coughing and slowly dying from acid smoke poisoning, their brutish fighter turned Mayan scholar might be their only hope for survival.

"The Mayans spent a lot of time studying the stars," Gunnar continued, "so all the books talked about it. I know a few of their favorite constellations, but I don't know their positions in the sky."

"Give us what you have," Mala said. "Quickly, now."

Gunnar rattled them off. "Turkey, scorpion, death god, vulture, sun lord, night lord, maize god, armadillo, crocodile."

"The Crocodile of Calakmul!" Mateo cried. "The Lord of all Suns! But that's two that match—which one do we choose?"

Will scanned the drawn faces of the group. Eyelids drooping, hands twitching, no one was able to speak without coughing.

They didn't have time for a mistake.

Gunnar leaned over Mala as she lay on her side, choking. "Will a healing potion help?"

Selina shook her head. "It would buy her a few minutes, at most. The gas would simply re-enter her system.

Everyone seemed to be looking to Will to decide. He ran a hand through his hair, all too aware of the price of failure. "The Lord of all Suns is my choice," he said finally. "From what you said, that's the legacy he would prefer. Not the image of a crocodile."

From the ground, Mala nodded in silent agreement.

Will asked the question he was afraid to ask. "Does anyone know the stars in the Mayan constellations?"

"That one, yes," Gunnar said, and Will released the breath he was holding. "It mirrors one of our own."

The warrior bent over the map and pointed out seven stars Will knew as the Big Dipper. Part of Ursa Major. Will didn't waste any time: he assigned everyone a single star except for himself and Gunnar, who he assigned two. The group hovered over the map, memorizing the route to their designated lever. Will knew if his guess was off, or if someone pulled the wrong lever, they were doomed.

As the party lurched to their feet, Will couldn't shake the feeling that something was off. That the choice between the two constellations had been too easy.

It smelled of a red herring, and he remembered something Gunnar had said about Yiknoom. "Wait!" he shouted. "Gunnar—didn't you say the sorcerer king revered the Babylonians?"

"Yes," he said, giving Mala a worried glance behind her back. "And?"

"Do you have the common zodiac here?" Will asked.

Mala scoffed. "Of course. I've known it since I was a child."

"Yiknoom revered the zodiac," Gunnar added.

"That's interesting," Will said, "because the common zodiac comes from the Babylonians. Who he also revered." As eyebrows rose around the group, he continued, "Can anyone pick out the constellations?"

"I can," Selina said. "Which one?"

Will ticked the zodiac signs off in his head, then gave a grim, satisfied smile. There was only one choice, and it felt right. He could feel it in his bones. "Taurus."

"The Bull of the Heavens!" Mateo said. "Another of Yiknoom's favorite names."

Selina hurried to point out eleven stars forming the horns and body of the bull.

"Choosing between two seems too random," Will said. "Taurus is my choice."

Everyone agreed. Will divided up the levers again, this time taking three for himself. He gave three more to Gunnar, and two each for Mateo and Selina.

"What about—" Mala said, coughing too hard to finish her sentence. She started to swoon, and Will caught her.

"You're coming with me," he said, sheathing his sword and scooping her in his arms.

Gunnar looked ready to protest, but Will didn't give him the opportunity. He didn't know how much the toxic gas had affected the big warrior, or how much mental fortitude he possessed. Nor did Will care. He knew how far he had to carry Mala to pull the levers, and, despite his lethargy and coughing fits, he *knew* he could do it. Knew he could press through the pain and poison and whatever else it took to have a chance of saving the mysterious dark-haired girl hanging limply in his arms.

When he looked down at the greenish pallor of Mala's skin and heard the rattle of her breathing, he felt as terrified as he ever had, even when cocooned alive in the web of the spider people. He didn't understand why she affected him so much, but then again, he had never understood anything about love.

Stay with me, Mala.

Everyone sprinted in opposite directions. With his sword swaying on his back, Will ran as fast as he could down the corridor, cradling her like a child. "Put me down," she said, though her whisper sounded far away. "I can walk."

He ignored her.

"Will the Builder." She tried to wag a finger. "This is my expedition."

He took a right turn, past two intersections and down a long passage on his left. The first lever came into view. He raced to it, pulled, and kept on running.

She reached up to stroke his cheek. "Will the Builder."

"What?"

She giggled. "What's your favorite color?"

Will ran faster.

As the black-walled corridors flew by, enmeshed in silver light, it did feel as if he was racing through the night sky, reaching for the grandeur of the stars.

Her arms were wrapped around his neck. After a prolonged coughing fit, she buried her face in his chest and released a deep sigh.

"Don't fall asleep!" he shouted. He rounded a corner and saw a long passage leading to the second lever on his route. He shook Mala to keep her awake, and she laughed lightly. "You play rough. Do you know what I like about you . . ."

She trailed off, the light in her eyes dimming. *No*, he whispered to himself. *You have to stay with me.*

Two more right turns, then a straightaway. His legs felt full of lead, arms cramping from the strain. A curve to the left. Mala sank in his grasp, her head lolling to the side. After two more intersections, the final star-shaped handle came into view, gleaming at the end of the passage. Drool seeped out of Mala's mouth. He had no idea how many levers the others had reached, whether his plan would work, or what would happen if it did.

Gasping for breath as she slipped in his arms, he stumbled the final few feet to the lever and shifted her prone form to his left hand, sweating under the strain. With his right, he reached out to grasp the star-shaped handle.

And pulled with all the strength he had left.

25

Caleb woke on his back beside a silver stream. Dawn light filtered through the trees. Marguerite lay beside him, stroking his hair. A few feet away, the Brewer had started a fire and was heating something in a small pot.

As Caleb blinked and sat up, Marguerite leaned on an elbow and smiled. She smelled good, like warm spice and a buttery leather jacket. "There you are, love," she said.

"What happened?" Caleb asked. He felt groggy but fine.

The Brewer glanced over. "What's the last thing you remember?"

"Singing. Rolling." He shuddered. "Almost being turned into a giant mushroom."

"I held them off long enough to get away, and they didn't give chase. Fairies never stray far from their rings." The Brewer took the pot off the fire and lined up three tin cups. "Coffee?"

"Yeah. Thanks. And thanks for saving our lives." Caleb turned to Marguerite. "How'd you find us?"

"I was afraid I'd lost ye, honestly. When ye never came back, I noticed all the mushrooms and figured the fairies took ye. I slept during the day and searched the forest at night, looking for a ring. They never pop up in the same place twice. I s'pose I got lucky."

Caleb swallowed. *Lucky.*

"But I wouldn't 'ave given up," she said, staring him in the face. "Not ever."

He drew her close and gave her a long kiss.

The Brewer took his coffee and sat by the stream, grinning into the morning sun. "Didn't think I'd ever see another sunrise."

"So, the singing," Caleb said. "Are you a wizard?"

The Brewer laughed. "Hardly. Back home, music has power, too. Its own kind of magic. Just not as strong as over here. Whatever ability I had to affect people with my music . . . it's amplified on Urfe. By a lot."

"So you're some kind of . . . bard?"

"You can call it that, sure. There are others like me." He grinned again. "Though none who can belt out a Freddie Mercury tune."

With his brothers gone, it felt incredibly comforting to talk to someone from back home. "Where's the flask? If I ever needed a drink, it's after that experience."

Marguerite looked him in the eye. "Didn't ye notice the horses are gone? Someone raided the camp the first night I went looking for ye, including the grog. We only have the pack I was carrying."

"Oh."

"The Brewer's going with us to the Blackwood Forest," she said. "He'll help us forage and drink from the streams."

"Safety in numbers," he said, glancing at Marguerite and then back at Caleb. "If you don't mind."

"Nah, man, that's great," Caleb said, and meant it. "Where're you headed after that?"

"Dunno. I've been wandering the Ninth since I landed here. Don't care for the Congregation too much. The only thing worse than religion is being told I can't have one."

Caleb chuckled. "Word."

Marguerite looked confused by the conversation, and Caleb knew they needed to have a long talk, very soon.

Luckily, she had a compass in her pack, and they headed north, towards the Blackwood Forest. As they trekked through the pine needle-strewn wood, the two men chatted about home, forging an instant bond. The Brewer wasn't sure how long he had been on Urfe, though he estimated ten years. His last year back home was 2002. It made Caleb's head hurt to think about the time differential, so he didn't bother. Will had come to believe that it swung erratically and was impossible to pinpoint.

The Brewer gathered berries and roots as they walked. After they set camp and had dinner, he sang a few songs for them, which helped relieve Caleb's itch for a drink. Long and deep and haunting, one song in particular moved Marguerite to tears, and made Caleb feel calm and reflective.

"Did you learn that here?" he asked, not recognizing the language.

"Icelandic ballad," the Brewer said, his voice faraway. "Beautiful, isn't it?" He lay on his back with his hands clasped behind his head. Minutes later he was snoring.

Caleb drew Marguerite close, gazing at the stars while he whispered in her ear. "I've missed you."

"More than the grog?"

He kissed her neck until she purred. "Much more."

"More than any other woman?"

Caleb thought about it and gave an honest answer. "By a long shot."

His hands moved under her shirt, and she cupped his face in her palms. "Now there's the man I once knew."

Over the next few days, as they traipsed through the beautiful and unspoiled wilderness of the Barrier Coast, Caleb felt at peace for the first time in a very long while. Happy, even. More so than back home, except for missing his brothers.

And the main reason was Marguerite.

He and the gray-eyed rogue fell into a natural rhythm, made easy by their mutual attraction. They frolicked through fields of wildflowers, bathed in streams, and spent long nights in each other's arms after the Brewer fell asleep. Caleb loved how she stretched like a cat in the morning and how her brow furrowed as she wrote poetry in her vellum notebook as the sun went down. She kept him laughing and never judged. Even her disapproval of his drunken state in Freetown, he knew, came from a desire to see him whole.

A born storyteller, the Brewer entertained them with countless tales from Urfe and back home. He had traveled up and down the Ninth, from the Sea of Grass to the Burning Desert, from the Lost Islands to the tops of the Fǎgras Peaks. He had braved a dragon's lair and explored the ruins of lost civilizations, wooed a dryad princess and played the lyre at the court of a mountain troll king, stolen an egg from a rukh's nest and sold it to an ogre-mage.

Or so he said. Somehow, Caleb believed him.

One afternoon, a passing line of Devla worshippers, clad in gray caftans and bearing the distinctive triangle of blue dots on the backs of their hands and foreheads, forced Caleb and the others to scurry off the trail and take refuge in the trees. Unlike the last group they had seen, these worshippers carried staves with sharpened ends in addition to their scrolls.

"You're afraid of them?" he asked the Brewer.

"They've never done me harm, but I've never seen them armed, either. Makes me nervous."

"Is there a God in yer world?" Marguerite asked.

The night before, Caleb had told Marguerite that he and the Brewer hailed from a world across the stars. He told her with a sly wink, ready to pretend he was joking, but she took it as she did everything else: calmly, with a dash of good humor and a helping of practicality. *That explains the oddities*, she had said.

Oddities?

The way you move, talk, make love to me. It's different, eh? Otherworldly.

The Brewer had explained to Caleb that morning that, in a place where spirit mages traveled the dimensions and fought among the stars, it was easier for people to conceive of life on other worlds.

"We have lots of people who think there's a God," Caleb said with a dismissive wave of his hand, in answer to Marguerite's question.

"I'm no theologian," the Brewer said in response, "and I'm certainly no saint, but doesn't being on Urfe make you think . . . I dunno, about where it all comes from? Technology, magic, reality, myth? It seems to me there's something lurking back there, in the wings."

"I don't believe in God," Caleb said quietly. "If there was one, I don't believe he'd do this to us."

"Do what, love?" Marguerite asked, but he never answered.

They had been traveling through a region of sycamore and golden meadows, skirting the foothills of a mountain range. The next morning, just after setting out, they topped a knoll and saw a vast emerald forest sprawling to the north. Not far away, plumes of black smoke rose above the tree line, besmirching the blue sky.

"That looks deliberate," Marguerite said grimly.

Caleb swallowed, remembering the smoking remains of villages they had seen when he and Will and Yasmina were marched to the mines by wart-covered tuskers. The corpses stacked like firewood beside the stream.

"Whatever it is," the Brewer said, pointing at the sweep of dense woodland, "you're looking at the start of the Blackwood Forest."

*   *   *

Once he entered the forest of his ancestors, Caleb forgot about the ominous plumes of black smoke polluting the sky in the distance. His father's homeland was the most beautiful place he had ever seen: old-growth oaks and redwoods bearded with moss and lichen, streams pouring like quicksilver through boulder-strewn gullies, wildflowers bursting over a rich palette of green.

It made him feel all weird inside. Confused. Longing for memories and a childhood he had never known on this world, yet desperate to see his own home once again.

The farther they walked, the stronger the acrid stench of burning leaves grew. Soon they saw vultures circling a column of smoke rising through the canopy.

Wary of a forest fire or a lingering war party, they cautiously followed the plume into a dirt clearing, where they encountered the smoking remains of a Romani settlement. Judging from the dirt-encrusted stable posts and brick latrines, it was an established outpost.

The Brewer sang a mournful dirge as they walked the perimeter and took in the bodies of men, women, and children splayed around the charred frames of the wagons. A few tuskers were interspersed among the dead, identifiable by their curved tusks and strands of long oily hair knotted in filthy clumps on the ground.

Silent tears streamed down Marguerite's face as she helped the Brewer study the evidence of battle. Caleb stumbled into the forest and vomited. He waited on a tree stump with his head in his hands as Marguerite and the Brewer finished. The bodies of the children hovered in Caleb's vision, and he started to shake.

Why would sentient creatures do this to one another? he wondered. *Why must there be violence and war?*

Why is there so *much* of it?

Marguerite soon joined him, white-faced and rigid. He took her in his arms and held her as the Brewer finished his lament, giving voice to the voiceless.

"No more than a day or two old, I'd wager," the Brewer said, when he joined them in the forest. "By the looks of it, the tuskers had a far superior force."

"What now?" Caleb said, in a toneless voice. He looked down at the *pura vida* tattoo he had acquired in Costa Rica, on the inside of his left biceps. *Pure life*, it meant, and he had loved the philosophy behind the popular local saying.

Now it seemed false and shallow.

"I don't suppose we 'ave much of a mission, anymore," Marguerite said.

Caleb toed the ground and said, "What if there's a survivor in one of these settlements? A child hiding in the woods?"

"Tuskers aren't known for their thoroughness," the Brewer added. He glanced back at the ruins of the camp. "Not usually," he muttered.

"We could skirt the edge of the forest," Marguerite said. "Check the closest villages for stragglers."

The Brewer had taken a long rapier with a leather-wrapped hilt from one of the bodies. He tested the blade and said, "I wouldn't mind meeting a few tuskers along the way, too."

Both looked to Caleb to decide. His instinct was to run as fast as possible in the opposite direction, to never stumble upon a group of tuskers or witness such a horrific sight again. But the unblinking eyes of the slain children wouldn't let him look away.

Face grim, he ran a hand through his hair and pushed off the stump. "Let's keep going."

26

Hours later, when Val and the others stopped for water atop a small knoll, they spotted their first band of roving demons. Synne saw them first, whispering for everyone to flatten down behind a boulder. Val followed her finger to a brown-stubbled valley off to their left, where a dozen toad-like creatures the size of bulls bounded over the moor. They fought as they moved, jockeying for position, grunting words in a garbled language.

"Disgusting creatures," Adaira whispered.

"And dangerous," Rucker added. "Those are vrog demons. Their skin is poison and they'll swallow ye whole."

The party hunkered down until the toad demons passed out of sight. Pushing to his feet, Val trudged onward, unsure how long ago they had left the town. The passage of time felt irrelevant in the blue mist. He had never thought about it, but he realized the separation between day and night added flow and purpose, heft, to the daily routine.

Bands of roving demons became common sightings. The type of demon varied: bipedal monstrosities with multiple sets of arms; demons that resembled terrifying versions of familiar animals; demons that bore no relation to any living creature Val had ever seen, things born of flame and nightmare.

Fearful of the moor's open vistas, the party kept as low a profile as they could, hiding in the spongy, knee-high shrubbery whenever a band of demons came within sight. The ground dried out as the party topped a particularly long slope, the heather a blanket of rust on the hillside. When they reached the top, they gazed down upon a comely vista in the distance: A city of golden stone and stately towers cradled by the undulations of the moors.

Rucker leaned his good arm on a knee. "So it's true. Wherever we are, Badŏn exists here."

"It's quite beautiful," Adaira said softly. "Just like in the history books."

"*Was* beautiful," Rucker corrected. "Now it's a demon pen."

True enough. As Val looked down at Badŏn, he saw a swarm of dark forms massed outside the gates. He shivered. How were they supposed to make it into the city alive, not to mention finding and capturing its ruler?

A shriek came from overhead. Val looked up and saw a demon-man with leathery skin and dragon wings hovering in the sky. The creature shrieked again and pointed down at the party. In the distance, a pack of demons near the city turned towards the hill.

"Shut it up," Rucker said hoarsely.

The demon danced back and forth in the sky, continuing to betray their position. It was too far away for his fledgling Spirit Fire, so Val opted for a different spell he had been practicing. An amalgamation of the Moon Ray spell in his father's notebook, adapted to the only light source on offer: the blue mist.

Except he had yet to test it in battle.

Synne herded the group back down the hill, below the sightline of the city. The demon parties in the distance could no longer see them, but the man-demon tracked their position from the air, shrieking and pointing.

Val gathered his magic and held out the tip of his staff as a focal point. He pretended he was shooting an arrow of magic, then suffused it with the essence of the blue mist. Drawing forth and channeling the light from the sky was much harder than a simple illumination spell, but after a tense wait, a beam of blue light shot out from his staff and struck the flying man-demon in the chest.

The beast gave an inhuman cry and darted backwards, trying to escape the ray, but Val followed it, channeling the beam until the demon burst into blue flame and dropped from the sky.

Not as powerful as Spirit Fire, Val thought, but not too shabby.

Adaira gripped his arm as the party sprinted back down the slope. If they could reach the ridge they had just traveled over, a series of smaller dales and hillocks awaited, presenting better options for concealment.

The clacking of a pack of demons arose behind them. How far would they pursue them, Val wondered? How fast were they?

He picked up Rucker, and they all flew low to the ground in order to stay out of sight. With a burst of speed, the party topped the ridge and then landed, surveying the stippled landscape. To their left, a stream cut an S-curve through the hills. On their right was an uneven valley pockmarked with knobby mounds of granite.

Yet topping the next ridge over, running and flying and hopping straight towards them, was a horde of demons of all shapes and sizes, at least a hundred strong.

"Queen's Blood," Rucker whispered.

The party whipped around and saw another group of demons, even larger than the first, racing towards the slope they had just climbed. Val looked skyward, thinking they might escape through the air, but instead he saw a dozen man-demons approaching, the rasp of dragon wings flapping out an obscene leathery rhythm.

The horde of demons bore down on Val and the others from all sides. He tried to force away the terror that had buckled his knees and scooped a hole in his gut. "Should we try to surrender?"

"Demons take no prisoners, boy," Rucker said, hefting the battle-axe he had taken from Myrddin's tomb. "We stand our ground and kill as many as we can."

Adaira fingered her necklace and stood next to Val. Synne flexed her fingers, hands loose at her sides, eyes flashing and ready for battle. As Val summoned his magic, prepared for a futile display of power, thoughts of his brothers flooded his mind, of the good times they had enjoyed together, of the years that could have been. Surprising to him, the same acute sense of loss surged through him for Adaira.

"You should escape if you can," Val said to Dida, as the howling demons thundered down the hillsides. "Through one of your dimension doors."

The Zimbabwean mage had closed his eyes and was whispering to himself. At Val's words, Dida opened his eyes and calmly folded his hands in front of him. "Such spells are for elder spirit mages, I fear, not bibliomancers. I could hide in a Rune Box until the air ran out, assuming the demons couldn't see me. But I prefer to stand with my brethren."

Rucker roared and brandished his axe. He cut an impressive figure, though Val knew he was a sapling in the face of the hurricane that approached. Fear turned to rage, and Val trembled with helpless fury. In desperation, he twisted the ring he had found in Myrddin's tomb. When nothing happened, he waved it at the sky. Still no response. Out of options, he picked out a demon on which to unleash the last of his Spirit Fire.

"Hey—over here!"

At first Val thought he was imagining the raspy male voice, because there was no one else in sight, but the words came again, more urgent this time. He whipped his head to the left, towards one of the knobby mounds that dotted the slope of the ridgeline like thimbles.

Was that a hand waving them in? Or a hallucination born of despair? He peered closer, to where the side of a waist-high mound rubbed against the slope of the hill, not ten yards from where they stood. A man's face, hard-eyed and unshaven, popped out of the mossy undergrowth wedged between the hill and the mound. By now the rest of the party had noticed.

"Quickly, now," the man said, "unless you aim to be demon food. I'm closing up on the count of three."

Val exchanged a quick, desperate glance with the rest of the party, then turned and bolted for the mound.

"Shield yer entrance if you can," the man said. "I've been following you all day, and I know yer wizards."

Dida waved his hands, blurring their forms to match the color of the vegetation. It was a crude disguise, useless from up close, but it might create confusion from a distance.

The man's face disappeared. Val panicked for a moment, thinking it was a trick, but as they drew to within a few feet of where he had emerged, Val saw a thin vertical crevasse where the mound met the ridgeline, a fold in the quilted landscape invisible from a dozen feet away.

A dirt-encrusted hand extended. Val took it and squeezed through, into a musty chamber the size of a walk-in closet. A rectangular tunnel, framed by rough-cut standing stones, led into the darkness of the hillside. Val rushed into the tunnel, allowing the others to enter. The man concealed the narrow opening with a moss-covered strip of wood.

"Hurry," the man said, picking up a torch and striding down the tunnel. "They might pick up our scent."

"And if they do?" Rucker asked.

"The barrows are a maze of tunnels. Maybe we lose them, maybe not. We can talk later."

He didn't wait for an answer, and the party didn't have a choice. Val followed the others as they followed their savior deep into the earthen tunnel system. It was not until they had run a few hundred yards that Val noticed what the man had wrapped around the waist of his tattered patchwork clothing.

A black sash.

Val caught his breath. The first group of black-sashed gypsies he had encountered had stabbed his friend Mari to death, and the second had tried to
kill Val and his fellow students in an alley.

Maybe the man had taken the sash off of someone else. Maybe things were
different in this world.

Or maybe they were going to have a serious disagreement.

None of it mattered at the moment. The man was their lifeline, and they followed him blindly through a series of intersected tunnels barely wide enough
to squeeze through. At times, the ceiling dipped and Val and Dida had to duck
their heads.

No sounds of pursuit echoed from behind. They ran for at least a mile before slowing to a walk, yet still the man continued, leading them deeper and
deeper into the warren of passages formed by beaten earth and standing stones.
The tunnels smelled of soil and musty stone, and they took so many turns Val
quickly lost track of the route. The size of the stones, as well as the crude construction, recalled the architecture of the cemetery on the moor. Dolmens and
menhirs and megaliths, harbingers of an ancient culture attuned to the natural
world.

"Who are ye?" Rucker asked at last.

"A traveler, like yerselves."

"What mean ye? From Londyn?"

"Ye know what I mean. From the other Urfe."

Rucker used the butt of the battle-axe to spin the man around in the middle
of the corridor. "Speak plainly."

The man stopped to catch his breath, his eyes flicking into the darkness of
the tunnel. "We're deep enough inside that ye'll never find yer way out. Even
if ye did, there's nothing but death out there. So take yer hands off me and let's
have a civilized discussion."

With a glare, Rucker lowered his axe.

"I assume ye came for Tobar?" the man asked. "Sent by the Congregation?"

No one denied it.

He lifted the end of his sash. "Then ye know what I represent. Doesn't matter over here, though. Demons don't care about black sashes and wizard stoles,
gypsy or free, who's taken a blasted Oath or not. They eat and they kill and
that's the whole of it."

"Where's Tobar?" Adaira asked.

He shrugged. "Dead with the rest of 'em, I presume. There were five of us came through. Demons swarmed us soon after we came over. I fled like everyone else, got lucky and stumbled on an entrance in the barrows." His mouth tightened. "No one else made it."

"How long?" Rucker said roughly.

The man shrugged. "A year? Maybe more."

The time period matched what they knew. Val gave a small shudder. *A year in this hellhole.* "How do you survive?"

"I hunt and forage close to the entrances. The demons either don't know or don't care about the tunnels."

"And your plan is what," Adaira said, "live like an animal until you die?"

"What would you have me do, lady? Run a hundred miles across the moor and pray no one sees me? I'm no wizard. It's death out there for me." He smirked. "Which is why I saved ye."

"What do you mean?" Val said. "What can we do?"

"Probably nothing. But if there's a chance to escape this accursed world, it must lie with the crown Tobar stole."

Adaira nodded. "We suspect as much, too."

"What about the wizards who tried to follow him?" Val asked.

"Is that what they told you?" He gave a rough chuckle. "Tobar didn't flee. He stood his ground. When they tried to blast him out of existence, the crown glowed like the birth of a star, everything went black, and we found ourselves here. Tobar tried everything to get it to work again."

"So where is it?" Rucker asked. "The crown?"

"The last thing I saw before I ran away was a demon with the face of a man, and as tall as two men, carrying Tobar away. Crown and all."

"Carrying off a full spirit mage?" Dida said, doubtfully.

"Just telling ye what I saw. Why would I lie?"

"How does that help?" Rucker asked. "Unless ye know where to find him?"

"We arrived near the town of golden stone. The demon carrying Tobar was headed right towards it."

"Badŏn," Adaira murmured.

The black sash gypsy pressed his lips together and said, "I don't want to believe it. But it looks just like the legends say."

Rucker leaned his arm on a knee. "Whether it's truly Badŏn or not, what good does the knowledge do us, with a few thousand demons around the gates?"

The man returned his gaze with one almost as hard, and even more desperate. "Because I know a way inside."

The black-sashed gypsy's name was Ferin Siralaw. As tall as Val, broader at the shoulder, a year of living underground had carved out hollows in his cheeks and stripped his flesh of fat. While they walked, he twirled a pair of short scimitars with black handles like he knew how to use them.

When they reached one of the wider intersections, Ferin bowed and swept a hand out, showcasing a bed of moss covered by a filthy blanket. There was also a pair of old buckets filled with water, a pile of berries and dried mushrooms, and a cracked mirror.

"Welcome to my palace." He picked up the mirror, grinning at his grimy reflection and stained, uneven teeth. "Got to make sure I'm still handsome, after all. I found the buckets near the city. It never rains here, but the streams are always full. The work of the demons, is me guess."

Dida's face turned quizzical. "Why do you sleep in an intersection of tunnels?"

"So he can see what's coming," Rucker said.

Ferin passed the water around. "Don't know who built the tunnels or why, but they're sturdy and go for miles. I know of at least a dozen exits onto the moor. They've kept me alive so far."

"Do you have a plan?" Adaira asked. "Once we reach the city?"

"Get the crown or die trying, lady. I don't even know if it will take us back. That's yer job. I just know I can't live like this anymore."

She gave his sash a disdainful glance. "How do we know we can trust you? You'd slash our throats if you had the chance."

Ferin's smile was cold. "Don't believe everything ye hear. But I could say the same to ye, no?"

"Not without due cause, or in cold blood."

Ferin gave a harsh laugh. "Due cause? Do ye know what's happening in the Ninth, or even in yer own city?"

"Do you?" Val said. "Hiring an assassin to target students?"

"How else should we fight the Congregation? We live like dogs in the street." Fists clenched, Ferin worked to bring his anger under control. "Ye don't know the way to the city, but I don't stand a chance without ye. We need each other. I propose a truce. Find the crown, return home, and go our separate ways."

"We'll find it ourselves," Val said.

"It'll take weeks, and ye better pray the demons don't hear ye."

Adaira laid a hand on Val's arm. "We accept your offer," she said to Ferin. "Nothing more, nothing less."

Dida gave a sigh of relief, Rucker looked bored, and Val noticed that Synne had edged closer to Ferin.

Val backed off, knowing Adaira had made the right choice. He understood Ferin's anger, had seen the Fens and the poverty, but killing innocent people was never the answer. Moreover, while the Congregation had once seemed like a terrifying entity, Val realized his viewpoint had started to shift. The rule of wizards on Urfe was far from perfect, but at least its streets were mostly peaceful, and its cities clean. Earth, too, was a messy place, and sometimes hard choices had to be made. He had also just had a firsthand education as to what happens when ignorance and prejudice were allowed free reign: charlatan druid-priests holding a town hostage; Adaira almost strung up in a tree for healing a child. Not to mention Val's own horrific encounters with the black sash gypsies, the murder of Legate Wainwright, and Urfe's history of wizard persecution during the Age of Sorrows.

He would choose an imperfect government over anarchy, any day of the week. Progress over superstition.

They had not had a proper rest in ages, and decided to take the opportunity to recharge. Not trusting Ferin, the party posted a guard and got a fitful night's sleep in his hideout.

In Val's dreams, everywhere he went, the village girl he had killed floated above him, her hair a halo spread around her, damning him with her eyes.

After everyone woke, they had a cold meal and resumed trekking through the gloomy tunnels. Except for the rats and voles, they saw no signs of life, heard nothing from the world above.

What a lonely existence, Val thought, looking at Ferin with a grudging respect. An entire year down there alone. The human desire for survival, to claw out an existence on even the worst of terms, was a powerful thing.

The black sash gypsy led them out of his hovel and through a convoluted series of passages before the barrow opened into a wider tunnel with smooth stone walls and a trench running through the center. An ancient sewer, Val guessed.

Ferin stopped to speak in a hushed voice. "We're beneath the city now. I know of two entrances. We want the second."

"Why?" Rucker asked. "What's yer plan?"

"I'll show ye soon enough. Quiet, now."

He ushered them through another confusing section of tunnels, creeping along in silence. A rancid odor drifted into the passage. Not long after, they saw a ray of weak blue light spilling down through a sewer grate. As the party edged around it, Val looked up and caught a glimpse of a golden stone tower shadowing a broad avenue. A foot with a giant spur on the heel crashed onto the grate not a second later, causing everyone to still and Val's heart to thump against his chest.

Whatever demon the foot belonged to kept thundering down the street. Val scurried past the grate with the others, his pulse still pounding. A hundred yards further, they encountered a smaller tunnel branching to the right. "Entrance number one, if ye don't count the sewer grate," Ferin whispered. "I followed the tunnel once. It led to a cellar in the southwest corner of the city."

Val wanted to know why Ferin thought the second entrance was better, and he soon got his chance. When another side tunnel appeared, sloping upward and to the left, Ferin said, "This is the one."

"What happens if we keep going?" Rucker asked.

"The passage is blocked. Cave-in."

They followed the side passage until it dead-ended at a stone door. Ferin eased it open, revealing a set of spiral steps. Face tight with concentration, he led the way as quietly as a mime, pausing with every step to listen. Nothing accosted them, and the stairway ended at another stone door.

Ferin eased the iron handle to the side. The door opened without a sound. They stepped into an old, cobwebbed basement filled with casks of ale. He curled a finger for them to follow, leading the group up a set of wooden stairs and into the house proper. After bypassing the first and second landings, which opened onto tiled hallways filled with tapestries and beautiful murals, he continued to a rug-lined hallway with a series of closed doors. Howls and strange cries emanated from the street outside.

Moving with the wariness of a wild animal, Ferin slunk to the second doorway and eased it open. It contained lacquered cabinets, a plush rug, and a four-poster bed with gauze curtains. The bedroom of some nobleman, Val guessed.

Ferin made them crawl on the ground towards the window. When Val peered under the bed, he saw a bloodstained wooden floor and two skeletons clutched in each other's arms, both with gaping holes in their ribcages. As if something had found them under the beds and ripped their hearts out.

The black sash gypsy crawled to his knees and risked a glance from the bottom of the window. Moments later, he motioned everyone forward. Val gripped the windowsill and saw a portion of the city sprawled below.

Directly across from their position loomed an ivory citadel with a pair of spires and ornate trim. Lining the street below were two- and three-story buildings made of the city's signature golden-hued stone. Every window looked broken, most of the doors had been smashed, and there were jagged holes in the walls, as if giant bodies had crashed through. Demons of all sorts roamed the town, and Val pulled back with a gasp when he saw live gargoyles squatting like vultures on one of the rooftops.

"What are we looking for?" Rucker asked, in a rough whisper.

Ferin pointed on a northeast diagonal. In the distance, Val saw what he thought was a grassy courtyard in the middle of a large rectangular building. He looked closer and realized the grass was a basin of emerald water, the size of a municipal swimming pool, surrounded by statue-columns that supported a roof terrace. Steam rose off the water, and dark shapes slipped in between the statues, disappearing into alcoves or stepping into the basin. More demons congregated on the rooftop in small groups.

"Best I can tell," Ferin said, as he ducked below the sightline, "that bathhouse serves as their palace. If the crown is still here, that's my guess as to its location." He moved away from the window, turning to face them with a grim expression. "Somehow, we have to get inside."

27

Grilgor, the pig-faced leader of the tusker raiding party, gripped his spear as the line of people in gray caftans approached, a dozen men and women trekking single file through the valley. The triangle of blue dots painted on their foreheads marked the humans as followers of Devla.

It also marked them for death.

Following a bizarre memory loss that Grilgor still couldn't explain, he was demoted from captain of a slaving crew and ordered by his masters in the Protectorate army to roam the middle portion of the Ninth, the vast plains and old-growth forests, searching for gypsy caravans and other Exilers.

The devout followers of Devla were the greatest prize of all. A hundred Devlan scalps would have Grilgor promoted back into the far more profitable profession of slaving.

Concealed just inside the forest, shielded by a group of beech trees with gnarled limbs, the tusker leader crouched, eager, as the worshippers drew near. Grilgor had thirty armed tuskers, battle veterans all. As usual, the Devlans were armed with scrolls and good intentions.

Grilgor licked his thick lips at the thought of another slaughter.

As the worshippers passed by the grove, he gave the signal. The tuskers rushed out of the trees, clubs and spears raised, huffing and snorting and whooping. The last two groups of worshippers, cowed by the might of the tuskers, had either fled or awaited their fate with bowed heads, secure in their faith. Silly, dead fools.

This time, the lead worshipper broke rank first—only she stepped *towards* the charging tuskers. Grilgor was even more surprised when she threw back the hood of her caftan, revealing skin as black as deepest night, inch-high dreadlocks covering her scalp, and an intricate, sapphire blue tattoo twisting around her arms and torso.

But the greatest surprise of all came when the woman produced two boomerangs from the folds of her caftan, flicked her wrists, and knocked two of Grilgor's charging warriors senseless.

As he roared at his men to kill the woman, the rest of the Devlan shucked back their hoods and drew a variety of weapons. Grilgor snarled. *So the fanatics have decided to fight.*

Still he didn't worry. Except for the dark-skinned woman, the Devlan did not look like seasoned warriors, and the tuskers outnumbered them three to one. It was not until the last Devlan in line, a thin young man with flowing mahogany hair and stormy eyes, raised his arms and swept Grilgor's men off their feet with a blast of gale-force wind that the tusker leader cringed in fear.

Wizard, Grilgor whispered.

A geyser of earth exploded skyward. The young mage whipped his hands in a circle, and a tornado of rock and earth tore into the tuskers, blinding and wounding and driving them to the ground. With the tables turned, the rest of the Devlans rushed forward, tearing into the fallen enemy.

Grilgor reeled from his hidden vantage point inside the forest. He debated fleeing, but this would be his second failure. The Congregation would never forgive him. Even his own people would shun him. After a moment of indecision, he puffed his chest out and remembered who he was. Grilgor the Gargantuan, twice the size of a regular tusker, born into battle on the plains of Paragoth Teer.

There was only one wizard, and he had yet to spot Grilgor. The wizard looked young, untested, and probably of weak gypsy stock. If the tusker leader could kill him, they could still win the battle.

Weak the wizard might be, but he was still mage-born. Grilgor would have one shot and one shot alone.

The tusker leader hefted his spear, took aim, and heaved with all his might. The math was simple: if the wizard was well-trained and put his Wizard Shield in place, then Grilgor's attack would fail, and the wizard would kill him. If the wizard was unshielded when the spear hit, then he would die instead.

Secure in the simplicity of his logic, Grilgor snorted and stomped in disbelief as a whirring object flew out of nowhere and met his spear midway, knocking it down before it reached the wizard. He turned in time to see another boomerang thrown by the tattooed woman, right before it struck him in the temple.

It was the last thing he ever saw.

*   *   *

The dreadlocked woman stood above the fallen tusker leader, toeing him to ensure he was dead. He was an enormous specimen of his kind, much taller than the others and as thick as a tree trunk. She stared down in disgust at his necklace of desiccated human ears.

"Allira!"

She stood, wrinkling her nose. The tusker smelled of rotting garbage. Behind her, the young mage was walking towards her, leaving to the others the task of dragging the dead tuskers into a pile. Soon they would light a pyre and offer the sacrifice to Devla, thanking Him for the victory.

"Elaina caught a spear in her side," the mage, whose name was Branyn, said. "She requires your attention."

Allira nodded and saw a wiry blond woman lying on the ground, jaw clenched, bearing her wound in silence. The bleeding was substantial. Allira squatted, reached into her pouch, and cleaned the wound. After that, she applied a paste to stem the blood flow.

When she finished, Elaina thanked her and tried to rise. Allira eased her down with a smile.

"We'll set camp close," Branyn said when he returned, after meeting Allira's gaze and hearing her unspoken request. "She can walk in the morning?"

Allira tipped her head in response.

One of the Devlan lit the pyre. The tusker corpses burst into flame. Branyn floated Elaina beside him as the group of Devlan left the battle site, trekking far enough into the forest to escape the smell, which would alert predators. They set camp by a lazy creek and conducted a short worship service. After that, they dispersed to forage and shield the perimeter of the camp with loose foliage. Ward-craft was not a skill Branyn possessed.

When camp was set, Allira slipped into the forest to sip her tea and commune with nature. The canopy of ancient beech calmed her spirit. Her scouting party was one of several sent by the Prophet to roam the Ninth, striking back at the Congregation's death squads.

The genocide carried out in the privacy of the wilderness west of the Great River, far from prying eyes, caused her thoughts to roam to another place and time, a land far across the ocean, a dry, wild place of unimaginable beauty. Allira's birth land. An ancestral lineage that had stretched for eons until wizards from an island empire arrived on cloud steeds and brought Death at their heels, crushing Allira's peaceful tribe as a mortar grinds spice against the pestle.

All except her. Spared by a stroke of fate she would forever resent, the eight-year-old Allira had been sent to a lonely water hole in the desert before the attack, a punishment by her mother for stealing honey. When Allira returned that night, cold and starving, to find the massacred remains of her family and friends, she wept so long and hard that when she was finished, she found she no longer possessed the power of speech.

She had not uttered a word since.

After years roaming the harsh landscape on her own, Allira emerged into a coastal village with a beach like crushed stars. A young girl belonging more to the desert than to human civilization, she learned to communicate in other ways, and people seemed to understand her. One could learn an entirely new language, she realized, when one did not use words to speak.

Restless, she did not stay in the village for long. Honoring the tradition of her people, she healed those she could, and decided to help others without a voice. The soles of Allira's feet could recount many experiences. Many. Back in New Victoria, she had spent long months in the Fens, easing the pain of those poor forgotten souls until her supplies ran out. She debated finding more roots and herbs and returning, but decided that instead of dabbing at a fever with a cloth, she could do more good by fighting the infection at the source.

Allira's scouting party returned to the main Devlan settlement, a sprawling tent camp hidden in plain sight within the endless brown plains west of the Great River. Thousands had joined the cult in recent months.

Not a cult, Allira corrected, eschewing the demeaning terminology the Congregation had imposed. The Devla were a religious tradition spanning millennia, surviving against all odds into the present.

She had also joined the cause, though she considered the particulars of the religion unimportant. If she did believe in God—after what happened to her tribe, she had her doubts—then she believed that the same God served many different peoples, under many different guises. The god of the sky was the god of the desert was the god of the seas.

Picking her way among the canvas tents and prayer blankets, Allira made her way to the pavilion housing the Prophet. The great man wanted a report from her. Allira commanded respect from her dual role as the camp's best healer and one of their most potent fighters. Still, she sensed her presence both pleased and saddened the Prophet. Like the rest of the Devlan, he was painfully aware that Allira's skills were of the earthly variety, and that no true cleric walked the land.

The Templar, the one who prophecy foretold would lead them into battle and secure their freedom, still had yet to appear.

According to the canticles, the Prophet was supposed to herald the arrival of the Templar, and many had tried. Was the current prophet another charlatan, Allira wondered? There was something about this one . . . the confidence in his wheat-colored eyes, the inner peace . . . no, he was no charlatan. This she knew for sure. Misguided or insane, perhaps.

But no fraud.

Still, it was only a matter of time before the Congregation found them and hunted them down like vermin. They were doomed without the Templar or, if not the fulfillment of that legend, then another miracle.

Allira's people had a saying about that, however. That a true miracle will only happen to someone who is not looking.

And no one, she thought, absorbing the quiet desperation of the Devlan worshippers and the blind faith they placed in their leader, helpless stalks of corn awaiting reaping by the Congregation, longed for a miracle more than they.

28

As soon as Will pulled the final star-shaped lever, the black marble floor disappeared, and he went into free fall. He barely managed to keep hold of Mala's unconscious form as they plummeted into a dimly lit pit.

Something sleek and silver gleamed next to him. A wide pole of some sort. He lunged for it with one arm and managed to grasp onto it. As he wrapped his legs around the metal surface, shifting to get a better grip on Mala, he realized the surface of the pole was slick with an unknown substance. Not slippery like oil, but greasy enough that Will was slowly sliding down it, unable to maintain his position.

Trying not to panic, he took in his surroundings with a glance.

And then he panicked.

He was suspended near the top of an enormous pit that stretched at least a hundred feet across. Writhing, crackling blue fire—the source of the weak light—comprised the walls in every direction. Ten feet above him loomed a stone ceiling with no visible openings.

Dozens of identical silver poles, at least thirty feet long, extended down from the ceiling like metal stalactites. They started wide at the ceiling and tapered down to sharp points. Below the poles was a bottomless abyss.

Will had slipped a third of the way down his spiked pole, edging towards a drop into that well of blackness. For a moment, he couldn't think. The predicament was too awful. The toxic gas had weakened him, and Mala was slumped in his left arm, unconscious. There was no apparent exit. Fire all around, and death below.

Stay calm, he told himself. Stay calm and *think*. The poison mist was gone, at least.

He couldn't search for an escape while holding Mala, couldn't do anything other than slide to his doom. Clutching the pole with his legs to free up an arm, he started fumbling in Mala's pouches for a familiar green bottle: an ointment of healing.

The strain was enormous. Just as he thought he might drop her, he found the bottle, which gave him a burst of hope.

Would it even work on someone unconscious? It might heal her, but would it wake her up in time?

There was only one way to find out.

He uncorked the bottle and poured it down her throat, trying his best not to spill the precious liquid, praying it would bring her back.

Within moments, she spluttered and sucked in a deep, gasping breath. A few seconds more and her eyes popped open. She took in the situation and was able to cling to the pole by herself. Energized, feeling a bit stronger himself, he tried to climb the pole. While he didn't slide down as fast, he still lost ground. He estimated they had less than a minute before they fell to their deaths.

Mala didn't waste time on small talk. "What have you tried?"

"Nothing. We arrived seconds ago. I was about to drop you so I gave you a potion."

"Quick thinking."

"I dropped the bottle when I finished," Will said as he looked down, realizing they had slid halfway down the spire pole, "and never heard it hit."

Mala grimaced. "The walls or the ceiling, then. The exit has to be one of the two." She tried to climb the metal surface of her pole and failed. "We can't go up, so there must be an exit through the fire."

Will had a sudden inspiration. "What about your magical rope? Can we use it to reach the ceiling?"

"I lost it," she said, then pointed to his left, at the nearest wall. "*Go*."

Five feet separated each spiked silver shaft. Will jumped from pole to pole in the opposite direction, until he came to the last pole and felt the heat of the blue fire.

"The fire is real!" she called out, from the other side of the pit. "I tossed in a cloth and it ignited."

"What do we do?"

"Travel the perimeter and search for an opening. We might have to suffer a burn to survive."

Will glanced down. Ten feet of pole remained below him. He did as Mala suggested, leaping from pole to pole along the perimeter, dropping a few more inches with every jump. Halfway along the wall he was exploring, tucked behind the wall of flame, he saw a set of tight spiral steps.

"Mala! The exit!"

She vaulted across the spiked poles faster than he thought possible, then threw a dagger at the staircase. It clanged off the stone. No illusion. Yet the flames appeared to extend all the way to the steps. Would they burn to death before they reached the top?

"Do you have a potion of fire resistance?" Will shouted.

"You'd know already if I did. It's a ten-foot leap. Can you make it?"

The staircase extended all the way to the bottom of the wall of blue flame. He couldn't tell if there was anything beneath it. "I think so."

Mala snarled. "Bloody sorcerer king."

Just before she jumped, Will had a sudden thought and yelled at her to stop. "Do you have any rope?" he called out.

"Of course."

"What about your expandable stick?"

"Yes."

"Give them to me."

"Why?"

"*Do it.*"

She complied, extracting a coil of rope and a six-inch jade rod from her largest pouch. She shook out the rod to a length of six feet. "Whatever you're doing, it best be fast."

Will refrained from looking down. He knew they had seconds to spare. Heart thudding in his chest, his fingers flew across the rope, tying it to the bottom of the rod. The lower they dropped, the less margin of error he had to jump for the staircase. But he didn't trust the sorcerer king and his too-obvious exits.

Holding the rope in one hand, feet clamped onto the pole, Will lowered the stick into the abyss. It dropped three feet below the end of his spiked pole, then five more. He started to lose faith in his idea. Yet how could there be a bottomless pit in the middle of a pyramid? Was it a trap carved out of stone by magic and running through the other levels? A rip in space-time?

Or just a devious red herring?

The stick reached ten feet down. Still nothing. If he slid any farther, he might not be able to make the jump to the staircase.

He let himself slide a few inches farther down the metal pole. Just before he reached the point of no return, the jade rod struck a solid surface.

"It hit!" Will said.

"I heard nothing."

"The illusion must be soundproof. Like the entrance on the surface."

"What if it's another ruse? Spots of congealed magic, designed for just what you're doing?"

"What if it's not?"

"We have to choose, Will the Builder. The fire or the pit. *Now*."

He looked at the spiral staircase shimmering through the fire, the promise of a quick climb to freedom luring him in like a siren's call. Below him was nothing but faith and the gnawing suspicion that the staircase was a trap.

"I choose the path less traveled," he muttered, and leapt into darkness.

Moments later, he landed on an invisible but solid surface, jarring his knees. The illusion of a bottomless abyss remained beneath his feet, causing him to sway with vertigo.

"Let go!" he shouted, releasing a breath he hadn't realized he was holding. His voice rang clear, but he realized there was a soundproof veil between him and Mala, and she couldn't hear him.

As he waved frantically up at her, she finally let go and dropped through the air, landing on the invisible platform with him. Her eyes went wide as her feet found solid ground amidst the illusion of an abyss. "You're brave, Will the Builder. Rash but brave. Why did you choose to jump?"

"The staircase felt wrong. Hidden enough to draw our attention, but a little too convenient. Why'd you choose to follow me?"

"Because you're usually right," she said, then pointed behind him.

He turned and saw, twenty feet away, the bottom portion of a translucent crystal staircase visible beneath the wall of blue fire. Feeling her way in the darkness with the jade pole, testing every step like a blind person, Mala led the way to the bottom of the steps.

The staircase felt firm. They climbed side by side and, while they couldn't see through the blue fire to the chamber of spiked poles, they could see far enough inside to make out the set of spiral steps they had first seen. It lay directly within the fire. Just before they finished the ascension, Will gripped Mala's arm and pointed at the top of the staircase.

It dead-ended at the stone ceiling.

"What do you bet you can't see the stairs we're on from the spiral staircase?" Will said.

"*Queen's Blood*. Burned alive with the real exit a jump away."

Will swallowed.

They emerged from the crystal stairs into a cavernous jungle made of naturally colored limestone. In every direction, as far as they could see, trees and animals and insects stood frozen in time, carved with a precision that made him catch his breath in awe. Macaws clustered on the branches of a ceiba tree, tarantulas poised on the forest floor, jaguars peered out from hidden vantage points in the foliage, iguanas basked in an artificial dusk light whose origin, yet again, remained unknown.

Will turned, gawking at the epic forest. He rapped on a few trees to make sure they weren't real. Twenty feet overhead, a canopy of limestone vines and branches hung from the ceiling. "Is it like the first level?" he wondered out loud. "An entire jungle frozen in time?"

"I don't believe so," Mala said, equally awed. "I believe this is the creation of geomancers and artisamancers—teams of them—working for who knows how long. The scale of this . . . it boggles one's mind."

"Yiknoom knew how to make an impression," Will muttered.

Remembering the lethal traps they had encountered, he and Mala crept through the grotto, wary of the slightest sound or movement. Nothing stirred, and they reached a solid limestone wall. They backtracked and tried the opposite direction. Before long, they heard the faint sound of rushing water, and eventually the jungle broke to reveal a broad underground river lined with banks of rose-colored sand. In the distance, the steady roar of water suggested the presence of a waterfall.

Will bent to let the pink sand sift through his fingers. It felt cool and soft. "Crushed limestone?"

Before Mala could reply, Mateo and Selina strode out of a different section of the jungle, looking weary but unharmed. Will rushed to greet them. "Did you fall into a pit?" he asked. "With spikes and a wall of blue fire?"

"Aye," Mateo said, a little sheepish. "I tried to reach the side, but was so exhausted I slipped off the pole and landed on the bottom."

"And lucky for me," Selina said, "that particular trap was not designed for mages. I flew down and tested the bottom, though not before I contemplated flying through the fire to reach the false staircase. A devious trap. And my magic is almost spent."

A moan came from behind them, followed by the sound of someone crashing to the ground. Will and Mateo exchanged a glance. They rushed into the stone forest, Mala and Selina right behind them. A hundred yards away, Gunnar lay crumpled on the ground, his leg bent at an awkward angle and much of his body covered in blistered burns.

"Tried to jump . . . to the staircase," he gasped. "Too weak to make it. Fell through the fire to the floor. Broken . . . leg. I crawled up the stairs."

"That fall saved your life," Mala said, cradling his head. "Will—bring a potion!"

"There's less debate when it's someone you love, I see," Selina muttered. "Tamás warned me you were selfish."

"I'm practical," Mala snapped. "He can't go on like this."

Will handed Mala the last healing potion, ill with worry for Gunnar. She slowly poured the viscous substance onto his broken leg and the worst of his burn wounds. Gunnar stopped her with the bottle half full. His leg had reset, but the blisters on his arms had only partially healed, and he looked exhausted to the point of delirium. The man had reached three levers all by himself, Will remembered.

Though relieved the big warrior would survive, Will's ears still rung with Selina's words. *Someone you love.*

"Everyone—look!"

He turned to find his cousin pointing at the river, where a long blue canoe had drifted into sight, close to the bank and heading in the direction of the waterfall. The sides of the wooden vessel were covered in runes, the raised stern and bow fashioned to resemble the head and tail of a serpent.

"The way to Xibalba," Mala murmured. "In Yiknoom's day, the Mayans believed Xibalba could be reached through an underground river that plunged into the deepest cenote in the world."

"According to legend," Gunnar said, still grimacing with pain, "a giant water snake would ferry dead souls on the journey."

"Whatever it is, it's about to disappear," Will said, stepping towards the bank and eying the canoe.

Mala gripped his arm. "Selina's magic is spent. Gunnar is barely conscious. We haven't slept in days. If we do not rest, we won't survive the next trial. We have to trust the canoe will appear again, or there is another way forward."

"She's right," Mateo said, approaching on Will's other side. "We have good visibility on the bank, and there are no obvious threats. Does it not almost feel as if we've been given a place to rest? Perhaps a final reprieve?"

"An entire artificial jungle in which to contemplate the magnificence of Yiknoom Uk'ab K'ahk," Mala said grimly. "And dwell on the impending descent into Xibalba."

Will sank to the ground, too exhausted to argue. "What do we know about the mythology of Xibalba?"

"The name means 'the place of fright.' "

"That's lovely. What else?"

Mala flicked her eyes at Gunnar. He accepted a flask of water from her, managing to lean on an elbow as he spoke. "The Mayans believed the underworld was a place, just like the surface of Urfe, with its own cities, forests, trials, and monsters. I don't know much more, except Xibalba was ruled by five powerful Death Lords named Pus Master, Bloody Claws, Bone Scepter, Skull Devourer, and Blood Gatherer."

"Gunnar," Will said with a swallow, "you can stop talking now."

Fifteen minutes after the serpent canoe disappeared from sight, an identical vessel appeared at the opposite end of the river, drifting slowly into view. They came at regular intervals, on and on and on, validating Mala's theory. The party watched the procession in silence, knowing they soon would have to embark on the next leg of the journey, descending into the madness of the sorcerer king.

After a cold but filling meal on the sandy bank, Will walked to the river's edge and peered inside. He could see through to the rocky bottom, twenty feet below. After probing the river with his sword, he removed his shirt and splashed water onto his face and chest. Somehow, the temperature in the grotto stayed warm and humid, making the river a pleasurable wash.

Before he finished, Mala approached with her wavy hair unbound, removing her pouches and sleeved vest as she walked. Will tried not to stare at her ridged stomach or the copper swell of her breasts beneath her leather halter-top. Two more scars, longer than the vertical scar marking her forehead, crisscrossed beneath her left ribcage.

She walked right up to him and reached around to place her hands on his back, her hair brushing his chest. The neutral look in her eyes belied the comfortable, almost intimate, nature of her touch.

"Your scars," she said, "were not there before."

"From the tusker lashes. Yeah. Those hurt."

The proximity of her scent, sweat and leather from the journey, the faint trace of sandalwood and cinnamon from her perfume, coursed through him like a drug.

He wanted to ask if she remembered the flight through the constellation maze, her arms wrapped around him and the question she started to ask. He wanted to tell her how he felt, but his pride, wounded from her rejection on a moonlit night beside the sea, led him in a different direction. "You never told me what happened with Zedock's majitsu, when you disappeared."

"Ah, Will the Builder, perhaps one day we will exchange tales from the past." She removed her hands and gave him her signature smile, mocking and sure. "And perhaps not."

"Is that right? And what will that depend on?"

She turned her head as she took off her boots and stepped in the water, lips still upturned, violet eyes teasing. "Whether or not we return alive, of course. Or was there something else you had in mind?"

Instead of answering, Will met her gaze and reached up to gather his chin-length hair into a ponytail and squeeze the water out. Even without flexing, he could feel the muscles rippling in his chest, back, and arms.

She laughed as she turned to wash her face, her last gaze flicking approvingly over his physique.

*   *   *

The party collapsed into a tight circle to sleep. Will took second watch, after Mala. She awakened him by tracing a finger across his cheek and then his lips, slowly, savoring the touch. Or so he thought—when he opened his eyes, she was squatting beside him with an indecipherable expression on her face, and he realized he had simply been dreaming of her touch.

She bid him goodnight and lay down next to Gunnar. Will turned away with a hollow feeling in his chest.

Will's shift passed without incident. The stone jungle was as still as a postcard, the river a soothing babble to his right. An hour or so later, he woke Selina, and the sylvamancer disengaged from Mateo with a yawn. Will decided to join her on watch for a moment. There was something he wanted to ask her.

Selina sensed his question before he posed it. "You want to know about lycamancy," she said, when he sat next to her in the sand.

"I've been curious," he admitted.

She gave a sad smile. "It's better than being terrified, or prejudiced. The usual reaction."

"Is it . . . discipline? Something you learn?"

"It's an innate form of magic. Something you are born with. Though it does take practice—and ideally a teacher—to learn the skill."

"Can you transform into any animal?"

"Within reason, yes. There are size limitations. And it's risky. When I transform, I become both the animal and myself. Every hour, every minute, that I remain in an altered state, the harder it is to return to human form."

"Who taught you?"

"My mother. It tends to run in the women of our family."

"Is your daughter one, too?"

Mateo had told Will about Lynestra, Selina's twenty-year-old daughter to whom she had given birth at the age of sixteen. Soon after the child was born, Lynestra's father had left them to join a ship bound for Catalonia. He had sailed away and never come back.

The sylvamancer pressed her lips together, as if the question made her uncomfortable. "Yes."

Another of the empty canoes drifted by in the unchanging light. "Are you teaching her?" he asked, sensing a story untold.

She fell silent for a moment. "My daughter has grander aspirations than do I. She's also a stronger wizard. A year ago, she took the Oaths and enrolled at the Abbey."

Will looked down, unsure how to respond.

"I know she wanted a different life, but her decision was hard for me to understand. I love my clan and my forest, and want nothing more than to live my life in peace, with my people."

"I knew a geomancer named Alexander, once," Will said, toeing the sand at the memory. "He was a good man, with his own views and his own code of ethics. He passed his tests but didn't join the Congregation. Maybe your daughter will follow the same path."

"Thank you for that," she said quietly. He sensed a finality to her response, as well as a deep sadness, something that went beyond what she had told him.

He rose and squeezed her shoulder. "Good night," he said.

She reached up and squeezed his hand, as if grasping onto a lifeline. "Thank you for listening," she whispered.

Will woke feeling stiff but refreshed, thankful nothing terrible had befallen them during the night. It did feel that the peaceful riverbank was a lull before the slaughter, a moment for survivors to reflect on the eternal might and grandeur of the sorcerer king.

After a quick breakfast, the party donned their gear and waded into the river as the next canoe approached. Gunnar tried to hold the vessel in place but found he couldn't stop it, causing everyone to scamper aboard. Neither the movement nor the weight of the passengers altered the canoe's course even an inch.

"Selina, can you fly ahead to investigate?" Mala asked, as the roar of the waterfall grew louder. In the distance, obscured by a spray of mist, the river disappeared into a jagged tunnel that resembled the jaws of some giant beast.

After concentrating for a moment, the sylvamancer's face paled. "The entire river is warded. I cannot access my magic."

"By the Queen," Mala swore. "I don't like this."

"But this is surely the way," Gunnar said.

"I realize that," Mala said. "I just said I didn't like it."

The pounding of the cataract grew louder and louder. Will wondered how big it was, and whether they would survive a fall.

"Maybe we should explore the rest of the stone jungle first," Mateo said, trying to peer into the darkened tunnel. "In case there's another exit."

"Good idea," Will muttered. He tried to dip his hand into the water, but was unable to push through an invisible wall surrounding the canoe. "Except I don't think we're allowed to leave."

The others tried, without success, to reach out of the ensorcelled vessel. No amount of rocking or pushing altered its course, and the five of them were forced to surrender to the inexorable current, pawns on the sorcerer king's ancient chessboard, unlucky holders of a one-way ticket on a demonic carnival ride that was drifting slowly into the unknown.

The roar from the falls thundered in Will's ears as the canoe slipped into the tunnel. It picked up speed in the darkness, moving faster and faster as a cold wind pressed into his face, so fast he felt like an astronaut in G-force training and his chin trembled and the blood pounded in his head as the wind roared around him with the force of a hurricane. Just as he thought the pressure would tear him apart, a flash of green light revealed the top of a towering cataract, and the canoe slowed as it tipped forward. The vessel teetered for an instant at the edge, cocooning them in spray from the falls, then plunged into the abyss.

29

Instead of stragglers and lost children, Caleb and the others found only death. Camp after camp of it, the putrefying stench of it, the soul-numbing futility of massacred lives.

Just before dusk of their third day in the Blackwood forest, they stumbled upon their ninth destroyed Romani settlement. This one sprawled for half a mile, and Caleb counted fifty-five wagons. No telltale smoke heralded the slaughter, and the wagons and bodies were cold to the touch, picked over by carrion. The day before, Marguerite and the Brewer concluded that the tuskers had started north and moved south.

Outside the main circle, they found a wagon untouched by fire. They ran to it, praying to find a hungry, dirt-smeared child stowed inside. A spark in the darkness.

Instead they found a cabinet full of grog, an unmade bed, and chests full of clothing, maps, musical instruments, and weapons.

"They took the coin," the Brewer said, picking up an empty purse, "and left everything else. Why? Tuskers don't care for human grog, but they could have sold the rest."

"They're traveling light," Marguerite said. "Killing and moving on." Her face darkened. "Collecting more coin from the Congregation for burning wagons than they gain from selling swords."

Caleb grabbed a jug off the shelf.

"Please, Caleb," Marguerite said.

"Their faces, Marguerite. I can't take it anymore." He stumbled outside and into the woods, away from the smell of death. He tore the stopper out of the bottle and drank until his throat burned. The liquor tasted like bad rum and cinnamon.

A wide, fast-moving river ran through the forest a hundred yards from the settlement, downstream from a cataract whose roar pounded a steady rhythm through the woods. Dimly aware that Marguerite and the Brewer were setting up camp without him, Caleb sat on the bank and drank with a vengeance, trying to obliterate the horrific memories of the last three days.

After a while, the Brewer brought over a skin of fresh water and offered it to him.

"What's that for?" Caleb said.

The older man smirked. "Done feeling bad about the world?"

"Not even close."

"That won't get you anywhere, you know. I'm stuck in an alternate reality, and for the last year I was trapped as a sex slave for a goblin-faced faerie queen. I could spend the rest of my life complaining about it, or I could move on and enjoy the sunshine."

"Those kids don't have any more sunshine to enjoy."

"I know," the Brewer said quietly. "But you do." He glanced at Marguerite. "And so does she."

Caleb's eyes slid over to where Marguerite was sitting disconsolate by her bedroll, staring into the forest.

"She kinda likes you, you know," the Brewer said.

"I kinda like her."

The Brewer squatted next to him. "Then put this stuff away and show her." He put a hand on Caleb's shoulder. "Value yourself, kid. The universe is cruel, but it's not your fault."

Later that night, after Caleb had sobered up and poured out the rest of the jug, he slid into the bedroll next to Marguerite. "I'm sorry," he said.

"For what, love?"

"For me. For the drinking. It's just . . . it's the kids, Marguerite," he said in a husky voice.

She looked up at him with red-rimmed eyes. "I know."

A tear traced his cheek, and he lowered his face. She brought his head to her breast, pressing her lips to his forehead, holding him close as he wept.

After breakfast the next morning, they heard a cry in the woods nearby. At first they thought it was a bird or even a cat of some kind, but when the cry repeated, more shrill and terrified, they realized it was a human cry.

A child.

Caleb leapt to his feet, trying to discern the direction of the sound.

"There!" the Brewer said, pointing upriver, in the direction of the waterfall. "It's coming from over there!"

With the others close on his heels, Caleb took off through the woods, tearing through brambles and thorns, climbing over rocks and fallen trees in his haste to follow the river and reach the source of the voice. The cries increased in intensity as the cataract came into view, a forty-foot whopper that plummeted into a jumble of boulders and frothy brown water at its base.

"Help me! Please help me!"

It was hard to tell, but Caleb thought the voice belonged to a little boy. He scanned the river, trying to find a way up the steep, rocky terrain that climbed both sides of the banks. He would scramble up if had to, though he feared it would take too long to reach the top.

Marguerite had veered deeper into the forest, away from the waterfall. Just before Caleb and the Brewer started climbing, she called out that she had found a path. They rushed over and saw her racing up a dirt trail that wound through the foliage. Using his long stride, Caleb overtook her, bursting out of the woods and into a clearing at the top of the ridge. His eyes whipped towards the water, where he saw a curly-headed boy of eight or nine clinging to a raft in the middle of the river, approaching the waterfall at a fast clip. The river grew wider and swifter at the top, right before it plunged over the cataract.

"Hold on!" Caleb shouted. "I'm coming!"

The boy turned his head and clutched the raft tighter, his tanned face pale with fear. A small pack lay on the raft beside him. Caleb realized he must have gotten caught in the current and was unable to reach the shore. Why in the world was he on the river by himself in these dangerous woods?

It didn't matter. Caleb just knew he had to help him.

Without further thought, he cut a long diagonal as he dashed to the bank of the river, creating some distance from the waterfall without overshooting the boy. Tearing off his boots so he could swim faster, he stepped over the sharp rocks at the water's edge and dove out as far as he could. A blast of cold water cut through him, and the current seized him at once.

"The waterfall's too close!" Marguerite cried out. "You're not going to make it!"

He risked a glance and realized she was right. The boy was drawing closer and closer to the falls, and if Caleb didn't turn back that very instant, he was going over, too.

He didn't care. He wasn't letting that little boy go without trying to save him. In that instant, the boy on the raft became all those lives snuffed out by the tusker raiding parties, all the children on all the worlds that Caleb couldn't help, all the sadness in his soul. He swam faster, without a plan, just knowing he had to reach him.

The boy was poised on the edge of the raft, watching the inexorable approach of the falls. Caleb swam harder, arm over arm, then spied a boulder just beneath the surface, invisible from shore. Caleb veered closer and clamped onto it with his legs.

Seconds remained. The boy saw that Caleb had grasped onto something, and started frantically paddling the raft in his direction. He wasn't nearly strong enough to affect the current, and it wasn't going to work.

"You have to jump!" Caleb cried, when they were twenty feet apart. "I'll catch you!"

The boy looked from the raft to the falls to Caleb, transfixed by fear. He shook his head.

"You have to!" Caleb shouted, then realized he was only scaring the boy. "Please," he begged. "I'll catch you, I swear."

Ten feet separated them. The boy swallowed and, at the last moment, pushed off the raft with his back foot and jumped into the air. Caleb stretched as far as he could, willing his body to extend, ready to jump into the water with the boy if he didn't make it, planning to shield him with his body as they plunged over the falls.

He didn't need to. The boy was a good leaper, and Caleb caught his wrists. The current gave one final tug, trying to rip the boy free, but Caleb pulled him into his arms and hugged him tight.

With the Brewer and Marguerite forming a human chain to help them reach the shore, they got the boy to safety and wrapped him in dry clothes. After returning to camp, the Brewer made a fire as Caleb and Marguerite gently questioned him.

"What's yer name?" Marguerite asked.

His soft blue eyes peered up at her, trusting, underneath the mass of brown curls. "Luca."

"How long were you on the river?"

He thought for a moment. "Three days?"

Caleb sucked in a breath. "Where are your parents?"

The boy lowered his eyes and fumbled with the sleeves of Caleb's shirt, which hung a foot off his hands. "They put me on the raft and said they would find me. I had a pole," he added. "It fell in the water."

"Why'd they put you on the raft?" Caleb asked gently.

He swallowed again, and gave a knowing but slightly ashamed look, as if he possessed knowledge he knew he wasn't supposed to have. "I heard them talking. About the bad things that were coming."

Caleb exchanged a glance with the others, fearing the boy's parents had set him on the river just before a tusker attack.

If so, the boy wouldn't have a home to go back to.

Marguerite patted him on the hand. "We'll take care of ye, yeah? For as long as ye need."

He looked at her for a long moment, as if judging her intent, then gave a small nod.

Though relatively healthy, the boy was starving and tired. Whatever clothes and provisions his parents had given him had been lost on the river. After dinner and a short discussion, they decided to stay in the camp another night and let him recuperate. Later, Caleb strode back into the settlement to find some children's clothing, covering his nose and mouth to alleviate the smell of death, vowing not to let the boy see the devastation.

When he returned, Marguerite was stroking Luca's head and singing softly to him by the fire. Caleb laid a blanket over him and tucked his head on a woolen sweater he had brought back from the camp. Once the boy fell asleep, Marguerite went to Caleb and kissed him, long and passionately.

"What was that for?" he asked, feeling dazed as she broke away.

"What you did this morning, Caleb? That was the bravest thing I ever saw."

30

The Prophet woke in a cold sweat from the dream, his body shivering and mind reeling. It was the middle of the day, and he was lying on his back by a cold gray stream. The last thing he remembered was bending down to fill a water skin. Though accustomed to the sudden onset of his waking dreams, his advisors were gathered around him, worried.

No, not a dream, the Prophet thought. Dreams did not seize him in the middle of the day, cause him to lose consciousness, and seem so vivid and tangible he could still see the ocean in his mind's eye, smell the wildflowers, and hear the clamor in the streets of Freetown.

Dreams drifted away right upon awakening. They did not remain in the mind forever, as indelible as any memory.

What he had seen was a vision.

He started to shake with the memory. The boy! The coffer! The power!

Though rare, the visions had come upon him before. The first one, a glimpse of worlds beyond worlds and celestial beauty that left him speechless for weeks, had caused him to leave his clan as a teenage boy and seek refuge in the forest, wandering alone, surviving on mushrooms and insects, searching for clarity and enlightenment. During this period, which lasted for years, he had many strong dreams, and many visions. He had learned to distinguish the two, though he considered dreams just as powerful, in their own way. How else was the Maker of All supposed to communicate with His creation? A painter cannot step into his own painting, can he? Yet the Prophet could see evidence of the Master's brushstroke all around, in the trees and tall grass, the whistling of wind on the prairie, the depths of an owl's gaze.

After wandering for years, he emerged from the forest, his only regret that he had not seen his parents again before they died. They were caught by a Protectorate patrol near the Great River and banished to the Fens. A distant cousin heard they had succumbed to dysentery but didn't know for sure. The daily atrocities that happened on the Fens were nearly impossible to verify, the corpses of the deceased fed to alligators.

As his sermons began to attract followers, he reluctantly assumed the mantle of a prophet. When one of his visions came to pass, a flood on the plains that he foretold and which had saved the lives of many villagers, he became known as *the* Prophet.

But no dream or vision had affected him like this. He stood by the stream, still in shock, wrapping his leather belt tight around his coat of coarse wool. As his disciples hovered, waiting for him to speak, he gazed around the muddy tent camp, watching his people trudge about their daily tasks. Despite the recent influx of followers and a few small victories, their raiding parties lost more fighters every day. Their scouts returned with heavy hearts and a lack of hope, detailing the torched settlements.

Where was their God, they cried? When would He come to save them?

Yet not only had Devla failed to appear, He had not answered the call of their parents' generation, or their parents' parents' generation, or a hundred ones before that. He had not made His presence known to His people for millennia of persecution and toil.

The Prophet knew what the Congregation said about him. That he was just like all the others, heir to a long line of pretenders and charlatans, of filthy gypsy liars who used the mantle of prophet as a way to obtain wealth and power and lure concubines into his tent.

He knew his motives were pure, but maybe they were right about the rest. Who was to say whether or not he was a true prophet? Or more importantly, whether he was the prophet foretold by the canticles, the one who would herald the arrival of the last true cleric, the Templar, the fist of Devla who would free his people as he breaks the will of the world?

In fact, the very thought of such a thing terrified him. It was hubris, sheer hubris, to believe that he might be the conduit for such a man.

Yet the vision had been so clear! And it was not a man he had seen, but a boy.

A child of sun-kissed skin and curly brown hair, blue of eye and quick to smile. In the Prophet's vision, the boy had approached the Coffer of Devla, hand outstretched and ready to lift the lid, just before the unleashing of a great power had seared into the Prophet's mind and flung him awake. There were other people in the vision, but the Prophet had focused on the boy. All his life, he had expected one such as he, an innocent vessel of pure heart and mind, the perfect avatar for the Creator's designs.

Devlan scholars believed a warrior would come to free their people. But the Prophet thought otherwise. The Creator never did the obvious. He worked in mysterious ways. And what better lesson of his power than to work through a helpless child?

Visions were never exactly as they seemed. He knew this. If the past was any judge, then he had glimpsed but a tiny piece of the puzzle, a veiled portent of the future.

Still, this was the most powerful vision he had ever had, gripping him like a seizure. He *knew* Devla had been speaking to him.

Go. Find the boy. Help him fulfill his mission.

During the evening meal that night, as the winds keened around the tents of the worshippers and threatened to coalesce into deadly funnel storms, the Prophet sat among his people, breaking bread with his neighbors, accepting no special privileges. All of his closest supporters were present except Allira, his favorite of all, and whom he did not consider a disciple. Though she traveled with him, he knew she did not possess the same faith, which made her presence and loyalty all the more remarkable. A gift from Devla she was, this silent healer from afar.

Except for a growing atmosphere of despair, it was an evening like any other in the Devlan settlement—until the Prophet called for quiet and leapt atop one of the tables, his eyes ablaze with the fervor of belief. Those closest to him lowered their utensils as the Prophet raised his hands, his wheat-colored hair unbound and falling to his shoulders.

"The Templar has come," he said, his voice ringing through the dining hall. With a conviction that sent chills up and down his arms, and caused his followers to leap to their feet in elation, he repeated the words he had waited a lifetime to speak.

"He has come, I tell you! The Templar has come to Urfe, and it is our duty to find him!"

31

"Impossible," Rucker said, as he stared out of the window of the abandoned house, down at the demon-infested streets of Badŏn.

"We'll be spotted at once," Val agreed. He wondered whether Badŏn was Urfe's equivalent of the Roman city of Bath in England.

Ferin waved a hand. "Why do you think I've never left this building?"

Adaira approached the window. "Dida, can you create a one-way, translucent ward? Such that I cannot be spotted from the window?"

"Indeed," Dida said. He stepped forward, outlined the perimeter of the window with his hands, and concentrated. "Done," he said, after a few moments.

"Thank you," Adaira said. "Now, I need some time." She remained standing in front of the window, shrugging off questions. When she turned around, Val saw a look of determined satisfaction in her eyes. "A sewer grate lies but two blocks from the bath house. On the left rear side."

"How do you know?" Val asked. "What spell was that?"

"Owl Vision. It adjusts the size of the retina and blocks out non-essential rays of light, allowing one to see into the distance."

He filed the knowledge away, and Rucker shook his head. "What's yer point? That's still too far."

"Think about how we came in," Adaira said. She pointed in the direction of the sewer grate. "In relation to the baths."

Val exchanged a confused look with Dida. Synne and Rucker also looked stumped, but Ferin pushed off the wall, excited. "The blocked tunnel. The sewer grate is right in line with the blocked tunnel."

Adaira tipped her head in acknowledgment. Her sense of direction was much better than his own, Val realized.

"But have you the power to clear it without alerting the demons on the street?" Ferin asked. "Or collapsing the tunnel even further?"

"Probably not," Adaira said, and then looked at Val. "But *he* might."

*   *   *

After sneaking away from the abandoned house, the party hustled back to the collapsed portion of the tunnel. Once they arrived, Val examined the pile of rubble. Ferin had nailed the problem: any of the three mages might have cleared the debris, but doing so without collapsing more of the tunnel and alerting everyone within earshot—that was the trick.

He considered the possibility of using magic to dig above or below the collapse, and try to create a parallel tunnel. The more he thought about that, the less practical it seemed. He was no geomancer, and even if possible, the process would consume too much energy. Nor did they know how far the collapse extended.

Rucker proposed having Adaira or Dida create another tunnel collapse behind them as a diversion, then letting Val plow through the tunnel. Still too risky, but another option came to him.

"Dida, how strong are your wards? If I were to lift the collapsed section of the tunnel a few feet into the air, could you support the weight?"

Dida studied the tunnel. "Doubtful. It would depend on how far it extends. Given the height and width of the collapse, I estimate I could create a ward that would support the pile to a radius of ten feet."

Val considered his answer. "What about a moving ward?"

"What? I don't—*oh*. I see. Very clever."

"I don't see," Rucker said. "What the bloody hell are ye talking about?"

"Can you?" Val asked Dida.

The bibliomancer rubbed his narrow chin. "Yes. Yes, I believe I can. It will take some time, though."

Rucker raised his axe in a threatening manner.

"I'm going to disturb the rubble as little as possible," Val explained. "Both to reduce the chance of extending the cave-in, and to avoid notice from outside. I'll lift and compress the pile enough for us to slide under, and we'll crawl forward while Dida protects us with a moving ward."

"Ye want me to crawl on me belly underneath a few tons of rock and a ward he's never used before?" Rucker said. "Do I look like a mad delver to ye?"

"Dida," Val said, "how certain are you about pulling this off?"

The bibliomancer performed more calculations in his head. "Ninety-five percent, and we can pretest the weight. The issue is longevity. A moving ward, not static by nature, will require a great amount of energy. I estimate I can maintain the ward for one hundred and thirty seconds. Be warned, that will exhaust my magical reserves."

"That's a chance we'll have to take," Val said. "So, we go a minute out, and if we're not out by then, we head back."

As Rucker shook his head, Ferin said, "I'll risk anything to leave this cursed world."

Adaira squeezed Val's hand in consent, and Synne agreed as well.

Rucker snarled as he flung a hand at the rock pile. "Get on with it, then," he said, then muttered, "I don't like tight spaces. Got trapped inside a tube worm's burrow in the Gobi desert once, for three days straight, with all its disgusting little worm babies. Never thought I'd see sunlight again."

As the old adventurer continued to mutter, Dida spent almost an hour fine-tuning the casting of the "Walking Ward," as he dubbed it. With the others guarding the tunnel, Dida had Val lift a portion of the rock to get a sample of the weight, and then Dida performed whatever calculations genius bibliomancers performed in order to perfect the spell.

"I believe I am ready," Dida announced.

"You *believe*," Rucker said, "or you *know*?"

"Can one ever be certain of anything?" Dida asked, with a sniff. "Val and Adaira and I will proceed first, in case the volume of rock should change. Be warned—you *must* stay right behind us. I compressed the diameter as much as possible to conserve energy."

As Rucker fumed, Val lay on his back at the edge of the cave-in, with Dida to his right and Adaira on his left. "Ready?" he asked.

"Indeed," Dida said.

With a deep breath, Val focused his magic and lifted the pile of rubble two feet into the air. Though lighter in weight than the cave-in he had lifted off of Will in the abandoned clay mine, the tonnage was substantial.

The difference lay in Val's strength. He was a far stronger mage than before. It was not a simple matter to lift the rock pile, but neither did it expend as much energy as summoning Spirit Fire.

Yet it wasn't a single, quick lift. Once Dida inserted his invisible ward, Val and the others slid beneath the suspended pile of rubble and, with a leap of faith, Val released the rocks over their head.

The ward held. Val breathed and lifted the next portion. On a count of three, the party slid on their backs or crawled on their stomachs, depending on their preference, as Dida moved the ward. Once they got moving, Val and Dida worked in tandem, Val lifting and releasing at the same time Dida edged the shield forward. Adaira was tasked with muffling the noise from the released piles, which she did by using a powerful reverse Wind Blast against the bottom of the rocks, easing them down. Still, anyone within earshot would hear the settling of the pile.

Rucker had gone pale even before they started crawling, so Val tasked Synne with counting off the seconds. "Eighteen, nineteen," she called out, after they had moved a dozen feet.

The plan was working, but crawling on his back while maintaining the Walking Ward had taken a greater toll on Dida than he anticipated. "One hundred seconds more," the bibliomancer said through clenched teeth. "That is my limit."

He shaved off ten seconds, Val realized.

"Thirty-one," Synne called out.

"We go back at fifty," Rucker called out. "Not a second more."

The pile of rocks and debris loomed inches from Val's face as he crawled. He could see the mud and insects coating the bottom, smell the dampness of the stone. He focused on lifting and releasing in a regular rhythm. *Lift release breathe. Lift release breathe.*

"Thirty-six!"

The volume of Val's next lift seemed less than before. "It's thinning!"

"*Push*," Ferin said.

"Forty-two!"

Still no sign of the tunnel on the far side. Maybe Val had imagined the lighter load. If they had to crawl back, Dida would be spent, Val would be in rough shape, and they would be back at square one.

"Fifty!"

"Turn back," Rucker said, through clenched teeth.

"No!" Ferin said.

Val debated for half a second, then decided to gamble. They could push harder on the way back, he told himself. Whatever it took. If they didn't get through, they might not have another chance.

He asked Adaira to use her Owl Sight, then focused his magic on raising the next portion of the cave-in, this time extending farther out than he had before, much farther than Dida's ward would extend. Val knew they couldn't go that far and still make it back, but if he could just reach the end . . . he probed even farther, testing the limits of his strength, lifting an enormous amount of rock a few inches off the ground, just enough to peek through—

"I see it!" Adaira cried. "It's not far ahead!"

Val eased the rocks down with a shudder, then resumed the original plan, lifting a smaller portion while Dida inserted the ward.

Fifteen seconds later, they were through.

As Dida collapsed on his side, breathing hard, Adaira took a glow stone out of her pack and illuminated the new portion of the tunnel. Rucker lurched to his feet and paced back and forth, muttering to himself as he brushed off the soil.

Dida clapped Val on the back. "Well played, my friend. A moving ward. I do believe you just supplied me with a graduation thesis."

Exhausted by his effort, Val couldn't help but grin. Stuck in a world full of bloodthirsty demons, crawling through a sewer tunnel towards an uncertain fate, and Dida was thinking about his senior paper.

Adaira squeezed Val's hand. "How do you feel?"

"Drained, but okay."

"What about ye?" Rucker asked Dida.

The bibliomancer had taken a knee while he recovered. "I'm afraid the task took much more from me. One-quarter strength left, at best."

"We should move," Synne said. "Our access to provisions and a safe haven is now lost."

Her comment caused the mood to sour. She was right. There was no going back.

Axe in hand, hunched in a fighting stance, Rucker led the way through the unexplored portion of the tunnel. A hundred yards in, a grate appeared overhead, and Adaira floated up to check their position.

"It's the right way," she said, excited. "We're on a direct path to the bathhouse."

The walls had become slick with moisture and algae, and puddles started to appear on the floor. As they walked, the puddles morphed into a thin layer of murky, foul-smelling liquid, probably excrement. Before they knew it, they were wading through knee-deep muck, trying not to gag from the smell.

Val noticed Rucker moving through the sludge more easily than anyone else, as if the soupy liquid wasn't affecting his movements. Val asked him about it.

"If ye think I'm all I appear to be," the crusty warrior said, "then ye don't know me very well."

Val had no idea what that meant, but Rucker refused to answer more questions.

The sewer tunnel spilled into a round chamber easily a few hundred feet across. The narrow conduit continued on the other side, and four other tunnels exited the room at regular intervals. Val tested the water with his staff as they edged forward. The depth appeared unchanged.

"Why don't one of ye float us across?" Rucker asked. "I don't like the looks o' this."

"Wise counsel," Synne said.

As Val linked arms with Rucker, Adaira and Dida held Ferin between them. The mages took flight while Synne followed below, skimming atop the water with the floating jump-step of the majitsu.

When they were halfway across, a creature the same color as the sewer muck rose out of the water. It had the broad flat face of a salamander, and its elongated torso sat atop a stubby tail that allowed it to slide back and forth through the water as if on wheels.

Val started as five more of the creatures emerged, popping out of the water like jack-in-the-boxes, scooting back and forth and making glugging sounds as they watched the party.

"Those are demon grub, not demons," Rucker called out. "Just fly around them and don't make contact. The skin is poisonous to humans."

"Perhaps they're food," Ferin said, unsheathing one of his scimitars, "but what's eating them?"

As if on cue, the strange creatures disappeared beneath the sludge, and a flurry of humanoid bodies covered in bristly gray fur rushed into the chamber from a pair of tunnels. A foot taller than Val and ropy with muscle, the demons had intelligent, rat-like faces and a ridge of sharp plates running down their backs. Each carried a short sword carved from bone, notched along the sides, and the rat-demons in the lead hefted spears of the same material. Without breaking stride, they tossed a barrage of spears at Val, Dida and Adaira, recognizing them as mages and knowing they were vulnerable during flight.

The bone spears whizzed through the air and forced Dida and Adaira to crash into the muck, sacrificing flight to erect a Wizard Shield. Val tried to do the same but didn't get his shield up in time. Just before a bone spear pierced him through the chest, Synne leapt in front of him and batted it away with a ridged hand.

Val dropped into the thigh-deep filth of the cistern. The seven-foot tall rat demons rushed forward, tossing another round of spears as the party struggled to find their footing on the slimy bottom. The mages erected Wizard Shields in time, but one of the spears grazed Ferin on the arm, spinning him around. Rucker lowered his head as a missile shattered on his horned helm.

"Rakatori!" Rucker shouted. "They're clever fiends, so watch yerselves!"

Val estimated there were a dozen of the creatures. Half stayed back to toss spears at the wizards, keeping them occupied, while the other half rushed to engage Synne and Rucker and Ferin. The rat demons looked formidable and intelligent, but Val would still bet on the team with three wizards.

Until the rat demons' own wizard stepped forward.

Shorter and leaner than the fighters, wearing a tattered brown robe over his fur, the long-nosed rakatori mage raised his hands and swirled them in the air. A moment later, three balls of hardened muck rose out of the cistern and shot towards Val, Adaira, and Dida. The slimy globes of magic burst against the Wizard Shields and rocked the three of them back.

A few more like that, Val thought grimly, *and one will get through.*

He felt confident they could have taken the rat mage alone, but they also had to contend with the fighters throwing bone spears. If Val lowered his Wizard Shield, he risked opening himself up to a spear attack or the rakatori mage. He couldn't maintain the shield the entire time—that was very draining—but the constant barrage kept him on the defensive. He guessed the rat demons planned to eliminate the party's fighters, wear Val and Adaira and Dida down, and pick them off one by one.

It was a sound strategy, except the party's fighters were not normal fighters. Synne met the charge of the rat demons in front of one tunnel, and Rucker and Ferin stepped forward to defend the other. Ferin proved to be a vicious and dirty combatant, blocking the short sword of his opponent with one of his scimitars, then lowering to slice out the legs of the rat demon with his twin blade. The demon screeched and fell into the water, legs spurting green ichor.

Despite Synne's display of agility when she blocked the bone spear, Val guessed the rakatori had never seen a majitsu before, because they attacked her as if she were a slight, weaponless woman surrounded by a pair of hulking rat demons.

They attacked her, and then they died.

Synne hurled herself at the first attacker, hitting him with a flying kick to the chest before he could react. Her next kick drove through muscle and bone, throwing the demon back a dozen feet. Recovering impossibly fast, she spun and blocked a sword thrust with her forearm, then delivered a combination that snapped her attacker's head back and dropped the rat demon like a thunderclap.

Rucker was almost as impressive. Somehow he moved as if fighting on dry land, despite the fact the scummy water reached almost to his waist. Val had begun to suspect Rucker's strange, multicolored ring afforded him freedom of movement in varying terrains and substances.

After blocking the first swing with his spiked vambrace, Rucker stepped back and caught a rakatori in the chest with his battle-axe. The gleaming blade sliced through the demon as if it were air, leaving a trail of smoke where it passed. The scream of the rat-faced creature echoed off the walls. Val caught the corner of a grim, surprised smile on Rucker's lips, and the warrior twirled his new blade and cut down the next demon.

Just as Synne was about to finish off another attacker, the rat mage shot three spheres of hardened muck at her. She dodged the first two, but the third hit her square in the chest, sending her sprawling.

Without thinking, Val flew across the cistern to help her. Two bone spears whizzed by his head, narrowly missing, and he erected a Wizard Shield just in time to protect himself and Synne from another round of projectiles. He scooped her out of the water, holding her head in his arms as he continued to shield them.

The remaining rakatori were squared off against Ferin and Rucker. With the rat mage distracted, Adaira stepped behind Dida's shield and tried to slice through the throat of a rat demon. A green line appeared, but the skin must have been thicker or a different consistency from that of a human, because the rakatori kept fighting. Adaira tried a different tactic, sending waves of water crashing into the fighters, distracting them while Rucker and the black-sash gypsy cut them down.

Yelling for Dida to protect Synne, Val advanced on the rat mage, picking up discarded bone spears from the muck and flinging them at the demon with his mind. This kept the rakatori pinned against the wall and forced him to erect a constant Wizard Shield. Before he could escape, Val saw a blur of silver and heard a loud thwack as Rucker's axe buried itself into the back of the rakatori. Its spine severed, the rat mage fell to the ground, twitching as it died.

The cavern fell silent. Val looked around. None of the rakatori was left standing.

Rucker spat. "Filthy beasts. Got them all, at least." He retrieved his axe and ran an admiring eye over the smooth surface. "Me and Demonbane, we'll get along just fine."

Val rushed back to check on Synne. She had regained consciousness and was easing to her feet.

"How bad is it?" he asked.

She tried not to wince as she probed her chest and ribs. "I hardened my skin before it hit. A minor blow."

Hardly minor, he thought. It had knocked her unconscious. He knew that a Wizard Shield, though extremely useful, was no panacea. It took an enormous amount of energy to maintain and was susceptible to the magic of a stronger mage, or even an extremely powerful blow. The ability of a majitsu to harden his or her skin—a weaker form of a Wizard Shield—was meant to protect against fists and blades, not a blast of magic or a dragon's claw.

"We have half a jar of healing salve left," he said.

"Don't be absurd," Synne replied, gasping with the effort.

"Thank you," he said. "For saving me again."

"I took an Oath to protect you. There is no need for acknowledgment." She looked down in shame. "I should thank you, instead."

"How about we mutually acknowledge that there is no need to continually thank each other for saving each other's lives, as often as needed?"

When she lifted her head, the hint of a smile graced her lips, the first Val had seen since the journey had started.

*   *   *

As the party continued slogging through the tunnel, wary of encountering more rakatori, Val wrinkled his nose at the fetid odor. Finally the sewer tunnel sloped uphill, and the water level lowered until they were walking on dry ground again.

"Why were you sent to prison?" Val asked Synne quietly, moving up to walk beside her.

The majitsu stiffened and didn't respond. He could tell by her labored breathing that her injury was still affecting her.

"You don't have to tell me," he said. "But somehow, I think a grave injustice was done."

She turned to him, eyes flashing. "My family has been majitsu for many generations. For longer than the Order has records. *Nothing* was more important to me."

"Was?"

Synne tightened her lips. He didn't think she was going to respond, but after a moment she said, "I have a younger sister. She sought entrance into the Academy during my final year. One of the Head Dons—" Val noticed her left fist clenching—"entered the bedchamber of my sister during the Testing. When she refused his advances and reported him, he denied it and had her expelled. No one questions a Head Don." Her voice turned bitter. "Their standards of honor are legendary."

"That's terrible. What happened to your sister?"

"She hung herself."

"My God," Val muttered. "I'm sorry, Synne."

The majitsu was quiet for a long moment. "My sister was not like me," she said. "She was born weak, with but a trace of power. But the pressure to succeed from our family was immense. The headmaster knew this when he approached her. He offered her acceptance into the Academy."

"How did you end up in prison? Did you speak out against him, too?"

"I challenged him to a duel to the death," she said calmly. "He accepted."

Before Val could process her response, leaving him wondering how Synne had bested a powerful don while still a student, the party rounded a corner and saw a sewer grate twenty feet ahead. Ferin rushed to it and peered up at the street. "I can see the top of the bathhouse," he said in an excited whisper.

Val and Adaira levitated up to take a look. To his right, Val saw the columned green tower marking the corner of the sprawling building that housed the baths. His line of sight was limited, but he saw no sign of demons on the street in either direction.

Adaira peered closer with her Owl Vision. "I think there's a window on the ground floor. No sign of activity on the street."

Rucker waved his axe. "We can scratch our arses down 'ere and wait for more rakatori to wander by, or we can get on with this."

Val didn't like it. They had no way of seeing inside the bathhouse, no idea of where to find the crown. But Rucker was right. Standing around and talking about it would only expose them to more danger.

"How's yer strength, boy?" Rucker asked.

Val wiped a bead of sweat from his forehead. "Decent."

"Save what ye can. I've a feeling we'll need it."

Val floated up to remove the grate, checking the street and seeing nothing but a corridor of handsome stone buildings. Strange growls and shrieks arose in the distance, a chorus of demon chatter that caused a wave of gooseflesh to prickle his arms.

One by one, the party climbed or drifted out of the sewer, and Val replaced the iron grate.

Lord Alistair pushed away thoughts of his daughter and forced himself to concentrate on the five assembled members of the War Council, some of the most influential figures in New Albion.

The Chief Thaumaturge had long felt that the members of the War Council—the five unanimous votes needed to usher the Protectorate into war—should reside solely with the Congregation. Soon, he would make that a reality. For now, the makeup of the current assembly suited his purpose. In fact, he expected the lone dissent to come from Dean Groft.

In the gray-walled, musty War Room located in the magically-secure basement of the Sanctum, decorated with world maps and portraits of the monarchy, unused for official purposes in over fifty years, the other members waited for Lord Alistair to present his case. As he ordered his thoughts, the Chief Thaumaturge gazed down from his dais, casting an imperious eye on those present.

First there was Yasir Ookar, First General of the Protectorate Army, a half-breed reptilus with a genius for battle strategy and the most commanding gaze Lord Alistair had ever encountered from a common born.

Next to him was Kjeld Anarsson, Tenth Don of the Order of Majitsu, a mountain of a man from the wild northern fringes of the Realm. Kjeld, Alistair knew, had exhibited enough magical proficiency to be accepted into the Abbey, but his love for the fighting arts—for physical violence—was so great that he chose the path of the majitsu instead. Kjeld was the most feared non-mage in the Realm.

Neither Yasir nor Kjeld, Alistair knew, would blink at the prospect of war.

Seated to Yasir's left was Alaina Whitehall, the common-born Governess of the Protectorate, a woman who dealt in financial markets and diplomacy. A shrewd and powerful woman, her interests were aligned with those of the Congregation.

And, finally, his orange eyes gazing at Lord Alistair with unsettling calm, was Dean Groft. Long ago, out of respect for the wisdom, public service, and awesome power of the spirit mages, the Congregation and the Protectorate Governors had made the joint decision to include the Abbey's Dean of Spirit-mancy in the War Council.

How utterly inconvenient.

No removal mechanism existed to remove current members of the War Council, and Dean Groft might retain his position at the abbey for decades to come.

Another solution was called for.

"I'm sure you've all heard by now," Lord Alistair began, "of the terrible murder of Garbind Ellhorn."

A round of grave nods.

"What you may not know is the identity of the murderer."

"Has to be another wizard," Kjeld rumbled. "An elder mage. No one else has the power."

Lord Alistair folded his hands as he stood atop the floating dais of spirit he had formed when he arrived. The others were seated in stern, high-backed chairs, including Dean Groft, who had an annoying tendency to put the common-born more at ease in his presence.

"Unfortunately," Lord Alistair said, "you're mistaken. Garbind's body was reduced to ash, and a black sash laid on his bed."

Kjeld snarled and flew to his feet. "That wasn't reported!"

"I don't understand," said Yasir. "Does that not confirm a wizard was to blame?"

"No gypsy wizard is strong enough to defeat an elder mage of the Congregation. Above the sash, the image of a sword was carved into the bedpost. Based on the carving and recent events on the Barrier Coast, we believe this to be the murder weapon. A blade powerful enough to cut through Garbind's defenses. We suspect the blade took his life, and a gypsy mage burned the body."

How convenient, Lord Alistair thought, that the spirit lieges are so thorough. Not even the Conclave suspects the truth.

Alaina paled. "The rumors of Zariduke returning . . . they're *true*? And the Black Sash has the sword? By the Queen . . ."

"Yes," Alistair said somberly. "I'm afraid so."

Yasir placed a gloved fist on the table. Lord Alistair had always admired the professionalism of the commander-in-chief. Even now, in the face of such dire news, he exhibited an eerie calm. "Shall I order raids in the slums?"

Alistair nodded in approval. "A wise sentiment, though I fear another course of action is needed. My belief—gleaned from various sources—is that Zariduke is on its way back to the Barrier Coast."

"What sources, pray tell?" Dean Groft asked. His red beard flowed over his brown cassock, and his orange eyes, often tinged with paternal warmth, flashed a challenging stare. Gripped in Groft's left hand, a little too tightly for Lord Alistair's liking, was the Dean's staff, a solid quarterstaff of blackthorn with an azantite handle.

"You doubt my sources?"

"I doubt the wisdom of what I suspect you're about to propose," Groft said. "More so without the soundest of evidentiary foundations."

"As you know," Alistair said evenly, aware of the disturbance among the others the rift was causing, "we have spies within the gypsy community. All of whom report that Zariduke was used to murder Garbind, and is now westward bound."

"Conveniently headed for Freetown, I assume? Out of reach of the Congregation?"

Alistair locked eyes with the Dean.

Kjeld pounded the table. "This cannot stand!"

"My aides reported another attack on a pleasure garden last night," Alaina said. "Claimed by the Black Sash."

In retaliation to the growing persecution, Black Sash gypsies across the Protectorate had increased their militant activity, often carrying out terrorist attacks in the larger cities. The rationale, Lord Alistair knew, was to raise awareness for their cause. Instead, it was scaring the populace and playing right into his hands.

Lord Alistair hung his head. *How terrible*, his gesture said, *that the world has come to this.*

The table set, he served the main course. He described the damage a weapon like Zariduke could do—had already done—in the wrong hands. An elder mage slaughtered. A Revolution empowered. He recounted tales of massacres of Congregation sympathizers in the Ninth Protectorate. Told lies about the atrocities committed by the Devlan worshippers. Described how a fractured Protectorate would appear weak to its enemies to the south and across the oceans.

Laying the groundwork for his larger scheme, he spoke of how the Arch-Governors in the Mayan Kingdom had begun massing troops along the border, preparing for an incursion.

When he finished with his speech, Lord Alistair placed his hands on the dais and summoned his gravest expression. "Our Realm has enjoyed long decades of peace and prosperity, but nothing lasts forever. Let us delay no further. Before one more innocent life of an Oath-fearing citizen is taken—be it mage or common born—let us take control of the Ninth Protectorate once and for all, and root out every unlawful occupant of our cities. We delivered a gentle rebuke in Freetown, but the message was not received. Gentlemen, I propose that we declare war against the gypsy people. Find Zariduke, bring the Revolution to heel once and for all, and secure our border with the Mayan Kingdom."

Through it all, Dean Groft sat quietly, damning Lord Alistair with his eyes. The Dean had a trump card, a veto, and he knew it.

But so did Lord Alistair.

Dean Groft crossed his legs. "So it's war, is it?"

"I'm afraid so."

"A gentle rebuke?"

"A final attempt at peace."

Dean Groft leaned on his staff and stood. "I'm afraid I have to dissent."

"Would you care to say why?"

"Oh, I believe you know."

"I'm afraid I don't."

One by one, Dean Groft cast his melancholy gaze on the other four members of the War Council. No one spoke. All except Yasir averted their eyes.

"When you have a proposal worthy of my time," the dean said to Lord Alistair, "I'll be happy to reconvene."

As Dean Groft left the room, Alistair seethed on his dais, resisting the urge to sear the infuriating dean with Spirit Fire. He resisted because it would be antithetical to his purpose, and because, truth be told, he was not sure who would emerge the victor of that battle.

Instead, Lord Alistair let the other four members join him in silent contemplation of the aging academic who was afraid to defend the Realm. A man whose cowardice, it would soon be reported, had driven him to take his own life.

Immersed in the roar of the cataract, the serpent canoe plummeted for so long Will thought surely they were doomed, until the vessel leveled off in midair and took them on a demented roller coaster across a mythic landscape, racing across a roiling sea of tears, skimming the peaks of razor-tipped mountains, plummeting down rivers of blood and slime and pus as monsters out of Will's worst nightmares fought pitched battles and tormented human prisoners. A throbbing crimson light exposed the canoe journey in flashes, the smell of sulfur-tinged water suffused his nostrils, and he did not know how long the voyage had lasted or whether it was all a waking dream, a nightmarish thrill ride engineered by the mad genius of the sorcerer king. All he knew was that he could not leave the canoe, could not blink or close his eyes, could do nothing except stare in terrified awe until it was over.

When the motion finally stopped, Will blinked and fought against the nausea the ride had induced. The others wobbled unsteadily around him. There was no sign of the canoe or the river or the stone jungle. Instead they found themselves in the corner of what appeared to be the inside of a vast, traditional pyramid: gray slabs of stone stacked together without mortar, gently sloping to a ceiling fifty feet above their heads.

Aglow with the purple hues of dusk, a replica of an entire Mayan city sprawled inside the pyramid. He saw squat stone buildings and thatch-roofed huts, a wide flagstone boulevard, courtyards and terraces and fountains. Four terraced, smaller pyramids towered over the city at various intervals, their flat tops almost brushing the cavern ceiling.

"Xibalba's city of the dead," Mateo said, his voice hushed.

Jittery with apprehension, Will busied his mind by studying the angle of the walls and the size of the chamber. If he strained, he could see the far end. "I have a theory about this pyramid," he said, "though you're not going to believe it."

"Which one?" Gunnar asked, peering at the silent city.

"Not one of those pyramids—the whole thing. Yiknoom's tomb. This is the fourth tier, right? I've been doing my best to get a handle on the size of each level, and they're definitely shrinking, despite their size. Shrinking by a substantial and uniform amount, if my instincts are correct. And when it comes to construction, they usually are."

"Shrinking?" Mala said. "So this cannot be a pyramid."

"Actually, I think it is. I just think it's *upside down*."

After a moment of stunned silence, Selina shivered and folded her arms. "Inverting a normal pyramid to reflect life after death, a journey into the underworld." She looked at the imposing stone walls looming above their heads. "I know not how we arrived, or how to name the magic that drove the illusion of the canoe ride."

"About the only thing certain," Mala said, stepping onto the first flagstone of the boulevard, "is that the only way forward is down."

One of the four smaller pyramids lay at the end of the first stretch of boulevard. In fact, the road was the only way through, since a contiguous line of huts and stone buildings fronted the byway. Will and the others fell into step behind Mala, weapons drawn, wary of the next test and knowing it would come soon.

It started as soon as they passed the first hut. The decomposing corpse of a Mayan warrior lurched out of the entrance, followed by two more. They attacked the party with spears and bone knives, gaining fluidity as they moved, as if just awakened from the grave. Mala and Mateo slew the first two, and Will cut through the third, his blade snipping the life force of the zombie as easily as it had Zedock's undead creations.

Not true undead, he thought: creations of a necromancer.

Before the party could wipe their blades, a host of dead Mayans stumbled out of the buildings, blocking the way forward. The wounds on the corpses were gruesome, testaments to the violent manner in which they had died: entrails spilling out of stomachs, eyes hanging from sockets, flesh stripped from bone.

Will shivered as he swept Zariduke through a pair of moaning corpses, trying not to think about the hell into which they had descended. He remembered what Xibalba meant. *The place of fright.*

Selina blew the horde back with a Wind Push, giving the party a chance to regroup. Will looked behind them and to the sides. There was no place to run.

Mala pointed towards the pyramid looming at the end of the street. "That must be the way!"

"I can use magic," Selina said, "but I cannot fly. The air above is warded."

"Then we fight our way through."

Though skilled, the Mayan undead did not have a coherent battle plan, and were no match for the prowess of the party. Selina saved them from being overwhelmed by sheer numbers with periodic blasts of wind, and the party made steady progress down the boulevard. Fifty feet from the end of the street, Will spotted a darkened entrance at the bottom of the small pyramid.

He pointed it out to the group, and they surged forward. Will shepherded everyone inside, cut down two more of the ensorcelled undead with a touch of the blade, then slipped inside.

Darkness, utter and complete. The smell of dusty stone.

"Mala!" Will called out. "Mateo! Selina! Gunnar!"

No answer.

He tried to back through the entrance, but it seemed to have disappeared. He felt blindly for a wall or ceiling. Just as he suspected he had entered a sensory deprivation chamber, he heard a low, ominous growl.

Will whipped around and saw two curved yellow eyes shining in the darkness from ten feet away. The animal growled again and then roared, a familiar sound from the jungle.

Jaguar.

The yellow eyes lowered as if about to spring. Will might be blind, but he liked his chances with his sword, as long as he could track the big cat's eyes. He crouched in defense, gripping his weapon with both hands.

The eyes leapt forward. Just before Will swung, he heard another growl from behind, within striking range. On instinct, Will rolled to his left and felt claws rip into his left shoulder. He screamed and jumped to his feet. He could see them both now, on his right and left, stalking forward together. Fast as Will was, he knew he had little chance if they lunged in tandem.

He feinted a rush to the left, and the one on the right closed in. Will darted back. They weren't going to let him isolate them.

The two pairs of eyes moved closer. Will's eyes had adjusted to the darkness enough to make out the vague outlines of the jaguars. Fifteen feet separated each one. His shoulder stung but he had full range of motion. Knowing he had to take a risk before they pounced, he decided to use their tactics against them. He rushed the cat on his left again, committing fully this time and turning his back to the second cat. Just as the cat in front of him sprang, Will turned and swung his sword in a high arc, cleaving through flesh. As Will suspected, the second cat had tried to take his back.

Instead of screaming in agony, the cat disappeared in a snip of blue-white light. *Magic.* Will didn't pause. He dove forward and rolled twice before springing to his feet, knowing he was vulnerable. As he rose, he felt hot breath on his face and saw eyes glowing in the darkness from a foot away. He lurched backwards as the cat sprang. Shadowy claws disturbed the air an inch from his face as Will stabbed upwards, ripping through the chest of the creature.

Another snip of blue-white. The eyes disappeared. He shuddered through a long breath in the darkness, trembling from adrenaline. A light appeared on his right, and he spun, both hands gripping Zariduke. The light expanded to reveal an exit cut into the stone. Before Will sprinted through the door, he took a quick look around and noticed the battle had taken place in a small, featureless stone chamber.

Outside, Mala and Selina were waiting on him. "Jaguars?" Will asked, and both women gave a grim nod of assent.

Gunnar stumbled outside soon after Will, his arms covered in claw marks and with a hunk of flesh torn out of his leg.

Will and Selina exchanged a look of concern. *Mateo,* Will thought. *Where's Mateo?*

Mala retied her sash and hurried over to Gunnar. As she inspected the leg wound, Will took in their surroundings. They appeared to be on the other side of the pyramid they had entered, standing on a ten by ten platform of mosaic tile at the edge of another boulevard. The tiles displayed a scene of two Mayan brothers battling their way through a blasted landscape filled with ghouls, monsters, and fiery torments.

Will glanced down the boulevard and saw another portion of the underground city sprawled before them, with a second pyramid waiting at the end.

"Four tests," Gunnar said through clenched teeth, pushing Mala away and struggling to his feet. He pointed at the scene depicted on the mosaic. "Hunahpu and Xbalanque were Mayan warrior twins trapped in Xibalba. They had to pass four tests to escape."

"Mateo!" Selina shouted.

Will turned and saw his cousin walking out of a new opening in the pyramid. As soon as he exited, one of the huge stone blocks lowered without a sound, resealing the entrance.

Mateo strode calmly forward, sword in hand, a tight smile creasing his lips. He was sweating but unharmed.

"Thank Devla!" the sylvamancer said, throwing her arms around him.

When she disengaged, Will clapped his cousin on the back, bursting with relief. "Like I said—better than most with one hand."

"What were the tests?" Mala asked Gunnar.

"The Dark House, The Chamber of Cold, The Blade Forest, and . . ." He frowned. "I cannot remember the last."

Gunnar refused to take any more of the final healing potion. As soon as the party stepped back onto the boulevard, the corpses returned, leaving their eternal rest to respond to the sorcerer king's call.

Selina tried again to take flight. This time, a host of zombies grabbed onto her, forcing her back down. She blew them back with a shudder.

Yiknoom is forcing us to take the tests, Will realized. *Shepherding us to the pyramids*.

The battle along the second portion of the boulevard was tougher than the first, but they fought through unharmed. The gruesome zombies felt symbolic to Will, part of the horrific imagery of Xibalba rather than integral to the challenge. Still, every battle, every use of magic and every swing of the sword, chipped away at the party's reserves.

He entered the second pyramid side by side with Mala. As soon as he stepped inside, he plunged straight into a pool of icy water, the cold so intense his brain could think only of survival. He managed to hold his breath just before he submerged, but his body temperature dropped so fast he started to shiver uncontrollably.

Pale blue light filtered through the water. Out of the corner of his eye, he saw movement and realized it was Mala, swimming for the surface. Above her, through a shimmer of transparent water, Will saw that they had dropped into a cenote at the bottom of a cylindrical cavern with sheer walls. Ten feet above the water, a set of crude stairs cut into the wall led to a door at the top of the cavern.

An exit, if they could stay alive long enough to reach it.

A burst of adrenaline gave Will the strength to swim to the surface, though he felt sluggish and disoriented. He looked down and saw Mateo and Selina struggling to reach the surface. Mateo was closest. Will gave him a hand and pulled him up, and Selina used magic to propel herself through the water.

After a few moments of frantic searching, Will spotted Mala treading water. She was looking back and forth between the set of stairs and Gunnar's flailing form ten feet below.

She turned to dive for Gunnar. Just before she submerged, she screamed at the sylvamancer. "Fly us out! To the stairs!"

Good idea, Will thought, except when Selina rose out of the water, a hailstorm began raining down chunks of ice as big as golf balls. The storm forced her to drop back into the water and cover the party with a Wizard Shield.

"This will drain me!" the sylvamancer said. "We have to submerge!"

Mateo pointed out the obvious. "That's certain death."

Mala burst out of the water with Gunnar, taking refuge under Selina's shield as huge lumps of hail battered it. The warrior's lips were blue, his eyes glazed over and his speech slurred.

Will guessed they had less than a minute before all of them succumbed to the cold. The hypothermia caused his brain to wander, and a flood of memories flashed through his mind. Racing down a warped New Orleans sidewalk on his bike with Caleb, shyly asking Val to play a board game, their father stroking Will's hair as his mother read bedtime stories. Another piece of his subconscious reached through the fog, a darvish girl trapped in a basin of water with her palms glowing red, forced by her delver captors to heat water for their barracks.

Will shook off his lethargy. "Heat it!" he said to Selina. "Use your magic to heat the water!"

"The basin is too large," she replied, her teeth chattering as she mumbled her words. "It will take too long."

"Just around us," he said. "Form a bubble. Use our body heat."

Selina cocked her head sideways, then raised her eyebrows in sudden understanding. "I can't keep the shield and heat the water."

"Then we go under," Mala said.

Selina grimaced, then commanded everyone to link arms and huddle together as they slipped beneath the water.

The water numbed Will's face and stole his breath. Everyone pressed close together, sharing as much warmth as possible. Mala breathed oxygen into Gunnar's slackened mouth.

Selina had moments to work her spell. Will's lungs burned as the cold seared through him. Just as his breath gave out, a tingle of warmth grazed his fingertips and spread along his nerve endings. It was one of the most exhilarating experiences of his life. He let himself drift, enjoying the warmth. A corner of his brain told him he was dying, and he laughed when he saw Selina waving her arms frantically through the water, pointing upwards.

Strong arms yanked Will to the surface. The hailstorm had ended. Someone slapped him on the back, over and over, and after Will vomited water he realized his cousin was holding him.

Though blue in the face and disoriented, everyone had survived. They huddled within the protective arms of Selina's bubble of warmth until their body temperatures returned to normal, the water as warm as a sauna, and then paddled to the side of the cenote underneath the rough-hewn stairs. Afraid the hailstorm would return if Selina used her magic to fly, the party erected a human pyramid to reach the bottom of the steps. Gunnar formed the base, and once the rest of them had ascended, Will and Mateo used Mala's jade stick to pull the big man out of the water.

Sword at the ready, Will led the climb up the stairs. Blackness loomed above them, as if a starless night had consumed the jungle. As soon as his head cleared the top of the cenote, the whole scene disappeared, and Will found himself standing on another mosaic tile, just past the second pyramid, at the edge of a new section of boulevard.

He shuddered at the awesome power of the sorcerer king.

"A brilliant solution," Selina said. "Heating the water."

"An old friend gave me the idea," Will replied.

Mala's eyes flashed with anger. "How does he do it? Limit your magic after death?"

"I believe it to be a controlled warding," Selina said. "Specific to certain spells."

"Taking away our easiest options for escape," Will said, glancing at the third pyramid in line, a hundred yards down the boulevard.

"Or maybe the sorcerer king is still alive," Mateo said softly. "Watching us as we stumble into his home."

Mala scoffed. "For a thousand years and more?"

Will snarled to cover his fear, and strode forward, onto the first paving stone. The dead Mayan warriors attacked again, even more than before, but the party tore through them with a fury and raced inside the next pyramid.

As soon as Will stepped inside, he found himself at the edge of a clearing surrounded by jungle. The landscape was similar to that outside Ixmal, vines and spiky aloe interspersed with thickets of slender trees. Will could smell the musky air, hear the chirping of the birds and insects.

The goal was clear: on the other side of the clearing, a hundred feet away, an open doorway set into the bottom of a huge ceiba tree beckoned for them to enter. A small pile of bones was scattered in front of the doorway.

Will barely had time to notice the hundreds of obsidian knives littering the dirt floor of the clearing before the blades attacked, rising into the air and coming at the party from all sides. *The Blade Forest.* He had half a second to prepare, wishing he had his shield, worrying about the other members of the party. Gunnar had taken a beating in the last two chambers, Mateo only had one hand, Selina's Wizard Shield may or may not be enough to save her, and Mala, well, Will always worried about Mala, even though she was the most capable of them all.

The knives attacked in unison, lunging at him from multiple sides. He lowered his head and hunched his shoulders to protect his vitals, giving up his forearms, shins, and sides of his thighs as he batted away the knives attacking his face and stomach. When they struck, the weapons pierced his leather armor, though every time Zariduke met one of the ensorcelled blades, the smaller weapon dropped to the ground in a snick of *white-blue* light.

A quick glimpse told him how the others fared. Mala had her short sword and dagger in hand and seemed to be parrying five knives at once, spinning and striking and blocking, making steady progress towards the door. Mateo fared almost as well, not as fast as Mala but meeting the knife thrusts with great precision, the whip-like motion of his urumi sword able to take out multiple blades at one time.

At first Will couldn't see Selina, but then he noticed a giant tortoise on the edge of the clearing, lumbering towards the door, the thick shell absorbing blow after blow.

Gunnar was struggling yet again. The strongest but slowest of the party, he couldn't keep up with the spinning knives, and had not advanced a step. Blood poured from a dozen wounds.

Will ran to help him, batting away the knives surrounding the big warrior. Will arched in pain as a knife stabbed him in the side, penetrating an inch into the thick muscle. He spun away and redoubled his efforts, snapping his wrists as he whisked his sword back and forth. Gunnar roared and barreled forward beside him, taking cuts as he ran. Mala tried to fight her way to them, but the sentient knives sensed her intention and clustered to bar her way. In response, she reached into one of her pouches and withdrew a weighted net. She swept it back and forth, clearing the air. The knives shredded the net within moments, but it gave Gunnar a pathway to the door. He sprinted forward, almost making it before three of them pierced his back, driving him to the ground.

Will and Mateo tried to reach him, but neither could fight his way through. It was all they could do to protect themselves. More whirring knives slammed into Gunnar's prone form. Mala had almost reached him when a trio of knives forced her to stop and fight. She recovered at the last moment, crouching and spinning, blocking knife thrusts faster than Will could follow.

He watched in horror as one of the knives streaked towards Gunnar's face. Just before it hit, the tortoise blurred into human form and Selina created a shield in front of the warrior. The knife bounced off it. Another caught the sylvamancer in the arm before she could defend herself, and she stumbled backwards. A dozen more came at her, and she was forced to erect a Wizard Shield and sprint for the end of the clearing.

When Mala reached Gunnar, the big man was unmoving. Using one hand to defend them both, Mala poured the remains of the last potion over Gunnar's back. She grabbed her other sword and fought off the attacking blades as the big man blinked and slowly regained his feet. Mala took two more cuts to the arm and one to the thigh as she covered him. Not once did she cry out.

Side by side, muscles aching and sweat pouring into their eyes, Will and Mateo fought their way to the door and joined Selina. Moments later, Mala and Gunnar arrived. The knives came all at once as the party dove through the portal.

Again they appeared on the other side of a stone pyramid, on another tiled platform at the edge of a boulevard. The fourth and final pyramid loomed before them.

Though no one collapsed or moaned, everyone gasped for breath and stood on unsteady feet, streaked with blood from the knife wounds. Will wondered how they would survive another test.

"You should have let me die," Gunnar muttered. "I've become a liability."

"Hush," Mala said. "You've saved us more than once, and your turn came."

Will remembered the undead Mayans never left their houses until someone stepped foot on the boulevard. He got a surge of hope that they might be able to catch their breath but, as if the sorcerer king had read his thoughts from beyond the grave, the first dead Mayan warrior emerged into the street.

"Queen's Blood," Mala swore. "*Run.*"

The party dashed forward, gaining as much ground as they could before the streets filled with the undead. Selina used more Wind Push than usual, and everyone arrived unscathed at the entrance to the fourth pyramid.

Mala led the way inside.

Darkness, and then a jaundiced light.

Glistening within that sickly glow were strands of woven silver, tens of thousands of them, a network of finger-size filaments interlocking to form a pattern of beautiful but deadly design.

A spider's web.

Filling the entire cavern.

A soundless scream bubbled in Will's throat. He recoiled and brushed against another portion of the web, which caused him to flail his arms and shout. Shaking with fear, he forced deep breaths through his nose, then turned to survey his surroundings.

The web stretched for hundreds of feet in every direction, anchored between the walls of a giant underground grotto, wrapped around the tips of stalactites and stalagmites.

Not this, Will whispered. *Not a web.*

Was this the final test? Defeating a massive spider in battle? It would fit the subterranean theme.

For the first time on the journey, the icy talons of panic—true panic—clawed at his throat. As he remembered his imprisonment by the spider people, awaiting a gruesome death within the cocoon, he felt the familiar punch of desperation, the shortness of breath that preceded a full-blown panic attack.

You're past this, Will. You're a warrior now. A leader of this expedition.

He told himself this, but still the anxiety swelled within him, a geyser building towards eruption. Will reached deep and channeled his primal self, the reptilian portion of the brain that knew only two things: fight or flight.

And he chose battle.

Stomping down his fears with booted feet, flinging thoughts of the past away like a handful of lice, Will snarled and strode deeper into the web, owning his panic but leaving him saddled with the knowledge of his predicament.

Alone in the home of whatever creature had made *this*.

At least he had freedom of movement. Why that was, he had no idea. He swung at the web and sliced through it, though it didn't disappear. So it was real, then. Not made of magic.

He reached a section of the web marked by six-foot wide funnels of silk. Down one of them, a flash of movement. He started to turn and run the other way, then looked closer. There was someone trapped in the web, waving for help. Someone human.

Why weren't they shouting? Was the giant spider nearby?

As Will advanced, the person in the web took shape. It was a human female with her back stuck to the web, facing Will. *Why is she stuck and I'm not? Is it my sword, or something the spider did to her?*

The woman had freed one hand and kept waving it at Will. A flicker of light splayed off a jeweled ring. Will moved closer, towards a T-junction of funnels. The woman's head took shape: long black hair splayed against the web, dark brow, a narrow face and hooked nose.

Mala.

He darted forward, though when he passed the T-junction, he saw more movement down a funnel to his right. Another form trapped, another hand waving. A man, this time.

At first he thought it was Mateo, but when he looked closer and realized who it was, saw the fine-boned face and olive skin of his brother, Will released a strangled cry.

Caleb managed to rip away the silk covering his mouth. "Will! Get me out of here!"

It was Caleb's voice. Will started to sprint forward when Mala called his name, too. He turned and saw her struggling to free herself. "Hurry, Will! The others are trapped nearby!"

Behind Mala, a huge, bulbous shape scuttled into sight, closing in on her position. The spider looked as big as a small house. Mandibles longer than Will's arms clacked as it approached, and his knees turned to jelly, palms slicked with sweat.

Unless he intervened, Mala would never free herself in time. Caleb shouted his name again, and Will turned to see another spider approaching behind his brother.

He turned towards Mala, then back to Caleb again. Of course one or both could be an illusion—but they could also be real. He had no doubt the sorcerer king had the power to pluck his brother out of Freetown and bring him here. It made more sense for Mala to be real, since she was in the pyramid with them—but what if *Mala* was an illusion? That would be the sort of devious trick the sorcerer king would play.

He couldn't tell.

But he didn't have time to save them both.

"Caleb! If that's really you, what was the name of my first pet?"

"What? Spike the Gerbil! Now get over here and free me, little brother!"

It was the right answer, unknowable to anyone else on Urfe. Delivered exactly as Caleb would speak.

"Hurry!" Mala said. "I've no more time!"

She was right, he knew. He had about two seconds to decide which one of them to save. While it hurt worse than he could have possibly imagined, as much as his father's death or his mother's breakdown, Will knew what he had to do.

"Will the Builder, where are you going?"

He shut out the panic, the suffering, in her voice as he ran. He couldn't bear it.

"You'll never finish the quest without me! Our people will suffer!"

That gave him pause, the knowledge that saving Mala might be for the greater good. But Will was a man of passion, and that sort of argument had never won the day with him. Caleb was his brother.

"Will, I love you!"

No, he thought as a lump formed in his throat. Don't say that to me. Not now. In that moment, as he moved farther and farther away from her and condemned her to die, he knew that he loved her, too. Maybe that love didn't make sense, but he knew it as certainly as he had ever known anything.

But deep down, he didn't believe Mala would say those words to him. One day perhaps, but not yet. Not even to save herself.

Though maybe he was wrong, and his brothers were right about her. That she was selfish and acted only in her best interests.

Just before Will reached his brother, he heard a scream and turned back to see the spider sinking its fangs into Mala's throat. It began to feed as he turned and sprinted the last few yards to Caleb, reaching him just ahead of another mammoth arachnid. With tears blurring his vision, devastated by the choice he had been forced to make, Will freed his brother from the web. Caleb's lopsided smile of gratitude, the terror in his eyes: it all looked exactly as it should. Yet as soon as Will turned and raised his sword to fight the spider, Caleb's hands wrapped Will's face from behind, obscuring his vision, and a voice as ancient and moldy as a funeral shroud rotting in a thousand-year-old tomb whispered into his ear.

"Greetings, Will Blackwood."

34

The first night with Luca in the Blackwood Forest passed without incident. After a solid dinner and a long night's sleep, some of the color had returned to the boy's cheeks. In the morning, Caleb scrounged around the Romani camp and brought back a pallet of eggs, which the Brewer turned into a mushroom omelette. Luca gobbled up a huge portion.

Just as they finished breaking camp, a distant whinny caused everyone to stop moving. Hoofbeats followed, and Caleb's eyes flew to meet the Brewer's.

"It's not tuskers," the older man whispered. "I know the sound of their steeds." As Marguerite nodded in agreement, he added, "but that doesn't mean it's not bandits."

Though the boy had a stoic set to his mouth, his eyes had gone wide with fear. Caleb put his hands on his shoulders and gave him a reassuring squeeze, then lifted his eyebrows at his companions, silently seeking the best course of action.

"Go to the waterfall," Marguerite said. "The noise and the smell of water will help hide ye. I'll join ye soon."

"What!" Caleb said in a loud whisper, as the hoofbeats grew louder. "Why aren't you coming with us?"

"We need to know if it's friend or foe. If a friend, they might bring news. If foe, there may be others."

"Let me go."

She flicked her eyes at the boy. "Better you stay here."

Caleb gripped her arm, terrified at the thought of losing her. "It's too risky."

She reached up to pat his cheek. "They won't see me. It's what I do, love."

"I don't like it," the Brewer said, "but she's right." He looked at Marguerite. "*If* you're as good as you say."

The corners of the young rogue's mouth upturned, and there was a flinty edge to her gaze. After disguising the remains of the fire as best they could, she shooed them away. "Quickly, now. To the river."

Caleb didn't like it one bit, but Marguerite was already slinking into the trees. She disappeared without a sound, almost right before their eyes, which gave him a small measure of relief.

Oh, she's good. Very good.

As the Brewer led the dash back to the waterfall, the boy looked so small and lonely that Caleb took him by the hand. As soon as their palms met, the boy squeezed him tight, as if he had been waiting for the gesture. Hand in hand, they slipped through the forest behind the Brewer, searching for a place to hide as they hurried up the path beside the falls.

It was the boy who found it: a patch of space under a fallen log half-covered by a nest of brambles. The thorns scratched their cheeks as they hurried into the tiny space, grateful no snakes or rodents called the alcove home. There was just enough room for the three of them. Once inside, the Brewer reached back and covered the entrance.

The river drowned the hoofbeats. The only other sounds were a pair of robins chirping above their heads. As they waited, Caleb found himself breathless with worry for Marguerite. The feeling of anxiety expanded into a well of fear in his stomach so dark and deep he found himself shaking beside the boy.

I can't lose her again.

Long minutes later, someone yanked away the brambles covering the entrance. As Caleb shrank back, Marguerite's head popped into the hole, her gray eyes twinkling. "And here I thought I'd caught me some rabbits for dinner."

The three of them climbed out of the cramped hole. Caleb groaned as he stretched to his full height. He gave the Brewer a hand, and the boy scampered out like a monkey. After giving Marguerite a bear hug, she laughed and eased him away. Caleb said, "How'd you find us?"

"I told ye. It's what I do."

"Who was it?" the Brewer asked. "Did you see them?"

"Aye. It's a group of gypsies, and they're waiting for us by our camp."

The new arrivals turned out to be a war party of sorts, a few dozen men and women from a settlement farther north that had heard of the raids and sent out volunteers to battle the tuskers and search for survivors.

"Cleared out three bands of 'em already, we did," said a raven-haired woman with a colorful scarf tying back her hair. Though taller and not as dangerous-looking as Mala, she wore a similar weighted sash around her waist and carried a short sword, reminding Caleb of the adventuress. "Ye've saved us some time, too," she said. "Now that we know you're from Freetown, we'll turn east instead of south."

The entire party was heavily armed. A few carried strange, flexible blades called urumi swords.

One of the men spat on the ground. "It cost us," he said. "Lost a dozen ourselves. But I'll gladly give up me own life to stick a few of the filthy tuskers raiding our camps."

As a chorus of agreement broke out, Caleb sent Luca to the river to fill water skins, then helped Marguerite give an account of what they had seen. After providing chilling information on the number of destroyed settlements, the new arrivals listened to the news of Tamas's call to arms with grim satisfaction, vowing support from the clans to the north. They said they would take over the task of spreading the word, suggesting it was too dangerous to proceed without the protection of a large group. After a short discussion, Caleb, Marguerite, and the Brewer decided it was better to return to Freetown and relay what they had learned.

The war party gave a detailed account of the clans and settlements in the north ready to join their brethren, and promised to communicate with Freetown via messenger pigeons. As with the council in Freetown, the attacks and massacres across the Ninth had spurred the clans into action. Though aware of what they were facing, the news of the sword and the search for the coffer had provided a spark of hope up and down the Barrier Coast.

"If anyone can bring the coffer back, the wielder of Spiritscourge can," one of the men said. "We 'eard he slew three dragons in the Battle of Freetown. Have ye seen him, then? Is he really as tall as two men?"

It took Caleb a second to realize they were talking about Will. He hiccupped a laugh and held a palm under his chin. "He's about this tall, and trust me, you've never seen a bigger dork in all your life."

"A dork?" one of the men asked.

Caleb laughed and rolled his eyes, filled with a rush of longing and pride for his brother.

The war party stayed around for a late afternoon lunch. They were well-stocked and knew how to live off the forest. After making squirrel stew, they replenished the party's rations. Before they parted company, Caleb pulled the leader of the war party aside, a slender, hard-eyed man named Merrin.

"We found the boy with us on the river yesterday," Caleb said. "Should he . . . go with you instead?"

"Best if he stays under your care," Merrin said. "We would only put him in danger."

Caleb agreed, and felt a rush of relief. "What about his family? He said they lived near the water, and his parents put him on a raft three days ago.

"Upstream, then?"

"Yeah. Has to be."

Merrin's face darkened. "We've seen all the settlements around here, every direction but south, inside a two week's ride." He glanced over at the boy, sitting near Marguerite with downcast eyes, whittling a stick with a small knife. "There's nothing left but smoke."

Later that night, after Luca and the Brewer were asleep, Caleb took Marguerite by the hand and led her back to the intact wagon in the camp. The war party had buried the bodies, and what stench remained was unnoticeable inside the wagon. Still, to help perfume the air and erase bad memories, Caleb burned a stick of vanilla-and-cinnamon spiced incense he found in a cabinet. Surrounded by the ghosts of his kin, he made love to Marguerite, filled with a sadness that her warm body, her tangible humanity, helped alleviate.

Not just alleviate, he thought, but heal. The presence of the beautiful wanderer who was both tough and gentle, rough around the edges but secure in her own skin, had filled him with a strange and constant fluttering in his gut that he had never before experienced. Despite being born on a different world, maybe in a different universe, they operated on the exact same wavelength, as if they were two halves of the same intergalactic soul.

So this is what love is like, he thought.

Caleb was lying on his back. Marguerite reached over to stroke his cheek. "What's on your mind, love?"

"Luca."

"Aye," she said, after a moment. "We might be all he has left."

"I know," Caleb whispered. "I don't know how to tell him about his parents."

"I think, in his own way, he already knows."

Caleb stared at the roof of the cabin, a lump forming in his throat.

Marguerite took his hand and snuggled up beside him. Her auburn hair, cropped short when he had met her, had grown past her chin. It brushed his face as she leaned over him, but he sat upright and put a finger to her lips. "Did you hear that?"

"What, love?"

"I thought I heard footsteps.'"

"It's probably the Brewer," she said, though she slid off the bed and reached for her trident dagger.

"He wouldn't interrupt us. Not unless something was wrong."

In the camp outside, Caleb heard a series of sounds that chilled him to his core. An exchange of snuffles and grunted commands in a language he didn't understand, but which he had heard before and would never forget.

Tuskers.

Caleb's eyes went wild with fear.

"Get dressed," Marguerite hissed. "We'll hide here and hope they pass us by. They're just looking for survivors."

That rationale did not make sense to Caleb, but what was there to do about it? With shaky hands, he slipped on his boots and leather pants and ruffled shirt, donned his father's vambraces, and picked up a foot-long metal candlestick with a pointed end. Caleb abhorred violence with every fiber of his being, but he had people to protect. A woman he loved. A child.

He hovered over Marguerite's shoulder as she crept to one of the circular wagon windows overlooking the camp. As she eased aside the lace curtain, he saw three spear-wielding tuskers stomping between the wagons. Two of them had spiked clubs strapped to their backs, the third a sword.

By their relaxed posture and the loose way they carried their spears, Caleb knew the tuskers thought the camp was deserted. *They're looting*, he reasoned. *Looking for something they might have missed the first time around.*

"They're coming straight for us," Marguerite said. "To search the wagon."

Caleb gripped the candlestick. "What do we do?"

"We surprise them."

"Can we beat all three?"

"If I kill one before the battle even starts, maybe." She looked Caleb in the eye. "If you 'elp me."

Caleb swallowed and gave a slow nod. "I'll do my best."

She squeezed his arm and told him what to do.

As Marguerite hid beside the door, he tiptoed to the window facing the forest and eased the wooden shutters open, cringing at the creak. He froze, but the tuskers kept snorting and conversing as if nothing had happened. Caleb crouched by the window and waited, devastated by the thought of Marguerite facing off against a monster half again her weight.

The tuskers drew closer. Caleb's hands shook, and his stomach heaved like a ship's deck in a hurricane. He choked back the urge to vomit.

When the door swung open, the first tusker stepped inside and noticed Caleb crouched by the window, drawing its attention. Before the creature could cry out, Marguerite sprang from behind the door and knifed the tusker in the throat.

The monster gurgled and clutched his neck. Caleb dove through the window, rolled when he hit the ground, and sprinted to the front of the wagon. "Hey pig-face! Over here!"

He had to divert the attention of at least one of the remaining tuskers. Marguerite was no match for them both, especially in the confined space of a wagon.

Caleb rounded the corner and got his wish. One of the tuskers was waiting on him with a raised club and a spear. On pure instinct, Caleb ducked the club swing and met the thrusting spear with his left bracer. The spear shattered, causing the tusker to step back in surprise. Caleb swung his candlestick like it was a tennis racket, smacking the tusker on his arm. The creature grunted and raised its club.

From the corner of his eye, Caleb saw Marguerite dive out of the wagon, just beneath the sword thrust of the third tusker. Behind her lay the prone and bloodied form of the first attacker.

Caleb's opponent feinted, then kicked him in the chest. He stumbled backwards and raised the candlestick threateningly, like a landlord with a baseball bat, aware it was an inferior weapon he didn't know how to use. The tusker came at him and swung low, at his feet. Caleb stepped back and blocked downward. His bracer made contact but didn't splinter the wooden club.

So it only destroys metal. Helluva time to realize that.

Confident its opponent was outclassed, the monster shook the club above its head as it advanced. Caleb knew he couldn't defeat him on his own, and a brief glimpse told him Marguerite was locked in a battle for survival. He looked to the side, desperate for another solution, and saw three more armed tuskers running into the settlement, their bare ugly feet slapping the ground, squat bodies jiggling with fat and muscle.

Oh, God. There's more of them.

Marguerite saw them as well. She screamed, "Run, Caleb!"

The new tuskers reached the center of the settlement, twenty yards away and closing. Caleb feigned a run into the forest. His opponent followed. Faster and more agile, Caleb twisted to the side, blocked a club thrust with his bracer, then sprinted back to help Marguerite.

"No!" she cried. "Flee!"

Her opponent never saw Caleb coming. He brained it in the back of the head with the candlestick, and Marguerite followed up with a wicked thrust to the gut. They turned and saw the four remaining tuskers approaching with evil grins, knowing they had Caleb and Marguerite backed against the wagon.

"At least we'll die together," he said.

Marguerite squeezed his hand and crouched, brandishing her three-pronged trident dagger. Caleb was dizzy with fear. As the tuskers attacked, snorting and rushing their prey, the knowledge of an easy victory gleaming in their eyes, a forceful baritone interrupted the battle. As if entranced, everyone stopped to listen. The voice sang a song of warriors, a tune whose words Caleb could not understand but which he knew spoke of valiant deeds and courage in the face of danger, of good triumphing over evil, of a knight on a windswept cliff bringing death and justice with the sword clenched in his gloved fist.

The Brewer strode into the clearing, blade in hand, singing at full volume. As the tuskers drew back in confusion, Caleb felt a surge of confidence and adrenaline unlike anything he had ever experienced. He sprang forward and swung the candlestick with all his might, again and again. Marguerite leapt to his side, ducking under a club swing and slipping her three-pronged dagger into her opponent's side.

The tuskers recovered, but the Brewer entered the fray, twisting to the side to avoid a spear throw, then rushing forward to engage the nearest tusker before the rest could coordinate an attack. He sang as he fought, taking down his first opponent with a flurry of sword thrusts, then engaging two more while Marguerite and Caleb faced off against the third.

Caleb blocked another swing while Marguerite slipped behind their attacker and sliced its jugular with her dagger. They turned to help the Brewer, who had already dispatched another tusker, and the battle was over in moments.

Breathing so hard he couldn't speak, Caleb put his hands on the other man's face, drew him close, and smacked a kiss on his cheek. Marguerite whooped and added another, causing him to break into a wide grin.

"Where's Luca?" Caleb asked.

"He's safe," the Brewer said. "I hid him in the forest before I came."

The older man's grin slowly faded.

"What?" Caleb said.

He waved for quiet. In the forest north of camp, what at first sounded like the rustle of an animal moving through the woods actualized into the stomp of multiple pairs of feet, crashing through the brush.

After the footsteps came voices, grunting and huffing and snorting.

More tuskers. Many more.

The Brewer's eyes flew upwards. "*Run.*"

35

As Val and the others climbed out of the sewer and hurried down the street of the demon-infested town, the forms of the party started to blur, as if they were a mirage. Dida's work, Val knew.

Rucker snarled at the bibliomancer. "Kill it. Most demons can see through a quick illusion, and some can sense magic. Best just to get off the street."

Dida canceled the spell, making Val feel even more vulnerable. Every step on the blue marble paving stones sounded to his ears like a herd of buffalo charging down the street.

The stench of demonkind permeated the air, overlaid by a growing odor of sulfur from the hot springs. The party stopped at the next intersection, edging forward to peer around the corner before sprinting across. Val caught his breath as two different groups of demons came into view. To their left, a block away, a circle of horned albino humanoids was hunched over a motionless form on the ground, scooping out hunks of flesh with long black talons.

Down the street to their right, twenty yards away but walking in their direction, was a trio of towering cyclops demons with six arms, and thighs as big as Val's body.

"Back in the sewer?" Ferin asked.

Rucker swore. "No time."

"I'll create a diversion," Synne said. "Then meet you inside as soon as possible."

Rucker waved a hand. "Too risky, and we need you with us."

"Then what?" Adaira whispered. "We're out of time!"

Rucker turned to Dida. "Shield us the best you can. We have to risk it."

As their forms blurred, Val wondered if a mad dash across the intersection was the extent of the plan, until Rucker hooked his axe on his belt and whipped another hunting knife out of its holster. With a snap of his wrist, he flung the knife around the corner at the group of albino demons.

Val heard a scream that turned into a series of raucous shrieks. Bare feet slapped against stone, and a dozen horned, pale humanoids with blood-flecked mouths hurtled past the intersection and tore into the trio of cyclops. The larger demons swatted them away like flies, but the albinos regrouped and attacked again, their superior numbers making it a fight.

"I vote for running," Rucker said.

Val cursed as the party sprinted forward. *Some time for Rucker to develop a sense of humor.* With a sidelong glance, he glimpsed the pitched battle between the two groups of demons as the party raced past the intersection. Farther down the street, when he checked over his shoulder again, he saw that one of the albino demons had tumbled into the intersection, probably batted away by a cyclops. The demon noticed the fleeing party and leapt to its feet. Adaira saw Val's face and turned, then made a furious slicing motion with her hand. The albino demon shrieked and clutched its throat as rose-colored blood erupted from a long gash. The demon stumbled but didn't die, and Rucker followed up with a knife to the creature's heart.

The columned green tower lay just ahead. With a burst of power, Val ripped out the wooden slats on the boarded-up window as they ran. Heavy footfalls pounded down the streets in the surrounding blocks, no doubt demons drawn to the melee going on a block away. All it would take was a single glance to raise the alarm.

The tower was squatting on the corner of another intersection. Propelled by fear, Val led the dash across another portion of open street and dove through the ground-floor window of the baths, tumbling blindly onto a slick tile floor obscured by a cloud of steam.

After ensuring everyone was inside, Val observed his surroundings. They had landed on a tiled floor, slick with moisture, on the edge of a pool of murky green water. A dense vapor rose off the surface, eddying in the air and suffusing the room, limiting visibility to a dozen feet. The room reeked of rotten eggs, the smell of sulfuric water heated deep within the earth.

"Watch yerselves," Rucker said in a low voice, as they crouched on the tiles, praying none of the demons outside had seen them enter. "Anything could be in here."

The tiled floor extended to the left and the right, a three-foot walkway that hugged the wall as it wrapped around the basin. Val peered through the steam and saw frescoes in colorful but faded pigments covering the ceiling. Steps led into the basin at various intervals, and a marble archway opposite the window gave access to the interior.

Val and Synne crept to the left, the others took to the right. When they reached the archway, Rucker peered through, then waved everyone into a narrow, stone-walled corridor. Haze seeped out of archways on both sides of the passage. Splashing and grunting and the plop of demon bodies stepping into steaming baths could be heard in all directions.

"What now?" Adaira whispered.

Rucker shook his head. "I don't like this. We were lucky that bath was empty."

"Can you use your sight?" Val asked Adaira.

The cuerpomancer concentrated as she gazed down the hallway. "I can't see through the steam to the right," she said finally, "but there are stairs to the left, at the end of the corridor. Fifty feet away."

"I fear these alcoves are infested," Synne said. "Perhaps there is less company below."

Everyone agreed to try the stairs. Proceeding two by two in the corridor, they crept through the misty hallway, scurrying past the open archways. The dense steam spilling out of the rooms and swirling in the hallways was a godsend, because it shielded the party from observation. Still, Val knew it was only a matter of time before they ran afoul of a group of demons.

It happened just after they passed the last archway on their left before the stairs. A demon with mottled brown skin, tusks, wings, and distended jaws stepped into the corridor on hooved feet, right behind Dida. Before anyone could react, it lowered its head and barreled into the bibliomancer's chest, driving him to the ground. As it stood, Rucker cut off the creature's head with a vicious swing of his axe.

Val thought everything was fine until Dida didn't get up. He curled into a ball and coughed, grasping his side. Rucker slapped a hand over Dida's mouth. "Quiet, lad!" he said in a harsh whisper.

Ferin waved a hand at them to hurry. After carrying Dida and the dead demon into the alcove, the black sash gypsy pushed the demon into the basin. As its lifeless form sank to the bottom, Adaira probed Dida's side. "Three broken ribs," she announced quietly. "I can heal him, but it will take hours, at least. Internal wounds are complex."

"We don't have hours," Dida gasped. "I can continue."

Val raised his eyebrows at Adaira, asking a wordless question.

She pursed her lips. "He will survive, but the pain will be hard to bear."

"I'm fine," Dida said, gritting his teeth and pushing to his feet. "I'm staying with you." He took a step and swayed, and Val caught him before he fell.

"We need him," Rucker said. "Give him the ointment."

Over Dida's protests, Adaira rubbed the last of the healing salve onto his side. Within minutes, he was up and walking again. Val was thrilled his friend had recovered, but he knew that was the last reprieve.

Despite Rucker's misgivings—the lower level of a dungeon was never safer—the party felt the better option was to continue down the stairs and hope for a less populated level. Just past the alcove, a set of limestone steps covered in lumps of green and brown algae materialized out of the steam.

Strange, Val thought. *Those steps look almost . . . diseased.*

The steam was even thicker on the staircase. Val could only see to the third step as they approached. Just before he and Synne began their descent, he noticed two ash-colored humanoids sitting on their knees, almost childlike, at the bottom of the staircase. They had gangly limbs, crimson eyes that glowed through the steam, and three long fingers ending in claws that looked like iron. Apart from their eyes and knife slash mouths, their faces were featureless, smoke congealed into skin. Their only reaction to the presence of the party was to tilt their heads upwards and regard them with lidless eyes.

Synne clutched Val's arm and jerked him away. "Fall back," she said. "*Fall back.*"

Val stumbled away from the staircase, wondering what had spooked the majitsu. Yet as the party lurched back down the corridor, there was no sign of pursuit from the two strange beings. As far as Val could tell, they had not moved at all, simply observing the party with eerie calm.

Rucker led them back into the room they had just cleared, edging away from the archway. Adaira said, "What are those things?"

"Death is what they are," Synne answered, with a shudder. "Impervious to most magic and weaponry, as fast as I am, and with claws as sharp as azantite."

"Not to mention their bite," Rucker said. "A poison with no antidote. On Urfe, they're known as gethzul."

"What the hell are they doing sitting on those stairs?" Val asked.

Rucker spat into the water. "They're guard dogs for the demon lords, or so the legends go. Never seen one meself."

"Won't they come after us?"

"Whatever it is they're protecting, I don't think they much care who is at the *top* of the stairs."

"We studied them at the Academy," Synne said. "Many generations ago, six of our Order descended with a spirit mage into the Thirteen Hells, on an intelligence gathering mission. They encountered a pack of gethzul. All of our Order was slain, and the spirit mage was forced to flee."

"I thought them to be legends," Rucker said.

Ferin's eyes were wild. "We can't go forward, and we can't go back."

"We have to go somewhere," Val said grimly. "I wish we could get a look at the rest of the level. Remember, we only have to find Tobar."

For some time, Val had been trying to recreate the spell that had allowed him to view the layout of the dungeon beneath Leonidus's castle. A Spirit Map, it was called. So far he had been unsuccessful. His father's spell book had only hinted at it, and Professor Azara had said with a smirk that such a spell was far beyond his present abilities. He refrained from telling her that he had already cast it in Leonidus's dungeon.

"I might have a solution," Dida said slowly.

All eyes turned his way.

"As you know, we bibliomancers do not employ many offensive spells. Combat is not part of our ethos. But we do have certain spells that can be adapted to fit certain situations. For instance, I am proficient in a Mirror Ward that renders the protective barrier not invisible, but reflective of the environment."

Rucker waved his axe. "Yer talking in riddles again."

"To the observer," Dida said, "the warded zone appears to be a reflection of its own form."

"Are you saying you can make us look like demons?" Val asked.

"*One* of us," Dida said. "And the spell will not enable you to appear as a demon, but merely reflect the form of the observer. However, given that we are surrounded by demons, I see the logic in your supposition."

Everyone except Ferin volunteered for the task. Val argued that the strongest mage should be the guinea pig, in case things went south. Dida protested that it was his spell and his duty, and Adaira clutched Val's arm and begged him not to go, contending she was the most expendable mage and should take the risk.

Val won the argument by sheer stubbornness, shrugging off Synne's protests and Rucker's appeal to wisdom and experience. "Except for Ferin," Val said, "we're all here because of me. Getting us home is my responsibility."

No one liked the idea, yet everyone agreed it was the best plan they had. They would risk trying to pass the gethzul if no other option arose, but it might be unnecessary, if Tobar and the crown were stowed somewhere on the upper level.

As Dida slowly walked around Val, casting the Mirror Ward, Val gripped his staff and threw the hood of his cloak over his head. He felt nothing except a slight prickling of his skin.

When Dida finished, everyone looked at Val with widened eyes.

"Remarkable," Adaira murmured. "I'm in need of a good wash."

"Ye look much more handsome now," Rucker quipped.

"Can you see my staff?" Val asked.

"You mean my axe?"

"Excellent."

After a round of pleas for caution, Val took a deep breath and strode into the hallway. A thousand things could go wrong. Death was all around. He turned right, away from the staircase, sensing the gethzul would react if they saw another of their kind, since they were so rare. He strode down the passage, terrified but understanding that a projection of strength and confidence was his best ally. That and discretion. Engage no one, stop for nothing. He lowered his head as he passed two demons conversing in an alcove. Neither gave him a second glance, and the steam helped cloak his face.

When he reached the next alcove, Val stepped inside and found himself in yet another steam room with a basin of water in the center. A dozen reptilian forms lounged on the tiled walkway and drifted through the steam bath. Val tensed. It might look awkward to walk through the chamber without stopping, but he had already committed.

Head down, lips compressed, Val tried to ooze confidence as he strode all the way around the walkway, towards the alcove on the other side. He had to step over two demons who reared up to address him in a guttural language. Val ignored them and kept walking, praying they didn't look at his face and see an exact replica of their own.

He felt tension hovering in the room, but none of the demons accosted him as he walked out of the room and found himself in an inner hallway with a tiled floor and rounded ceiling. He looked left and right. Alcoves and steam in both directions.

Just when he thought the entire level was a warren of tiny steam rooms, he crossed the hallway and entered a covered colonnade that spilled into a gigantic open-air basin of steaming water. Due to the outside exposure, the vapor was thinner, and Val could see that the colonnade wrapped all the way around the rectangular pool. Archways led back into the building at regular intervals, and marble statues supported the rooftop terrace they had viewed from the tower.

The basin, colonnade, and entrances to the alcoves teemed with demons. Val froze, unsure what to do, trying not to gag from the smell, forcing himself not to flee from sheer terror. Before he could decide, a seven-foot tall demon with a misshapen head and three horns rose out of the water, pointed a talon at him, and shouted something in a demon tongue.

Val tried to stay calm as he walked down the tiled walkway surrounding the steaming central basin, away from the three-horned demon that had singled him out. To his dismay, the ugly seven-foot tall beast followed, bellowing and making threatening gestures whenever Val looked over his shoulder. None of the other demons seemed concerned about the aggression. A normal occurrence in demon land. There had to be a few hundred of them milling in and around the steam pool.

Should I ignore him, Val wondered? *Stand and fight? Jump into the basin? Run away as fast as I can?*

None of those seemed like good options.

He waved a hand without turning, dismissing the demon, trying to feign confidence. The brute ran up and shoved Val in the back. Not weighing half as much, Val tumbled to the tiled floor and skidded across the moist surface on his stomach. He barely managed to hold on to his staff. The demon roared and tried to kick him. Val rolled to his side, then jumped to his feet as the demon swung a gnarled fist. He ducked and shoved the beast in the chest, enhancing the maneuver with a wisp of magic. He felt more eyes on him, heads turning to watch the fight. Not good. The demon stumbled and then barreled forward again, head lowered to spear Val with its horns.

Just before he was forced to use a stronger spell that would surely draw attention, another demon tackled the misshapen beast from the side, sending them both into the basin. Hot water splashed in Val's face, and the smell of sulfur stuffed his nose.

The new combatant was a toad demon. The fight in the pool turned into a brawl, drawing more and more demons, and Val exhaled as the rest of them ignored him. *Of course*, he thought. *Everyone thinks I look like they do. The toad demon probably thinks the three-horned demon just attacked his brother.*

He hurried away from the battle, walking the length of the walkway and peering into every alcove, searching for Tobar but finding nothing except groups of demons loafing or playing dice games. Just as he started to despair, he passed a grate in a corner of the walkway, set between two alcoves. He almost walked right by it when he noticed movement below.

He stooped, not caring if anyone noticed. He had to take a chance while the battle in the central basin was still raging.

The sight of what lay beneath the grate caused him to clench the iron bars and suck in a breath. Thirty feet below, he saw a chamber that mirrored the structure of the open-air courtyard. Yet instead of green-hued spa water, a pool of molten lava bubbled within the basin. Rough-hewn rock comprised the archways, and the walkway was a moss-covered path dotted with enormous, misshapen fungi. Women in various stages of undress lounged in the mouths of the alcoves, using the fungi as furniture. Not women, Val realized as he noted the bat wings and barbed tails, the pointed ears and forked tongues.

Succubi.

He scurried around to get a better look, keeping an eye out for approaching demons. A few were already giving him the eye.

A multi-tiered obsidian platform sprawled along one side of the lava basin. On the third level—the top of the platform—a tall and shockingly handsome demon lounged on an ivory throne. Two ram horns curved back from his head, jeweled rings covered his fingers, and black veins pulsed across his pale, bare torso like a living tattoo. Fear rolled through Val at the sight of him. The eeriest thing of all was how human his face looked. Except for the horns and his height—nine feet tall, at least—it could have been a dark-haired movie star lounging on that throne.

A succubus stretched out like a cat in his lap. Two more sprawled at his feet. On the second tier of the platform, a brown-haired human male in a filthy patchwork cloak occupied a much smaller throne. The man looked dazed, as if not quite present, and Val caught his breath when he noticed his eyes were missing. Atop the man's head was an elegant crown with a bluish-white hue that Val recognized from Cyrus's briefing.

A crown made of congealed magic. The Star Crown.

Tobar.

Fascinated by the macabre scene, Val almost didn't notice when the handsome demon tilted his head towards the grate, as if sensing Val's presence.

Val flung himself backwards at the last moment, praying he hadn't been too late, sensing the immense power of the being.

No outcry was raised. Grimly satisfied with the discovery but shaking at the knowledge of what he had seen, Val returned through the steam-drenched warren of passages, flinching at every turn. He arrived without incident and described the throne room to the others.

"Yer sure about the tall demon?" Rucker asked.

"I'm sure," Val said. "Why?"

The adventurer and Synne exchanged a glance. "Because that sounds like Asmodeus," Rucker said slowly, with the only flicker of fear Val had ever seen cross his face.

"Who's that?"

"A Demon Lord of the Thirteen Hells," Synne said. "A cambion, they say, born of a succubus and a human."

Ferin clutched his hair as he paced back and forth. "The legends are true, then. Asmodeus came to Badŏn, and now he's taken Tobar." He stopped pacing and looked around the group. "We can't fight that sort of power. He'll kill us all."

Val turned to Rucker. "Is he right?"

"I don't know," he said slowly. "Probably."

"I don't understand," Adaira said. "Is he trapped here? Why bother with this realm?"

Rucker leaned on his axe. "Maybe this is an alternate dimension, or maybe we're in his world. Or maybe he came through with Tobar and is trying to cross the veil, like we did, to gain access to the real Urfe."

Dida's face turned quizzical. "How can we help him gain access to Urfe?"

Rucker threw his hands up. "I don't know. Maybe he needs someone from our dimension to manipulate the powers of the crown." He turned to Val. "A stronger mage than Tobar."

Val swallowed. Impossible odds or not, as far as they knew, there was only one way out of this dimension, and it lay through Asmodeus and Tobar. "He's immune to magic, I assume?"

Rucker pointed his axe at him. "Boy, no matter what the books or anyone tells ye, *no one* is immune. Magic resistance is a relative thing. I'm sure he's powerful, maybe too powerful for the likes of ye, but he's not immune."

"That is correct," Dida said. "At least for the beings and worlds catalogued by the mages of Urfe."

"Asmodeus," Ferin muttered again, sinking against the wall and running a hand through his dirty hair. "They say he flays humans alive and keeps them as pets, to torture for all eternity."

"Maybe we can't defeat him," Adaira said. "But we don't have to, do we?" All eyes turned her way, and she gave a calculated smile that belied the trembling in her hands. "We just have to get the crown."

"And do what with it?" Rucker said. "We still don't know how to get back."

"She's right," Val said. "We can worry about that later. But we don't have to kill Asmodeus. We just have to escape with the crown."

Ferin threw back his head in mock laughter. "We just have to steal it from underneath a demon lord's nose and slip through a city full of hell spawn undetected. Is that all? It must be nice to possess the false confidence of a privileged birth."

As Adaira turned an icy gaze on Ferin, Dida wagged a finger and said, "If we can retrieve the crown, I could hide us inside a Rune Box until our enemies have dispersed."

"Do you have enough magic left for that?" Val asked.

"I'll manage."

"What are the chances Asmodeus can see into one of those?" Rucker said.

Dida grimaced. "Probably good. We'll have to construct it someplace clever."

Val scanned the faces of the group and knew they needed him to make a decision. "If that's our best option, then we'll have to make it work."

36

Caleb, Marguerite, and the Brewer slipped back into the forest moments ahead of the regiment of armed tuskers. A quick glance over his shoulder told Caleb the newcomers were at least thirty strong. They would find their dead compatriots and see the freshly spilled blood and give chase through the forest, tracking them with those huge ears and snouts.

Oh Christ, Caleb thought as they plucked Luca out from inside a cluster of ferns where the Brewer had hidden him. *They'll catch us in no time.*

They grabbed their packs and fled through the darkened woods opposite the main trail. A full moon gave them just enough light to see by. The Brewer changed his tune from a rousing battle song to a series of chirps, hoots, and other avian cries that possessed a ring of authenticity. It helped to mask the sound of their movement and allowed them to move more swiftly through the undergrowth. Luckily, the forest was not too dense in that region, and they made good progress. Luca looked terrified.

Marguerite risked another glance and almost tripped over a tree root. Caleb caught her by the arm. "What about their noses?" she asked. "I've 'eard they can smell humans from a mile away.

As she asked the question, they heard the faint sound of large bodies crashing through the forest.

"Do I really need to answer that?" the Brewer said.

Caleb grabbed the boy's hand and ran faster.

A short time later, breathless and on edge from the sounds of pursuit, they caught a break when the Brewer spied a bed of plants that resembled a cross between leeks and garlic. He raced over, got on his hands and knees, and started digging out the bulbs.

Caleb recoiled at the familiar, urine-soaked smell. "Stinkweed?"

The Brewer nodded as he bit into a bulb and crushed the brown pulp in his hands, then wiped it on his arms and clothes. Remembering the allergic reaction that had almost killed Yasmina, Caleb hesitated, then realized they had no choice. He and Marguerite and Luca grabbed their own bulbs and followed suit. The boy's hands were shaking, and Caleb helped him finish.

"Will this fool them?" Marguerite asked the Brewer.

"Sure, until they start wondering why the stinkweed is getting farther and farther away."

After a few sips of water, they fled through the forest again, covered in the foul-smelling herb. Marguerite had an uncanny knack for finding the easiest path through the undergrowth, leaving Caleb in awe of her abilities. After another hour of clambering over roots and rocks and suffering the constant slap of branches, she spied an old game trail, and they picked up the pace even further. Caleb asked if anyone had any idea where they were headed, but the Brewer could only shake his head, too tired to respond. Caleb remembered the man was quite a bit older than he and Marguerite, and had just spent a year in captivity.

By the time the game trail spilled into a sizeable stream, twenty feet across at the widest point, all sounds of pursuit had faded, and the Brewer collapsed in exhaustion at the edge of the water. Luca hugged his knees and took in huge gasps of air, and Marguerite sank to the ground beside Caleb.

After quenching their thirst and refilling their water skins, they followed the river downstream, away from the mountains and towards the coast. The thieves that had robbed Marguerite after the fairy attack had also taken her compass.

Tracking the stream by the light of the moon, they walked through the night, not daring to stop. At times the riverbank grew too dense, and they had to wade through the cold water, struggling over submerged boulders and fallen trees. Caleb had to carry Luca much of the way.

With dawn came a whisper of hope. They had heard no sounds of pursuit for hours, and the river would help confuse trackers. They reapplied stinkweed two more times, and no one complained about the forced march. The memories of the destroyed settlements hovered around them, driving them on.

Wary of fairy rings and predators, they finally decided to stop when, close to dusk, they saw a rock slab in the middle of the stream large enough for them all to sleep on. They foraged for dinner and made their bed on the cold hard stone. Luca laid his head in Caleb's lap, asleep in moments to the gurgle of water. Caleb stroked his hair as Marguerite snuggled tight against him.

Two days later, the forest broke to reveal a rolling meadow of orange poppies spilling down to the ocean. They had seen no sign of the tuskers. With a cry that sounded closer to a sob than a whoop of delight, an outburst of repressed emotion, Luca ran circles through the wildflowers and collapsed on his back in the middle of the meadow. Marguerite jumped into Caleb's arms and hugged his neck as the Brewer broke into a familiar song.

"Really?" Caleb asked. "The Sound of Music?"

"What?" Marguerite said, as both men roared with laughter.

As they headed south along the coast towards Freetown, the tenor of the trip changed, becoming less foreboding and more alive with the promise of a safe return. Luca began to open up, dashing through the surf when they bathed and asking constant questions about the marine life they could spot offshore. As did most children that age, he prized adventure above all else, and listened in rapt attention as the Brewer lifted his spirits with child-friendly tales of his travels.

Still, a sadness lurked in the depths of Luca's blue eyes like a plundered shipwreck at the bottom of the ocean, a place once full of treasure that was gone from the world forever. Caleb noticed it most at bedtime. More than anything in the world, he wished he could ease the boy's pain and make him whole again. They had still not discussed his parents, though when they reached the ocean and turned south, Luca had stood quietly facing in the opposite direction, towards his homeland, knowing his life had changed forever.

Near dusk on the fourth day along the coast, just a day or two from Freetown, the Brewer stopped to inspect a set of enormous footprints in the sand trailing down from the coastal hills.

"Too small for giants," Marguerite said, peering down. "And too big for human. Definitely not troll."

"What's that swishing thing in between the prints?" Caleb asked.

"A tail," she guessed, which earned a nod from the Brewer. With a grimace, the older man stood up straight and announced that the tracks belonged to a shibomos.

Marguerite wrinkled her face in confusion, but Luca looked stricken by the mention of the name. The Brewer noticed and squatted down to talk to him. "Don't believe everything you hear. I've met one before, and they're not nearly as bad as their reputation. They can even be quite friendly."

Luca peered at him with a dubious expression. "They can?"

"Sure," the Brewer said, with a wink. "Especially if you give them the right mushrooms covered in honey."

"What? Shrooms covered in *honey*?"

"Indeed," he said gravely. "It's their absolute favorite."

As the boy pondered his words, the Brewer stood and pointed at the ocean. "Is that a sea lion?" he asked, prompting Luca to whip around. "Why don't you go see?"

As Luca ran towards the shore, the Brewer's face darkened. "The shibomos really aren't as bad as the stories. But still dangerous."

"What is it?" Caleb asked.

"Think of Bigfoot with green fur."

"What?" Marguerite said.

"A big hairy man-beast that lives alone in the forest. Extremely solitary creatures. I've only seen their tracks one time, and *no one* has reported a sighting on the beach. My guess is the raiding parties are forcing them out of their homes."

Caleb cast an eye towards the edge of the forest, a hundred yards in the distance. Sloping gently upward and covered in lichen and scraggly wildflowers, the area was much rockier than most of the hills hugging the coast. "How dangerous are they?"

"Oh, they could do us in, if they wanted. But they're not usually aggressive."

"Usually?" Caleb said.

"Exactly," he replied, putting a hand on his sword as he called for Luca to return. "They're a wild card, for sure. No one knows much about them. But I do know they're nocturnal, and, if the stories are true, they hate caves and will never go inside. I know these hills. They're limestone and porous. If we can find a cave before dark, we can hole up for the night, set out at sunrise, and be long gone by the next nightfall."

"Why don't they like caves?" Caleb asked.

The Brewer shrugged. "I hear they're afraid of the dark."

*　　　*　　　*

They delved back into the forest, tracking as close to the beach as they could while searching for a suitable place to camp. Moss-covered boulders abounded, causing them to flinch at every turn, wary one of the fuzzy green mounds would reveal itself as a shibomos and rise up to attack them.

The shadows lengthened inside the forest, heralding the night. After a half hour of searching, the Brewer disappeared inside a crevasse set between a pair of boulders. Most of the openings only penetrated a dozen feet or so into the hillside, not deep enough for his liking.

He was gone so long Caleb began to worry, but finally he emerged holding a brass oil lantern, no bigger than a coffee cup, which he kept in his pack. The Brewer gave a tight smile and held up a thumb.

"Yeah?" Caleb said.

"Yeah."

Luca's eyes grew wide as he stared inside the cave. Marguerite linked arms with him as they went inside, claiming she was afraid and needed support. The damp narrow passage, strung with cobwebs and tree roots, soon widened into a smooth-walled grotto the size of a two-car garage. Other than a dried bed of sticks and pinecones that looked long abandoned, it was empty.

The Brewer set the lantern down well away from the entrance, gathered everyone close, and said, "Just to be sure, we should eat quietly and turn in. Might as well have an early night."

No one disagreed. After dining on nuts, berries, and salted beef sticks, they set out their bedrolls and turned off the lantern. The darkness was silent and complete, almost tangible, a second skin both alien and familiar.

As usual, Caleb slept between Marguerite and Luca. As soon as the light went off, as he did every night, the boy scooted closer to Caleb and pressed his head against his shoulder. Caleb reached for his hand and squeezed it. Luca didn't let go, and they lay like that deep into the night, Caleb comforting the boy's fear of the dark, and the boy easing Caleb's fear of being useless.

The Brewer was softly snoring, and Marguerite's breathing had assumed a steady, quiet rhythm. She, too, made Caleb feel things he had never felt before. Not just the electric dizziness of love, but the selfless, freeing feeling of living for another human being. With that came fear, of course. Fear of rejection, of betrayal, of bodily harm to his lover.

But that was okay. That was all human. He could live with those kinds of fears.

Yet the boy provided something that even Marguerite did not. Caleb knew that while his gray-eyed paramour truly loved him, and even respected him, she didn't *need* him. Marguerite was an accomplished member of the New Victoria Rogue's Guild. She could kick his butt with one hand tied behind her back, had skills he could only dream of, and made her own way in life.

The boy, on the other hand, needed him. At least right now. While Luca was affectionate towards Marguerite and entranced by the Brewer, it was Caleb's hand he always sought when scared or tired, Caleb's shoulder he liked to lean on after a meal. Caleb's eyes he gazed into whenever the memories trapped in his head or the trauma of the last week became too much to bear and the haunted look consumed him, the incomprehensible loss of his family washing over his fertile young mind like a tidal wave.

A rustling from outside the cave broke Caleb's reverie. Something pawing through the brush they had piled up to conceal the cave mouth.

Caleb stilled, and his mouth grew dry. Should he wake the others? He didn't want them to make any sudden sounds. The noise from outside grew in volume, and he swore he could hear a shuffling and then a sniffing sound, as if something on two feet had stuck its nose in the entrance of the cave and was searching for prey. Luca trembled beside him, gripping his hand and scooting even closer, until he was almost on top of Caleb. The Brewer and Marguerite were still asleep, and he realized the boy must have been awake the entire time.

Just as Caleb was about to sound the alarm, the rustling faded into the undergrowth. The boy's quivering continued for some time, and Caleb whispered soothing words and stroked his back until he relaxed again. After a while, the sounds of the night returned, an owl hooted outside the cave, and the boy laid his head on Caleb's chest and grew so quiet that Caleb had to lean up to hear his breathing, just to make sure he was okay.

As Caleb lay awake in the darkness between Marguerite and Luca, as far from his friends and family and everything else he knew as one could possibly get, he had the surprising revelation that, despite the ever-present dangers of the journey and his utter lack of knowledge as to what the future held, he had never felt so at peace.

37

Both the spider web and the moldy voice in Will's head disappeared. Instead, he found himself standing with Gunnar and Mateo and Selina near the top of a staircase made of huge limestone blocks. His stomach lurching with emotion, Will spun, looking for Mala and his brother.

There was no sign of Caleb, but Mala was standing on the step behind Will, her hand on the hilt of her dagger and looking just as confused as everyone else. He pulled her fiercely into a hug.

Instead of pulling away as he expected, she gripped his arm, then looked at Gunnar and back at Will, as if she, too, had faced an impossible choice.

So none of it was real, then. Somehow the sorcerer king reached out from beyond the grave, outside of the pyramid and across Urfe and into his brother's head—Will steepled his fingers against his temples. *Of course he didn't do that. The answer to the question about my past was right here, inside my own head. As was everything else. His feelings for Mala, his fear of spiders . . .*

Will turned and slammed a palm into the wall. "We're coming for you, you bastard! Do you hear me?"

The pyramid was as silent as a tomb.

As Will's anger ebbed out of him, the fear returned in full. With a shudder, he forced himself to concentrate on his surroundings. A few steps above him, the staircase dead-ended at a wall. He walked up to probe the barrier with his sword. It was solid stone.

Fifty feet below, a white light beckoned. Nowhere to go but down. As the party descended, Gunnar said in a numb voice, "I remember the nature of the fourth test now. What it was supposed to involve."

"And?" Mala asked, when he didn't continue.

The warrior's eyes slipped towards Mala. "The heart. A terrible sacrifice of the heart."

When they reached the bottom step, the origin of the light source was revealed. A short passage with a rounded ceiling led into a huge arena of some sort, lit by a bleached white glow that illuminated a rectangular playing field of packed dirt. On either side of the arena, high stone walls slanted up and away from the ground.

Wary and uncertain, the party stepped into the arena. High above loomed a ceiling made of rough black granite. The dirt floor was smoothly groomed, like the infield of a baseball diamond. Will pointed at the wall on the far side. Fifteen feet up, the face of a circle, two feet in diameter, had been cut into the stone.

Will knew what this was. He had seen pictures back home of the ancient ball game played by the Mayans and other Amerindian cultures. Though he couldn't remember all the details, he thought the object was to throw a ten-pound rubber ball through the circle. It seemed simple, but it was a violent game with no rules. Serious injuries and death were commonplace.

And that was on Earth.

As if in response to his thoughts, a thump emanated from the far side of the field, and he looked up to see a gray ball the size of a basketball rolling across the field. It stopped just short of them, crunching softly into the dirt.

Will turned to inspect the wall above the passage they had just walked through.

There was no corresponding stone circle on their end.

After Mala toed the ball with her foot, Will bent to pick it up. It was made of dense rubber and was quite heavy. If he stood right under the circle, he thought he could toss the ball high enough to get through, but it wouldn't be easy.

As soon as he picked up the ball, a doorway cut into the wall on the far left side of the arena creaked open, and out stepped five beings from Will's darkest nightmares. The leader was a nine-foot tall skeletal humanoid with a forked tongue as long as Will's arm, a necklace made of shrunken heads, and a rigid black snake that served as its staff. The shortest creature, about Mala's height, was a squat green monstrosity covered in pus and open scabs and wielding a spiked club. A third had skin like bark, thick branches growing out of its skull, and a coiled rope ending in a noose in each hand.

Another walked with a simian lope, had gray skin and arms that dragged the ground, and tentacles that writhed on either side of its mouth. Last was a hulking crimson beast bunched with muscle and almost as tall as the skeletal leader. Tiny suckered appendages covered its arms and legs, and it carried a broadsword, as well as a bag slung over its scaly shoulders.

"The Archdukes of Xibalba," Gunnar whispered. "Devils. Hell spawn."

"How are they beaten?" Mala asked. "In the stories?"

Gunnar gripped his war hammer, still bleeding from the knife wounds the healing potion hadn't closed. "They aren't. But myth tells of how Hunahpu and Xbalanque escaped Xibalba by defeating two of the archdukes in a ball game."

"Lucky us," Will muttered. "We get five."

"One apiece, then," Mala said, twirling her sash as the five creatures fanned out in a line and advanced on the party. Diseased flesh dropped off the pus devil as it walked.

Will shook off his dread and focused. "Might as well try this the easy way. Selina, can you fly with that ball? Try to throw it through the circle?"

The sylvamancer used her magic to pick up the rubber ball and soar into the air. The archdukes kept advancing. Twenty feet separated them from the party. As Selina flew over their heads, arms extended to toss the ball through the circle and hopefully end the trial, the bark devil turned and launched one of his ropes at her. The coiled rope unfurled and the noose snagged one of her ankles. The creature yanked and brought her crashing to the dirt. She arrested her fall at the last moment, landed on her feet, and thrust her hands at the monster's chest. Will heard the rush of a wizard wind, but the bark devil and the other archdukes barely flinched.

"Magic resistant," Mala said grimly. "I feared as much."

Those were the last words before the battle began in earnest. The huge crimson beast stalked towards Gunnar, and Will noticed in horror that its suckered appendages were little fanged mouths that opened and closed in hunger.

As the pus devil squared off against Mateo, Mala threw her sash at the tall bone devil. The skeletal being grinned as the weighted ends wrapped around his neck and clanged against his skull without effect. Short sword and curved dagger in hand, she sprang forward to cut him down at the knees, but he blocked both blows with a sweep of his snake staff. On the backswing, the head of the staff came alive and lunged at her.

Will didn't have time to watch his friends or keep track of the ball. The gray-skinned devil flung both of its long arms at Will, scraping at his leather armor with fingernails as sharp as daggers. Will stepped back and blocked the blows with Zariduke, disappointed when the monster didn't disappear with a snip of blue-white light.

Whether these beings were actual archdukes from the Mayan hell dimension or some twisted hybrid creation of the sorcerer king, they weren't going to disappear with a touch from his sword.

Instead of falling back as Will expected, the devil thrust its head towards him, and the tentacles around its mouth tried to latch onto his face. As Will recoiled in horror, the gray devil's fingers reached around to lash his back, ten dagger tips stabbing him from behind. He screamed.

Stay calm, Will. Stay calm or you're dead.

Will shook off the pain and created distance with a snap kick to the monster's chest. Closing in for the kill was not an option, he realized. Those tentacles would tear his face off.

His sword thrusts took nicks out of the gray man's long arms, but the creature didn't react to the pain and never seemed to tire. Will risked a glance to the side and didn't like what he saw.

Mateo's sword had a greater reach than the pus devil's club, but his cousin's supple blade didn't seem to cause any damage when it connected. Non-magical weapons, Will realized, could not harm the archdukes. He thought the two combatants equally matched until the pus devil tore off hunks of its own flesh and tossed them at Mateo, causing a smoking wound wherever they made contact.

Selina had managed to free her ankle from the noose but, her power waning and far removed from her preferred sylvan battleground, she was in a fight for her life against the bark devil. Will feared the fight was over when the devil snagged Selina's foot again and dragged her forward, its head lowered to spear her with the branches growing like antlers out of its head. Mateo noticed and rushed to her defense, whipping the bark devil with his sword. The weapon had little effect, but it distracted the monster long enough for Selina to transform into a small rhinoceros that burst out of the noose and met the bark devil head to head. A fierce battle ensued, and Mateo paid for his decision with a club lash from behind.

Gunnar and the crimson behemoth stalked each other in a slow circle. As the big man kept his eyes trained on the broadsword, the archduke flung the sack on its back at Gunnar's feet. The warrior leapt back as the sack burst, causing gallons of red liquid to splash over him. The crimson devil roared in delight as Gunnar slipped and fell, covered in blood.

Will started to despair. The archdukes had the edge in battle and did not seem to tire.

But the party didn't have to win, he reminded himself. Assuming the arena was not a cruel diversion, they just had to put the rubber ball through the circle at the far end.

This fight would be won with their minds, not their swords.

It was hard to think of a viable strategy while keeping the gray-skinned devil at bay, but Will had no choice. He dropped back slowly, allowing his opponent to gain ground but freeing his mind to think. He forced himself to eliminate the human component of the battle, the terrible price of defeat.

How can I move my chess pieces to win this battle? What are my advantages, my variables?

He fought his way next to the Selina-rhinoceros. "Create more of them," Will said.

The powerful animal tilted its head in a quizzical manner.

"The rubber balls," Will said. "Can you make more?"

The rhino snorted and backed away. Moments later, Selina transformed back into human form and caused nine more of the rubber balls to appear, right beside the real one, which was lying near the passage where they had entered.

"Send them through," he said. "All at the same time."

With a sweep of her arms, the sylvamancer caused all ten balls to rise into the air and commingle, then speed toward the circle cut into the stone. Will felt a rush of elation until the bark devil threw a rope at the real ball, ignoring the other nine as he yanked the rubber sphere out of the air and sent it hurtling back towards the party. Mateo ducked before the ball flattened him. It bounced off the rear wall and settled at Mala's feet.

So much for that.

Mala got the hint and called out a series of battle commands. As the archdukes advanced, the party formed a spearhead in defense, leaving Mala alone in the middle and Will at the point, engaging the skeletal leader and the pus devil at the same time. He wouldn't last long against both archdukes, but he didn't have to. As the two sides engaged, Mala broke away, picked up the ball, and took off for the side wall.

Instead of pressing their numeric advantage, all five archdukes broke off and went for Mala. Will sprinted after her, but the archdukes were as fast as he was, and he would never catch them in time. Horrified, he could only watch as the crimson demon caught up to Mala, raising his broadsword to cut her down from behind.

She was halfway across the arena, slowed by the weight of the huge rubber ball. Despite Will's shouts, she didn't seem to notice the approaching devils, until the last second when she dropped the ball and whirled, blocking the crimson devil's attack with her short sword and shoving her dagger to the hilt in his chest. The archduke roared and staggered back.

At some point, Mala had retrieved her sash. She twirled it in the face of the bark devil, smacking him twice in the forehead while keeping hold of the weapon, then letting the sash fly at the skeletal leader. The weighted ends curled around his head and smashed one of his eyes, causing him to clutch his face.

Mala picked up the ball and kept running. The gray man loped after her, the pus devil steps behind. The rest of the party had drawn closer. Gunnar threw his hammer across the field and hit the pus devil in the back, causing it to stumble.

The gray man reached out with a long arm and caught Mala by the shoulder. She screamed as the fingernails dug in, whipping her around. She turned with blades up and fought like a wounded animal, driving him back with an acrobatic kick to his chest.

After grabbing the ball again, she closed the distance to the far wall. Will and the others were steps behind the archdukes. With a triumphant shout, Mala bent low and heaved the ball in the air.

It bounced off the wall a foot beneath the hole, fell to the ground, and rolled back towards her feet.

Will sagged in despair.

Mala wasn't strong enough.

As the fight commenced anew, the rubber ball soared back into the air and shot towards the hole. *Selina*, Will realized. He froze, holding his breath as he followed the ball's trajectory. Inches before it sailed through, the bark devil lassoed it and jerked it backwards. It bounced and rolled right up to the skeletal leader, who cackled, bent double to pick up the ball with a bony hand, and threw it all the way back to the other side.

Will's heart sank. The archdukes converged on Mala, but she whipped out her expandable acrobat's rod and pole-vaulted over them. At the height of her trajectory, the gray man reached out with a long arm and raked her leg in midair. She collapsed in a heap at Will's side, bleeding in a dozen places.

He pulled her to her feet. "Can you fight?"

Her eyes flashed. "If I'm breathing, I can fight."

She called out another battle formation, this time with Gunnar as the ball carrier. The attempt failed when the crimson devil caught the big man as he was dashing across the arena along the side wall. The archduke's tackle put the big man flat on his back and left a string of bloody wounds on his side.

Teeth marks, Will realized with a shudder. From those horrid little mouths.

Mala kept trying to push Gunnar through, but the battle went downhill. Selina was forced to morph into rhino form to stay alive, Mateo looked ready to collapse, Gunnar heaved with exertion, and Mala looked frustrated and desperate.

We need something different, Will thought. *Some way to fool them.*

As the pus devil advanced on him, he wracked his brain for a new strategy, a way to harness their strengths or exploit the situation.

One ball, he told himself, *through one single circle. That's all it takes.*

The pus devil swung his spiked club. Will blocked it. Again and again. His strength was fading. The archdukes were barely injured and looked as energetic as when they had stepped out of their stone doorways.

As Mala called out a new formation, a thought came to him.

"Different plan!" Will called out. "Selina, I need you!"

The sylvamancer broke away from her fight with the gray man and morphed into mage form, flying backwards to meet Will.

The ball was too big to hide, he knew, and the archdukes could pick it out of a crowd.

But what if they made it disappear?

"Gunnar, get ready!" Will called out, then ran to the rubber ball and picked it up. When the big man cast a quick glance over his shoulder, Will winked at him, praying he would get the hint.

Will turned towards Selina, not bothering to lower his voice. He wanted the archdukes to hear. "Can you cloak the ball with magic? Block it out with light?"

"I believe so," she said, breathing hard as she darted back and forth along the rear wall to avoid the gray man's reach. The archdukes pressed the attack, sensing the party's reserves were spent.

"Then do it!" Will shouted. "Now!"

He knew wizards could work with light. He assumed Selina could use the white illumination in the arena to form a barrier around the ball that would cloak its presence. Whether it would fool the archdukes was another matter. He doubted she could hide the ball itself, but maybe she could create a barrier the archdukes couldn't see around.

Whatever spell she used, it worked. Though he could still feel the heft of the rubber ball, it disappeared in his hands. As soon as it did, he called Gunnar's name and pretended to toss the ball to him.

The big man seemed surprised at first, causing Will's heart to sink, but he caught on at the last moment and feigned catching the projectile, *oomphing* and falling backwards as if it had caught him in the chest. Clutching his arms around a bundle of empty air, Gunnar feigned a step forward and then darted to the side, around the crimson archduke. Dashing for the far wall.

The devils broke off from their opponents and converged on Gunnar. Will's spirits soared. *They bought it.*

While the battle raged around Gunnar, Will sheathed his sword and took off at a dead sprint down the center of the arena. As soon as he started running, the ball reappeared. Selina's spell must not have been mobile.

The pus devil noticed first. With a shriek, he babbled in a strange tongue and pointed at Will. The other archdukes broke away again and gave chase. If Will was unencumbered, he would have made it free and clear to the far wall. But the ball was *heavy*.

The stone wall loomed ten yards away. He debated a desperate heave but knew he had to get closer. Right to the bottom of the wall. Not only did he have to throw the ball high enough to reach the circle, he had to be accurate, and he probably had one chance to get it right.

Five yards away. Will wanted to shout with victory. He was going to make it. The closest archduke, the skeleton, was too far away to reach him. Will reached the wall and bent his legs for extra power.

Before he could propel the ball upward, something scaly wrapped around his neck and tightened. He dropped the ball, gagged, and clutched his throat. A flat serpent's head darted for his eyes, fangs glistening. Will stuck out a hand and grabbed it by the neck just before it bit him.

Will unsheathed his sword with his other hand. He could hear the archdukes rushing towards him. The skeleton man must have thrown his staff all the way across the arena.

Will swung hard. His sword cut deep into the coils, shearing the snake in two. It fell lifeless to the ground. In one smooth motion, Will sheathed his sword and picked up the ball. Too late he noticed the bark devil right beside him. The massive being thrust its horned head right at Will's chest, aiming to impale him.

The attack had come fast, but another attack came faster. He heard a war cry from his cousin and saw the pliable blade of the urumi sword snap in mid-air and smack away the bark devil's attack, an inch before the deadly branches pierced Will's chest.

The other four archdukes were a step behind the bark devil. But Will had the ball, and a step was enough. He hurled the rubber sphere at the circle, praying his aim was true, willing it to go through.

The bark devil snarled and tossed one of his lassos at the ball, seeking to foil the attempt just as it had the last two.

Mateo's sword snapped again.

The rope split in two.

The ball soared through the circle.

38

After strategizing until confident they had the best plan available, Val and the others left the safety of the steam room. Before they confronted Asmodeus, they had to get past the gethzul, a task none of them felt confident they could accomplish. Again, they were driven by necessity rather than choice. Trying to drop down through the iron grate would draw every demon in the building, and in addition, Val had sensed powerful wards on the iron bars. They had tried removing a few portions of the floor, but had found nothing but packed dirt, as far as they probed. Either something strange and interdimensional was going on, or they would have to blast through so much floor it would alert every demon in the baths.

A dozen feet before the staircase, Synne laid a hand on Val's arm. "Promise you will do as we agreed. Do not engage the gethzul. Queen willing, we'll join you soon."

Val cracked a grin. "You don't trust your wizard?"

"I know how he thinks."

He clasped her arm in return. "Good luck, and come back to me. I need my majitsu by my side."

Her eyes flashed with emotion. With a short nod, she turned away and flexed her fingers, preparing for battle.

At the top of the stairs, Synne and Rucker fanned out to the sides. The eyes of the gethzul once again flicked upwards, watching the party with cool disdain through the swirling vapors. Rucker twirled his axe and grinned, locked eyes with Synne, and sprang down the stairs. The majitsu followed on the opposite side, taking five steps at a time with graceful leaps.

The gethzul on the right rose fluidly to its feet, awaiting Rucker's charge. At the last second, the demon spun away from his axe swing and raked backwards with an extended hand. The creature moved far faster, but Rucker had somehow anticipated the maneuver and lowered his head. The gethzul's black claws rasped harmlessly across his helm.

When Synne engaged, the two seemed evenly matched. The movements of the gethzul were not methodical in nature like the trained majitsu. Instead they were primal, animalistic. The smoke-colored demon slashed with its claws in whip-like motions, keeping Synne on the defensive. When she pressed the attack, the demon absorbed punches that would have shattered bones. Once or twice the gethzul stumbled backwards when Synne connected.

Val watched the fight with a hollow space in his stomach. Once the battle started, he led a second charge down the middle of the staircase, followed by Dida and Ferin and Adaira. The three mages erected Wizard Shields around the group as they raced down the stairs. Both gethzul broke off and tried to attack Val and then Adaira, but the Wizard Shields held—barely. Val felt the magic start to tear, and he knew a few blows from those black claws would rip right through the magic. Synne said the gethzul were immune to most spells, so they had no choice but to hurry through and leave the battle to the warriors.

A wave of thick hot air assaulted Val at the bottom of the staircase. Molds and yeasts and mushrooms covered the rock walls and floors, sometimes forming strange symbols and patterns, as if the fungi were sentient beings.

Ten feet past the stairs, Val turned and saw Rucker take a piece out of the gethzul's shoulder with his axe. Black blood dripped from the being's ashen skin, though it continued fighting in silence. With anticipation that seemed supernatural, Rucker avoided or blocked most of the blows, using his helm and bracers and even his boot spurs as shields. When one of the gethzul's claws tore through his left spur, ripping it in half, the crafty warrior responded by jamming the end of his axe blade into the monster's stomach, causing it to stumble backwards and trip over a step. Rucker swung down for the kill but the gethzul sprang away at the last moment.

Synne was connecting with more frequency than Rucker but causing little damage. Val could tell she was too wary of the gethzul's poison bite to move inside for a killing blow. Blood streaked from wounds on her arms and oozed through her shirt.

What she needs, Val thought, *is a weapon*.

"Synne," he shouted, "catch!"

He launched his staff over the head of the majitsu. Synne leapt high into the air to catch it, blocking downward with the staff as she landed to defend another blow. Val breathed a sigh of relief when the staff held up to the claws of the gethzul. With a lightning-fast combination, Synne found an opening and ripped a large gash through the creature's chest with the crescent moon tip.

Val expected the gethzul to step back and regroup. Synne must have, too, because she was caught by surprise when the gethzul pressed through the awful blow and sprang onto her like a jungle cat, wrapping its legs around her waist and biting deep into her neck.

Synne dropped the staff and convulsed, her scream ricocheting through the hallway.

Stunned at first, Val recovered his wits and dashed forward, ignoring Adaira's shouts of protest. Synne lay helpless on the floor, the gethzul still attached to her neck. Black energy sprang into Val's hands, roaring through him, and he channeled the Spirit Fire into the demon's back.

The gethzul arched and emitted a high-pitched moan. The Spirit Fire didn't consume the gethzul as it did most things, but it burned a hole into its back, and Val kept pushing. Synne was still slumped on the steps. When the demon turned for him, somehow pressing through the pain, Synne lurched to her feet and picked up the staff. She swung with both hands at the gethzul's torso, snapping her wrists so hard the azantite edge almost severed the demon in half. It fell to the floor, dead, and Synne collapsed beside it.

Val extinguished the Spirit Fire. He turned and saw Rucker locked in battle with his opponent, taking blow after blow from its claws and narrowly avoiding a bite. When Val picked up his staff to join the fray, the gethzul broke off from fighting Rucker and lunged at Val too fast for him to react. Val screamed as the gethzul raked his chest and arms with its claws, opening deep gashes as it sprang forward with its mouth agape, four long incisors prepared to clamp onto Val's face.

His Wizard Shield came too late. The sickly sweet breath of the gethzul pressed into his face, then faded away as the monster slumped to the ground. Val looked down and saw Rucker's magical axe embedded deep into the demon's spine. An incredible blow. A killing blow. Rucker walked over, spat as he put a foot on the demon's back, and yanked out his axe. "Teach the bloody thing to turn its back on me."

"Adaira!" Val called out, shaking from the fading adrenaline and the pain lancing through his chest and arms. "Synne needs you!"

The cuerpomancer was already rushing over. After casting a worried glance at Val's wounds, she bent over the majitsu. Adaira took in the blue pallor of her face and the bite wound in her neck.

Rucker's words rang in Val's head. *A poison with no antidote.*

Adaira moved everyone back and hovered over Synne. As the rest of the party watched the stairs and the hallway for signs of trouble, Dida caused the air to shimmer, shielding the party from casual observance. If anyone had heard the screams, Val realized, then they would assume the gethzul had claimed another victim.

Adaira face had paled and she broke into a cold sweat as her hands moved in a slow circle around the wound. The work of a cuerpomancer was a mystery to Val, but he gathered that Adaira was very talented, and she looked as exhausted as he had ever seen her. He brought her a drink of water and stayed by her side, but could do little else except look on in concern. Though incredibly painful, he sensed his own wounds were a shadow of the poison coursing through Synne's system.

Val grew more nervous with every passing second. He guessed many of the demons could see through Dida's spell, and it was only a matter of time before one wandered over. Or maybe the strange, luminescent life forms on the walls were reporting their presence, and Asmodeus was already waiting on them.

At last the majitsu coughed and opened her eyes. Adaira swooned and fell into Val's arms. "The poison was so strong," she said weakly. "Unlike any I have ever encountered. Had I not reached her at the very moment of injection, she would have had no chance."

After drinking an entire skin of water, Synne hobbled to her feet. The color returned to her skin, and she flexed her hands and rolled her neck. After a deep bow to Adaira, she signaled with a curt nod that she was ready to continue.

The cuerpomancer was slumped on a step, barely conscious. "I can walk," she said, struggling to her feet, "but I'm afraid my magic is spent."

Val gritted through his own pain and stood beside her. Besides the physical wounds, he guessed half his magic was depleted.

Synne recovering from a brush with death. Rucker bruised and battered. Adaira and Dida almost drained, Val at half-strength, and Ferin of little use against the sort of adversaries they were facing.

As the party started down the humid passage glowing with the bioluminescence of demon-spawned fungi, marching towards a final encounter they might not be able to survive, Val wondered, as did all leaders, whether the choices he had made that led to that moment were the right ones. Whether he could have done better.

In response, he tightened his grip on his staff, filled his mind with images of his brothers, and prepared to steal the crown.

39

Dean Groft jerked awake and sat up in bed, his subconscious mind tickled by an abnormal fluctuation of spirit. It was probably nothing, a spirit mage honing a late night spell or a ripple from a distant battle of wizards or a bubble in the space-time continuum. He knew his subliminal awareness was more attuned to the presence of spirit than was his conscious self.

Instead of falling back asleep, he rose for a drink of water. Unlike the vast majority of his peers, Dean Groft did not have a towering stronghold with a colored spire in the Wizard District. Though spirit mages themselves, his parents had raised him to be a public servant, and he had married a common-born woman who had long since passed. The dean lived a block off St. Charles, in a quaint, ivy-covered cottage across from the stately public library. A modest house compared to his neighbors.

That did not mean his residence was unprotected. Everyone knew who lived there, and attempting to encroach on the property of an elder spirit mage was, well, it was simply not done.

Clad in a linen bed-robe, his bad knees creaking, the dean's eyes passed over the portrait of his wife on his bedside table. The warm smile and eyes like melting glaciers, hair as red as flame, a woman whose kindness surpassed even her beauty.

After Helena died of old age, the dean lost much of his will to live. What kept him going was not a desire to live forever—on the contrary, Groft had no children, his parents and siblings were long deceased, and he desperately missed his wife and looked forward to the day his spiritual energy reunited with hers.

No, his motivation was his sense of civic duty.

Lord Alistair had always been ambitious, but ever since his own wife had perished, his lust for power had consumed him, warping his perspective. Though an effective leader, and one of the most powerful mages to grace the Realm in hundreds of years, the Chief Thaumaturge did not believe in egalitarian rule. He believed in the superiority of the mage-born.

Extreme loyalty to one's own people was not a positive character trait, Groft knew. It simply made one insensitive to the plight of others. Not only that, but a world ruled by the privileged few could only lead to inequality and ruin. The growing disparity in the Realm had bred anger and desperation. Revolt was inevitable.

The Congregation would crush the Revolution, of course. Yet what kind of world would result? One of slaves and masters, cruelty and prejudice?

That was not a world in which the dean wished to live.

Groft knew he was the only mage powerful enough to challenge Lord Alistair's bid for authoritarian rule. Many looked to the dean as a stabilizing influence, and he feared what would happen should he die and leave the Realm in Alistair's hands.

With a deep sigh, he padded into the kitchen. He poured a cup of water from a pitcher and added a few chips of ice from the frost chest.

That drink of water saved his life.

When he stepped back into the bedroom, he saw two black shadows in human form flow through the walls and converge on his bed. Hands extended, streaks of silver light pulsating up and down their bodies, they reached for the rumpled bedcover that had concealed Groft's sleeping form not moments before.

His first thought: how had they gotten past his wards?

His second: what in the Realm *were* they?

As the two beings realized the bed was empty and turned to face him, he at once sensed the warped magic that had been forced into these creatures. Knew they were perversions of humankind and spirit.

He also sensed their power, and that a touch would mean his death.

The shadows flew right at him. Groft blasted them with a Spirit Wind that pushed them back. They regrouped and pressed forward. He raked them with Spirit Fire but it disappeared into their shadowy forms, as if joining with their energies.

He had moments to act. None of his plentiful magic items would help him. He guessed only a handful of items in the Realm could combat these beings. He tried a few more spells in rapid succession, just to be sure. Fire Sphere from a shattered lamp, Spirit Ray, Mind Whip. Nothing worked.

Forced to take defensive measures, the dean skipped the inferior Spirit

Shield and went straight to Spirit Skin, a highly advanced spell that bonded spirit to the outer layer of the epidermis and created the strongest barrier known to man. Dean Groft experienced a grim relief when the shadow creatures tried to grab him and were repelled.

The problem was, Spirit Skin was incredibly draining. If maintained, he had perhaps ten minutes before his magic ran dry. It gave him a reprieve but little else. A scintilla of time to formulate a plan.

The shadow beings seemed to sense this and hovered just out of reach, watching him.

Waiting.

He looked closer and noticed in shock that he recognized the faces of the shadow beings. Both were former spiritmancers who had died over the years: one a student who had perished during the Planewalk; the other a young mage who had disappeared while exploring the Place Between Worlds. Or so they had been told. Lord Alistair had presided over the failed Planewalk attempt, and spearheaded the search party in the Place Between Worlds.

Alistair, the dean whispered in horror, *what have you done?*

He contemplated flying into the Wizard District, rousing the Conclave, and letting the members bear witness to these beings. If traced back to Lord Alistair, his deed would land him in the Wizard Vault for life. Perhaps spell his execution.

What stayed the dean's hand was worry for the safety of others. Only a dozen or so mages in the Realm could form a Spirit Skin, and these beings would destroy all others who stood in their path. Would destroy *him* if he didn't figure out a way to combat them.

Congealed spirit was the rarest and most powerful of all magic. The might of a spirit mage molded over time and distilled into an item of arcane power. He did not know exactly what these hybrid beings were, but he sensed they were formed of spirit during a long and arduous process. He could not even imagine the suffering those poor souls must have endured.

He also knew the one thing that could combat congealed spirit was a higher purity of magic. This was why Zariduke was so feared. It cut through lesser magic without fail, and must have been made by a supremely powerful arch mage. Salomon himself, if the legends were true.

But Groft did not have Spiritscourge, or another item even close to that level of power. His greatest offensive weapons—spells born of spirit—would only inconvenience these beings. Groft could fight them by making a weapon of equal or greater strength, but that would take time. Years.

Yet offensive spells were not his specialty. A true spirit mage focused on exploring the nature of magic itself, probing the dimensions, unlocking the secrets of the multiverse.

Let us see, he thought, *if I can defeat them in another way.*

Let us see if they can follow where I lead.

As the shadow beings watched, streaks of silver light heaving up and down their forms, Dean Groft clapped his hands to create a rift in spirit, and then stepped into the Void.

A tunnel of endless dark.

Boundless. Formless.

He extended his hands and flew, not with his body but with his mind, down and down and down, faster and faster, unlocking his power, whisking across the fabric of reality.

He looked back. The shadow beings had followed.

Deeper into the tunnel, twists and turns and loopholes, a maze of blackest night before bursting through a veil of spirit into a starscape stretching to infinity and littered with impossible geometric shapes, doorways to other planes slipping in and out of existence, dancing along the edges of worlds, skirting the rims of universes.

A younger spirit mage might be dumbstruck by the journey, awed by the specter of divinity, the order within the seething chaos, but Dean Groft had traveled the pathways of spirit many times before, deep into the cosmos. He ignored the spectacle and focused on the purpose of the journey.

Another glance confirmed the presence of his pursuers, flowing steadily behind him.

They're tracking my spirit signature, he realized.

With a sinking heart, he realized why Alistair had used spirit mages as the subjects of his unholy experiments. They could go to the same places Groft could, and he guessed they could endure longer than he, with their unnatural infusion of pure spirit.

Just to make sure, he passed through a few hell dimensions and then up to the empyrean realms, shielding himself with spirit as he burrowed through the elemental planes.

Nothing fazed the two beings.

There was only one thing left to try.

With a burst of power, he opened a rift to the Place Between Worlds. Most beautiful of all places in his home universe, a primary plane of reality that Dean Groft had oft visited but did not truly understand, it was a fitting site for what he planned to do.

He wondered briefly whether it mattered where souls die and if they could travel the same pathways after death, whether his plan jeopardized his reunion with his wife.

Not all things can be known by the mind of man, he said to himself.

Not all things should.

His world exploded in color as he entered the Place Between Worlds. Otherworldly hues preserved in solid state, melted rainbows forming tubular passages and wide open plains stretching to infinity, no sky or ground, just a primordial soufflé of grottoes and tunnels and conduits of color, polyhedra and spirals and archipelagos, the building blocks of magic, of reality, of the awesome unknown power of creation.

Groft ignored the flat, one-dimensional circles that signaled the entrance to new worlds. Likewise, he avoided the Astral Wraiths, long and fluttery shapes similar in composition to the shadow beings following him. The Astral Wraiths were terrible adversaries who devour the essence of wayward travelers, and which no one knew how to kill. They might serve his purpose—he had no idea what would happen if the shadow beings came into contact with an Astral Wraith—but flying too close was risky. He had a different goal in mind.

Most of the time, the Place Between Worlds existed in silence. Yet eventually a high-pitched whine arose, a whistling rush of air akin to a boiling teakettle. The Astral Wind, bringer of chaos and buffeter of souls. Something even a spirit mage feared. No one knew what happened to those caught in the wind, because no one had ever returned. His guess was that the Astral Wind spanned dimensions and universes, or perhaps broached an entirely new plane of reality. Spirit mages could find their way to new dimensions, but if they could not keep track of their progress, lost in the wind, they might never get back.

Instead of ducking into another world, Dean Groft kept his course straight and true. If the shadow beings caught and killed him, they could follow his spirit signature back to Urfe and wreak havoc.

Sensing them at his heels, he whirled and cast Astral Cord, connecting his essence to that of the beings following him. He felt the invisible cord attach, and tested it with a sudden burst of speed.

The cord drew taut, jerking him backwards, closer to the shadow beings.

For better or worse, their fates were linked.

The wind keened louder. Groft kept flying. He turned and saw blasts of silver light heaving through the forms of the shadow beings, as if anxious or fearful.

As the Astral Wind overtook them, screaming into Groft's ears, the sound of reality itself splitting, he used the last of his magic to encase himself in Spirit Skin, a final desperate measure that might help shield him from whatever lay ahead.

The Astral Wind spun them so violently that Groft lost all sense of direction. He vomited as he spun in circles through worlds and dimensions and realities so fast his vision could not keep up. Yet as he whirled through time and space, snapping the link to his adversaries as his Spirit Skin weakened, he felt at peace with the knowledge that the return pathway was scrambled and the three of them were hopelessly lost in the multiverse, with no way back to Urfe.

What came next, only the Creator knew.

40

As the rubber ball flew through the hole in the stone, the ground gave way beneath Will's feet. He fell through a trap door that hinged open, his momentum slowed, and then he was floating inside an enormous hall with columns of jade and a floor made of gold.

He looked up. The trap door had swung shut behind him. There was no sign of the archdukes, but his companions had fallen through the floor with him, drifting slowly downward as if caught in a featherweight spell, droplets of blood from their various wounds suspended in midair. At first he assumed Selina had arrested their fall, but when he saw her struggling to right herself, he knew the magic had come from a different source.

The floor was thirty feet below them. Soft golden light, a captured sunrise, illuminated the room. With nothing else to do as he descended, Will absorbed his surroundings.

The jade columns portioned off a smaller square, about the size of his high school gym, within the larger rectangle of the vast hall. Outside the jade columns, ingots representing a huge variety of gemstones formed the walls of the chamber, diamond and sapphire and opal stacked in neat rows from floor to ceiling. Thousands and thousands of them. Will caught his breath. Whether melted in a forge or shaped by the hand of an alchemancer, he couldn't begin to grasp the amount of wealth those walls represented.

Gemstone statues, glass display cases, and a cornucopia of other treasures filled the space inside the columns. An exquisitely carved urn cradled butterflies of spun gold. Swords and goblets and full sets of armor, cloaks and girdles and helms, priceless works of art from a plethora of cultures. Some of the artistic styles looked familiar to Will, and some looked fantastical, either created by societies endemic to Urfe, shaped by mages, or from another world entirely.

"By the Queen," Mala whispered, as she gaped at the treasure.

In the center of the hall, a circle of twelve marble sarcophagi surrounded a golden statue on a pedestal. The statue was of a tall Mayan chieftain with arms spread wide, as if showcasing the room to his visitors. A headdress of sunrays crowned the figure, and he grasped an azantite rod beset with a variety of gemstones.

As the party touched down, they regained freedom of movement. Mala approached one of the display cases. Inside was a violet amulet matching her eyes, embedded with pieces of azantite that formed a nine-pointed star.

"The enneagon of Kirna Tuluth," she breathed. "A legendary talisman."

After walking around the room and inspecting the various items, touching them to ensure they were real, no one needed to question where they were. They had arrived, Will knew, in the treasure room of Yiknoom Uk'ab K'ahk, and the only question that remained was what sort of guardian lay in wait. Somehow, it made him more nervous that nothing had appeared yet.

Maybe someone had found this place already, he thought with a nervous chuckle. But if that was the case, then why was all the treasure left behind? The room looked untouched for millennia.

Keeping a wary eye on the circle of marble sarcophagi, silent sentinels carved in Egyptian style, Will stepped onto the pedestal and tapped his sword against the gold statue. It was solid. "Yiknoom, I presume?"

Gunnar peered up at the statue. "Aye," he said, at the same time a voice sounded in Will's head. The same raspy voice, full of rot and power, that had whispered in his ear in the spider web.

I am pleased you bear witness to my cathedral.

Will spun, just as he had the last time, but there was no one to be seen. "Did anyone else hear that?"

"Aye," Gunnar said again, raising his war hammer and crouching into a fighting stance. Sash and short sword in hand, Mala whirled one way and then the other. Mateo and Selina pressed close together, scanning the room.

As Will jumped off the pedestal, his head swiveling to find the source of the voice, it spoke again.

An accumulation of the greatest my age had to offer.

At that moment, Will understood. He knew why they had floated softly down through the ceiling, why the room was laid out in such an orderly fashion, and why no terrible guardian had approached them thus far.

The disembodied voice belonged to the sorcerer king himself, his thoughts or his essence somehow preserved through the millennia. And what the spirit of the eldritch mage desired above all else, the last pleasure available to his vain and putrefied soul, was for them to bear witness to his glory.

To *see*.

"Show yourself!" Mala commanded.

A spray of laughter echoed in Will's head, the rustle of dry leaves in a cemetery. *I am where I have been for eons, daughter of the wagon wheel, and will remain for eons to come. The Lord of All Suns to your children and your children's children, a thousand generations bowed before me, all bearing witness to my glory and trembling at my everlasting might.*

Humility, Will thought, was not a strong suit of the sorcerer king.

I commend you on being the first to survive my trials. You may observe my riches as your lives expire, but be warned, to touch my possessions is to incur my—

The sound of shattering glass broke the monologue. Will whipped around to find Mala standing in front of a large azantite chest covered in runes and engravings and surrounded by shards from the smashed display case. Two pairs of azantite rings, attached to each side of the coffer, provided a means by which to insert poles and carry the chest.

Mateo's face broke into a reverent expression. "The Coffer of Devla."

Stop.

Mala whipped out a canvas bag that somehow expanded to encompass the entire artifact. She fitted the bag around the corners and slid the fabric across it. Once the coffer was concealed, the bag shrank to normal size, and Mala stuffed it into a waist pouch. After that, she strode three display cases over, smashed another one, and withdrew a glove made of chain mail.

Stop!

"Catch," she said, and tossed the glove to Mateo.

STOOOOOPPPPPP!!!!!

The sarcophagi at the base of the pedestal shuddered open. Twelve mummies encased in swaths of gold-plated wrapping climbed slowly out of their tombs, shaking off their eternal rest. Each held a razor-tipped iron staff with handles shaped like ankhs.

Mala paled as she unsheathed her sword. "True Egyptian mummies. Human servants encased in molten gold by alchemancy, then imbued with unnatural life by a sorcerer. Abominations. Deadly ones."

Each of the beings was as big as Gunnar, and they advanced on the party with fluid movements, staffs clenched in their golden hands.

Mateo struck first, dropping the glove Mala had thrown and snapping his blade at the nearest mummy. The weapon vibrated as it clanged off the metallic skin.

The mummy feigned a kick and jabbed the staff at Mateo's chest. Without his shield, the one-handed fighter was forced to scramble out of reach. The mummy pressed the attack, causing Will to leap to his cousin's defense.

"Put on the glove!" Mala shouted.

Will wondered what she knew, but Mateo was in no position to retrieve the item. Will staved off the advancing mummy's attack and thrust straight into its chest. His sword only penetrated an inch or so into the monster's gold-plated armor, and there was no snip of blue-white light.

The gold is real, despite the alchemancy that fused it together.

The mummies swarmed the party, outnumbering them almost three to one. Highly skilled warriors who seemed impervious to attack, Will wasn't sure what to do. He had resorted to using Zariduke as a defensive weapon, blocking thrust after thrust from the iron-tipped staffs.

Mala and Gunnar were on their heels. The battle was too tight for Selina to use Wind Push or a similar spell, so she flew straight up, trying to create distance, but a mummy launched its staff at her and pierced her through the leg. She fell screaming to the ground, yanking out the staff and arresting her flight just enough to break her fall. Mateo roared and ran to her defense. Will noticed he had picked up the glove and that it had somehow, magically, attached to the stump of his left arm. Before he reached Selina, the sylvamancer swept away the advancing mummies with a thrust of her palms, sending them crashing into a pillar.

Two more guardians rushed the sylvamancer from the side, and she morphed into a giant tortoise and retreated into her shell. The mummies used their staffs as bludgeons and battered her. When the shell started to crack, Selina morphed back into human form. Will and Mateo arrived just in time to defend her, Will's eyes widening when his cousin stopped an iron tip from piercing his side by catching it with the palm of the chainmail glove. Mateo looked just as shocked. He backhanded a mummy in the face with the glove and sent it sprawling.

Selina could no longer walk, and Will could tell her power was almost spent.

"The eyes, Will!" Mala shouted. She and Gunnar were both locked in a desperate battle. "Go for the eyes!"

Fighting to keep the horde of mummies away from Selina, knowing he and Mateo were about to be overwhelmed, Will stared into the golden orbs of his opponent and, with a flash of insight, understood why Mala had cried out. The mummy's liquid gold eyes moved like magma within the sockets.

They moved—which meant they were not as solid as its skin.

Which meant he might be able to pierce whatever lay underneath the gold plating, perhaps the magic that kept the thing alive.

He whirled to the right, isolating one of his opponents. An iron tip grazed Will's side as he slid inside the blow, coming face to face with the mummy. The monster grabbed Will's neck with its hand, squeezing so hard Will couldn't breathe, but he reared back and jabbed his sword upward, into its left eye.

The blade slid through and, with a blue-white pop, the life force of the mummy dissolved. The shell of gold armor fell to the floor.

Will didn't waste time. He dashed behind one of the mummies attacking Mateo, planning to jab it in the eye by surprise. The mummy turned at the last moment, and Will switched his grip and slashed horizontally across the mummy's face, right between the eyes. Another *snip* of light.

Ten to go.

Three mummies charged Will. They must have processed what occurred, because they guarded their eyes as they fought, heads lowered and keeping their distance with their staffs. They pressed him hard, pinning him against a column.

Will was beginning to tire. He couldn't break through their defenses, and the mummies were enormously strong. One slip-up meant an iron-tipped staff through the chest.

He risked a glance to see if anyone was close enough to help. Mateo had dragged Selina to one of the marble sarcophagi and was using it to guard her back while he fought off an attacker. Mala slipped through a mummy's defenses and jabbed it in the eye with her dagger. The tomb guardian didn't disappear, but it stumbled away, clutching its ruined orb. Then Mala noticed that, just like Will, Gunnar was surrounded by three attackers and about to be overwhelmed. An iron tip caught the big man on his left arm, spinning him around. Sensing a victory, the others pressed harder.

One of Will's attackers rushed him. He didn't have time to aim for the face. Gripping Zariduke in both hands, he swung a mighty blow that severed the mummy's staff. The guardian dropped its weapon and wrapped Will from behind, underneath his arms. Will couldn't shake him and had to defend against the other two attackers while the third mummy tried to drag him to the ground.

He had seconds before the mummies overwhelmed him, as did Gunnar.

Mala noticed.

She glanced at both men, first at Will and then at Gunnar, trying to decide whom to save. Expressionless, she sprang onto an emerald pillar to her left, using it to vault high over her remaining two attackers.

When she landed, she sprinted straight for Will.

"No!" Will roared, redoubling his efforts to free his arms. "Go to Gunnar!"

An iron tip slipped through Will's defenses and jabbed him in the thigh. He screamed and dropped his sword arm in pain. The third attacker's staff came straight for his heart, but Mala entered the fray just in time, batting away the blow with her short sword. She spun and swung at Will's head. He got the hint and ducked, and Mala stabbed the mummy holding Will in the face, just missing an eye.

Gunnar cried out, a prolonged scream that gurgled in his throat and caused the hairs to raise on Will's arms. A quick glance revealed a group of mummies surrounding his friend, jabbing him over and over.

When the screams ended, the mummies surrounding the fallen warrior straightened and fanned out to converge on the remaining members of the party. Will felt like vomiting. Mala didn't cry out in reaction to Gunnar's death, but she attacked the mummy in front of her with a vengeance, driving it against a pillar with a furious combination of attacks. The mummy took a desperate swipe with his staff, missed, and this time Mala's aim was true. She lunged forward with her two blades, piercing the mummy through both eyes at the same time, blinding it.

Will did a quick count in his head. Two mummies killed, two blinded. Eight still fighting.

It was too many.

Selina was down. Gunnar dead. Mateo was losing the battle against his lone attacker, and another was heading right for him. He'd never hold them both off. As Will blocked two staff thrusts and rushed to his cousin's defense, limping on his wounded thigh, a staff swept out his legs at the ankles, and Will fell hard to the ground, dropping his sword.

Before he could recover, three mummies rushed him, staffs poised to run him through.

41

The lower floor of the baths reeked of rot and decay, reinforcing Val's impression that the entire level was diseased, contaminated by the arrival of Asmodeus and his demonic minions. The party's boots squished on disgusting molds and toadstools as they strode warily through the rough-hewn passages. Patterns continued to form and then disperse in the thicket of moss and fungi covering the walls and ceilings.

When exposed, cracks in the plaster revealed rudimentary brick walls. The passages were tighter and more convoluted than the first level, the rooms much smaller. Steam drifted up from shafts bored into the rock floor.

"This level appears to have no correlation to the one above," Adaira said. "Where is the water source for the upper level? Why the abrupt temperature change on the staircase?"

I don't think we're in Kansas anymore, Val thought.

"Could this be another dimension altogether?" Dida pondered. "Perhaps a nexus between this world and the domain of Asmodeus?"

"Who knows what that blasted crown did," Rucker said. "There's no sense fretting about it. Let's get it back and return to the surface."

As they followed a curving passage deeper into the interior, a peal of wicked laughter emanated from farther ahead.

Rucker spat. "Succubus. Vile temptresses."

"We must be close to the throne room," Val said.

The rooms they had passed so far, irregular chambers with steam whistling up through bore holes, had all been empty. They ducked into the next one, an alcove with walls covered in green slime, and began to implement their plan.

Dida set to work creating an invisible Rune Box big enough to fit them all inside. The plan was to steal the crown, flee, and hide inside Dida's magical contraption until things calmed down. Retrace their steps to the tower or, if forced, make a mad dash through a different section of the sewers.

As the bibliomancer spoke in a low voice and twisted his fingers to inscribe intricate shapes in the air, Val prepared a spell he had been working on the entire journey, an advanced form of Wizard Shield based on condensed spirit instead of hardened air.

After Dida finished, the party rehearsed the plan a final time. Once the bibliomancer drew within sight of the crown, he would form a Rune Passage that would allow him to travel across the room undetected, snatch the crown, and return. As opposed to opening a door of spirit and traveling through the dimensions, Val gleaned that a Rune Passage was some kind of advanced mixture of magic and mathematics that allowed a bibliomancer to warp time and space within a limited range.

If Dida failed or was detected, the party would create a diversion and try to cause enough chaos to escape to the Rune Box. It was not much of a plan, but Val agreed it was their best hope. Another option was to wait until Asmodeus left the throne room, but time was not on their side, and Val preferred to take proactive steps. Better to make a play for the crown than have their hands forced.

After what everyone had been through on the journey, no words of encouragement were needed. No speeches made. One by one, they filed grimly out of the chamber, knowing this might be their lone chance to return to their home world. Val and Adaira exchanged a look that spoke volumes, a mutual desire for a future that might never come to pass.

Molds and yeasts and puddings pulsated with green and amber light as they crept down the passage. Another round of laughter, musical and unhinged, drifted through the corridor. Closer than before. Growing nervous, the party waited while Dida cast a spell to mask the sound of their footsteps.

Fifty feet later, a red glow appeared as the passage spilled into a cavern dotted with four-foot tall toadstools and slimy tendrils hanging down from the ceiling like gelatinous horses' tails. Just past the cavern lay the basin of seething lava Val had seen from above. As the party fanned out to hide behind the mushrooms, Val caught a glimpse of Asmodeus on his ivory throne, on the far side of the lava basin.

A pair of succubi, their backs to the party, reclined on a bed scooped out of a giant blue mushroom, steps away from the obsidian walkway that surrounded the lava. Val noticed the succubi were eating live scorpions out of a silver urn, giggling as they dined.

He caught Dida's attention and raised his eyebrows. The bibliomancer shook his head. *I can't see the crown from this angle*, was the unspoken reply.

Val tensed as his friend, ever so slowly, edged to the corner of the mushroom and peered around. Not liking what he saw, the bibliomancer returned to his position and, after expelling a silent breath, tried the other side.

Dida stayed in position for so long Val felt sure someone would notice him. His friend's lips were moving, his hands tracing patterns in the air beside the mushroom. As Val watched in dread and then awe, Dida stuck his arm out from behind the mushroom. Yet instead of exposing his position, the bibliomancer's limb disappeared into midair. Dida slid the rest of his body into the invisible Rune Passage, and Val exhaled with relief.

A waiting game ensued. Val ran through his spells in his mind, keeping the magic on a razor's edge, ready to bring forth Spirit Fire or erect a defensive shield at a moment's notice. Adaira's back was pressed into his, her scent drifting to his nostrils, a touch of humanity among the horror. He reached for her hand and squeezed it.

The seconds ticked off in Val's head. A full minute passed, then another.

What was taking Dida so long?

It was only supposed to take the bibliomancer a few moments to fly through the Rune Passage, grab the crown, and return. Asmodeus must be watching his prized possession closely.

A bead of sweat trickled down Val's forehead. At any moment, one of the succubi might decide to walk to the back of the cavern. He exchanged a grim look with Rucker, who was squatting behind the next mushroom over. Synne and Ferin were to Val's right.

Asmodeus is torturing Tobar, he told himself, and Dida simply has to wait it out.

A few moments later, a deep chuckle boomed through the cavern, as if amplified by a megaphone. The very sound of it caused a shiver to whisk through Val, vibrating his nerve endings and turning his muscles to slush.

"I AM WONDERING HOW LONG THOU WILST WAIT ON THY FRIEND TO RETURN," the powerful voice said. It sounded as if someone was shouting in Val's ear. "BUT MY PATIENCE HAS EXPIRED. COME, HUMAN WHELPS. SAY HELLO TO MY COURT. EXTEND A PROPER GREETING."

Val swallowed over and over as he tried to control the trembling that had overcome him at the sound of the demon lord's voice. As the members of the party exchanged a worried glance, unsure what to do, a scream tore through the cavern.

A human scream, familiar and wracked with pain.

Dida.

The leering face of a succubus peered around the mushroom, clapping in glee when Val and Adaira jumped back in terror. The demon-spawn flew out of reach as Rucker roared and charged her with his axe.

"I'll scatter yer bones across the cavern, wench!"

The succubus cackled.

"COME, SPIRIT MAGE FROM ANOTHER WORLD. COME AND PAY HOMAGE."

Shaking like a leaf, unable to get a grip on his fear, Val gripped Adaira's arm and felt her shaking as well. A glance at Ferin told Val he was in even worse shape. Synne looked rattled but in command, and only Rucker seemed unaffected by the words of the demon lord.

Adaira's eyes flicked towards the return passage. Val shook his head. He wasn't leaving Dida behind.

When Val emerged from behind the mushroom, he realized at once how badly they had miscalculated. How foolish they had been.

Earlier, when he had peered through the grate, he had not been able to observe the entire chamber. Now he could see four hulking humanoids, formed of flesh and fire, standing with arms crossed at the corners of the lava basin. Giant curved swords hung from ruby scabbards on their backs. Far more succubi and incubi than Val had realized filled the alcoves surrounding the walkway. Dozens of them.

Val's eyes fell to the ivory throne atop the obsidian platform, and Asmodeus boomed another chuckle when he noticed the party's reaction.

"DOST THOU THINK THE PRESENCE OF MY MINIONS TIPS THE SCALES IN MY FAVOR? DOST THOU THINK THOU HAD A CHANCE TO DEFEAT ME WITHOUT THEM?"

The chuckle turned into a belly laugh that vibrated the air and stole what remained of Val's courage. The sheer presence of Asmodeus overwhelmed him, the immensity of his physical form combined with the eldritch magic suffusing his being.

He sensed that Asmodeus wanted him to walk forward. Val complied, as if his legs were under the control of the demon lord. As he left the mushroom cavern and emerged onto the obsidian walkway, he saw something that caused his shivering to increase.

To Val's left, directly across the lava basin from Asmodeus, was a giant portal in the middle of the air. The circular gateway was tall enough for even the demon lord to step through. Val gazed through the gauzy surface and saw madness incarnate. A realm of black-spired cities and misshapen forests and seas that burned, tortured souls and disease-wracked bodies and beings out of nightmares whose form and substance, whose very existence, twisted Val's mind to the point of breaking.

Trembling, he forced his gaze away. The glimpse of Asmodeus's realm had stripped even more of his resolve, and he had the overpowering urge to lay prostrate on the walkway and beg Asmodeus to end his life. Anything to avoid being sent through that portal. The compulsion became so strong that Val started to kneel, head bowed, his mind overcome and his legendary will broken.

As his eyes lowered, moving from the demon lord to the base of the three-tiered platform, he saw another thing.

He saw Dida.

The bibliomancer's arms and legs were stretched apart and attached to an iron wheel. Dozens of dagger-like barbs protruded from points all over Dida's body, pinning him to the blood-drenched contraption. Val had no idea how he was still alive. Two incubi, their smooth male faces grinning in pleasure, slowly spun the macabre device.

Shudders coursed through Val again, though they stemmed from a source other than fear. If the demon lord had not tormented his friend, Val might not have summoned the strength to fight. Instead, his rage gave him the fuel to shake off his terror and regain control of his mind.

Spirit Fire surged to his fingertips. With a roar, he flung his hands at the two incubi spinning the wheel, lancing them from across the lava basin. The two male demons didn't even have time to scream. They simply disintegrated.

Asmodeus gave a chilling smile. "SO HE COMES TO PLAY. THANK

THEE FOR DEMONSTRATING, MAGE CUB, THAT THY POWER IS ENOUGH TO SUIT MY PURPOSES."

Val lifted his arms and focused twin bolts of Spirit Fire on Asmodeus, aiming for the center of his chest, infusing the spell with as much power as he could muster. The magic flared as it streaked through the black veins covering the demon lord's torso, then dissipated as Asmodeus stood to his full height and roared with laughter. "AN ATTACK BY A SCHOOLCHILD? ONE NOT YET OUT OF WIZARD SCHOOL?" He flicked a wrist. "ENTERTAINMENT, PLEASE. LEAVE THE MAGE WHELP FOR ME."

As Val despaired, shocked by the easy absorption of his magic, the lesser demons in the room surged forward, the succubi screeching and taking to the air, wingless incubi racing down the obsidian walkway, the four fire demons striding across the lava basin.

"It has to be my axe," Rucker said, in a low voice beside Val. "It's our only chance to defeat him."

Not our only chance, Val thought.

He doubted it would matter, but he had a final card to play.

Ferin screamed as two succubi lifted him by the arms and carried him towards the portal. Rucker noticed and raced to free him.

Val handed his staff to Adaira, so she would not be defenseless. "Synne," he said, "watch my back."

He lanced Spirit Fire into the ranks of demons surging towards them, annihilating the front ranks and causing the rest to scatter. He turned to attack the fire demons but, while the spirit magic hurt them and halted their attack, the cost was too great. He was running out of fuel, and doubted he had enough to deal with all four. It would also leave him defenseless against Asmodeus.

Rucker freed Ferin and raced out to meet the fire demons, running right across the lava, his movements again strangely unaffected. *That's a powerful ring*, Val thought, as the first fire demon swung a vicious, two-handed blow that Rucker rolled beneath. He came up swinging, and his axe bit deep into the leg of the demon, bringing it down with a familiar wisp of smoke. Rucker moved on to his next opponent, his head barely reaching its chest, whipping the axe back and forth as if it were a toy blade. Whenever the ensorcelled weapon met one of the demons' fire swords, the blade shattered as if made of glass. Rucker spun to block another attack, but a different demon backhanded him, causing him to drop his axe as he tumbled across the lava. Just before the fire creatures converged, Val levitated Rucker out of harm's way, then whisked the axe back into his hand.

Synne destroyed anything that dared approach Val on foot. Succubi used their wings to swoop down from above, but Adaira fended them off with Val's staff. One evaded her swing and got behind her, but made the mistake of grabbing her choker. With a sizzle and a flash, the necklace turned the demon into ash.

Though the party withstood the initial attack, the battle went downhill. The three remaining fire demons realized Rucker was no easy foe and attacked in unison. It took everything he had to stay alive, and they had him surrounded in the center of the basin. Ferin was fighting a losing battle in one of the alcoves, Adaira's arms were tiring, and Val could tell Synne had not fully recovered from the poison. Even if the party staved off the attack of Asmodeus's minions, they would have nothing left against the demon lord.

Through it all, Dida whimpered in pain on the wheel, and Tobar watched the battle with unseeing eyes, sitting on his mock throne like a marionette on a shelf, the crown shoved low on his head. Val tried to whisk the crown across the room, but it was somehow grafted, through magic or other means, to the mage's head. Val even tried to lift Tobar himself, but realized he was attached to his chair.

Asmodeus laughed at the failed attempt. "PREPARE THYSELF TO TAKE TOBAR'S PLACE, YOUNG ONE.

Val knew the demon lord meant to crush his spirit. While Asmodeus's words terrified him, they also fueled his anger, and revealed that the demon lord didn't mean to kill him. At least not before he tried to syphon Val's magic to harness the power of the crown, then fling his dried-up soul into hell.

"Adaira," Val said, "do you have enough magic to fly me across the lava?"

She fended off a clawed attack from above. "I think so."

"Then I'm going for Asmodeus. Synne, I'll meet you there."

As the majitsu took off down the obsidian walkway, clearing away the lesser demons with a flurry of attacking limbs, Val shouted across the lava basin.

"Rucker! Ferin! Now!"

Rucker turned his head and noticed Synne pulling Ferin into a sprint towards Asmodeus, while Val and Adaira linked arms to take flight across the basin. With a superhuman effort, Rucker fought through the ring of fire demons, taking a terrible blow to the back that almost brought him down. He stumbled but regained his footing, racing across the lava just before they could grab him.

Asmodeus boomed another chuckle. "THOU COMEST FOR ME? LET US PLAY, THEN."

The demon lord stood and grabbed a six-foot scepter off the side of the throne, a black rod topped with a cluster of gray baubles. When he pointed the scepter at Val and Adaira, a cone of gray light shot forth. Anticipating the maneuver, Val erected a wall of Spirit Armor in front of them as they flew. The gray cone slammed into the invisible barrier. Val felt the air shudder, but his Spirit Armor held.

"THOU HAST POWER, WHELP. I GRANT THEE THAT. BUT NOW FEEL MINE."

Asmodeus opened his mouth and roared. A blast of air assaulted Val and Adaira, far more powerful than any Wind Push Val had ever felt, blasting through the Spirit Armor and tossing them all the way back across the chamber. Val and Adaira slammed into a rock wall and slumped to the ground, fighting to stay conscious.

Synne had reached the bottom of the throne. She leapt up it, clearing ten feet with every bound, and drove her fists straight into the chest of Asmodeus. The demon lord didn't even flinch. He grabbed Synne by the neck, thrust his thumb through her eye, and flung her at the lava.

"No!" Val shrieked, halting her descent just before she landed in the bubbling magma. As Synne swooned in pain, he whisked her across the cavern and to his side, trying not to look at her bloody eye socket.

Ferin, trailing behind Synne but unwilling to attack the demon lord, dropped to his knees and begged for his life. Asmodeus reached down, picked him up, and flung him at the portal.

Ferin saw where he was headed and screamed. Val tried to levitate him back, but Asmodeus overpowered his attempt, thrusting Ferin faster and faster through the air. Val reeled as the black sash gypsy shrieked a final time before he sailed through the portal and disappeared into the hell dimension.

Asmodeus reached down and spun Dida's wheel, inducing a fresh round of screams. As the demon lord stepped off the throne and onto the obsidian platform, Rucker leapt out of the lava and swung his axe with all his might, taking a chunk out of Asmodeus's calf.

Black ichor gushed from the wound. The demon lord bellowed and stumbled back. He pointed the scepter at Rucker and another gray cone of light shot out, slamming into Rucker's chest and throwing him into the lava.

"Save him," Val said to Adaira, as Rucker sank unconscious into the molten fire. His ring might protect him from immolation, but it would not keep him from suffocating to death.

Rucker had given them a final chance to succeed, a sliver of hope, and Val meant to take it. While Asmodeus was distracted, he flew towards the demon lord, low and silent across the chamber, almost reaching him before the giant being took notice. When ten feet separated them, Asmodeus stepped forward to meet him with open palms, amused.

Val drifted closer. Asmodeus smiled. Just before they met, Val removed the stopper from the tiny azantite container concealed in his hands, and threw the soul jar right into the face of the demon lord, propelling it with magic.

The jar will take the first breath it feels when it opens.

Asmodeus caught the soul jar in his hand, an inch from his mouth. Close enough to work, Val hoped as he sucked in a breath, praying for the success of this last desperate attempt.

After a look of surprise at the puny thing in his hand, Asmodeus broke into a slow, wicked grin. "A SOUL JAR? FOR THE LIKES OF *ME*?"

The demon lord crushed the azantite jar in his fist, and his laughter stripped away Val's last shred of hope.

"COME, WHELP. ACCEPT THY FATE."

Val stumbled backwards on the walkway. Asmodeus stepped down off the platform, taking his time, knowing the fight was over. As Val shrank away, overcome by the horror of the situation, his eyes fell on Tobar and the crown, and a final desperate idea sparked in his mind. A cruel and ruthless gamble that would probably fail, and even if it did not, might damn him forever. Forcing himself to be strong, he overcame his revulsion of the idea by thinking of his companions, Adaira, and his brothers.

"ART THOU READY TO WORSHIP?"

The demon lord took another step forward. Val stood rigid before him, feigning obedience. Adaira screamed in the background for him to wake up and run. Asmodeus beckoned with an open palm, urging him to pay homage.

Val took a step forward. Asmodeus looked pleased. Val took another step, turned, and incinerated Tobar with Spirit Fire.

A hush fell over the chamber as the gypsy mage turned to ash. The clang of the crown against the empty throne broke the silence, and before Asmodeus could react, Val whisked the crown into his hands and reached as deep inside himself as he could, summoning every ounce of magic he had left. He channeled that magic into a spell for which he had no name, a suffusion of sheer power that he poured into the crown, as if it were a magical battery to be recharged.

A blast of multicolored light obscured Val's vision, and a shockwave of energy exploded outward.

42

That night in the cave, Caleb and the others never saw a shibomos, or any other creature. As the first rays of dawn spilled through the entrance and stirred them awake, they hurried outside and resumed trekking along the beach, seeing no sign of oversized footprints. After lunch, Caleb asked the Brewer if he could teach him how to sing.

"Of course," he said. "Who do you like? Eddie Veder? Bono? The Stones?"

"I don't mean sing a rock song. I mean sing like you do. You know, with the power to affect people."

"I'm not sure," the older man said, after a moment. "I've never thought of it like that."

"I'm not a very good thief, and I figure I need a skill in this world besides slinging drinks and teasing my little brother. Why not be a bard?"

"Huh," the Brewer said. "Why not?"

It turned out that Caleb could carry a tune, and over the next few days, the Brewer tried his best to coax out some of the enchanted reactions his own voice evoked. Yet try as he might, despite Marguerite's claims to the contrary and Luca's delight, Caleb couldn't produce any of the same effects.

"My guess is you have some magic inside you," Caleb said quietly. "Like a wizard, only your voice is your spells."

"Maybe it just takes time, love," Marguerite said. "Wizards, they practice for *years*."

"Yeah," Caleb said. "Sure."

Marguerite slipped an arm through his, and he gave her a sad, easy smile. She fulfilled him, but the closer they became, the more he wanted something to add to the equation.

Later that day, just before they crested a rolling plateau, the Brewer drew to a stop as the sinking sun turned the horizon into a blood-red stain spreading across the sky. He pointed out a craggy peninsula in the distance, jutting into the ocean like an elbow. "We're about to get our first glimpse of Freetown."

Luca's eyes shone with excitement at the mention of the renowned city.

Caleb draped an arm across the boy's shoulder and, as they topped the hill, enjoyed watching him point in awe at the sea of colorful tents and pavilions. Even after the attack, enough remained of the skyline to induce a sense of wonder, and the distance hid much of the damage from view.

After a quick wash in the ocean, they set camp and had their last dinner under the stars, the excitement of the return to Freetown like an electric current dancing among them.

Night fell. The breeze stirred. The Brewer fell asleep and started snoring as he always did, and Luca soon dropped off. Caleb listened to the surf with Marguerite in his arms, thinking for some reason about the tusker he had helped kill, yet another living creature harmed by his hand. While he didn't regret the act itself, he regretted the stain on the soul that resulted from all acts of violence.

Yet something had changed. Somehow this woman from another world, with her honest eyes and throaty laugh and skin like warm milk, had made the crushing sadness and pain he felt, the ache of existence itself, more bearable. He didn't know why things were the way they were. Why evil thrived. Why children suffered. How different universes could exist, what it meant to be born of two worlds.

What he did know was that he loved the woman beside him.

Marguerite stroked his arm as her toes curled in the sand. "Caleb?"

"Yeah?"

"Tell me about your world."

"What do you want to know?"

"Everything."

He laughed and kissed her neck, and she wriggled away. "Do you . . . want to go back?"

"Ah," he said. "I see. Of course I do."

She fell silent.

Caleb whispered in her ear. "But only if I can take you with me."

She looked up at him, not saying anything, showing him with her eyes how much his words meant.

"Would you go with me?" he asked. "To see my world?"

After a long moment, when she still didn't respond, he figured he had asked too much. He knew firsthand what a terrifying thing it was to travel across the stars. But then she grabbed his hand and said, in a husky voice, "When it comes to you, Caleb, I figure I'd go about anywhere."

His heart started to beat faster, and his throat felt dry.

Caleb didn't understand anything about this insane thing called human life. Especially after coming to Urfe and discovering a whole new world revolving around a whole new sun. He knew he didn't know much, wasn't good at very many things. He was even less useful on Urfe than back home. He sure as hell wasn't a warrior or a wizard, and he sucked at being a thief, too.

There was one thing, though, he was sure about. More than he had ever been about anything. Something that was right for *him*. After a glance at Luca's sleeping form, he weighed his decision one last time, knowing he could never look back, wishing his brothers were by his side to bear witness.

He reached into his pocket and took out something he had been holding since the last Romani camp. He had noticed it inside the lone intact wagon on their first pass through. Unable to steal from a camp full of his dead kinsmen, he had let it be, only to pick it up again when he and Marguerite had returned to make love.

Because this was different. A way to honor the fallen.

With a deep breath, he stood and held up the silver ring he had found concealed in a cabinet. A wedding band inset with sapphire gemstones in the shape of tiny suns. He dropped to a knee. "Marguerite, will you marry me?"

She pressed her hands together and looked so stunned Caleb wondered if this world even had the same ritual. But then tears streamed down her eyes, and she cried out in joy and threw her arms around his neck. "Aye, my love." She peppered him with kisses. "I will."

"Good," he said, in a husky voice, "because I want to adopt Luca, and I want him to have a mom."

She drew away but kept her hands around his neck. "I think I would like that very much." She glanced at the sleeping boy. "Why wait, though?"

"What do you mean?"

"I'm from the gutters, where life is cruel and short. I'm not much for a fancy wedding, Luca needs a home, and I don't need any Protectorate magistrate signing me papers . . . so why not tomorrow? In our own way?"

He thought about it, and realized he felt the exact same. Especially on Urfe, where he didn't know whether he would be alive or dead from one day to the next.

"Rock on," he said.

The wedding took place in a waist-deep pool of water near the base of a waterfall, just a short climb into the hills on the way to Freetown. A spot the Brewer knew from past visits.

A slender cataract, much gentler than the one that had threatened Luca, spilled over red rocks into a basin the color of melted emeralds. Soft evening light bathed the river in pink and golden hues. Gushing water drowned the sounds of the forest.

Caleb was shirtless and barefoot; Marguerite wore a sequined white dress he had also found in the wagon, planned to give to her as a gift, and stuffed in his backpack. After the Brewer belted out a medley of tunes, everything from classical ballads to a few stanzas of Dire Straits's *Romeo and Juliet*, the couple exchanged vows. Marguerite read a poem she had composed late into the night, and Caleb recited a heartfelt declaration of love and support he made up on the spot. As sunlight slatted through the canopy of redwoods, the Brewer gave a shout out to the Great Architect of Time and Space and Love, then delivered a moving speech about the two people he knew at first sight were destined to be together forever.

Luca carried the silver wedding ring through the water, smiling as he frog-kicked to their side, and handed the ring to Caleb. He hugged the boy tight to his chest, lifted him high, and threw him back into the pool, to Luca's great delight. Once the boy returned to shallower waters, Caleb slipped the ring onto Marguerite's hand.

She threw her arms around his neck. The Brewer declared them husband and wife.

Caleb kissed his bride, and they fell laughing into the water.

They decided to camp for another night. The Brewer prepared a gourmet wedding meal of fire-roasted quail, wild asparagus, and mushrooms sautéed with garlic and onions. Luca ate so much he complained of a stomachache.

After hours of dancing and singing by the fire, once the child and the Brewer fell asleep, Caleb took Marguerite by the hand and led her to the beach. Sheltered by a high line of dunes, he made love to his new bride, thinking he had never been so at peace.

As they lay together under the stars, Caleb realized he didn't need to be a warrior or a wizard or a bard. All he wanted was to spend the rest of his days with the woman lying beside him, and with the curly-headed boy asleep by the fire. Those two needed him not for the things he could accomplish, but just for who he was.

And that, he knew at last, was enough.

43

Sprawled on his back and at the mercy of the mummies, Will realized he was no longer the same fighter that had started the journey. Instead of balling up on the ground or looking for Mala to save him, he assessed the situation with icy calm, rolled to the side to avoid a thrusting spear, and thrust himself between the legs of his closest attacker. As the mummy stabbed downward, Will managed to turn to the side and avoid the blow by inches, then grabbed the spear and used it to leverage himself to his feet, grimacing away the pain in his thigh. He retrieved his sword just in time to block another staff thrust.

Whirling and dodging, parrying and counterstriking, he risked a glance at his companions and saw Selina morph into a king cobra that reared to strike one of the mummies attacking Mateo. The snake's fangs clamped onto the mummy's face, missing its eye but saving Mateo from certain death. The other mummy snagged the cobra on the end of its staff and flung it away. The snake flopped on the ground and then changed back into an immobile, ashen-faced Selina.

This isn't working, Will thought, as he narrowly avoided a spear thrust to the chest. Gunnar is dead, Selina gravely injured, and the rest of us are barely hanging on.

As a pair of mummies advanced, Will did his best to isolate his brain and think while he fought. Had the mummies lain dormant in their sarcophagi all these centuries, then awakened on their own to fight?

He didn't think so. He thought someone had called them to life. The same someone who had affected their journey in various ways during the descent, the same someone who had called out to them and made his presence known.

He remembered Mala's comment about the mummies. *Imbued with unnatural life by a sorcerer.*

Will never had the chance to ask Val what had happened to Zedock's creations. The hordes of skeletons and zombies in the cemetery. But the fact that Val was alive spoke volumes. In Will's mind, the only explanation was that the necromancer's death had severed the bond to his creations, stripping them of life.

Which meant killing the sorcerer king might be another way to destroy the mummies and end the battle.

He was here somewhere, Will was sure. Talking in their heads and influencing events. Though he was not at full strength—how could he be?—he was here nonetheless.

But where?

Will blocked a staff thrust, saw a rare opening, and took it. As he lunged for the mummy in front of him, aiming for the exposed eye, Caleb appeared in the mummy's stead, cringing as Will's sword descended.

On impulse, he broke off his attack, knowing as soon as he did what had happened. The Caleb-thing grinned and thrust the tip of his iron staff at Will's gut. As he twisted, the staff just missed his vitals, raking his side instead.

Of course I am here, rasped the sorcerer king.

The second mummy morphed into Val. Holding his side, Will stumbled away and saw his remaining companions in similar states of confusion.

Is fratricide not to your liking? Perhaps patricide suits you better?

Caleb and Val became Will's mother and father. He gritted his teeth when his parents lowered their weapons and walked towards him with open arms and pleading eyes. Will stumbled back, unable to raise his sword.

The hall shimmered and became a spider web, the mummies giant arachnids rearing up to attack. Will spun first one way and then the other, his pulse hammering, not knowing what was real.

Shall we choose again, perhaps? Condemn your love to the grave once more?

Mala's voice rang out. "Close your ears! He spins nothing but lies!"

Will overturned a crystal zelomancy board to block the spiders' advance. He looked to his left, hoping to gain confidence from the sight of his companions. Instead he saw Charlie stumbling in a circle, face ravaged by decomposition, and Lance fighting a losing battle with one arm.

I can't do this, Will thought. *He'll show me things I can't bear to see until I stumble.*

He snarled and raised his sword in defiance. "Where are you, Yiknoom?"

Dry, rasping laughter echoed through the hall.

The spiders morphed back into mummies. Will scrambled away from the staff thrusts, again and again, desperately seeking an answer. The sorcerer king had yet to reveal his true physical form. Odd for such a vain ruler.

Think, Will. Is he coiled like a dragon, sleeping beneath his treasure? Hidden on a different level of the pyramid?

Have we passed right by him and not known it?

No. Yiknoom is arrogant. As proud as any who has ever lived. If his essence is trapped somewhere for eternity then it is here, smothered in gold and coin, watching over his domain. Taking pleasure in our demise.

A thought struck Will like a thunderclap, almost allowing a spear to run him through. He spun away and repeated his own words. *Smothered in gold and coin. Watching.*

"Selina!" he shouted, his voice frantic. The mummies had assumed the forms of Mala and Allira, coming at Will with welcoming arms he knew were iron-tipped staffs. "Do you have any strength left?"

"Barely."

"Are you able to melt something?"

Her voice gasped with pain. "Aye, if I have a heat source."

A glow stone appeared in the hand of the Charlie illusion. Mala's voice rang out. "Break it, and you have fire."

The adventuress tossed the glow stone at Selina as their enemies pressed the attack. Will heard Mateo scream. "Melt the gold!" Will cried. "Off the statue in the middle!"

Selina smashed the glow stone on the ground. A flame burst forth, and the sylvamancer channeled it into the statue of the gold chieftain standing on the pedestal, arms raised, overlooking the scene with haughty disdain.

At first nothing happened, causing Will to wonder if his guess was wrong or if Selina had enough power left to melt the statue. But then gold started to drip onto the ground in molten plops, like icing from a cake.

Fools. Minions. Weaklings. Your souls will feed my eternal journey. Bow before my power!

The hall pulsed and morphed into a jungle, the mummies into crocosaurs that rushed Will and his companions, snapping with thrusting jaws. He spun away, staving off the elongated rows of teeth. "More, Selina!"

The jungle became the surface of a sun, throbbing with orange light that stole Will's vision. He fled backwards, blindly waving his sword in defense. A scream reverberated in his head, not a human cry of pain but something greater, older and vaster, parched by a millennia of clinging to a magical half-life.

The searing light dissipated, and the hall returned to its natural state.

Will's eyes flew to the pedestal and saw that much of the gold exterior had melted off the statue, exposing pockets of waxen flesh held together by a blue-white light tinged gray, as if the magic had degraded over the centuries. A single red eye blinked and roved back and forth within the socket, desperate and exposed.

The light also revealed Selina, surrounded by mummies and impaled on the end of a staff, her hands fluttering weakly for release. Mateo cried out in dismay as Will absorbed the situation.

Eight mummies remained. He had no idea how injured the sorcerer king was or how long he could live without the protection of his golden shell, but it didn't matter. Will knew how to end this. As he ran towards the statue, Yiknoom's voice reverberated in his head, uttering lies and then screaming in rage, trying to distract him. The mummies converged as one, coming straight at Will with their staffs raised, a line of gold and iron.

I will flay you alive, lock you in stone for eternity! Eat the souls of everyone you hold dear!

With the mummies steps away, Will ran forward and launched Zariduke like a javelin, straight at the abomination on the pedestal. He saw Selina's dying eyes pick up the trajectory of the missile with the last of her power and speed it forward, striking a devastating blow in the center of the sorcerer king's chest.

With a *snip* of blue-white light, Zariduke pierced the unnatural amalgamation of flesh and magic, and Yiknoom crumbled into dust.

At once, the mummies toppled to the floor, their life force extinguished. Mateo moaned and rushed to Selina's side. He started to ease her off the iron-tipped staff but she gripped his hand to stop him. "I'm sorry," she said, her face twisting from the pain.

"Stay with me, my love," he said. "There has to be healing aid in here."

Her head lolled forward as she strained to remove a slender copper necklace from beneath her shirt. "Take it," she whispered, when her hands failed her.

Distraught, Mateo eased the necklace off her, and she closed his palm around it. "It was all for her," she said, and then breathed her last breath.

Will held the spear while Mateo, his good hand trembling, eased Selina's body off the iron tip and held her in his arms. Mateo pressed his lips to hers, then sank to his knees and lowered her body to the ground.

Will approached from behind and touched his cousin's shoulder, letting him know he was there. Mateo reached back and took his hand, gripping it tight.

Mala squatted next to Gunnar's body, taking his hand in silence. She pressed her lips to his forehead for a long moment, folded his hands across his chest, and rose to approach the pedestal. At the base of the melted statue, beneath the ashes of the sorcerer king, an iron pull ring had been exposed.

Will left Mateo to grieve in silence, paid his respects to Gunnar, and stepped over the puddles of liquid gold to join Mala on the pedestal. She took a cloth out of a pouch and used it to wrap the superheated iron ring. Together, they tugged on the handle. A trap door opened to reveal a set of stone steps.

"What was he?" Will asked, toeing the remains of the sorcerer king as they stared into darkness. "In the end."

"Who knows," she said. "A perversion of man and magic, stripped of humanity. If he had any to begin with."

Will swallowed as he looked at Gunnar and Selina's prone forms. "We should bury them."

"Yes."

A rumble arose from above, as if the earth itself had groaned. The sound increased in volume as chunks of obsidian began falling from the ceiling.

Mala's eyes flew upwards. She dashed away to inspect the remaining glass cases.

"What are you doing?" Will shouted.

"Go!" Mala yelled back. "I'll follow soon!"

Larger pieces started to fall, and Will feared the entrance to the staircase would be blocked. He had no idea where it led, but he had seen no other exit. After picking up a wooden shield from the floor in case he needed cover, he pulled his grieving cousin away from Selina and hustled him to the staircase. Mala was still running around the room, frantic, pawing through the remains of the treasure.

An enormous piece of stone dropped a foot away from Will, cracking the floor. "Now, Mala!"

"Go!"

He would gladly risk his life for her, but what he would not do was risk his life to help her find more treasure. After another futile plea, Will shook his head in frustration and hurried down the staircase after his cousin. He hated to leave Gunnar and Selina but they had no choice.

Enough residual light filtered down from above to make out a rough-hewn tunnel at the bottom of the stairs. They followed the passage for a few hundred yards and found another staircase leading upwards, almost vertical and only wide enough for one person at a time. A faint blue glow lit the staircase, though the light had started to dissipate into scattered turquoise motes.

Thunderous booms erupted all around as the magic holding together the pyramid of the sorcerer king came undone. Dust and loose stones plummeted from the ceiling. The floor cracked beneath their feet. His heart heavy, Will cast a final longing glance down the collapsing passage, then started to climb.

44

After he blasted the crown, the shockwave of magical energy pulsed, and the world disappeared. Val found himself drifting through a darkness as deep as outer space, though instead of stars he was surrounded by a panorama of multidimensional shapes in a constant state of flux, glowing with a bluish-white light, winking in and out of existence like the random shuffling of a million Rubik's cubes in 3-D.

Weightless, his body spinning out of control, he tried to right himself with physical strength and then with magic. Nothing seemed to work. He felt no pain, and wiggled his fingers to make sure he was still alive. Val twisted and caught glimpses of his companions: Synne with her bloody eye socket, Rucker floating unconscious below her, and Adaira struggling to reach Val. Dida was off to their right, semi-conscious and gravely injured from his wounds.

Everyone was floating towards a different portal. Whether another world or universe or dimension awaited inside, Val didn't know, but he suspected they would be lost forever if they drifted through.

WHAT HAST THOU DONE, WHELP? THOU WILT DESTROY US ALL!

Val looked up, towards the sound of the terrifying voice, and saw Asmodeus. The demon lord had managed to right himself. Feeling nauseated both by the sight of his wounded friends and the kaleidoscope of helixes spinning around him, Val tried to focus as the giant being fixed his gaze on the crown floating a few feet away from Val. He had lost his grip on it during the blast.

Trying to take advantage of the distraction, Val reached for his magic, only to realize his power was spent. He could only watch, cringing, as the demon lord flew straight for the crown. Once Asmodeus retrieved the artifact, Val had no doubt as to their fate.

Right before the demon lord snatched the crown, an old man wearing a wrinkled tweed coat appeared out of nowhere, ten feet away from Val. "That will be enough of that."

As soon as the man spoke, Val's body stopped moving, as if he were a spinning top that someone had just corralled. Looking around, he saw his companions frozen as well, hovering among the shapes with glazed stares and inert bodies.

The newcomer was a tall, angular man with wispy gray hair and a stoop to his posture. Though facing away from Val, the voice was familiar, and he could picture the sloping forehead and corkscrew eyebrows that Will had described, the silver eyes glittering with intelligence.

Salomon.

"I'm afraid I'll have to take the crown," the old man said, with a melancholy sigh. "It was never created for this."

Asmodeus turned to face the arch mage, towering over him as he spoke. WHO ART THOU? HOW DIDST THOU ARRIVE HERE?

Salomon ignored him and reached out towards the crown. It whisked into his hand.

With an annoyed scowl, Asmodeus pointed his scepter at the old man. A cone of gray light shot forth, bounced off Salomon like a bullet ricocheting off of metal, and returned to strike the demon lord in the chest.

The blow threw Asmodeus back ten feet and left him floating on his side. Stunned, he managed to regain his equilibrium and return upright, then roared and swung his obsidian rod at the elderly mage.

Before the blow landed, Salomon dissolved and reappeared behind the demon lord. Left off-balance from the swing, Asmodeus lurched forward, confused. As he turned, Salomon casually waved a hand, causing rays of light from the polyhedra surrounding them to streak towards the demon lord and wrap him in bands of blue-white energy.

Furious, Asmodeus tried to escape but found he couldn't move. His eyes widened as he looked at the arch mage with sudden recognition. IT IS THEE.

"Is it?" Salomon said mildly. He pressed his palms together and then spread them. A portal opened in front of Asmodeus similar to the one beside the lava basin, a realm of madness and black spires, death and chaos.

As the demon lord bellowed in protest, Salomon flicked his wrist and sent Asmodeus hurtling through the portal, then closed the doorway with another wave.

"Why?" Val said, thrilled that Asmodeus was gone but trying to process the sudden turn of events. "Why intervene now?"

"When I made the crown, I'm afraid I made a mistake by not accounting for the possibility of a powerful suffusion of spirit. Further abuse would disrupt more probability waves than would *not* intervening."

Val's face tightened. "That's not what I'm asking. Why now, and not before Synne had her eye plucked out? Before that monster put Dida on his torture wheel?" Val was shouting now. "Before Ferin was sent into that hellish place and I was forced to . . ."

He bowed his head at the thought of blasting Tobar into nothingness with Spirit Fire. The black sash gypsy mage was no innocent, he knew. Without killing him, Val would have lost the chance to help his brothers.

Tobar's mind might never have recovered anyway. He had chosen to go to war, and Val's brothers had not.

And none of that changed the fact that Val had killed him in cold blood.

Salomon's silver eyes turned sad.

An image of the redheaded girl in the village sprang unbidden into Val's mind. He swallowed and looked away. He could deal with the ramifications of his actions another time. Right now he had people to save. "Where are we?"

"Someplace even more elemental than the Place Between Worlds. You would not understand. Not yet."

"Between space and time?"

"Between, among, within, before, after."

Val corralled his fury, his utter hatred of this man and his godlike games, and focused on the situation. "My friends need urgent care."

Salomon pursed his lips and nodded.

"*Did you hear me!?*"

"They are in stasis," Salomon said quietly.

"What does that mean?"

"Time is different here. Their condition will not change under my thrall."

"Heal them," Val demanded.

"I'm afraid I am not a cuerpomancer."

"So you can stop time and toy with a demon lord but you can't make my friends better?"

"Magic is not omnipotence, Val. It is only magic. And I am but a single, tired old wizard."

Salomon pressed his palms together again, and another portal began to form.

"Wait," Val said.

The arch mage hesitated.

"Are my brothers still alive?"

Silence.

Val's voice turned low and deadly. "You owe me that much."

"I believe so," Salomon said finally. "But I do not know for sure."

"What do you mean? You know everything."

"I wish that were so. In this place, especially, my sight is limited. And I can only create a portal to places I have been."

"What about Asmodeus's world?"

Salomon didn't reply, and Val's eyes widened. "Why couldn't he use the crown himself?"

"Demons have innate gifts, but cannot employ true magic. As far as I have seen in my travels, magic is the sole province of humankind."

"Where were we? That weird world, the blue mist?"

"You give me far too much credit, Valjean. I have yet to scratch the surface of the multiverse. As best I can tell, when the opposing spirit mages clashed on Urfe, it triggered the crown's powers and created an alternate dimension. Thousands of years ago, when the wild mages of Albion battled the demons who overran Badŏn, led by Asmodeus, it was perhaps the most powerful release of magic that Urfe has ever seen. I can only assume the psychic signature of that event somehow interacted with the powers of the crown."

"Which *you* created."

"Yes, well," he mumbled, "I admit I lacked foresight with that particular endeavor."

"It's a time travel machine, isn't it?" Val guessed. He had been thinking about everything that had happened, including what he had seen during the Planewalk. "Only instead of going back in time, which is impossible for some reason, the crown creates an analogous alternate dimension."

Salomon was quiet for a moment. "Very good."

Val took a step forward. "You did it for the son you lost, didn't you?"

Salomon shuffled his feet and looked down.

"You wanted to travel back in time so you could be with him again, but you couldn't figure out how to do it. So you created a device that leads to alternate dimensions of your choosing. What happened, Salomon?"

The arch mage looked up with grief-stricken eyes. "I saw him," he whispered. "But I also saw myself, and I didn't want to deprive *that* father. Inflict on him the same . . . unbearable pain . . . that I have endured."

Val could only imagine what it meant to live as long as Salomon had, carrying that terrible loss and guilt.

After a moment, Salomon said, "I remained there for many years. Decades. Watching him unseen. Do you understand what that is like? What sort of torture it entails? It drove me mad. When I left, I lost track of time for many years. Decades, centuries."

"Why didn't you destroy the crown? You need to stop playing God."

The arch mage stared down at the crown for a long moment, as if deciding whether to use it again. "Quite frankly, no one except me has ever been powerful enough to use the crown in its proper application. I gave it to the Congregation as a symbolic gesture. I did not anticipate recent events and the loophole of direct force."

He read Val's unspoken question. "You have innate strength, yes. But true power entails far more than natural ability. It is an intense application of skill, knowledge, and desire over many years. Sometimes even lifetimes."

"How do I get stronger?" Val asked. "Become like you?"

Salomon's eyes met his, and Val felt dizzy as he locked gazes with the arch mage. "Be careful what you wish for," Salomon said, his voice sounding far away and his eyes expanding until they were all Val could see, a tunnel of silver that opened onto a glowing skyline and the hulking sprawl of wizard strongholds flanking the Thames river.

Val felt himself falling.

45

After a long vertical climb that sapped the last of Will's and Mateo's reserves, with chunks of rock cracking and falling all around, they finally reached an ancient stone door covered in runes. Will peered downward to see if Mala was behind them, but the light had almost dissipated and he could barely see. He shouted her name, over and over.

No answer.

With a worried glance at his grief-stricken cousin, Will turned the handle and the door slid silently inward, easing his fears of a final trap. On the other side of the door, a narrow ledge jutted over a cylindrical shaft at least fifty feet across. He looked down and saw, far below, the stippled tops of the statues dotting the floor of the first level. He prayed the life forces trapped inside them would finally be put to rest.

Above him, chiseled into the face of the vertical shaft, was a set of step-like indentations that led to the surface. Fresh air seeped down, and a few stars twinkled above like the lights of a rescue ship.

Mateo looked numbly at the sparkling heavens, no doubt thinking of Selina, of all that they had lost.

Will stood with a hand on the door. "I'm going back for her."

A huge rumble shook the pyramid complex, lasting for long seconds and shifting the ground beneath their feet. Mateo gripped his arm. "She made her choice, cousin."

Will hesitated. Indeed she had.

"Think of everyone back home, the Revolution. Think of your brothers."

Mateo was right, he knew. Mala did not deserve a rescue. Yet his earlier choice still haunted him, when he had left her at the mercy of the spider. Even though he knew it was an illusion, it felt like leaving her to die a second time.

Will sighed and shook his head. "I'll be back as soon as I can. I promise."

Mateo gripped his arm, then held the door as Will dashed back to the long staircase, shouting Mala's name as he descended, dodging pieces of stone that fell like hail from the ceiling. As darkness closed in, he came to a section of steps that had collapsed. Thirty feet beneath him, where the staircase resumed, he saw Mala standing at the edge of the top step, holding a cat o' nine tails.

"Foolish boy," Mala shouted up at him. "You shouldn't have come back."

"Shut up and help me think."

"Don't you think I already have? Go and save yourself. Return to your senseless Revolution."

"What about your javelin? How far does it reach?"

"It expands to ten feet. Don't you think I've thought of that?"

Will set down his sword and shield, lowered to his stomach, and reached down as far as he could. "You're going to have to jump."

Mala shook out the acrobat's stick to its full height, eying the distance between them. He knew it would be an absurd maneuver, even for her.

Another section of stone collapsed right beside her. After meeting his eyes, she looked down and took a jar out of one of her pouches. She opened it and dumped a chalky powder on the ground. Something to make the pole stick, he assumed. After that, she straightened and stuffed the cat o' nine tails in a pouch that made it disappear, sheathed her short sword, climbed down ten steps, and extended the pole out in front of her.

"Ready?" she asked.

"Ready."

With a deep breath, she dashed up the stairs to gain speed, planted the pole, and leaped straight into the air.

Will tensed as the pole scooted forward a few inches and then stuck to the ground, allowing Mala to extend. She soared upwards, holding onto the pliable shaft until the last moment, then shoved off it as a pole-vaulter would. Her body rose higher, drawing closer to Will's extended hand as she reached the apex of her trajectory.

His heart fell. She wasn't going to make it.

No, he said, and lowered himself even farther, extending his arm so far he felt as if his shoulder had come out of its socket. She reached as well, stretching until her fingertips brushed his wrist. Before she fell away, he locked onto her with an iron grip, smothering her small hand in his. He braced as her body weight pulled him forward, almost off the ledge, but he spread his legs and shifted his hips, stopping himself at the very lip of the broken staircase. He curled her up, amazed at his own strength, lifting her featherweight body with ease onto the ledge.

Side by side, she cupped his face in her hands. "Thank you," she whispered, then leapt to her feet. Together, they turned to sprint up the stairs in near-darkness.

Minutes later, Will heard Mateo calling his name, his voice hoarse from shouting. As he and Mala emerged, the shaft itself started to deteriorate, and the three survivors of the expedition navigated the vertical steps hewn into the cavern wall as fast as they dared.

When they emerged into the night, wary of finding a barren hilltop or a flock of angry arpui, their hearts leapt when they saw three simorghs and their Yith Riders, eying the collapsing hilltop with nervous expressions.

The simorghs took flight seconds before the top of the hill collapsed into a giant sinkhole.

Two weeks later, after a much longer return journey due to storms and a supply stop and the decision to steer clear of dragon territory, Will emerged from a long soak in his claw-footed tub feeling like a new man. After reapplying his bandages, he dressed in casual leathers and strapped on his sword—he went nowhere without Zariduke now—and settled into a chair by the fire at the Red Wagon Tavern, almost smacking his lips at the promise of a plate of fire-crisped meat. He was bitterly disappointed, and terrified, that Caleb was still wandering the countryside with Marguerite, who Will heard had arrived from New Victoria and traveled north with his brother. There was nothing Will could do about it that night, but in the morning he planned to set out for them.

The waitress tried to play it cool, but she ended up giggling with nervousness as she slid a mug of brown ale in front of him. Though Will and the others had only arrived that morning, word had spread of their exploits.

Get a grip, Will scolded himself. *The waitress is probably laughing at a joke someone told in the kitchen.*

Yet he knew it wasn't true. He felt the surreptitious gazes of every man and woman in the bar turning his way, trying to get a glimpse of one of the heroes of the Mayan Expedition that had returned the Coffer of Devla to its people.

It didn't matter. He cared about the eyes of one woman alone, and she did not seem any more impressed by him than she ever had.

After they arrived in Freetown, Will had asked Mala about the cat o' nine tails she had risked her life to bring back. In typical fashion, she had shrugged off his questions and proclaimed that her job was procuring magical items. She had remained behind, she claimed, to pick up several pieces she knew would command a high price.

He didn't believe her. Judging by the obsessive look in her eyes whenever he mentioned the scourge, and the way her fingers grasped the leather-wrapped base of the bloodstone hilt, he knew there was more to it than that.

Mala had kept to herself on the return journey, and Will suspected she was mourning the death of Gunnar. He knew the valiant warrior had never captured her heart, but he also knew she had loved him in a certain way, and that it had hurt her.

After Will finished dinner, Mateo walked in to join him, followed by Tamás. The revolutionary had requested the meeting. The three of them exchanged warm greetings and ordered another round. Will and the others had already handed over the coffer and described the journey, but had yet to discuss the future.

Mala arrived next, thirty minutes late, sweeping into the room with her hair unbound, hips swaying and nose stud twinkling and copper skin glowing, her eyes coolly surveying the room. She was dressed similarly to the first time Will had met her: black leather pants tucked into scarlet boots, a lace-up leather vest, and a long-sleeved shirt that matched her boots. The familiar blue sash hung from her waist, a choker of intertwined bronze graced her neck, and a stylized rose pendant hanging from a silver chain had replaced her old amulet. As always, she had her short sword strapped to her back and a curved dagger hanging from her belt.

There was no sign of her new weapon.

She met Will's eyes as she sat, her gaze as unreadable as ever, and signaled for a mug of ale. "I noticed the box has yet to open."

Legend held, Will knew, that the Coffer of Devla would remain shut until opened by a true cleric of Devla. Yet so far, the coffer had vexed the attempts of every single man, woman, and child in Freetown to open the lid and unlock its secrets. Tamás would not let anyone try to force it open or tear it apart, nor would anyone try. Superstition ran deep among the Roma, and the mysterious power of the coffer to lay low its enemies was known to every member of the clans.

"Perhaps you should have a little faith," Tamás said.

Mala scoffed. "A deep contempt for the ignorance of religion is the one value I share with the Congregation."

"What does faith have to do with religion?" Tamás said quietly.

"Bah. And what has this wishful thinking done for our people? We're condemned as outcasts, banished to the farthest reaches of the Realm."

Tamás pounded the table. "At least we have our freedom!"

Mala stared coldly back at him. "Until the wizards come and take it."

Everyone fell silent, remembering the horrors of the last visit from the Congregation.

"Where do we stand?" Mateo asked finally. He wore Selina's copper necklace around his neck, and the fingers of his chainmail glove flexed now and again, as if still getting used to its presence. Will wondered at its capabilities. Though he himself had acquired nothing of value from the expedition, he favored the battered ebony shield he had picked up in the treasure room. A teardrop buckler, lightweight and maneuverable, it felt right in his hand. He also liked the platinum edging and heraldic design, too faded to make out, which hinted at a more illustrious past.

Tamás took a swig of beer as the fire crackled at his back. "Word of the coffer has spread. Combined with the return of Zariduke, the spark of revolution has never burned brighter."

"A spark is one thing," Mala said, "an army capable of challenging the Congregation another."

He stared straight ahead. " 'Tis true, I'm afraid. The raid on Freetown demonstrated the advantage they enjoy over our own wizards. We can field an army, especially when joined by the clans in other Protectorates and the black sash gypsies—"

Mala smirked. "Be careful whom you invite into the bedroom."

"True again," Tamás said, "but as I was going to say, I'm afraid our army, even if joined by all the Oath avoiders from across the Realm, would fall short of the might of the Protectorate army alone. *Unless* the power of the coffer is unlocked."

"Is it that powerful?" Mateo asked. "Could it turn the tide in our favor?"

In response, Tamás began to recite in a soft, reverent voice that commanded the rapt attention of everyone within earshot.

> "Hear us, O Devla!
> This dream of dreams I have seen.
> A black night will come, stars asleep in their bower.
> Our people scattered
> Adrift in the sea of lament
> Ground under the wagon wheel
> When everything is ash.
>
> Who is this savior?
> When will he come?
> When shall we be free?
> O, Devla!
> Not until the prophet shall herald
> And the people shall hear
> The roar of the last true cleric of the age, the Templar
> Your fist, Your scorn, Your righteousness
> The one who unseals the coffer
> As he breaks the will of the world."

"It is worse than I feared," Mala said, her head swinging back and forth in disbelief when he finished. "You've pinned your hopes on a myth."

"So the Templar is the last cleric?" Will asked.

"So they say," Tamás said. "The one who will herald the dawn of a new age. Emissaries have been sent to the Devlans, in the hope they will come to test the coffer themselves. It's rumored their current prophet believes he might have found the Templar."

"What does *Templar* refer to?" Will asked. On Earth, he knew the name of the Knights Templars derived from their association with the Temple of King Solomon.

"In Devlan theology, the temple of God is everywhere," Tamás said. "Some scholars believe the *Templar* is a reference to mankind itself, though most of us believe the canticle refers to a specific person. Our savior."

With a weary sigh, Mala finished her ale and pushed away from the table. "I've heard enough."

"The wizards can outlaw religion and persecute us," Tamás continued, giving her a pitying look, "but they can never extinguish our spirit. Zariduke and the coffer have returned. Hope burns brighter than ever."

"Hope can die on the end of a blade, too," Mala said. "Or perish at the twitch of a wizard's hand."

Tamás slammed his hand on the table. "Go then, Mala of Clan Kalev. Walk the forests and mountains alone with your hardened heart, surrounded by your gold and pretty baubles, and leave your people to their fate."

Without a word, eyes blazing, Mala backed away from the table and climbed the stairs to her room. Will wondered again what had happened in her past to make her who she was.

And how to break through her defenses.

"Never forget," Tamás said, after she had left, "that it's the return of an *idea* the wizards fear. And ideas are much harder to kill than armies."

His words rang hollow. Will might not share Mala's cynicism, but neither had he bought into the wishful thinking of the revolutionary leader. After Mateo and Tamás turned in for the night, Will stared at the fire, surrounded by nameless faces among the casks of rum and ale. Even Dalen had plans for the night, one of his illusionist shows in the town square that he used to pay the rent.

Will slumped in his chair, feeling alone and unsure. He had no idea how to help Val, or how to go about finding Caleb.

"Why the long face, little brother?"

Will slowly looked up.

"I haven't seen you speechless since that time you put a tracking device on your sketchy ex-girlfriend's car and found out she had a husband and two kids."

Will leapt out of his chair, roared at the top of his lungs, and picked up his middle brother in a bear hug. He set him down and did the same to Marguerite. The other patrons clapped and stomped and whistled at the reunion.

"We just rolled in," Caleb said. "Glad to see the city's still here."

There was a little boy with curly brown hair standing off to the side. Though his blue eyes never left Caleb, Will wondered if he was related to the older, bearded man standing behind his brother. "Why wouldn't it be?" Will asked.

His brother and Marguerite exchanged a glance. "We saw some things. Bad things." He nudged his head towards the boy, and Will got the hint it was not an appropriate conversation.

The older man stepped forward and stuck out his hand. "The youngest Blackwood, I'm guessing?"

Will froze. "Um, why are you speaking in an American accent?"

The man grinned and introduced himself. Caleb and Marguerite disappeared upstairs to tuck the boy in, and once they returned, the four of them settled down to swap tales. The waitress gave Marguerite a jealous look as Caleb ordered a platter of food, a mug of ale for the Brewer, and a pitcher of water for himself and the gray-eyed rogue.

Will's jaw dropped as Caleb lifted his glass of water. "Excuse me?"

"Yeah, about that . . . a few things have changed." Caleb raised Marguerite's hand and showcased her wedding band. "We sort of got married. And that boy upstairs? He's sort of our adopted son."

Will stopped moving as if an anchor had dropped. Out of all the things he might have expected to hear, this was last on his list. Marguerite's grin split her entire face, and Will held up a hand. "Whoa there. Do you mean to tell me that during this journey, you got Caleb to stop drinking, and *then* he married you? And you have a *child*?"

Marguerite's eyes sparkled. "That's about it, methinks."

Caleb put his palms up. "Hey now, I didn't say I'm off the sauce forever. Just that I've got all I need right now. Luca's an orphan. We found him on the journey. We're all he has left."

Will saw the way Caleb looked at Marguerite, the love and compassion in his eyes when he mentioned the boy. Something had happened to his brother on the journey, Will realized. Something powerful. "Well," he said, "I don't know what to say. You're a husband. And a father. I thought I was the cheesy one in love."

"You still are," Caleb said. "Where is Small, Dark, and Deadly, anyway?"

"Upstairs, I guess," Will muttered.

"Don't forget what I've always told you. Give her the walking papers, and she'll walk right back to you."

Marguerite gave Caleb a playful smack on the head. As Will noticed their goofy grins and intertwined fingers, a rush of warmth coursed through him. He slapped the table and bellowed, "Come here, sis!" He picked her up in another bear hug, set her down, then climbed atop the table to address the crowd. "My brother just got married—drinks are on me!"

The Brewer broke into song, and the room exploded with merriment.

Hours later, after the excitement had died, Will recapped his journey to the pyramid of the sorcerer king as the others wolfed down their meal. Caleb's eyes grew wider and wider during the story, Marguerite shook her head in disbelief, and the Brewer looked as if he was taking mental notes for an epic ballad.

"Long story short," Will said, "we defeated the sorcerer king and brought back the Coffer of Devla. But no one can open it."

"I'm sorry about Gunnar and Selina," Caleb said quietly.

"Yeah," Will said, his eyes lowering. "Me, too."

"What's next for us? How do we find Val?"

Will pursed his lips and looked away. "I don't know. I'll think about it in the morning."

After the Brewer turned in, Will yawned and stood. "I'll leave you two lovebirds alone. I'm turning in."

Caleb gripped his brother in a fierce hug before Will left. "It's good to see you, little brother," he whispered. "I'm glad you didn't die on me."

"Right back at you."

Will climbed the stairs of the inn with a purpose. He wasn't as tired as he had let on. Seeing Caleb so happy made him ecstatic, but it also made him annoyed with himself. He was tired of pining for someone like a schoolboy. He had just returned from a journey where epic battles had been fought, ancient treasures unearthed, and dear companions had perished. Life was short and meant to be lived.

He knocked on Mala's door. No answer.

He knocked louder.

At last she opened up, her hair freshly washed and spilling over a white slip and leather pants she had pulled on to answer the door. She was holding a short sword pointed at Will in one hand, her sash in another. Always at the ready.

Her lips curled. "Yes?"

Will stepped inside, reached back to shut the door, pushed the blade to the side, and kissed her full on the mouth.

Mala didn't pull away, and he let it linger in case he never got another, her lips like warm plum and spice, a shudder coursing through him when he finally disengaged.

She peered up at him with a coy smirk, her face inches from his. "A bold move, Will the Builder. It seems I've taught you something, at least."

She hadn't moved, and her voice was low and throaty. As he moved to kiss her again, a knock came at the door, loud and insistent.

"Mala! Are you there?"

Dalen's voice.

She pulled away and reached for the door.

"I can't find Will, and you won't believe—" Dalen noticed Will as the door opened wider. The young illusionist looked at one and then the other. "Oh. *Lucka*, sorry to interrupt, but you both need to come. Now."

"What is it?" Will said, with a sigh. Dalen didn't look afraid, as he would if an attack had occurred. Whatever the news was, it had sabotaged his night with Mala.

"It's your brother. He just opened the Coffer of Devla."

46

The cityscape of Londyn whooshed by Val in a flash, a splice from a movie reel, and then he was standing in a familiar high-ceilinged room with a pearl chandelier, tapestries and heraldic banners covering the walls, golden sconces providing illumination.

Adaira stood beside him with a bewildered expression. Dida and Rucker were still ashen-faced and unconscious. Synne looked as confused as Adaira, and was shivering from the pain in her eye.

Startled by the sudden arrivals, two gray-robed Wizard Guards in the room raised their hands to cast a spell. As a dozen majitsu sprinted into the room, Val shouted at them all to wait, asked to speak with Cyrus Ravensill or the queen, and explained who they were. After a quick debate, one of the majitsu left the room and returned with Cyrus, the queen, and a score more Wizard Guards.

The tiny monarch, dressed in a diamond gown that matched her scepter, peered up at Val and Adaira. "Nearly a month has passed. We thought you lost forever."

Her words stunned Val. It had been impossible to keep time in the world of mist, but by his rough calculation, not even a week had passed. The journey to the other realm must have somehow warped the passage of time.

"My companions need urgent medical care," he said.

The queen swept an imperious gaze over the prone forms of Rucker and Dida. Her gaze rested on Synne for a moment, then returned to Val.

"The crown? The head of Tobar?"

"Did you hear what I said?"

The queen's eyes narrowed.

Adaira squeezed Val's hand, a signal to keep his cool. As much as it infuriated him, he knew that respectfully answering the matriarch's questions was the best way to help his friends.

"I destroyed the crown with Spirit Fire," he lied. "We were trapped. It was the only way I could think of to return."

"Trapped where?"

"I don't really know. Another dimension, maybe." He gave a very abbreviated account of their exploits, feeling as if Dida and Rucker's lives were slipping through his fingers.

The queen showed no emotion during the story. "Why, then, was another dimension not created when you left? As it was the previous time?"

"I don't know. Perhaps because I targeted the crown directly."

The queen compressed her shriveled lips. "How did you arrive here? Bypass our wards?"

"There was a flash of light when the crown exploded, and this was the last place I thought of."

The queen paced back and forth, tapping the scepter against her hand. Synne's eye was dripping blood, Dida was barely breathing, and Val wanted to scream his frustration. He took a deep breath through his nose and gripped Adaira's hand even harder.

Cyrus took a moment to step towards Val and whisper, "My brother?"

Val gave a grim shake of his head. "I'm sorry. But we sent the demon lord who killed him back to hell."

He squeezed his eyes shut for a moment, then clasped Val by the arm. "You wore the gray robe well."

Cyrus retreated, and the queen stopped pacing a foot away from Val. "The head of Tobar? As per our agreement?"

"In the final battle, I was forced to," he swallowed, "kill him with Spirit Fire. It was the only way to reach the crown." Val locked gazes with the frost-colored orbs of the queen, letting her see into his soul and glimpse the pain and dark deeds for herself. "I didn't realize the crown would explode. I did what I must, your Majesty."

"He speaks the truth," Adaira said. "I bore witness myself."

The queen rested her gaze on Adaira for a long time, no doubt weighing the truth of her words and the political implications of her decision. Finally she turned back to Val, her eyes boring into his, challenging him to flinch. The shallow rasp of Dida's labored breathing was the only sound in the room.

Head held high, Val returned the queen's stare until she gave a slow nod and turned to one of the Wizard Guard. "Bring the Spirit Mirror to the Gem

Room. Summon Lord Alistair. And alert the cuerpomancer that her services are needed."

Just before midnight on the third day after they arrived, Val left his quarters in the visitor's wing—he was no longer under personal guard, though still within the highly fortified walls of the castle—and padded down the hall to Adaira's bedchamber. The next day an airship was scheduled to fly them back to New Victoria. Val did not know why Lord Alistair had not arranged a portal, at least for Adaira.

To teach her a lesson? Or because it was not feasible to teleport others in such a manner, even for a spirit mage? He had no idea, and was once again reminded of how little he knew of this world.

He knocked softly on the door and wondered if Adaira was still awake. They had not spent a moment alone since their arrival. Debriefings and visits to the infirmary had taken up most of their time.

It had been close, but Dida had finally pulled through and regained consciousness. He would remain under the cuerpomancer's care for a while longer, but he had acknowledged Val's presence with a lopsided smile.

After Rucker regained consciousness, the hardened warrior refused all services from the cuerpomancer, instead asking that his fifteen-year-old niece in Londyn be healed instead. She had contracted a devastating wasting disease and the family could not afford the treatment.

The queen ordered the cuerpomancer to help the niece and asked Rucker to join her personal guard. With a twirl of his new axe, he refused her request, grunted his goodbyes, and stomped out of the keep.

The cuerpomancer had only been able to treat Synne's wounds and clean the empty socket. She could not replace the lost orb. The young warrior-mage adopted a silver eye patch instead, one that matched the new belt she would one day earn after her reinstatement—on order of the queen—into the academy of the majitsu.

Adaira opened the door in a blue nightgown. He stood before her in silence, knowing exactly what he wanted but also knowing what he still had to do.

What kind of future could they possibly have?

She gave him a challenging stare in return. Yet behind the pride, he saw eyes full of love, a look that said she would do anything for him—anything, that was, except trust him.

Not until he trusted *her*.

"I have two brothers," Val said.

She gave him a puzzled look.

He took a deep breath, not prepared to tell her everything but hoping it was enough, knowing his half-truths might come back to haunt him one day. On the other hand, if she trusted him, it could expedite matters. "They haven't taken the Oaths."

After a moment, she said, "Why not?"

What Val said next was as far as he was prepared to go, and even that was risky. "Our father was a gypsy. Our mother was not."

She took her bottom lip between her teeth, taking it all in. "That's why your family lived so far north."

He didn't answer, let her draw her own conclusions.

"You're worried someone will find out and use your brothers against you," she said. "You know you're bound to be successful, maybe even part of the Conclave one day. You don't want to jeopardize their safety."

Again, he let his silence speak.

She reached up and gently cupped his face. "I'm not my father."

"I know."

"I'll never breathe a word."

Val flashed a half-playful, half-serious smirk. "If I thought you would, I never would have told you."

She gave a soft smile in return. A sign that she understood what it had cost him to confide in her, and that he had only gone halfway. No names, no place of residence.

But he had told her.

"I'd like very much to meet them one day," she said.

"I'd like that, too."

She closed the door and removed her azantite necklace. As far as they knew, the necklace only lashed out against those who grabbed her in anger, but best not to take chances. After setting it on the bedside table, she took him by the hand and led him to the four-poster bed. Her voice was husky when she spoke. "Kiss me, Valjean."

47

Will raced into the mostly rebuilt town square, Mala and Tamás right behind him. High winds heralding a thunderstorm had rolled in, though the rain had held off. The night air was pregnant with unseen currents, the squall whipping into Will's face.

A huge crowd of people were gathered near the central fountain. Tamás had erected an open-air canvas pavilion to house the Coffer of Devla so everyone could stroll by and enjoy the sight of the legendary artifact. A pair of local wizards and four armed men stood by, a guard Tamás kept posted day and night.

As Will neared the pavilion, he saw the azantite coffer resting on a brick platform. The ancient relic always seemed the focal point of attention in the square, no matter what else was going on.

Glow orbs hanging in the corners of the pavilion illuminated a surprising scene. The lid of the coffer was hinged open and Caleb was standing right beside it, holding a black traveling cloak with silver stitching. Waves of heat lightning flashed in the sky above Will as Caleb bent over the coffer, examining the inside of the chest. The gathered people were staring at him with rapt expressions, though they had created a wide berth around the pavilion, as if afraid to stand too close.

Looking bemused by the whole scene, Marguerite stood beside her new husband, holding Luca by the hand. The boy was looking at Caleb with serious eyes, as if he knew something of grave import had just occurred.

"He's the Templar!" someone cried. "The prophecy is fulfilled! A true cleric has returned to the land!"

Murmurs of growing excitement rippled through the crowd as Will and Mala entered the pavilion. Tamás remained on the perimeter, dazed, looking back and forth between Caleb and the coffer.

Will leaned over to peer inside. The coffer was empty, an interior of smooth dark wood. "Caleb? What happened?"

His brother looked puzzled. "I don't know. Luca couldn't sleep, so we took a walk to show him the courtyard. I realized none of us had tried to open the chest yet, because why would we? Luca tried, and then Marguerite, and nothing happened. Just for kicks, I put my hand on it, but before I could even lift the lid, it popped open by itself. There wasn't anything inside except this cloak. I've no idea why—"

Will cringed as a deafening clap of thunder interrupted his brother. Twin flashes of lightning tore through the canvas roof of the pavilion, striking the two wizard guards in the chest. Both of them, a man and a woman, died on impact.

The screams of bystanders pierced the air. The lightning strike caused the roof of the pavilion to burst into flame, and people stumbled over their neighbors to flee, pushing and shoving to escape whatever power from on high had slain the two wizards.

Stunned, Will turned and saw three people who had appeared out of nowhere standing at the edge of the pavilion. One was a tall, bald, older man in a high-collared cloak. An orange, star-shaped pendant flashed at his throat. Just behind him stood a man and a woman wearing black robes cinched with silver belts.

Majitsu.

And a wizard.

The wind keened overhead. As another peal of thunder shook the ground, the wizard raised his hands and whisked away the burning roof of the pavilion, then sent twin bolts of lightning sizzling through the four armed guards.

"Lord Alistair sends greetings," the wizard said calmly.

"Electromancer," Mala breathed. "By the Queen."

"Enough!" Tamás roared.

The wizard gave the revolutionary a lazy glance and sent him, along with everyone nearby, tumbling away in a fierce gale.

The electromancer noticed that only Mala and Will, who was holding Zariduke in front of them both, had escaped the blast. The wizard's eyes widened. "Spiritscourge? The gypsy wench kept that from us. A boon indeed!"

Gypsy wench, Will repeated, as the Congregation wizard flicked his eyes towards Mateo, who was struggling to stand. Flashing in the center of his cousin's chest, born proudly in commemoration, was Selina's copper necklace.

And then, remembering her last words, Will understood. During the journey, Selina must have spied on them for Lord Alistair, through the necklace.

Why? he whispered to himself. Had it all been an act?

He didn't think so. He remembered the conversation when she had told him about her daughter, who was studying at the Abbey. Selina had seemed so sad, as if there was a story untold, and Will guessed the Congregation had threatened her daughter if she didn't spy for them.

None of that mattered now. The damage had been done. Keeping an eye on Will, the electromancer walked towards Caleb and the coffer. Will ran to help but the two majitsu cut him off, forcing him to adopt a defensive posture.

"Call the other mages!" Will shouted to Tamás.

"They are coming," he shouted back, though his voice was laced with uncertainty. *They're coming,* Tamás's tone implied, *but even if they arrive in time, they may not be able to touch a Congregation electromancer during a lightning storm.*

Everything seemed to be happening in slow motion. Painfully out of Will's control. He knew he was no match for both majitsu at the same time, and Mala was little help against them. He couldn't protect his brother and his new family. Rage bubbled inside him as the Congregation wizard strode towards Caleb and said, "You'll be coming with us."

"No!" Marguerite shrieked. In one smooth motion, she dropped Luca's hand and stepped in front of Caleb, then threw a dagger that bounced off an invisible wizard shield in front of the amused electromancer.

The wizard raised his hands. Lightning crackled at his fingertips, sparks trailing in the air around him, power leeched from the storm. Luca cringed and hugged Marguerite around the waist. Caleb reached for them, trying to pull them back, but before he could grab them, the wizard sent a bolt of lightning lancing into Marguerite.

Both she and Luca seized up as the electricity tore through them. The boy dropped without a sound, but Marguerite managed a prolonged scream before she fell and convulsed on the ground, her hair and clothing smoking.

As his loved ones twitched and lay still, slain almost instantly, Caleb stared down at them as if dazed, his face caught in an almost quizzical expression. Then a spasm passed through him, as swift and sure as the lightning bolt that had seized Marguerite and Luca. Caleb balled his fists and roared, a cry of rage and pain so intense it left a brand on Will's soul, a white-hot stain of emotion. As his brother staggered back against the coffer, the electromancer released another bolt. This time the lightning arced straight into Caleb's chest, yet instead of killing him, the bolt pulsed and bounced off his brother, returning to strike the electromancer.

Out of the corner of his eye, Will noticed the Coffer of Devla glowing softly with a multihued spectrum of colors, a rainbow of illumination that spread to envelop his brother. Snarling, Caleb raised his fists and stalked forward, causing the strange radiance to disappear when he lost contact with the coffer. But the electromancer had already fallen, struck dead by the reversal of his spell.

The two majitsu rushed Will. Before they reached him, the male screamed as a cat o' nine tails lashed into his back, the hardened azantite tips tearing deep into his skin. Mala hit him again before he could recover, the wicked barbs ripping out his throat and piercing his heart. Will had no idea how the weapon had pierced the warrior-mage's defenses.

"Feel the sting of Magelasher," Mala said, her words coated with vengeful satisfaction.

Will turned on the final invader and thrust straight for her gut. At the last moment, the majitsu spun away from the blade and sent a back elbow slamming into Will's sternum, doubling him over. Next, she shot a palm at Will's heart that he deflected with the side edge of Zariduke. Her hand dripping blood, the majitsu leapt at Will, fists and feet flying, forcing him backwards.

Another strike from Magelasher caught her in the side, ripping out a hunk of flesh. Stumbling, the majitsu managed to avoid Mala's next blow, but Will ran her through from behind. The warrior-mage stiffened and died on the blade. Will kicked her to the ground.

Caleb howled and fell between Marguerite and Luca's charred bodies, weeping as Will rushed to him. Caleb pushed him away and reached for the coffer, opening it as if trying to summon its magic. He closed his eyes, whispered a prayer too low for Will to hear, and opened them again.

Marguerite and Luca lay unchanged on the ground.

"Do something!" Caleb screamed as he picked up Luca's body and raised him to the sky. "If You exist, bring them back to me!" Will watched in horror as spittle flew from his brother's mouth. "*Damn You, do something!!*"

"The coffer!" someone yelled.

Will whipped his head around to see a wisp of a man hovering over the chest. He had a ferret-like face and was holding a shiny platinum bag that looked similar to the one Mala had used to ferry the artifact out of the tomb. The sack that held far more than it could possibly fit.

As Will watched in shock, the man stretched the mouth of the bag to fit over the coffer and, once the artifact disappeared inside, he pulled the drawstring tight.

Besides Caleb, who didn't even look up, Tamás was closest. He yelled as he sprinted towards the thief, followed by Will and Mala. Before they could reach him, the man threw a crystal sphere on the ground he had concealed in his other hand. The glass shattered and a portal opened in midair, revealing a dystopian cityscape of soot-blackened buildings, cracked arches, and a nest of crooked alleyways. The thief jumped through, and the portal closed as Tamás made a futile grab for his shirt.

Reeling, unable to process everything that had happened, Will sank to his knees as Caleb rocked on the ground beside him, inconsolable, moaning the names of his loved ones.

48

The evening after his return to New Victoria, Val eased into a soft leather chair as Lord Alistair poured them both a glass of granth. The Chief Thaumaturge's study in his St. Charles mansion was opulent beyond belief, full of stunning original art, glass cases housing bottles of rare liquors, and period furniture that reeked of wealth and privilege. A three-dimensional painting of the New Victoria Wizard District hung above the alabaster fireplace, and as Val stared at the piece, he realized he could actually shift the perspective of the painting with his mind and view the spires from different angles. Amazing.

The encounter did not intimidate Val. As powerful as Lord Alistair was, Val had risen to the top of one of New York City's most prestigious law firms on his own merit, navigating the hierarchy of the firm and some of the world's most influential business leaders along the way. He had studied at the Abbey, completed the Planewalk, and faced off against a demon lord.

Val was comfortable with power.

What unnerved him were the stakes.

Would Lord Alistair send him back to prison? Execute him? Banish him? Word had probably spread that he and Adaira had become an item. How would the Chief Thaumaturge react?

With a neutral expression, Lord Alistair handed Val a glass. "Granth from the Isles of Minos Krinn. The finest in the world, according to some."

Val accepted the offer and clinked his glass lightly against Lord Alistair's. "To your daughter," Val said.

"Yes," he murmured, as he took a seat.

"I never intended for her to go."

"I know that. She is quite willful, and now that she is of age . . ." Lord Alistair gave a shrug at the universal inability of fathers to control their daughters' behavior.

Val sipped his granth, which tasted like a rare whiskey infused with hints of vanilla and butterscotch. Delicious indeed, though Val barely noticed as he braced himself for the worst. Fighting was pointless; the house was heavily guarded, and Lord Alistair could snuff his life with the twitch of a finger.

Mere hours had passed since his and Adaira's arrival in New Victoria. Val's request to stop by his own residence to clean up before the meeting with Lord Alistair had been granted, though a majitsu escort had accompanied him. Val had showered, changed clothes, and on instinct, dropped off his staff. Though neither Adaira nor anyone in Queen Victoria's court seemed to recognize it, he guessed the Chief Thaumaturge was alive during Dane Blackwood's time in the Congregation. Val had no idea what their relationship might have been, but better not to raise uncomfortable questions. Not unless he had to.

"My daughter told me about Porlock, and of your encounter with the townspeople in the other world." His face tightened. "What they tried to do to her after she healed a little boy."

"Yes."

"Thank you," Lord Alistair said. "For saving her."

Val tipped his head in response, thinking of another child he had failed to save, gutted by the end of his own staff.

"I have also learned of your confrontation with the Black Sash gypsies during the hunt for the assassin."

This time Val's face darkened.

"Power is both a privilege and a duty," the Chief Thaumaturge said. "Hard decisions must sometimes be made. Decisions that not everyone will understand."

Where's he going with this?

"I believe you to be the kind of man with the disposition it takes to make such decisions." Lord Alistair's regal gaze locked onto Val. "A born leader."

"Thank you," Val said, confused.

"While you have much to learn, by completing the Planewalk you have technically fulfilled the requirements to become a spirit mage. I would like to make it official, Valjean. Join the Congregation. Join *me*. Help arrest the spread of ignorance and bring enlightenment and prosperity to the Realm. I will take you under my wing, see to your continuing education myself."

This was not at all what he had expected to hear. In fact, it was the opposite. "Lord Alistair . . . thank you. Again."

He didn't know what else to say.

The Chief Thaumaturge took a swallow of granth and leaned forward. "It seems my daughter has taken quite a liking to you."

Val didn't move a muscle. *Here it comes,* he thought.

"I have to say, the sentiment in our family is not hers alone. I want you to know that you have my permission, should the time come, to ask for her hand."

A master of his emotions, able to control his expression in the most chaotic of circumstances, Val found himself floored once again.

Lord Alistair leaned back, amused at the effect his words had imparted. "Understand that not everyone in the Congregation is ready to accept your role as my protégé. In their eyes, after all, you are a recently pardoned criminal who failed to return the crown."

Val nodded in understanding, still wondering where this was headed.

"We need to change that, in a very public manner. There is an item that has recently been lost to us. Stolen by a thief. An archaic religious object, a coffer, with symbolic importance to the followers of Devla. Should this item be recovered by the black sash gypsies, it will ignite more false hope among the people, and spark the Revolution. You've seen firsthand the dangers of this path."

"I have."

"Fulfill this task for us, recover the coffer, and I will be able to introduce you to the Congregation not just as a full spirit mage, but as my apprentice." He leveled his gaze at him. "And, I hope, as my future son-in-law."

Val's head was spinning, but he forced himself to stay calm. "I . . . don't know what to say. I'm flattered beyond belief."

"Then say yes." Lord Alistair finished his glass of granth, his tone implying an imperative rather than a suggestion. Not only that, but the silver bracelet Val could not remove, the one affixed to his wrist before the journey through the mist and which allowed the wizards to know where he was at all times, was a constant reminder that he was not yet a free man.

Still, he understood. He had broken their laws and narrowly escaped execution, and was still earning their trust.

The Chief Thaumaturge rose to clasp Val on the shoulder. "I'm confident of your answer, but I know you have much to digest. Go. Rest well. In the morning, you can inform me of your decision."

Val planned to take his advice, though he already knew his answer. He didn't really have a choice, and if successful, he could think of no better way to help his brothers.

Yet there was more to it than that. He did not find it distasteful—not at all—to agree to everything the Chief Thaumaturge was offering. He could not deny that he was falling in love with Adaira, though he had hardly considered marriage. Also, he enjoyed being a wizard and the power it conferred.

Nor was Val even sure, after the terrible things he had done on Urfe, that he belonged back home any more.

Keeping his conflicted emotions to himself, Val bowed and took his leave. Once he completed the new mission and found his brothers, he could deal with everything else—Adaira and his guilty conscience and the choice between worlds—when the time came.

After Val left, Lord Alistair poured another glass of granth, deep in thought.

Momentous events were in progress. After the mysterious disappearance of Dean Groft, the War Council would have the unanimity it needed to usher the Protectorate into war. At first Lord Alistair had thought—guessing Dean Groft had fled through the dimensions and died in some far corner of the multiverse at the hands of the two Spirit Lieges—that the lack of a body was unfortunate. He soon realized it was a boon. With no evidence to contradict him, the Chief Thaumaturge could spread whatever information about Dean Groft he wished.

Combined with the untimely death of Garbind Elldorn and the capitulation of Jalen Rainsword, who had not the stomach for lone dissent, Lord Alistair now had complete command of the Conclave. Except for the increasingly remote odds of that accursed prophecy, the one about the sword born of spirit, the path to his ascension was clear. The whispers of unease that floated about the Sanctum, the unspoken questions about the convenient disappearance of the dissenting mages, were too dangerous to speak aloud.

Recovering the coffer would reduce the odds of the prophecy even further, as would finding Zariduke. He would have to take the sword from its owner, a once-mysterious warrior whose identity had been revealed in a journal recently recovered from Zedock's obelisk by Lord Alistair's men. A touching missive that detailed Dane Blackwood's instructions to his sons should they ever travel to Urfe.

It was clear, from the confusing nature of their actions, that the Blackwood brothers never had a chance to read their father's journal. What a great irony that this same diary had helped Lord Alistair—the same man Dane Blackwood had warned his sons to avoid at all costs in the diary—to locate *them*.

The recovery of the diary had made Lord Alistair suspicious about the true identity of his talented young protégé with the enigmatic past. The evening before, the Chief Thaumaturge's suspicions were confirmed when Queen Victoria informed him of the return of a certain azantite-tipped staff.

A staff that had once belonged to Dane Blackwood.

Glass in hand, lost in the past, Lord Alistair rose to stoke the fire. The white flames were artificial, of course, and did not give off any heat. In a purely symbolic gesture, he tossed the journal of his old enemy into the fire, watched the light flicker around it, and then burned it to ash with Spirit Fire.

EPILOGUE

Atop a frozen plain in the Great Northern Forest, beyond the farthest reaches of the Ninth Protectorate, a lone traveler gathered her cloak against the wind and felt a stabbing pain in her side.

A pain that struck not at flesh and bone, but somewhere deeper. A pain of the mysterious regions of the heart.

Though she had just recently arrived, the lone wilder was eager to hone her craft and become a beacon of light to those in need. Proud and fierce she was, but also a lost young woman far from home, far even from her own world.

Following her intuition, she had asked the rukh that carried her away from the Yucatan to deposit her here, planning to study the northern climes before making her way south. She had no final destination, no method to her travels other than to act as a steward to the land and those it sheltered. Deep down, she knew that she, too, had something to mend, an aching spirit for the man she loved and a wrenching despair that she could not, no matter how much she tried, ever make him whole.

But something had changed, she knew, as she pressed her hand to her breast. Whether due to their past connection or the strange and magical energies that seethed across the surface of Urfe, Yasmina knew, without a doubt, that something had happened to Caleb.

Something terrible.

Owl staff in hand, a healthy harpy eagle perched on her shoulder, the wilder spoke softly to her mare as she gripped the reins. With a powerful neigh, the chestnut steed bunched its muscles and galloped south.

Atop a high and forested hill, at the foot of a mighty redwood, the Prophet's closest disciples gathered around their leader as he gazed through a silver monocle upon the chaos below.

Thousands more crowded the long slope of the hill behind the Prophet, most of them bearing arms concealed within the folds of their gray caftans.

The followers of Devla anxiously awaited word of what had caused the journey to stall. The long march to Freetown—weeks of arduous travel—had pushed their supplies to the limit. Yet the Prophet had insisted on traveling as fast as possible to the Roma capital, risking hunger and snowfall and bandits in the passes of the Dragon's Teeth, all in service to his vision.

They trusted him, but they needed a sign. Something to confirm their faith in his leadership. Now that they had arrived at the Barrier Coast, whispers of the ocean views and the shattered remains of the city drifted down from atop the hill. The followers were eager to know what had transpired.

Was he down there after all, the one whom they longed to lift up as their savior? The blue-eyed boy in the Prophet's vision?

Those surrounding the Prophet edged closer. All except Allira. Though she didn't have a spyglass, the silent healer was staring down at the city with a somber gaze, as if she, too, had seen the miracle that had transpired.

Slowly, the Prophet lowered the monocle to address his followers. O Devla, the power he had witnessed! The return of the coffer, the righteous fury arcing out of the vessel to consume the agents of the Congregation! A display of celestial might unseen in the Realm for millennia!

Shivering at the import of the events, the Prophet could barely manage his first few words. "I was wrong," he whispered, causing his disciples to edge closer so they could hear him.

No, not wrong, he thought. *The visions are never wrong. Just incomplete.*

"It's not the boy," he said, in a louder voice this time, his eyes moist from the tragic death of the woman and the poor child. After the man who had opened the coffer had flung himself across their broken bodies—clearly related to them—the Prophet had turned away from the scene.

The new age, it seemed, would be one born of tragedy.

"The Templar is not a boy," he said, his words gaining strength, "but a man. One who stands in the city below us at this very moment, in dire need of our aid and compassion."

As his words spread among the masses, causing a great commotion, one question was shouted above all the others, over and over. Voices crying out for guidance in the wilderness. "What do we do?"

The Prophet gazed down the hill at his followers. Though weakened to the point of collapse from hunger and the long march, his flock was no longer a defenseless body of worshippers, awaiting reaping by the Congregation.

They were an army now. A small army, yes, but one which would multiply tenfold once word spread that the coffer had been opened.

An army that would be led by a man far greater than he.

"What do we do?" the Prophet repeated as he drew to his full height, the power of conviction ringing in his voice, overcome by awe at the mysterious workings of the one true God. "We serve him."

TO BE CONTINUED IN
THE *RETURN OF THE PALADIN*,
BOOK FOUR of FIVE in THE BLACKWOOD SAGA

Please visit www.laytongreen.com to stay up to date on
The Blackwood Saga and Layton Green's other work.

Acknowledgments

I am deeply indebted to editor Michael Rowley for lending a guiding hand to the course of this series. Likewise, as always, I received invaluable input from my pocket aces: early readers Rusty Dalferes and John Strout. Cover designer extraordinaire Sammy Yuen designed another brilliant image, and proofreader / formatter Jaye Manus made sure the final text sang. Maria Boers Morris, Lisa Weinberg, and Bill Burdick provided excellent early reads. As always, during the writing of the novel, my family was the azantite pillar on which I leaned.

Finally, though the author of the *Canticles of Urfe* remains unknown, one might find similar inspiration in the moving poetry of Polish-born Roma Bronislawa ("Papuza") Wajs.

LAYTON GREEN is a bestselling author who writes across multiple genres, including fantasy, mystery, thriller, horror, and suspense. His novels have been nominated for multiple awards (including a finalist for an International Thriller Writers award), optioned for film, and have reached #1 on numerous genre lists in the United States, the United Kingdom, and Germany.

If you are new to the world of Layton Green, please visit him on Author Central, Goodreads, Facebook, and his website for additional information on the author, his works, and more.

www.laytongreen.com